LARCHFIELD

Polly Clark

riverrun

First published in Great Britain in 2017 by

riverrun

An imprint of

Quercus Editions Limited
Carmelite House
50 Victoria Embankment
London EC4Y ODZ

An Hachette UK company

HB ISBN 978 1 78648 1 924
TPB ISBN 978 1 78648 1 931
EBOOK ISBN 978 1 78648 1 948

10 9 8 7 6 5 4 3 2 1

Typeset in Monotype Fournier by CC Book Production
Printed and bound in Great Britain by Clays Ltd, St Ives plc

LARCHFIELD

By Polly Clark

for Lucy

Larchfield is a work of the imagination drawing on a handful of known facts about the life of W. H. Auden in Helensburgh during the years 1930–32. Some of the characters are inspired by real people he knew, some of them famous, and have been named for the sake of authenticity. They are, however, works of fiction, as indeed is Wystan himself. The town of Helensburgh is also fictionalised: certain landmarks and streets are named, but for the purpose of storytelling a great deal of the geography is invented, as are all the people. The school of Larchfield remains as a building, but its interior is completely imagined, as is the life of the school. Any resemblance between the characters in *Larchfield* and real people, living or dead, is not intended and purely coincidental.

Part One

ONE

Wystan

H IS JACKET IS WINTER-GREEN tweed with a herringbone stitch, and rather too large. The lining has come loose and a button is hanging by a thread, destined to drop before the train reaches Birmingham. Beneath the jacket: a grey shirt and a spotted tie. The shirt has a greasy stain down the front. His arms are huge, the arms of an ape, and he's lighting a cigarette as he gets settled for the journey from Oxford to Glasgow. Oiled or greasy, it's hard to tell, his hair is close shaved at the back and sides, with a fringe hanging louchely over his forehead. His left ear sticks out, the remains of the schoolboy. The impression made is one of pale, large fragility.

It isn't until he looks up that his attractiveness becomes apparent. His blue eyes flicker with a lively intelligence that animates all his features. It's as if one can see the thoughts playing in his mind. But this is an illusion; his friends will find they never really know him. Wystan is that terrible, isolating thing: *unreadable*. His hands are enormous, dwarfing the matchbox. He holds it gently, a giant lifting a farmhouse.

Every few minutes, he has to get up and walk around. He is recovering from an operation for an anal fissure, and it is still, after many weeks, unbearably painful. Though its refusal to heal is depressing him, he has started to consider the intimate, searing pain as a physical expression of the torment he feels all the time, which is sutured into his very biology. The wound that will not heal, that cannot be spoken of in polite company, is becoming a separate entity. He composes, idly in his head, as the train clatters along, a letter to the Wound. He wants to make peace with it. He wants to be forgiven.

There are two others in his carriage: a suited man whose bowler hat is neatly on the rack above, and a man with a florid face, sour with drink, who has fallen asleep against the window. The purple of his mouth is visible as he snores. Wystan studies them in between glancing at the pages of the *Criterion*. The two destinies of Man. Suited looks well fed and contented. He is reading the financial information at the back of the paper, and his face has an ageing softness that denotes a life free of depravity. Florid radiates ill health from every broken capillary. No wife, no children, no love. In time, Wystan is surely to become one of these men. Once we are all grown up, there is nothing else.

Wystan is going to be a Great Poet. He has decided it firmly, told all his friends. His philosophy of life is inspired by Emile Coué: you will become what you believe you will become. Eighteen months ago, he graduated from Oxford after a sensational three years, but with a very poor degree, and T. S. Eliot has, this very week, accepted his manuscript for publication with Faber and Faber. His cigarette glows in his fingers as the train hauls itself out of Coventry station and continues the drag and choke to Scotland.

His work is not where his doubts lie; that is not what draws his gaze nervously to Florid, snuffling before him. It is love. He shuffles in his seat to relieve the pressure on the Wound. It pulsates with its own torn language, telling him that he will never really know love.

Wystan rubs his white brow, pushes his fringe out of his eyes and rummages in his satchel, swapping the *Criterion* for a book. He's reading a lot of Freud at this time; it offers him little comfort.

Sheilagh snaps into his mind, her pretty frown causing him a pang. When he proposed to her, he was confident that, even if he was not in love, then he would be soon. She had accepted in the bemusing way women have of being excited about invisible things, and he found her endearing. Sheilagh was a nurse, and she brought that feminine practicality to their relationship. She knew about bodies, so he did not feel the need to be the oracle in this area, and she also knew about the way things were meant to be. Best of all, Sheilagh was nothing like his mother, which was certainly progress, for he deemed much of his problem to be his excessive attachment to his domineering mother. He was twenty-two at the time, surely old enough to know his own mind.

But then she started crying, quite soon into it all. She was disappointed in him, without saying why. Before this, Wystan had never been a disappointment, and it had not played well with him.

Hills swell beyond the window and a few drops of rain spatter the glass. The whistle blares at Carlisle station, doors slam, and Florid jolts awake, glaring round at his companions before reaching into his bag for a packet of sandwiches. They have been neatly wrapped in paper and tied with string. Who has done this for Florid? A wife? A mother? Has he perhaps done it himself? The smell of egg fills the carriage. Sniffing, the man reaches into his bag again and pulls out a bottle of beer. He flicks off the cap with a penny and sets it between his knees. Suited looks sideways with a sneer. The conductor, a half-pint man in a scarlet livery, appears in the doorway.

'Which way is the bar?' asks Wystan. He forgot about lunch, and didn't really appreciate how long the journey is.

The conductor points backwards. 'Two coaches down, sir.' He looks at his watch. 'Still a few ham sandwiches, I believe.'

Wystan nods. In a while, he'll wander along and see what there is. He sighs and observes through the window the almost imperceptible change from the greens and browns of Cumberland to those of Dumfriesshire.

The London establishment, which waits both to claim and judge him in a few years, shrinks to a speck. He is coming, for as long as they'll have him, to the briny shores, the promenade of hardware shops and grimy cafés, to the land of shallow valleys and low hills, of violet summers. His home will be the land of naval ships, with its seething hatred of outsiders, with its petty religious tyrannies. Soon, he will drop submarines casually into his poems; the sea will creep into his soul.

It's not his choice exactly. His trust money is about to run out, and he needs a job. His friend Cecil Day-Lewis has nominated him for this post of schoolmaster at Larchfield, though he has no experience of teaching and a severe distrust of the school environment. Florid coughs over his beer, drains it and fishes another out of his bag. Suited shakes his newspaper, expertly rolls it up and slips it under his arm before leaving the carriage, presumably to go to the bar. Wystan says, 'Shall I open the window?' and Florid grunts his assent. Cool Scottish air rushes in. Florid's hands are trembling. The sole of one boot is coming adrift and his laces are undone. Wystan knows he would rather end up as Florid than Suited, and indeed that is his trajectory. There's an honesty about Florid. He's given up trying to be what he is not.

When Sheilagh told Wystan his poems disgusted her, he knew that wasn't *it*, or wasn't it exactly. Her intuition that his poems were not about her, or anything she'd recognise, was certainly correct, but, as she sat sobbing into her hands, he wondered if he should press her to tell him what it was. At that moment, he hated her enough to humiliate them both. He might say, *So let's talk about disgust, then*, and see if it led to a conversation with any honesty in it. In truth, she bored rather than disgusted him; her body bored him, her deference bored him. Most of all, her safety bored him, even while he craved it. Should he tell her all this?

And yet, she loved him. On his side, there had certainly been tremendous hope. And is hope not the sibling of love? She wanted him to apologise for the poems in some way, to deny that what she thought was in them was in them. He couldn't do that, but he could apologise for himself.

Which he did. He cried while he did it, and he held her hand until he had finished. *Not cut out for marriage. You deserve someone better. A proper man.* She didn't look up when he left. When he reached home, he went to bed, where relief crashed over him and he cried until he was empty.

Wound is communicating its discomfort. Wystan gets up to walk to the bar. Why should this journey put him so in mind of Sheilagh? Perhaps he knows that, after her, there will be no love of the kind he wants. He has chosen the Wound over healing. The train sways, as if nodding its assent. Wystan feels suddenly tearful and digs his nails into his palm. Anyway, now is a new beginning. He could scarcely be further from Sheilagh and the hopes he had of change.

And the future? What of it? He cannot imagine a future where he fits. Wystan is travelling not into the future but into the heartland of – as he will soon describe it – the enemy. He does not know that he will be more alone than he has ever been, that he will love more deeply than he ever thought possible – and he will long for the consolations that poetry cannot give, at least not to the writer.

It has all been decided. He will live quietly, teaching English and French to the sons of Scotsmen, and he will get on with his work. He will be able to establish his routine for writing, he will be able to devote himself to it. Provided, of course, that he causes no scandals.

TWO

Dora

'AH! THE POETESS!'
Silver heads lifted. The voice materialised into Lois, a neighbour from along the road, who advanced through the guests on the lawn, her eyes full of amusement and intrigue. She planted a dry kiss on Dora's cheek and stepped back to take in the full measure of her pregnant belly.

In recent months, Kit had taken several unaccompanied trips up to Helensburgh, to finalise details of the purchase of Paradise, the mansion on whose lawn they were now standing, and to lay some groundwork in his new job. News had swiftly got out that a rather charming architect was moving into this part of town, and Kit had found himself with lots of new acquaintances, who accosted him for advice about their building projects. Lois had bagged him to help with designing some new windows for her listed coach house.

The owners of Paradise Lower, Matthew and Felicity, were the party hosts. They would be leaving the very next day, and Dora and Kit would be moving in. Matthew had constructed an ugly but effective barbecue out of an old mangle, and the smell of sausages drifted over the grass. Dora felt the oddness of her position as the not-yet owner, meeting guests on her not-yet lawn.

There was a little circle around them now. 'You know,' Lois said to Dora, 'I have been dying to meet you for ages. Kit's been hiding you! I thought he was making you up! Forever coming up and staying at that flat all alone and talking about his "wife". Poor sad soul, I thought.' Chuckles overcame her for a moment. Kit nodded, enjoying the game. 'And then,' Lois continued, 'I was behind Kit in the queue for the checkout at the Co-op and I saw, in his basket, he had *two* lamb chops and a bottle of wine! And I thought to myself, Aha! Something's up! Perhaps he does have a wife . . . or a girlfriend!'

At this, Lois collapsed into wheezy giggles.

Kit put his arm around Dora. 'No girlfriend. Just a wife.'

'Yes, a *poetess*. How wonderful. Tell me, Dora, should I have heard of you?'

Dora opened her mouth to attempt an answer, but the way the circle was staring gave her the uneasy sense that their attention had moved on and her poetry was not the main subject of interest. There was no other way to describe it: the guests were *gawping* at her stomach with perverted abandon. Never having had any contact with babies in her previous existence, she wondered if she was witnessing for the first time how women behave around infants or the prospect of them. Dora had become magnetic: the women's fingers began to uncurl as if irresistibly drawn to touch her. She was the centre of attention, certainly, even if no one was interested in what she said. The information that she was a poet had never produced this level of interest at parties.

Lois had Kit's hand now and was leading him towards the table where bottles and plastic cups were laid out. Plainly not invited to follow, Dora stared after them. What was going on? Her husband was stooping good-naturedly over another woman now, who was describing her conservatory, how perhaps he might take a look one evening.

She felt a hand on her arm and Felicity was standing with a hot dog for her. 'How are you doing?'

'Terrific, thanks.' Dora indicated the adoring circle around her husband.

'Handy, being married to an architect,' Felicity said.

Dora grunted. She considered being married to an architect no handier than being married to a poet. But there seemed no way to say that and not appear bad-tempered. She liked Felicity, who was about Dora's age and had a gentle, lilting Scottish accent. Liking Felicity had brought Dora round to the idea of living in a divided building in a faraway seaside town; if Felicity could thrive here, couldn't she?

Not only had Felicity thrived, according to her own account, but the house was perfect for a newly married couple with a baby on the way. When Dora and Kit were looking for somewhere to live, Dora had struggled to grasp that the kinds of houses she was used to – terraces, semi-detached houses: buildings that involved living side by side – barely existed here. Wealthy shipbuilders in the nineteenth century had built their country homes in Helensburgh, and now many were converted because of the cost of heating and maintaining such huge properties.

Paradise was a striking example of such a conversion. Blue, with a generous frontage that reminded Dora of buildings in Oxford somehow, there was no way of knowing from the front that it was divided into two; the grand façade with its ornate main door gave nothing away. Kit and Dora had bought the lower apartment with the main front door, and Paradise Upper had a staircase entrance at the back. Despite the house's beauty, it took Dora quite a few visits to agree with Felicity that it did suit them. She had scoured the estate agents for a family home that she recognised as one: a terrace with a courtyard garden; some small country cottage; a townhouse, even, tall and thin and looking out over the railway line at Helensburgh Central. But her choice emerged, simple and hard: a breathtaking mansion, which they could never have afforded, or part of one. Understanding this had taken her so long that several had been and gone from the market. They had committed to this one in some desperation.

Paradise's long front lawn stretched almost to the sea, separated only by a hedge and the narrow coast road. Dora had not got over the strangeness of having the sea so close, the incredible open emptiness of it, and the constantly changing colours of the sky and the water. This afternoon, the sea was a clear turquoise, hushing them gently from the shingle. There was so much outside space here. Dora had never seen such a huge garden in a domestic home. Alongside the massive lawn with its borders of shrubs and trees swept a wide drive, which became a forecourt in front of the house.

Felicity grinned. 'Yes, it's really yours! Your baby will be so happy here. Now, let me introduce you to a few people.' She took Dora's hand and led her back into the throng.

As the introductions started, Dora tried to retain the powdered faces with their attendant names. There were wives of the church elders; the lady who played the organ; the lady who ran the music society; the wife of the new minister; the new minister. A lady in a purple dress with a plunging neckline told Dora about her jewellery, which she made and sold. Perhaps Dora would like to come and see her workshop? Pointed questions and comments washed over her, hands brushed against her belly and Dora began to feel dizzy. How did anyone stay private – anonymous, even – here? Faces, accents, the landscape all demanded your attention, the luminous northern light searched you out, and look – the music-society lady was peering at her through thick glasses. Her eyes were huge behind them. She asked Dora a question – *when is it due*, probably – and now a man with a dewdrop on his nose was bending over her and telling her about the sewage system that lay under the road outside.

'Our best friends are your upstairs neighbours, Mo and Terrence,' said the jewellery-maker. 'Such *good* people. *Wonderful* people.'

'Oh, yes; I haven't met them yet.'

The woman said, 'They do such good work with the church. They *belong here*.'

Dora's husband was laughing again, relaxed and happy. His Edinburgh accent, which had always seemed so wonderfully exotic, blended in here, and did not seem like an accent at all. Kit had come home, in some fundamental way. It was the way Dora spoke that stood out. Kit caught Dora's eye and smiled. He looked like a complete stranger.

They belong here. The words wedged in Dora's mind, started a slow spin. They carried a clear implication, as yet unarticulated. What was it? That Felicity and Matthew had not belonged? Or . . . she and Kit? There was something accusing in the tone, or perhaps in the very words themselves. She braced herself to meet her upstairs neighbours . . . what would belonging here look like?

Dora suspected she had probably never belonged anywhere, but in the case of the city she knew best, Oxford, not belonging gave one a kind of exotic value. And because it was a university town, most people arrived there not really belonging. The daughter of northern teachers, Dora had never expected to go to Oxford, and indeed her mother had told her not to apply there, as she would feel out of place. Nevertheless, she had applied, had been successful; and to her mother's grudging alarm, for three years had immersed herself in the world that was most real to her: that of books and reading. A PhD on Wilfred Owen and the poetry of World War One had sealed her into its warm sandstone interior for another four years, and her own poetry had begun to emerge in that time.

Oxford had been a revelation. Poetry was a *real thing* in her gowned area of the town. Being clever was a good thing at Oxford, displaying your cleverness even better. After finally completing her PhD, Dora was offered a job at the university's publishing house as a lexicographer, which suited her interest in words and her temperament perfectly. And while many thought her shy and brainy to the point of passionlessness, they were wrong. There had been love affairs, mostly with young, intense and scruffy postdocs at the university. These had always fallen apart at the point where she was expected somehow to change, to accommodate them in some profound way. She never wanted to, enough, and they certainly seemed to have no notion of accommodating her, and her need to scribble and read.

It was a story – their story – that she and Kit liked to tell: how the unlikely couple met. A former tutor took pity on Dora's seemingly one-dimensional life and invited her to a dinner party at her former college, and Kit, a friend of a friend and newly widowed, was invited too, and there was an immediate connection between the brainy lexicographer and the gentle architect that no one could have foreseen.

Now that Dora was so heavily pregnant, she needed to go to the toilet all the time. The only advantage was that it was an opportunity to be alone, to escape when she needed to think. She excused herself from the jewellery lady and slipped away across the lawn towards the wisteria draping the front door's pergola like the entrance to a cave.

But as she crossed the forecourt and reached the step, with its promise of cool relief from the sun, she felt a hand on her arm. Felicity said, 'Ah, here they are, Mo and Terrence Divine – your upstairs neighbours.'

'Oh, but I . . .' Perhaps the introduction would not take long. Dora shuffled from foot to foot and turned to greet them.

Dora's most intimate neighbours were holding hands. They wore matching cardigans with a crest on the breast. Terrence's shirt was open at the neck, revealing a cross on a chain. His hair was combed back, creating an effect of rippled pewter, and he was wearing a pair of glasses with darkened lenses clipped on to them, but not pressed down, so they stuck out like two small visors. A faint scent of aftershave hung around him. He was unexpectedly handsome.

'Mo and Terrence, this is Dora. She's a poet!' With each word, Felicity eased herself further away, though her demeanour was impeccably friendly. She was now right on the invisible edge of what constituted their group.

'So. *Dora.*' An arm unfolded. Mo's little hand clasped Dora's.

Dora felt the cool fingers around hers. Her neighbour's hair was tightly permed and tinted a rather startling gold. On her forehead was an eye-catching mole that reminded Dora of a tiny nameless nation lifted out of a school map.

One more step back and Felicity would be free. She seemed anxious to be gone. Dora was puzzled. These people had lived together in Paradise for – how long was it? Five years? Felicity took that last step and vanished into the party, and Dora was alone with the new neighbours.

Mo watched Felicity disappear and then asked, 'Do you know the Lord, Dora?'

Dora's gaze roamed desperately and fell on the boat parked on the forecourt in front of the house. She was sure it hadn't been there when they came round to view. It was on a trailer and the tarpaulin had been rolled back to reveal, in curly gold writing, the name *Lady Maureen*.

'Um . . .' Dora didn't say the only thought to rise into the vacancy of her mind, which was, *Christ, that boat is enormous.*

'Jesus and the *Lady Maureen,*' said Terrence, squeezing Mo to him before releasing her like a spring. 'The twin pillars of my life.'

Mo said proudly, 'Terrence is an elder in the church. We've been here for – how long now, dear?'

'Oh . . . it must be fifteen years.' Terrence smiled down at his wife. It was a warm, attractive smile that left Dora feeling oddly envious. Terrence continued, 'It is Paradise indeed, here. Mo runs the Sunday school.'

Mo's attention turned to Dora's belly.

'When are you due?'

'November.'

'Our son, Theodore, is having his first child in the new year. Our first grandchild!' She studied Dora's swollen form, taking in every detail, until Dora blushed.

'Boy or girl?'

'Don't know.'

'You've a low bump, there. I think it's a boy. Terrence, don't you think it's a boy?'

Terrence looked startled. 'Oh, I don't know anything about all that. I'm more about the spirit than the flesh.'

Mo's voice was so breathy and sing-song that one word rustled into the next, making it necessary for Dora to concentrate hard, as if it were a complicated *Beowulf* lecture. The old lady went on: 'We'll be helping Theodore a lot with the wee one. My poor daughter-in-law knows nothing about anything, and my son, he's so busy with the double-glazing business. He's done so well. I don't understand the ins and outs, of course, but he's a real high-up now. So you'll be seeing a lot of us! Who is your birth partner?'

'My husband, Kit. Over there.' How she longed for him to come over. He knew how to talk to people. His easy social manner charmed everyone. He *belonged*. Dora was so tired and her bladder felt as if it might burst. As if to emphasise the point, the baby aimed a kick right on it.

Mo was talking again: 'It's wonderful to hear the voices of children, isn't it? Our friends love to visit us with their children. They *so* enjoy playing on the lawn.' Her eyes flicked up to her husband.

Dora reeled her attention back in, alerted by Mo's last whispered words. The long lawn at the front of the house, with the drive along-side it, belonged to Paradise Lower. The upper flat owned the rear garden, a neatly cultivated terrace with a summer house. In grappling with Paradise's divisions, Dora had seized on this ownership of the lawn as something that made her feel better about living at such close, isolated quarters with complete strangers.

She observed again the *Lady Maureen* dwarfing the Divines' parking space. She noticed the many cars parked in the drive for the party, and then she looked back at Mo, wondering how to formulate a reply. Had she, in fact, misheard?

Was she expected to say something like, *But you must let your friends run about on our lawn!* Is that what people did out here? Use each other's gardens?

Mo powered on: 'Felicity and Matthew . . . they loved to see children happy, laughing . . . enjoying themselves. Such *generous* people.' Her fingers crept to her neck, then her earlobes, then back to Terrence's hand.

Dora was getting a crick in her neck from leaning in. Finally, she could stand no more. 'Please excuse me. I'm so sorry . . . You know what it's like!' And she waddled towards the open doorway.

The gloom embraced her. She rested her head against the cool of the wall and took breaths until her pounding heart began to slow.

She looked around the beautifully corniced hall, with the wide decorative staircase at the end. Tomorrow, it would be hers. She and Kit loved the way that the lower apartment was largely untouched by the conversion. The staircase simply turned into a cupboard at a certain point. Dora's new home was fairytale grand with pan-elled walls and huge fireplaces and tall windows looking out over the lawn.

The original cloakroom in the hall was tiny, with an authentic Edwardian lavatory and high cistern. Dora had liked the space from the first time they had viewed the house. She thought she could see out the remainder of the party just sitting here quietly.

Dora was respectably married at last, to a man she could say without hesitation that she loved. They had bought the main apart-ment with a huge garden in the grandest house she had ever been in, and that, she had been sure, gave her a place. She could be like the ladies out there now; she could be a *hostess*; she could give her own parties on the lawn. Her child could grow up secure of his or her place in the world. Her child would be a Fielding, with a childhood home to love and remember.

This was the plan, and she loved it. She was a lucky woman. How many women really get what they want? All of it?

But unease crept and crawled all over Dora now. Alone in the Edwardian cloakroom, she pulled off her cardigan and scratched the skin of her arms until the red weals began to bead with blood. This steadied her mind a little, as did focusing on the sea and thinking up new ways to describe it. Waves strutting . . . a turquoise dress, off the shoulder . . . a submarine like a whale, with light breaking off its back . . . Waves strutting . . . or tutting? Perhaps at the shore . . . Perhaps the little waves tut at the shoreline . . . Dora smiled to herself, noticing, now, the fierce sting of the scratches on her arm. She ran the tap and dampened toilet paper and pressed it to the skin.

A knock at the door. 'You in there, Dora?'

Kit had come to find her. Exhausted, Dora pleaded to go home. They bid hasty goodbyes and, as Kit helped her into the car, anxiety sucked her words away. How she wanted to be a success, like her husband was. He seemed to have had a wonderful afternoon dispensing advice to the area's ladies. He had even chatted to the new neighbours and come out unscathed.

How Dora wanted to be the sort of woman a man is glad he married. Instead, all she could do was stammer, 'Kit, do you think . . . ? Do you think we've made a mistake? With the house?'

Kit's hand snapped out and covered hers. 'No . . . no, don't say that. You're just exhausted.'

There was a tap on the glass. Lois was signalling for Dora to open the window.

'I meant to tell you, Dora, dear,' she said breathlessly. 'There was another poet you may have heard of, here in Helensburgh. A long time ago, now. W. H. Auden! Do you know of him?'

'Really? In Helensburgh?'

'Yes, he taught at the boys' prep school, Larchfield, way back; I think it must have been 1930 or something like that. Anyway, I thought you'd like to know. Two poets! What do we call that? A brace? A couplet?' She giggled again. 'Well, I must be off. Lovely to see you both!'

'W. H. Auden?' Dora asked Kit in amazement.

'I remember something about that now.'

'Auden . . .' Dora repeated. 'That's so *unlikely* . . .' She trailed off, seeing the unlikeliness of Auden in this landscape suddenly very like her own. Kit kept his hand over hers as he drove them the short distance home.

Later, after they had eaten and Kit had fallen asleep in the bed-room of the bare flat they had rented for the move, Dora came into the moonlit sitting room, among all their boxes, and took out her notebook.

She rested her pen on the page.

(*Ah, the poetess!*)

Writing a few lines, beginning a poem, taking her fear out and studying it to make it into something – this was what she had always done to make sense of her life.

She wondered how it must have been for Auden, arriving into this strange place.

Did he, as she now did, lay down his pen?

Did he, too, find that suddenly, inexplicably, there was nothing to say?

THREE

Wystan

IT'S JUST AFTER FOUR when Wystan steps off the train at Helensburgh station. As the steam clears, he looks out for his friend Cecil, who got him the job at Larchfield and is the entire reason he's here. On the platform, a few women stand waiting for their menfolk, and a few men tuck their newspapers under their arms in readiness for the return journey to Glasgow.

Cecil is moving, that very weekend, down to Devon for his next job. It has been arranged that Wystan will just overlap with him, and see a familiar face before launching into the post as Cecil's replacement. Wystan's bags are heavy and he stops to rearrange them around his body. A wiry porter comes speeding up. 'I'll get them, sir,' he says.

Wystan indicates a bench a few yards away. The porter nods, a sandy fringe falling into his eyes. From a distance, he looks thirty; close up, he's much older. Wystan gives him tuppence and seats himself on the bench to wait.

Leaning against one of the platform's wrought iron pillars is a boy of sixteen or so, smoking. He has coarse ginger hair and is very lean; his trousers hang off him and his crumpled shirt is loose. His freckled face is pockmarked across the cheekbones, but in spite of this, or perhaps because of its slightly spoiled beauty, it is compelling. From his experience of loitering rent boys looking for trade Wystan knows the boy is not waiting for anyone in particular. Their eyes meet. The boy stares, drawing deeply on the stub of a cigarette as if it is his last. When Wystan looks back, the boy is still staring.

A skinny woman in a headscarf appears on the platform. 'Gregory!' she calls, and the boy starts. He tosses the cigarette into a barrel planted with spring flowers to his left. The woman – it must be his mother, surely – slips an arm through his, and off they go through an archway on the other side of the station. The boy doesn't look back. His big feet seem to trip over each other a little, as if the pressure to be a grown man, to be the stronger party, is making him clumsy.

'Wystan!' Cecil is there now, beaming, his hand out. 'Welcome to the Wimbledon of the north!' Wystan too throws down his cigarette, and embraces his friend. They have not seen each other since Wystan left university eighteen months before. Much has happened since then. Wystan's engagement is over, whilst Cecil has married his fiancée and they have been in Helensburgh for a little over a year.

Cecil is just three years older than Wystan, but his responsibilities make him seem more mature. He is flamboyantly dressed in a green shirt and striped trousers, and, with the glee of someone showing off his familiarity with a place, he gathers up Wystan's bags and ushers him out of the station to his waiting Austin. In less than two minutes, they are at Cecil's home: a narrow council house on West King Street. It is whitewashed, with a little stone arch over the doorway. The spring light glitters on the tiny windows and bathes the pocket garden in front, making it seem if not exactly nice then certainly not dismal. As they pull up, the front door opens and Mary waves in greeting.

How strange that in this leafy town, in this poor little house, such a happy meeting of two old friends should take place. Once inside, Wystan is shown to the room where he will stay that night before heading off to the school in the morning. All that remains are a bed with blankets and a lamp on the floor. Boxes are piled everywhere, filled with the Day-Lewis possessions. But it is still cosy; in the sitting room, the fire is lit and the sofa is drawn close. When Wystan comes down, they drink tea out of the three mugs Mary has kept back.

'So, tell me everything,' Wystan says. 'Will I survive?'

'There are a few things you should probably know. Perkins is insane, and his wife is dying of something. No one knows what it is, and he doesn't care. The whole place is falling to pieces, and you won't understand a word the boys are saying. The locals . . . well, I've barely met them, so cannot really say. We've rather kept to ourselves, haven't we, Mary?' He gives her a raised-eyebrow look over his tea. Her eyes dart over him as he speaks, checking the level of his tea, his expression, the cushions on the sofa.

'I've not been so well,' Cecil explains. 'But Mary is better than a mother at looking after me. Aren't you, dear?'

'I don't think the climate here is good for Cecil,' says Mary. 'We're looking forward to a bit of sun.'

'They light the place with gaslights still,' says Cecil. 'And the food is a horror. But I don't want to put you off. The boarders are quite amusing, and there's always Wallace.'

'Wallace?'

'A benefactor of the school. I think he's done a bit of locum teaching from time to time, knows a bit of history. He likes to meet any new staff, give his approval. He tracked me down in the first week. Got me blind drunk and babbling all my secrets.' He grins at Mary.

'So it's a lively sort of place.'

'I wouldn't say that. But, as I say, we've done a bit of motoring round Loch Lomond, and the rest of the time I've been teaching. It might be different for you, being single and living in the house.'

'There was a man on the train . . . a sort of vision,' Wystan says. 'Have you ever had that happen? You see someone, and it's as if he is you, twenty, thirty years hence?'

Cecil grins. 'Who was it, then? Mr Eliot?'

Wystan smiles, drops the subject. He reaches in his satchel and brings out a proof copy of his poems.

'When is it published?' Cecil flicks through the proofs, rubbing the corners gently with his fingertips. Cecil already has two collections out, but he knows that Wystan's work is going to eclipse them. Their friendship is intense, but with a kernel of awkwardness, because Cecil knows for sure that his future is going to involve hard work, unrelated to his poetry. There has been no financial support from his family and he is not rich. He has also opted to have a wife who must be supported. Wystan, though temporarily in financial need, is only playing with the real world. These poems are going to set him on a road leading far away. And yet it's impossible to blame him. He's so . . . Cecil looks again at the elegantly printed lines that he has seen in Wystan's terrible handwriting many times . . . He's so damn *clever*.

'To be published in September. I wish it was better, and so on.'

'Rubbish, man. And why are you squirming?'

'It's my backside. I've had a bloody operation and it won't heal. I'm sick to death; really, I am.'

A smell of cooking wafts in. Mary has made a stew and brings it on trays for them. It is a happy evening, and Wystan feels glad to be here. He wishes only that Cecil were staying, that he didn't have to face the school and the boys and his total lack of teaching experience alone.

FOUR

Dora

T HERE WERE THE BOXES, sealed and stacked.

    Ten belonging to her, filled with notebooks, drafts of poems and journals.

Just one belonging to her husband, Kit.

Dora was resting by the window of their Paradise sitting room. Around her was the chaos of moving: packaging strewn on the floor, teacups and plates forgotten on surfaces, and those boxes.

She sipped a cup of tea and studied the booklet of self-assembly instructions, noting that the first page had a diagram of two figures clutching screwdrivers next to the time estimate: forty-five minutes. For the last twenty minutes, Kit had been trying to balance three sides of a bookcase on his own in order to screw them together and, just as he brought all the edges together and made a grab for a bolt, one of them would slowly tip over with a sigh. The tension in the room heightened.

Putting down her tea, Dora now wrestled her pregnant body out of the chair and shuffled in front of him, holding the sides together

so that he could secure them. It was a wide bookcase and very awkward to squat at this angle with her arms stretched out. She winced
as pain flickered in her side.

'You're supposed to be resting,' Kit said.

'I know, but it needs two.'

'Well, I'm all right now. Thanks.'

'You know, it does help if you lay all the pieces out first and
read it through, like an exam paper, before you start.' Her hands
hovered over the pile of screws and bolts scattered indiscriminately
on the floor.

'Thank you for your input.'

Dora smiled and slipped back on to the chair.

'Well, I shall just watch you working then.'

'You do that.'

Through half-closed eyes, she observed her husband as he peered
at the instructions and grumbled through the bolts suspended in his
mouth. She still found it hard to believe they were married, with a
baby on the way and a new life stretching ahead. Secretly, she had
never believed it would get this far. First, because she was not the
sort of person anyone had ever wanted to marry, not since Isaac
from the trailer park when she was eight. Second, he was everything
she was unfamiliar with. He was older than she was by some fifteen
years – sixteen, for part of the year – with a whole previous life.
He was Scottish, although he had been away from Scotland for
over three decades. These, combined with his background of public
school, made him an alien creature in every respect. And yet, despite
(or was it because of?) their differences, they had been passionately
attached from the beginning.

When she opened her eyes, the electric screwdriver was whining in the bedroom as Kit tackled one of the new wardrobes. The bookcase was complete and standing against the wall.

Her gaze was drawn to the boxes again. It was troubling her that only one of them belonged to Kit. Also, she realised, as she yawned and altered her position gently, neither of them knew what was contained in the other's boxes. Perhaps that was odd; married people were supposed not to have secrets. And yet there they were, stacked neatly together in a harmonious little wall.

Dora's boxes had followed her all her life. She had ignored their growing inconvenience. She obsessively kept letters, cards, drafts, notebooks and they created a kind of past for her. Some people belonged somewhere and had a place their memories sprang from; Dora didn't. Her boxes grounded her, gave her a history like other people had.

Kit's single box was extremely tantalising. He never looked in the box; like hers, it seemed to fulfil its purpose simply by being there. And, until now, Dora had resisted the temptation to look in it herself. After all, the contents of her boxes were secret. She would have been furious if Kit had snooped in them. Her husband had, however, never expressed a wish to know what was inside them, and in return she had, reluctantly, never pried about the contents of his.

But now, wheezing with the bulk at her front, Dora found herself sliding over to the harmonious wall and pulling out the box. It was securely taped and she had to cut it open. It was hers to look at now, surely. They were married and would soon have a baby.

Photograph albums are what people carry through life into every new situation. Of course that was what was inside.

Her hands trembled at the cover of the first, then she snatched it out and opened it on her lap.

Two young people looked out from picture after picture, smiling by the sea, or at parties. Other young people surrounded them. There was a lot of laughter, arms around waists and shoulders. Dora's fingers strayed to her husband's youthful face to touch it, to be somehow part of the scene. She felt sick to see these pictures; nevertheless, she opened the next album.

These were wedding photographs. Kit smiling down at his new wife. Dozens of unknown people dressed up, smiling in groups. Dora scrutinised the faces of the bride and groom, trying to see in them some evidence that the wedding was a sham, that there was no love between them. The gaze they shared was unknowable. Was it happier than the gaze she and Kit shared in their wedding photographs?

Dora scolded herself, but for quite what, she wasn't sure. It was such a long time ago. The odd cut of the dresses and the oversized hairstyles should have been a comfort, but they weren't.

The last album was more recent. Two much older people stared out from the sofa or the garden bench, their eyes dark and inscrutable. Her – Mary's – expression was particularly changed. It was a little frightened. Her hands were twisted together in every shot. She had changed from a beautiful young woman into a thin, anxious figure.

And Kit, her darling Kit. He wore a forced smile, was pale and had shadows under his eyes. A cigarette smouldered in every shot.

Pity caught in Dora's throat.

'Ah, you decided to look at those, did you?'

She had not heard Kit come back. She flung the album to one side.

Kit sat next to her and sighed. 'It's all right. You've every right to see them.'

'I was just trying to work out what to do with all this . . .' She indicated all the boxes with a sweep of her hand. 'And I—'

'It's all right,' he said again and began to stack the albums back into the box without looking at them.

Dora wanted to talk about it, to talk about the happiness she'd seen in the pictures, about Mary. But also she didn't. She wanted to forget Kit had a past at all, to bury it in their own love affair. This had worked so far in the whirlwind of their year-long relationship.

Having secrets herself, Dora didn't know how to talk about someone else's. She opened her mouth to attempt something, but Kit interrupted: 'Is it time I threw these out?' He looked at her steadily.

'No. I didn't mean . . .' The thought whirled through her mind that perhaps she would have to throw her boxes out as well, which she really didn't want to do. 'I can't ask you to do that.'

'You're not asking me. I'm offering.'

Dora was determined not to cry. Crying when heavily pregnant was so uncomfortable. It squeezed and jostled the baby, and her constrained lungs struggled to gasp enough air. She dug her fingers into her palm and could not look at him. Shame bloomed across her neck and face: shame of her inability to have a grown-up conversation; shame of her blind fear that part of her husband would always be unavailable to her and the mythical Mary would hold him forever. Furthermore, she was ashamed of the smallness of her character, thinking only of herself and her baby when the woman was dead, and wasn't the poor man entitled to carry around a few photos?

'Do you miss her?' Dora blurted.

Kit suddenly looked very tired. He leant against the wall and paused to collect his thoughts. 'Look,' he said, 'I loved her, okay? But, for all kinds of reasons, well, she was unrealistic . . . Life dealt her bad cards and she played them badly. She wasn't strong.' His eyes met Dora's thoughtfully. 'Not like you.'

Strong? Me?

'Anyway . . . she couldn't cope with things . . . she started drinking really heavily after we were married – I mean, we all drank back then, but when I lost interest, she just carried on – and, well . . . basically . . .'

'What do you mean?'

'Did you never wonder why I don't have a family? Do you think I was happy about that? We couldn't risk it. I couldn't trust her. She couldn't trust herself. She didn't stop until . . . until she died. It took a long time. Longer than you'd expect.' Kit looked absolutely desperate.

'Oh,' said Dora.

'My wife . . .'

My wife my wife my wife.

'. . . was a lovely person. It torments me that I couldn't save her from . . . that. But when she died, it was a . . . relief.' Kit sank down in the corner. Dora's heart was beating so fast she began to feel faint. He said, 'So. I miss who she *was*, sometimes, yes, I do. But she turned into someone else. It's all so long ago.'

Dora stared at him. The information was an assault. She didn't know what to do with it. It was as bad – no, it was worse – than what she had spent time imagining. Finally, she said, with difficulty, for she feared the answer, 'Do you wish you were doing all this with her?'

Her husband's expression hardened as he looked up at her from the floor. 'It's more complicated than that, Dora.'

'No, it's not. It's perfectly simple. This is my only go at all this, and I've chosen you. Am I just someone who could give you the child you couldn't have with her?'

Dora could not believe she was uttering such questions. None of the answers were reassuring in the least. Perhaps this was why she had avoided such a discussion. If they had talked about all this early on, it would have been impossible to marry him. And she had wanted all this – him, the baby, the new life – so much.

Kit gave a deep sigh. 'Darling, if you ever decide to give up poetry, you could be a top-flight lawyer. You make an excellent case against me.' Then an expression she hadn't seen before slipped over his features. It was a meanness. 'I could, of course, ask you the same question. Have you only married a silly old fool like me to get the baby you want?'

Dora shifted to try and stand. She pulled herself up, and felt his arm under her, lifting her to her feet.

'Dora, darling . . . I'm sorry . . . I shouldn't have said that.'

'Leave me alone.' She pushed his arm from her. 'I feel sick.'

'Dora, listen. The truth is, I've failed at being married once. Failed in the worst way possible. I will regret that failure in some way perhaps forever . . . but there is something worse than that. Much worse.'

'What?' said Dora glumly.

'If I let *you* down. You are the best thing that has ever happened to me.'

'But what about Mary?'

'It's very hard to explain failure to someone who hasn't failed.' Kit managed a rueful smile. 'My greatest failure – if we are going to quantify them, and this is a lot of fun for me – is that I married Mary in the first place. Like I say, she was a lovely person, but we weren't really suited. I shouldn't have let it get as far as it did. I tried to make it better by honouring the words of our contract when I couldn't honour the spirit. So I never left her. I saw it through. Which, I realise now, just compounded everything. Do you see?'

'I think so.' The urge to leave the room subsided slightly. She said, 'I didn't marry you just to have a baby, you know.'

'It would have been fine if you did.'

'But I didn't. I want a life with someone who wants the same. Something more than just all my fucking boxes!'

'And that is what we are going to have.'

He took both her hands in his, and they stood in silence. Living a real life was very tiring, Dora thought. And she did feel sick and hot, even though something important had been sorted out. Perhaps because of it.

A FEW DAYS LATER, there was some furniture in the house, and the boxes were tidied away in the spare room. There was still a way to go before it would feel exactly like home, Dora thought, as she held up a print of some roses on the mantelpiece to see if it belonged there, but sunlight streamed in through the tall windows, and the space seemed to welcome her.

Footsteps creaked overhead and there was the crunch of wheels on the drive. Then the sitting room was plunged into gloom as the *Lady Maureen* moved with funereal slowness past the windows, pulled by the Divines' dilapidated jeep. They stared straight ahead as they passed Dora, and then they were gone. Silence and light enveloped the house again.

She was just opening her mouth to call Kit for his opinion when something happened. Fluid – only a small amount, but an amount – trickled between her legs, pattering on to the carpet. Her first thought was that she had finally lost all control over her bladder; she had certainly heard of women's pelvic-floor muscles being ruined by pregnancy and birth. Was this happening to her? Another warm patter on the carpet, just the same. And, with it, a very different idea, creeping coldly into her brain, from where she did not know – that the impossible was occurring and her waters were breaking. Such an event could not be happening, for she was only a little over six months pregnant. And yet . . .

Not able to compute what was happening, Dora laid down the print and shuffled to the bathroom, shutting the door. Sitting on the toilet, knowing the fluid starting to flow more strongly was what she feared, but still praying it was not, she pressed her head into her hands and tried to think. The outrageous physical problem crowded out everything else: nothing could exist alongside it. Panic rolled over her mind until it was blank.

Dora had not researched any hazards of this kind, having early on got lost in a miasma of birth plans, occult-seeming prohibitions and a burgeoning obsession about the sheer number of disposable nappies a child would get through before the age of three, which would *never rot*. There were ten weeks until her due date, and Dora had deferred most practical matters for the weeks ahead. She was not ready in any way to have an actual baby. She and Kit had no equipment; the room set aside for the baby's nursery was a dingy storeroom.

And yet . . . It was happening. After a few minutes, Dora emerged, no longer able to pretend there was nothing wrong, and went into where Kit was balancing a shelf in the dining room. Dora heard herself say, 'We have to go to the hospital,' and then his uncomprehending, 'What? Why?' But she was far ahead of him in the strange, dark tunnel they had now entered. For a few minutes, she wandered round the house, opening the drawers in a horrible parody of preparing the overnight bag every proper new mother has ready. How many pairs of pants would she need? Did she need a book? She had no Babygros or nappies, but perhaps this was no longer relevant in her case.

'What's happened?' Kit said, staring at her as she moved about the bedroom helplessly.

'My waters are breaking.' Her matter-of-factness startled even her.

'Isn't that impossible?'

'Yes. But it's happening.'

Kit stared at her for a moment, then went to get her coat and the keys, and put his arm around her to steer her to the car. 'Don't worry about all your things. I will bring them later. In you get.'

'But . . . ?' Numbly she obeyed and they clambered into the car. She tilted the seat back and propped her feet on the dashboard in an attempt to stop the flow of liquid. Kit squeezed her hand. He was the man she knew – the calm, gentle Kit – the only problem was that now Dora was changing into someone else. She stared out of the window, back to being a passenger watching the world blur by, as she had all the years of being a poet, before any of this, never driving, always watching.

The road twisted through the hills. On an otherwise deserted stretch, they got stuck behind not one but two giant logging trucks grinding up the slope barely faster than a bicycle. They were completely impossible to pass, wobbling with painful delay. Dora remembered then a friend from her childhood – what was her name? Anyway, she was adopted – a curly-haired gypsy girl from Hungary. And one day her parents were stuck behind a logging truck, just like this, and all the logs worked loose and fell all over their car and crushed it. The girl – what was her name? Dora shifted her feet, keeping her pelvis as raised as possible to keep the fluid from leaking out of her broken body, as if it mattered, as if it could be done anyway. The girl's father was killed and her mother brain-damaged, and little – what was her name? An only child, adopted – she lost all her spark and mischief, and did that thing that children overheard parents talking about: she went *off the rails*.

Perhaps Dora let out a whispered, 'Jesus!' Certainly tears crept out of her eyes, but there was also something muffling, insulating about the blanket of dread that now settled over her.

Where did the logging trucks go? They had vanished, and the motorway pressed on into twilight. Kit and Dora sat in silence, Kit's hand still over hers, and Dora wanted to say how sorry she was, for failing at being the one thing he had probably counted on. He thought she didn't understand about failure? He need only look at her now. It seemed that she did say something, because Kit said, 'Dora, I love you. It's going to be all right.'

It would have been pointlessly contrary to say, 'No, it's not,' though Dora knew with icy certainty that it was not all right, that there was a failure so enormous waiting to happen that it might just engulf them both, like those logs, enormous and lazy and stupid and deadly, and the parents of little – WHAT THE FUCK WAS HER NAME?

FIVE

Wystan

Make our hearts as bright and brave
as the mountain and the wave
so Scotland may be proud of you!

'Larchfield Song' by Cecil Day-Lewis

IT IS THE FIRST assembly of the summer term, 1930, and Wystan
Auden stands in Larchfield Hall with seventy-five pupils, a handful
of parents, the staff and Mr and Mrs Perkins. Miss Greenhalgh is
hammering the piano, her broad shoulders moving volubly beneath
her navy jacket. The refectory tables have been removed and the
benches set out as seating.

The boys' voices drift uncertainly into the rafters, carrying Cecil's
words. As he pictures his friend dragging out the clichés, a giggle
rises at the back of Wystan's throat, but somehow the purity of the
boys' voices lends gravitas to the song.

Mr Perkins, a ravaged-looking man with a skein of white hair, squints ahead. Wystan had his first formal meeting with him yesterday. Mr Perkins did most of the talking, handing Wystan a list of duties that includes minding the boarders, assisting Mr Jessop with drill, taking sports and, lastly, teaching English and French. Mr Perkins is from Edinburgh and has the sort of accent Wystan can follow. It gives Perkins a weary, superior air. Throughout the interview, Perkins had paused to rub his eyes, the swollen right one in particular, which contains yellow matter in the corner.

'WE'RE DOING THE BEST we can for the boys, Mr Auden. We have severely limited resources, which sometimes means we ask a lot of our staff. Your friend, Mr Day-Lewis, found the regimen a little too onerous, but there it is.' He leant forward. 'Times are hard, and I anticipate them getting harder. The parents don't like to pay, we're always chasing and forgiving, and the governors don't like to release money for anything at all, if they can help it. So my hands are tied about a lot of things. So there it is. For the sake of the boys. Now, any questions?'

Wystan shrugged. 'Whose is that car in the forecourt?'

'Oh, that's mine. Beautiful, isn't she? I can barely afford to take her out, but I can't get rid of her. No, no.' He rubbed his eyes again. 'My car is my pride and joy; she gives me so much pleasure in a life that, in all honesty, would frustrate the good Lord himself . . . So, if there's nothing else?'

'Thank you, sir.' Wystan left the dusty office at the back of school and had his first encounter with Jessop, the history master, heading off to do a round of the dormitories. Jessop was tall, blond and muscular – like a fantastic Viking, Wystan thought. He extended an eager hand to Jessop, even as his new colleague tried to sidestep him in the corridor.

'Wystan Auden,' Wystan said, catching the Viking's hand at last and feeling it cool and unwilling. 'First day . . .'

'Arthur Jessop. You can call me Jessop.'

They paused rather awkwardly, two tall blond men holding hands and with nothing to say to each other.

Jessop extricated himself. 'The boarders arrive this afternoon,' he said. 'I'll get them settled in. Then it's you.' His accent was a musical west-coast one, but his manner was furtive. When he finally edged past Wystan, his eyes were hard.

Wystan watched, disappointed, as he departed. What could have made him so repellent to the school's resident Adonis? Was it the bow tie? In an uncharacteristic moment of self-consciousness, Wystan reached up to the tie and considered taking it off, but then it did seem, with Jessop, that if it were not the tie, it would be something else. Still, it was only the first day: plenty of time to win over a sullen god.

After lunch, the cars began to arrive. Older boys said their good-byes, shaking hands with their fathers, hugging their tearful mothers, before immediately casting about for their friends. Jessop was on hand, carrying cases, directing boys and exchanging cursory pleas-antries with parents. Wystan watched a taxi pull up, from the back of which climbed a very small boy, who must have just turned eight. This was the late arrival: the new boy starting in the final term of the year. Wystan consulted his notebook. It was Jamie Taylor. The little boy clutched his satchel to him. His knees beneath short trousers were pink. On his cap was emblazoned *Potius ingenio quam vi*. His eyes were fixed on the gravel drive. Beside him stood his father, gaunt and tired. Wystan strode up to them, hand outstretched.

'Major Taylor?' he said. 'I'm Auden, the new schoolmaster. Can I help you with your bags?'

'Thank you.' Major Taylor's smile was brief, until it turned on his son, when it became huge and encouraging. 'Come along, Jamie. I've got your box.'

The little boy stared in disbelief at the empty taxi as they went through the gate. Wystan led them to the boys' dorm room and indicated Jamie's bed, which was a narrow cot between two others, with a locker on one side and a table with shelves on the other.

Parents and boys were bustling to and fro and a boy plonked himself down on the bed next to Jamie's and yelled across at a friend. Major Taylor and his son sat together on the bed, with the open box between them, as if there were no one else in the room. Poking from the top of the box was a teddy bear.

Major Taylor took the toys from the box and laid them carefully on the bed. It was a large pile, and it was clear there would be no room for them all in the tiny locker. He put his hand on his son's shoulder. 'We'll just go through them, Jamie. Pick which ones should stay and which I should take back with me.' The little boy began to cry silently.

'So, what do we think about Ted?' The major picked him up. He was too big to fit in the locker at all. 'Well, it looks like Ted's schooldays may not have started, eh?' As the toys were each picked up and looked at, they were either left on the bed or replaced in the box. When they had finished, the boy giving an almost imperceptible murmur of assent to this or that, all that lay between them was a tin soldier. Major Taylor put it in the locker, then pulled the boy's suitcase on to the bed and unpacked his clothes. Many of these had also to be taken back for lack of space. Pressed into the corner of the case was a cake tin.

'Look what Mummy made for you, Jamie. A cake! You can share it with your friends.' He laid it on the table, and then they were done.

The little boy gazed up at his father, chewing his lip. 'Daddy,' he whispered, 'I want to come home with you.'

Major Taylor wrapped the boy in his arms. 'Be a good boy, Jamie,' he whispered. 'I'll be back at the end of term.' And then he strode out of the room, straight-backed.

The little boy gazed around his bed, the room, the chaos of boys and parents, his face bright with tears.

Wystan stepped forward and put a hand on his shoulder. 'Come along, Taylor,' he said. 'I know a nice lady who will give you a biscuit.' Dumbly, Jamie Taylor followed him out of the dorm room, silent sobs wracking his tiny body. As they passed the bay window, Wystan saw the back of Major Taylor as he left the grounds. The back was bent now, and his hand was over his face.

Make our hearts as bright and brave!

The school song is coming to a close. Little Jamie Taylor stands steadfast at the front, trying to mouth the words, his eyes searching the audience for his parents. He still does not believe he is really here. Wystan glances round and catches Mrs Perkins' eye. She is sitting languidly next to her husband, encased in a green wool dress and jacket, with a hat and veil clamped on her head. She smiles at Wystan and raises her right hand very slightly and makes a tipping motion. Wystan guesses that this is the signal to come for tea later and he nods back at her.

After prayers, Mr Perkins stands at the wobbly lectern and manages to refrain from rubbing his eyes for the duration of a short speech. He welcomes the new boys, and the parents who have been able to join them on this first day of the new term. He introduces Wystan, peering down at his papers as if to refresh his memory. 'We have a new member of staff for English and French: the young and vigorous Mr Auden, who is fresh from Oxford and will bring, I am sure, a great deal to our community.' There is creaking and rustling as parents, boys and staff turn to look at him. Then the assembly is over and, when Wystan gets to his feet, he sees Olive standing by a table at the back with an urn and rows of teacups.

The parents immediately home in on Wystan, surrounding him in smart clothes and strange accents and enquiring about his experience and his background and is it true what they've heard, that he is a poet? Wystan nods and replies as best he can, but in the corner of his eye, Jamie Taylor hovers, searching the crowd for his father and mother. An older boy grabs him by the shoulder. 'Wee one!' he says. 'Get yourself in line!' And the little boy stumbles to the back as they file out, his hair sticking up, the gentle tidiness that denotes mother-love already slipping away from him, leaving him raw and naked in his clothes.

Dora

BIOLOGY. NATURE. DEATH. THESE were concepts that Dora had been able to take a view on or ignore when she was unmarried, living in a world of books, and had no baby.

Now they were raw and real. She felt them, not as words, not as ideas in her brain, but as muscle, vomit, sweat. Thinking was gone. Thinking was an outlandish, impossible luxury – a *Sandals* brochure in a war zone. She could hardly believe she had ever spent time thinking at all.

Due to her total lack of research, all information was new and quite amazing. For instance, she did not know that amniotic fluid replenishes itself: the foetus exists more in a waterfall than a bubble. If the amniotic sac breaks, birth usually follows within forty-eight hours, but sometimes the pregnancy can continue. The mother must simply lie completely still for the remainder of the term and new amniotic fluid will cascade over the foetus and through her.

Dora lay still in the room she had been allocated, observing her belly shift as the baby wriggled. She was a collapsed tent. Her baby was trying to make the best of it, but how could it survive in this broken place? The skin on her belly poked and dimpled as if a small rodent – a guinea pig, perhaps, or a squirrel – had mistaken it for a safe place and was trying to make a nest. It was pitiful, but also a bit frightening. Dora rested her hands lightly over the movement, perhaps to comfort the little creature, or perhaps to hide the sight from herself.

The door opened and Kit appeared with books and a teddy bear. Proudly, he laid *The English Auden* on the bed and, beside it, *The House at Pooh Corner*. In response to Dora's questioning look, he said, 'It's fun to read. You'll see.' Kit had made the room quite comfortable, with some photographs and a rug from home. The nurses observed this nesting process with ill-disguised bad temper.

Dora had not appreciated that the private room was for mothers at high risk of losing their babies. She was away from the ward and could not hear the cries of healthy babies, nor would she encounter proper mothers who had carried their babies to term. And, also, they would be spared the sight of her, with her leaking body and baby who would probably die. The nurses had not spelled this out. She had thought the room an act of kindness. But, as Kit took off his coat, a nurse came in and said, 'You're moving on to the ward tomorrow. We've got a really sick woman coming in.'

Kit clambered on to the bed beside her. 'How about a story?' he said. She nodded and rested her head on his arm, and Kit began to read *The House at Pooh Corner*, with all the voices. How had he known she would find this soothing, that it was about all her battered mind could accommodate? And it seemed that the little form inside her enjoyed it too, for it stilled, and somehow Dora began to drift off to sleep. She half woke as he left with a gentle kiss and a promise to return tomorrow, and dreamed of his fifty-mile drive back along the lonely roads to their empty house.

The night passed. The guinea pig/squirrel showed no sign of leaving. In the morning, Dora dragged herself carefully into a wheelchair, clutching without embarrassment the teddy that Kit had brought, and watched as all the homely additions were boxed up for Kit to take away. Then she was wheeled down to the ward.

It was worse than she had imagined. It was pure NHS Cinderella-department squalor. There were twelve beds – or maybe a hundred, the noise was so loud – crammed in. Babies were crying, or lying, enormous and still, in their cots like pupae. Beside one of the beds was a huge machine – Oh, God, was that some kind of milking machine? – to which a woman was being attached by her breasts. The curtains did not stretch all round the beds, and were uneven at the bottom, so that, even when an attempt at privacy was made, one could still glimpse the patients and the clogged feet of the nurses. Of course, one could hear everything. And what she mostly heard were admonishments.

'Oh, you've seen nothing yet, dear.'

'Wait till you have the second one!'

'The doctor won't be round for a while, I'm afraid.'

'No visitors till six!'

Into this bedlam, Kit arrived, and Dora grabbed his sleeve. 'Take me home. I can't stay here,' she pleaded. Perhaps she was, as everyone clearly thought, a prima donna, or some kind of weird ignoramus about the facts of life. Perhaps she was too posh to push and too snooty to lie in a dirty, noisy room full of strangers in their underwear. If so, she didn't care. Maybe these women were content to give birth in a cattle pen, but she, Dora, poetess, Oxford graduate and *human being*, was not.

Kit looked around him, bemused. Even he could see that this was the worst possible place to be if you were about to give birth to a baby who may die, and if you were one of the 'lucky' ones who carried on with their cascading pregnancy, how could it possibly be done here?

Visitors were not allowed until six, but it was apparent that, having driven fifty miles, Kit was not leaving. Grudgingly, a nurse told him that the boxes were under the bed for him to take away. He could stay for a short time.

'I want to go home,' Dora repeated. Nurses arrived and departed like compact white walls on wheels. Objects moved out of their way. Things, people, words collided against them and were lost.

Then a passing nurse, a young, impatient redhead, replied as though Dora had spoken to her: 'If you go home and you go into labour there, you won't be able to get here in time. Your baby will probably die.'

'Oh, God.' Dora was desperate. 'How about a hotel, then? There's a Holiday Inn down the road. All I'm doing is waiting. I need to be private. I need . . .'

The guinea pig/squirrel seemed to agree. It had gone very still inside the collapsed tent.

The nurse turned the wall of herself to face Dora. She had clearly never heard anything like this before. 'A hotel?' she repeated, almost wonderingly, looking at Dora anew, as if perhaps she were Oliver Twist and had said, *Please, sir, can I have some more?*

47

'I will be back in a minute,' the nurse said. She spun on her clog and glided out of the ward.

Dora sank back into the pillow, expecting to hear a roar of laughter from the nurses' station.

But then the redhead reappeared and, saying nothing, drew the tattered curtain around the bed.

'We're moving you,' she said to Dora. 'Don't *say anything*.'

Apart from when there was a total imperative, as in *I have to be somewhere else*, Dora generally did what she was told. Gratitude soared through her body, sticking in her throat.

'Thank you,' she mumbled.

'Hmm,' said the nurse. 'But you might have to leave at a moment's notice. And, if so, I don't want any trouble. I don't want any moaning.'

'Of course.'

'And no more talk of hotels, all right?'

'Agreed.'

What was this magical, mythical place she was being taken to? In her joy she almost sprang into the wheelchair. She didn't mind if it was another ward, as long as it was quiet and the curtains worked. She didn't mind if it was a broom cupboard.

Off they went, following the retreating back of the nurse, down a corridor, up a little ramp, round a corner, the echoing awfulness of the ward receding until it could not be heard at all. A single door on a long corridor. The nurse pushed it open and inside was a small but perfectly comfortable room. A proper bed, not a gurney. A television. A little window looking out on to the hills. No cot.

Kit helped her into the bed, with its lovely normal sheets and embroidered bedspread.

'Now, no unpacking,' said the nurse. 'You won't be here long. And, like I say, if we need the room, you're out and back on the ward without a murmur.'

'Where am I . . . ?'

Was it a promotion? Was it an ill omen? Was it better to go from the room kept for women whose babies may die, to the one for women whose babies have died?

SEVEN

Wystan

M RS PERKINS IS THE headmaster's dying wife. Her crinkly red hair is streaked with grey, and she is thin and flaccid from years of drinking, illness, morphine and immobility. She spends her days in an upper room of Larchfield, liking to hear the clang of the bell, the sounds of the boys rushing about their business, the admonishments of Mrs Clyde, the housekeeper. She wears an old housecoat, embroidered with flowers that look like rhododendrons. It was her mother's, and is grubby and threadbare. A plait runs down her back into which the greying fuzz of her hair is twisted.

Her illness is undefined, and her husband has grown indifferent. Mrs Perkins spends most of her time alone in the upper room, gazing out of the window and making notes in a school jotter. A bonus of the job is the unlimited supply of school jotters. Mrs Perkins has a whole bookcase of them, filled with diary entries, drawings of plants in the garden, lines from poems and many crossings-out.

She and Mr Perkins have no children. There was talk of it, then doctors said she was too fragile in mind and body for childbearing.

There is no mention of this in the jotters, but Mrs Perkins likes to meet all the new boys, and, for the youngest, she writes little rhymes, which they never see. Boys who are sick are brought to her, laid out on the daybed in the upper room and given warm milk with brandy.

She became ill shortly after marriage. It is an illness that she experiences as having a fiery core. It is consuming her, this fire. For the most part, she feels like a grate of dead ash, and then something happens, like the arrival of a new young master, and, deep beneath the ash, the core stirs. Though she has no conscious response to this, she finds it beneficial to increase her nightly drinks to three or four and to top up with a dose of laudanum.

The upper room is overheated with fug pipes and the southerly sun on the windows. But, when they are sick, the boys like to come and be fussed over by Mrs Perkins. She reads to them and hovers over them, brushing their hair from their faces with a thin white hand. She reminds them of their own mothers, who always look like this when they send the boys back to school after the holidays. When they are feverish, they often call her mother, and accept her kisses on their hot brows.

An audience with Mrs Perkins is one of the first duties of a new schoolmaster at Larchfield. And sure enough, on the morning after his arrival, Wystan is summoned to the upper room by Olive, the maid. He is curious about Mrs Perkins; according to Cecil, she is preferable to Perkins the headmaster. He makes a small effort at the washstand, splashing cold water on his face and applying some grease to his wayward fringe. But he forgets his teeth and does not polish his shoes. He is unconscious of the sight he presents to Mrs Perkins as she turns from the window and gazes upon him with her sad blue eyes. She is not in a housecoat for this meeting, having had Olive help her dress in a loose blue gown, which still fits her after almost twenty years. She too has made a partial effort, which feels like a whole one: her hair is in a neat bun at the back (Olive struggled with this for almost half an hour) and her face is pinked by a good splash of cold water and some rouge she rubbed in herself. But the dress smells of mothballs and she has forgotten to change her slippers, so the effect is diluted.

Nevertheless, the two partially tidy people meet with grace. Wystan gives a small bow at the door and approaches to take her hand. Mrs Perkins sees a most intriguing young man, odd to look at, certainly, with a long, ungainly face, fragile skin and large ears. He's very tall and unaccustomed to managing height, so seems to lope and flail. His eyes are pale blue and penetrating, however, and he has a manner about him that is unreadable. She cannot tell what he is thinking at all, unlike all the boys who parade in and out of this room.

Olive clatters in with tea, and Wystan settles himself on the daybed, where the boys usually recline.

'Mr Perkins tells me you're from Oxford,' she says.

'Well, I was studying there. For three years.'

'Albert and I always intended to travel, but then I became ill, and really since then I have been a terrible burden. Now, your room – is it satisfactory?'

Wystan's room is very bare, with just an iron bed with a horse-hair mattress, a desk by the window, a washstand and mirror. It suits him perfectly. He can see out on to a small forecourt where Perkins washes his Riley, and, beyond that, the gardens. The boarders are on the floor below, and through the floorboards he can hear the giggles, sobbings and arguings that are the life of small boys.

'Perfectly satisfactory, thank you.' His gaze falls on the shelf behind Mrs Perkins, upon which a bottle of gin is badly hidden behind some dried flowers.

'Your friend Cecil wrote us a lovely school song,' continues Mrs Perkins. 'We liked him. But I think he didn't like us so much.'

'I'm sure he did—'

'It's not a life that suits everyone,' says Mrs Perkins. 'Helensburgh is a small place, and young boys a long way from home are hard work. Well, this is what Mr Perkins tells me, anyway.' She takes a long breath and twirls the strands of hair which have worked loose from her bun. 'And you, Mr Auden? Will you be getting married soon?'

Wystan laughs, a bark of surprise. 'No, Mrs Perkins.' He leans forward conspiratorially. 'I was engaged not so long ago, but I'm afraid the lady broke it off.'

Mrs Perkins' eyes widen, and she too leans forward. An involuntary grin peeps at the corners of her pale lips. 'Really? Oh, you must be heartbroken!'

Wystan recognises, in the fading Mrs Perkins, a fellow gossip. A smirk dances across his face. He cannot keep it at bay.

'She found me disgusting, I'm afraid to say.' He watches how this volley will fall. Mrs Perkins stares at him. Colour has crept into her cheeks. This is a conversation! With actual information!

Finally, she says, 'And . . . are you? Are you . . . disgusting?'

Wystan slumps back, not breaking the eye contact between them. 'I'm afraid I am,' he says.

There is a silence during which Wystan can hear Mrs Clyde

instructing Olive in how to hang the pans, far below in the kitchen. Her fierce, almost impenetrable, accent snakes thinly into the room. Then there is another sound: a high-pitched whistle, or is it a wheeze? He realises the sound is coming from Mrs Perkins, who is pressing her pale fingers to her pale lips in an effort to staunch a wave of giggling. She winces in what looks like pain.

'Mr Auden. Forgive me—' Mrs Perkins surrenders. Her fingers slip away, she bows her head and her shoulders shake. The sound released is really quite raucous. Dirty, even, Wystan thinks. Mrs Perkins is not all she seems.

'I'm so sorry.' She gathers herself. 'You must remember I have been here for many years, and seen many masters come and go. It's so very dull for me. But never, in all my days, have I encountered anyone so perfectly unsuited to being here as you are. The mismatch is quite marvellous!'

Wystan's smile fades slightly. 'Mrs Perkins, I rather need this job.'

'Oh, Mr Auden, you are a breath of fresh air. Look at you! That is what makes you absolutely unsuitable, and also absolutely perfect. You will give Mr Perkins quite a run for his money, which is what he needs, between you and me.'

The lady clasps his hand. 'I can't tell you how I have longed to meet someone like you. Someone alive! Someone disgusting! And you simply must call me Daphne! No stupid formality between us. We shall drink and tell each other our secrets! We are going to be great friends.'

Wystan understands now. Beneath the surface of this wan invalid is an absolute subversive. 'And you must call me Wystan,' he says. 'Shall we make a dent in that gin you're hiding up there?'

EIGHT

Dora

D ORA'S EYES PUNCHED OPEN. Words ricocheted, as if whoever uttered them was right inside her brain.

So this was it. This was labour. The room was a hot, window-
less cell, full of people. Dora's knuckles were white as she gripped
the metal edges of the gurney. A young woman with an interesting
birthmark on her face was shouting at her. She noticed that she was
in tremendous pain, but it was as if she was outside it, as if she had
been amputated from herself. The gas and air suspended her com-
fortlessly above this warlike scene, with its bloody casualty.

The boys in the Great War came into her mind, all lined up behind
a rope, *like a fucking horse race*, one said, or more like a school sports
day, giggling and jigging about in the cold, nudging each other into
their racing stance . . . Dora flinched; the rough material of the
uniforms scratched the inside of her skull. The weight of . . . what?
She gasped and sucked on the gas and air in her hand; it did nothing
and her mouth simply opened and closed. *Innocence*. Their terrible
innocence felt as if it might crush her from the inside. The bang of

knowledge *with no time for book learnin', boys*! Knowledge of death, of pain; the full comprehension that an explosion was exactly that: the world in smithereens, beyond repair . . .

Even though the boys had signed their life-insurance forms, and even though they had written a letter home to be posted in the event of their sustaining injuries incompatible with life . . . they were entirely innocent of what that meant when applied to themselves. They had laughed about it. They were immortal, of course. Their mothers loved them and they were innocent of all true knowledge.

Until those words, there on the muddy starting line – *May God go with you* – and the bang of the rifle to set them off, wobbling under their packs as if they were doing a high octane egg-and-spoon race. They were no longer laughing; they were no longer saying anything at all because that unexpected prayer from a sergeant, who was not prone to any sentimentality, nor indeed any emotion at all, that prayer dealt them the first real blow of their lives, and in each of the boys now was a fissure, a creaking faultline in the clear window of innocence.

'What did he say?' asked Dora.

Kit's kind face looked down at her. 'He didn't say anything, sweetie.'

And Dora realised that it was she who had spoken – finally forced to articulate the terrible understanding she now had, but only the edge of it, only the manageable edge behind the starting line . . . She had said, 'Is my baby going to be all right?' And there had been no reply. The many people in the room all looked at the floor, or at their glinting lines of instruments, and her words, uttered with such effort, with such willingness through her pain to absorb the full implications of what was going on here, her words were not answered.

No one prayed for her. Dora was alone with her realisation. Life and death were real and in this room. It made sense only if one thought of it as a punishment. If this was a punishment, then perhaps there was a way she might be forgiven, and then it would stop and she might return to her previous state of innocence, rolling her eyes over *What to Expect When You're Expecting* and other flimsy shields against real knowledge.

Those boys she'd read about in her studies, now alive in her brain . . . most of them wrote no poetry; if they had any talents, most did not live long enough to see them flourish. They gouged each other to death with bayonets, blew bits off each other with ill-aimed grenades. Nineteen-year-olds cradled seventeen-year-old friends as they bled to death. Most were virgins; a few had never been kissed, except by their mothers.

Most of them cried for their mothers at the last, and, if they survived, cried for her back in the dugout. Dora, too, cried for her mother at the last. With bowed heads, the doctors and midwives seemed to accept what was to come.

Time, unquantifiable, passing . . . A man she'd never seen before, but who seemed nevertheless familiar, stepped out of the shadows and bent over her with curiosity. He was filthy, stinking of alcohol, his greatcoat drooping over his shoulders. His purple face was grave. It was the first time someone had regarded her closely since she had arrived in this room, and she tried and failed to speak coherently. The words came out as a mumble. He nodded to her, like a weary sergeant, and left the room.

Then a cry. No, more: a *protest*.

And a very small baby – not a guinea pig or a squirrel, but a *baby* – with a little wisp of hair and covered in blood, was placed in her arms.

The baby opened a gummy mouth and wailed.

And they took it away before she could give the baby the good news that one of them had definitely survived.

UNTIL THEY HAD NAMES, newborns were written up on the big whiteboard at the entrance to the neonatal ward using surnames with the prefix 'baby'. Having arrived far in advance of her name, Baby Fielding was placed, like a tiny Snow White, inside a glass box. Here she would stay, in her nest of wires and tubes, until she was big enough to go home.

And thus began the twilight world of driving. Fifty miles each way, every afternoon, to visit the little tank. Every night, they fell, exhausted, into bed; every morning, Dora dragged herself up to express milk, alone and freezing in bed, while Kit put in a morning's work. Then an afternoon in the car and the hospital. And the wheels of the car went round and round, round and round.

Why was Dora not afraid? Like her baby, she was marooned in a place that was a kind of anteroom to feeling. She knew nothing about prematurity, its alarmingly poor outcomes in many cases, nor its long-term consequences. Events moved so quickly that she had no time to find out. Baby Fielding was a *good weight*, that was all she knew. Dora's expression showed nothing more than tight-lipped bewilderment; meanwhile, her body continued to do its duty, to do as it was told. Never had she and Kit slept so darkly and deeply, the sleep of pure exhaustion.

Baby Fielding was still in the animal world, a world without language, with only need. She could not suck, being so young, and had to lap her milk from a tiny cup, like a kitten. This she did vigorously, supplemented with a feeding tube when Dora and Kit weren't there.

Dora fixed on the doctors who had miraculously saved her baby: the consultant who had been at her birth, and various young residents in creased white coats who could see two people when she stood before them holding her baby, rather than one creature-combination of mother and baby. They strategised and planned, pens galloping over clipboards, earnest faces enquiring after Baby Fielding's weight and Dora's health. They commanded regular formula feeding through the little tube to make the tiny soldier grow. If Dora could supplement this with breast milk by expressing it, this was excellent.

Tiny animals must grow. Need must triumph over ideology. Baby Fielding was in a medical situation.

Dora knew nothing about current trends regarding the feeding of babies and, in her battered state, it never occurred to her that there even was a trend. Surely everyone was here to help her help her baby? It took a midwife to sit Dora down and explain that everything was different now.

Dora *must* breastfeed. On *demand*. It was the *most important thing*. Otherwise her baby would not grow and she would not bond. Baby Fielding might even, it was hinted darkly, *not do so well*.

'But,' Dora protested at first, thinking still that this was a matter for discussion, not instruction. 'But she can't suck. She weighs less than four pounds. Isn't it more important to get her weight up?'

'Her weight will come up if you breastfeed on demand.'

'But the doctors say—'

'This is nothing to do with the doctors.' The midwife leant in, scrubs rustling. Her eyes were weary with the dozens, perhaps hundreds, of recalcitrant mothers she had had to explain the new world order to over the years. 'I'm telling you that you need to breastfeed your baby on demand, or she's not going to thrive.'

'But I'm only here for three hours a day!'

The midwife's eyebrows rose. 'Yes, I've been meaning to talk to you about that. You don't seem very . . . *concerned* about your child. Not very *committed*.'

Where was Kit when she needed him? Dora scanned the bleak room desperately. All that greeted her exhausted gaze was the shifty gleam of the walls.

The midwife sighed. She had met quite a few of Dora's sort before and was unperturbed. The brute facts of life always won in the end. It only prolonged a woman's torment to keep questioning everything. She rose beside Dora like a big grey wave. 'I'll be back,' she said.

In the short hard nights between trips to the hospital, Dora began to dream of being unable to feed the baby at all, of her starving to death in Dora's arms, or alone in the tank, far away. Dora was *uncommitted*. She was *unnatural*. She had been unable even to carry the baby to term. Dora began to worry that her daughter would die because of her mother's dogged adherence to feeding her formula.

If Dora thought she had ended some kind of argument, that everyone was going to agree to disagree, she was wrong. A few days later, the unit called to say that Baby Fielding was ready to go home and Kit and Dora should spend the night at the hospital in their family room and then take her home the next day. Stunned, they ran about arranging Kit's Mothercare purchases in the nursery. How could it be? She had a tube into her stomach and could fit in a hand. She didn't have a name – the only newborn still on the whiteboard without one.

When they arrived, they found their baby exactly as every other day, lying quietly in her tank with a tube in her stomach.

'But we can't take her if she still needs a tube,' Dora said.

A new midwife, uncannily similar to the previous one, said briskly, 'We'll take that out today and then she can go tomorrow.'

'I've never heard anything so ridiculous,' said Kit. 'We're not taking her home.'

'She's ready to go home.'

'No she *isn't*!'

The midwife glared at them both and left the room. Dora and Kit stood helplessly by the tank. Kit slid his little finger into Baby Fielding's hand and the fingers curled round it.

The door opened and the consultant from the birth came in, with a small group of midwives.

Holding his clipboard rather uncertainly, he looked at the baby in the tank with the tube and asked, 'You don't think Baby Fielding is ready to go home?'

'She's got a feeding tube in her stomach! She's plainly not ready,' said Kit.

The consultant blushed slightly and said, 'Actually, you're quite right. I'm not sure why we told you to take her home . . . ?' He looked enquiringly at the midwives, then seemed to remember something.

'There's been a question among the nurses and the midwives about your . . . er . . . commitment to breastfeeding, Mrs Fielding.'

'I have no commitment to breastfeeding! I have a commitment to *feeding*. You've been feeding her formula from the beginning.'

'I think it would help matters if we could agree that . . . er . . . *we* are going to hang on to Baby Fielding for a while longer, and, when you go home, *you* will be feeding her a . . . *combination* of breast and bottle . . . ?' He looked at Dora pleadingly. 'On demand . . . ?'

'Yes,' Dora said wearily. 'I will be feeding her a combination of breast and bottle. On demand.'

'Because, as we all know, demand-led breastfeeding is best for Baby, and supporting mothers with breastfeeding is NHS policy.'

He offered Dora a tiny smile at the ludicrousness of their exchange, while the midwives looked on sullenly.

They were left alone at last. It seemed that they had barely been left alone since the baby was born. Dora lifted her baby out of the cot and the three of them sat together on the edge of the bed.

'She looks like you,' said Dora to Kit. 'She's got your hair already. She's going to be a freckly Scot.'

'We should give her a name. Something really beautiful.'

'My grandmother was called Beatrice,' said Dora. 'I always thought that was a lovely name. We called her Bea for short.'

'Was she special to you?'

'She was the best,' said Dora. 'And you know what Beatrice means? It means "she who brings happiness".'

'Beatrice it is, then. Maybe we can squeeze my mother's name in there somewhere, as a middle name.'

The parents' hands crept together around the tiny form and their heads touched. It seemed to Dora that everything was as it was meant to be. She and Kit were the only possible combination to make this perfect little child. Bea's tiny fists had God-like powers; already they had dealt critical blows to the past, filled it full of holes through which the present poured. In that moment, there was no longer any past. None of it mattered. Everything people said about a child changing everything was true.

In a few days, Beatrice was ready to be discharged. Carrying her over the threshold of Paradise, they gazed upon her in amazement and disbelief that they had been allowed to keep her. After all the rules and prohibitions . . . What? You just took a baby home, without surveillance? Like a guinea pig?

Beatrice mewed and gurgled, and Kit and Dora delighted in this first for them both. Not even Dora's isolation or her unease about their situation could spoil it. Among the dozens of cards and vases of flowers sent for their daughter, they collapsed in a happy, champagne-enhanced humour, clinking glasses at their brilliance in finding each other, and in creating such a wonderful being as Beatrice. When she napped, they tumbled into bed together, celebrating with their bodies the triumph their bodies had produced.

NINE

Wystan

WHEN OLIVE BRINGS THE newspaper to the breakfast table on Wystan's third morning, Jessop snatches it from her hands. He says, without looking up, 'I have J3 for history first thing. Only chance.' His handsome features compose themselves into a sneer. It's unfair, Wystan thinks, that Jessop's bad manners do not detract from his beauty one jot.

'Oh, Lord, save us.' Jessop sniggers over his toast and turns the paper to face the group round the table, which comprises Miss Greenhalgh, Wystan, Mrs Clyde and, at a separate table, the boarders. The headline reads, *SHE'S MADE IT!*

Jessop reads aloud: 'Amy Johnson has landed safely in Australia! Her daredevil flight took her into the record books as the first woman to make the crossing. Glamorous Amy emerged from the cockpit tired but happy and waved to waiting crowds. It is said she undertook the flight with only a flask of coffee and box of frocks.'

Wystan says, 'There is something peculiar about women pilots.' The statement surprises him, and like other utterances that seem to emerge from him of their own accord, he stores it for later, to be unpicked in a poem.

Jessop snorts, 'Indeed there is!'

'Well, I think it's marvellous,' says Miss Greenhalgh. 'She's almost self-taught, you know.'

Jessop says, 'Miss Greenhalgh, the fuss is only because she's a girl.'

'I disagree, and I think the boys should know about it and how important it is.' She glances at the boys gobbling their bread and butter. 'She's a British heroine. I'm going to mention it in geography. She's flown across half of the whole world!'

'Well, it's not going into history. Anyone who's interested can see it in the paper.' Jessop tosses the paper down on the table as he scrapes back his chair. Wystan reaches for it. A huge photograph of Amy Johnson's face with its tight helmet and goggles adorns the front. He scrutinises the paper for a picture of the plane itself, the *Jason*, a tiny green Gypsy Moth. Halfway down page two, there it is: a blurry photograph of the plane, with Amy apparently in it, tilted over Hull. He is mesmerised by the photograph. He finishes his tea, delighting the younger company with an uninhibited slurp, tucks the paper under his arm and stands up. He and Jessop are about to leave the room together and Wystan takes a deep breath and holds the door open for his colleague.

'Jessop, perhaps you can help the new man out . . . ?' says Wystan, following Jessop's retreating back.

His colleague slows reluctantly, pulls his watch out of his pocket and looks at it with exaggerated hurry.

'Where does one go for some diversion in Helensburgh? I was thinking of a beer one weekend.'

'*I* spend my weekends sailing with the Wallaces,' says Jessop. 'I don't know what *one* does if *one* is without connection.' He shrugs, as if to say, *Is that it?* and turns to go. Wystan, baffled, stays him with a hand on his arm.

'Mr Jessop, I fear I have offended you. I am very sorry.'

The chiselled features regard him, aloof as a Michelangelo statue. 'Auden, I never wanted you here. You're not our sort. Cecil, before you, wasn't either, but at least he didn't parade himself around like a bloody peacock.'

'Whatever do you mean?'

'I'm sick and tired of you folk with your show-off clothes and your low morals making this school some kind of English outpost.'

'Jessop, I . . .'

But before he can work up some kind of excuse for himself, some effort at charm, Jessop is five strides or more away. He turns briefly to say, 'Before I forget – rugby next lesson, Auden. See you on the field.'

Wystan is left standing, speechless, in the corridor. Did this happen to Cecil? His friend never mentioned any reaction from the locals, but then, he wasn't in the building every day and night. At least he has glimpsed what lies beneath Jessop's hostility. To be despised for being English and without connection – how very novel that is. Wystan is well used to being something far worse, used to negotiating an alien world that would cast him in prison if it knew the truth. But such is the strength of Jessop's righteous feeling that, for a moment, Wystan's Englishness does *feel* illegal. He recalls those long weeks of school – far from home and all normal points of reference gone

– when *anything could happen*, when laws did not necessarily apply. Indeed, many things did happen.

He shivers. Is this a significant development, this resentment from Jessop? Will it spread? Wystan sighs. At any rate, he can now give up all hope of a friendship with his colleague. Wystan's act of resistance will be to admire his lovely form in secret.

Wystan takes the paper to his room for the treasured hour before the dreaded rugby. He carefully tears out the picture of Amy and the *Jason* and tucks it into his notebook. There's something about the big female smile inside the masculine machine that's compelling. Transgressive. He shivers, not as if *someone walked over your grave, there, my boy*, but somehow – yes – a touch from the future, a future that will be different. This sensation is always a sign that a poem is calling. He rushes to his desk and loses himself in scribbling the half-formed ideas down on the page.

An hour later, mist clings with a reptilian torpor to his skin. His bare legs have come out in goose pimples. When he moves, the shorts billow and a freezing draught gusts right up his groin. As he shuffles along the line, he feels hate gathering in his gut and travelling with a shiver right up to his hair.

'AUDEN!' Jessop's voice shoots through the grey, sharp as a ball, followed by the ball itself, which thumps into his chest and almost knocks him over.

Wystan picks it up from where it has fallen and jogs, as athletically as he can, into the cloud of boys who are all watching him.

'Yes?'

'Scrum to Foyle House. Seeing as you fumbled it.'

This is the problem that Cecil faced, only he faced it with more red-blooded manliness. There are often simply not enough boys to field a full rugby team, and usually a master is roped in to beef up the side. In this case, Wystan is replacing two boys. He has no idea why this should have been considered a good idea. Except that he's tall. Maybe he looks like he is worth two boys.

'Sorry.'

His team of damp twelve-year-olds regard him with a mixture of puzzlement and contempt, then turn and tramp back into their positions. They know they are going to lose, and this new master, with his funny accent and spindly legs, is going to make them lose.

At his own school, Wystan was a failure at all sports, being clumsy and large, with a mind always elsewhere. But somehow it didn't matter because he had other skills that interested small boys. He had views, and indeed *facts*, about God, and he also brought the facts of life into his year group, fascinating and disgusting the boys with his explanation of what awaited them all upon marriage – or before, if they were unlucky. His uselessness on the sports field was forgiven because, as one classmate would say, he was a 'witch doctor', and such earthly skills were not expected of him.

At Larchfield, however, witch doctoring or any form of outlandish ability is not appreciated and, indeed, should it rise to the surface, will likely be outlawed. Failure at sport is not an option. He had thought he would get away with refereeing, but Jessop seems bent on ensuring his humiliation by taking the refereeing himself and putting Wystan in the team. And one thing Wystan does not want to do is let his team down. He murmurs to himself as he jumps from foot to foot to get the circulation going in his legs, longing to shout across the pitch, *Look, boys! My spirit is heroic! It is just the poor ugly body . . .*

He doesn't object to watching a game, mainly because he can appreciate the patterns that bodies make on the field. Wystan loves machines, and a cricket game or indeed a rugby match well played has all the grace and mystery of a machine. But taking part in a match himself is a different matter. Running back to his position with a fervent hope that the ball will not come his way, he glances down at his skinny legs, his soft stomach beneath the mist-soaked shirt. This is not the material of which heroes are made. In a sense, his wish is granted, for the ball does not come anywhere near him; it has flown off in the hands of School House and a roar erupts, signalling a try.

McLeod belts in for the conversion. Mud spatters from his feet, lands in the curls of his hair and across his face. The ball disappears into the sky, then sails across the field in a lovely arc between the posts. Foyle House break into cheers and jump up and down. The School House team slump and glance resentfully at their grown-up teammate.

Being a disappointment is unbearable to Wystan. He is grateful for the mud on his skin because his face is burning. 'Come on, boys!' he says with sudden conviction. 'Now begins the fight back. Look, I'm worth two of them!'

Do they know what he is sacrificing for them, as he applies every ounce of his mind to that ball, concentrates every fibre of his ungainly body on not missing it? Do they know what love pounds in his heart, as a small voice cries across the mud, 'Mr Auden, sir!' and a boy's hands reluctantly trust the ball to his catch? Wystan quite simply gallops for it, his eyes fixed on it as if it were the answer, as if it were a gift from God himself. Is this what it is to be a man, to forget oneself, one's ugliness and uselessness and give all for one's comrades? Wystan reaches up, biting his lips, his blue eyes squinting. They are all watching . . . The ball is taking a physically impossible amount of time to arrive, because this is his test. This is the test of his character, of what he *must be*. He breaks into a wobbly sprint. Boys throw themselves at his knees and ankles to bring him down, but somehow the leather smacks firmly into his palms and he is still upright. 'Philip!' he cries, in that moment forgetting to use the sur-name and simply saying the boy's name as he would a brother – and he hurls the ball towards the muddy face.

His job is done. Philip Theakston catches with certainty, heads off into the mist. A cheer tells Wystan that Philip has scored, their defeat is not a shameful one. Caked in mud, Wystan suddenly wants to weep. His chest heaves.

At last Jessop blows the whistle and his test is over. As they troop back to school, he looks behind at the misty field, churned and barren. This is the space that heroes occupy, that men understand. Why does he not feel pride? Why does he feel so lost?

TEN

Dora

TERRENCE'S FOOTSTEPS WERE NOW familiar mournful creaks, long sighs in the planks above their heads. Mo's footsteps were staccato and urgent, more like the wings of something battering against glass.

Dora was sterilising some bottles, still half asleep. She jumped as the front door to the upper apartment opened and Terrence's shiny black shoes descended the iron staircase in front of her kitchen window, followed by his smart trousers and then the coat, black as a submarine. Terrence had good shoulders that filled out the sober uniform; she noted this, even as she pulled her dressing gown around herself in mortification that he could see her. Not that he was looking; Terrence was off to church. Dora did not know what elder duties involved, but they seemed to take up a lot of his time. The smart shoes clipped up and down in front of her kitchen most mornings. They really must get some blinds.

A rap on the front door.

Again, harder, full of confidence.

It was Terrence, his grin without warmth.

'You're blocking me in!' he said.

Dora looked cheerlessly out on to the drive. This happened most days now. The entire forecourt was a car lot, all in the shadow of the *Lady Maureen*. There were always strangers here, driving up and down, parking in front of the windows, dashing up the staircase to shout and stamp above their heads.

With nowhere to park their own car, Kit had squeezed it under the living-room window. Both front-room windows now looked out on to metal, with the dining-room window cast into shade by the magnificent flank of the *Lady Maureen*.

Dora sighed, pulled her coat over her pyjamas and laid Beatrice on a cushion in her playpen. She moved their car down the drive and on to the verge on the road. Terrence drove out in the jeep, nodding without looking at her. She tried not to be angry; being accommodating was what she was striving for.

As Dora walked back up the drive to the house, she saw Mo standing on the lawn. Hands on hips, she was surveying its potential . . . for what?

'Hello, Mo,' Dora said, in surprise. Mo mumbled something and turned away. Dora glanced at the upper window and saw a row of figures she did not recognise. They all stared as Dora went into the house, the hairs prickling on her neck and arms.

Dora tested the temperature of the milk on her wrist and then took the bottle into the sitting room, where Beatrice was waiting in her playpen. As she fed the child, she watched her neighbour on the lawn. Mo abruptly crossed the drive to return to the upper flat. She passed so close to the window that Dora stumbled backwards.

Dora scurried with the baby to the kitchen door and watched as Mo's comfortable loafers ascended the staircase. Unlike Terrence, Mo did look in as she passed and Dora cringed back into the gloom of the doorway.

The door upstairs slammed. Then, as always, the CD player went on. Singing and some kind of dancing bumped through the ceiling. Mo and Terrence had visitors again. Dora could not keep track of who arrived and left.

Jesus. Didn't anyone have a job? Or school? Again, as happened every day, the thought shuffled like an unlucky card to the front of Dora's mind: We have to do something.

Come down and have a drink, she wrote on a note. *Come and see the baby. Come and see our half of the house. Let's meet properly.*

Laying Beatrice back in the playpen, she slipped out of her door and round the house to the staircase. She had not set foot on it before, and it felt very odd, creaking past her own kitchen. She peered in as she passed, and was relieved that the light reflecting on the glass prevented her seeing much. The staircase was beautifully wrought and painted in black and gold. Dora noticed that the treads were made of words, and, though she dreaded being caught in her half-dressed state, she could not resist pausing to see what they said. Starting from the bottom step, they read,

And Jesus said
Let the children
Come to Me
And do not
Forbid them
For of such

Is the Kingdom

Of Heaven.

Dora shuddered. She hurried along the little balcony, with its window boxes of geraniums, and pushed the note through the letterbox of the red front door, where a little plaque read, *M. and T. Divine*, then scuttled as fast as her slippers could manage back to her door, panting with relief.

Beatrice lay where Dora had left her, gurgling in the playpen. As Dora gathered the plump shape into her arms and eased the teat into Beatrice's mouth, she marvelled at how reassuring was the unselfconscious greed of the baby animal, how real and warm, how the baby slurped with devotion until the bottle was all gone, and then fell back, eyes closing in ecstasy.

Fatigue crept over Dora; she felt her own eyes closing despite the noise from upstairs, but she dragged her lids open. Mothers who fall asleep with their babies roll over and crush them. Mothers who fall asleep in the day, when they don't have a job, are lazy and do not deserve the roof over their heads they have somehow managed to obtain, nor the little bundle of life they have been blessed with. She carried Beatrice to the nursery, and laid her on the changing table and changed her disposable nappy. The washable nappies were far too big for this minute baby she had produced, and lay in a pile tormenting her. As well as being prone to falling asleep, prone to desperate tears over nothing, unable to breastfeed and unable to *be contented*, she was also a polluter, like every other selfish woman, contributing to the filth and destruction of the world with mountains of disposable nappies.

As these thoughts pounded the rusty track of her brain, she sang 'Here Comes the Sun' to Beatrice. She buttoned the premature-size Babygro, rubbed the baby's back gently to release a burp, then laid her carefully down in the cot. Bea murmured a little and drifted off to sleep. In theory, Dora now had three hours to do something useful. There was laundry to put on, dinner to make – or some kind of attempt at it, at least – and definitely some cleaning to do. Instead, Dora wandered back into the sitting room and put on her *Friends* DVD, turning it up so that the canned laughter drowned out the noise from upstairs. She could probably watch half a series before she had to move again. She closed the curtains against the sharp winter sun and curled up on the sofa.

FOOTSTEPS CROSSED THE CEILING, descended the staircase, then crunched on the gravel outside the Fieldings' door. There they were, Terrence and Mo, having accepted the invitation to visit. Terrence had put on a stripy pink shirt, which suited him. Mo wore a plaid skirt and a jumper made of some kind of fibrous material that shimmered. She had made several visits to the front lawn over the course of the day, doing God only knew what. Dora and Kit had decided to bring the matter up carefully this evening.

With soil-engrained fingers, Mo handed Kit a paper bag. 'For the wee one,' she said. Inside was a miniature New Testament with a spill-proof white cover.

'She gives one to every new baby in the parish,' said Terrence proudly.

'How lovely,' said Kit.

Mo asked, 'Where is she, the wee babe?'

Beatrice was fast asleep in her nursery. She slept a lot, due to her prematurity, and had to be woken to be fed. In the cot, she looked like a doll. Reddish brown hair poked out beneath her little woollen cap.

Mo leant over the cot, pressed a finger to the sleeping baby's cheek. 'Oh, my Lord, it is a privilege. A privilege. That's what it is, isn't it, Terrence? To see this wee miracle.'

'It is,' said Terrence.

'We pray for her, you know, in church,' Mo said. Very fine fibres glowed in rainbow colours in her jumper when you got this close. As Mo leant over Bea's cot, Dora realised she was repelled by this apparently harmless woman. It was spiders on the skin. It was *revulsion*.

Mo had her hands clasped together now and was mumbling a prayer over Bea's sleeping form. Terrence bowed his head.

Kit said, 'How about a drink?'

Reluctantly, Mo tore herself away from the cot, gazing back at Beatrice as she left.

In the sitting room, Terrence accepted a sherry and said, 'You've got the grand front door, but we have the views.'

'You'll have to come up and see,' said Mo.

Terrence occupied the sofa comfortably next to Dora, while Mo took the armchair, accepted a bitter lemon and started talking. Dora and Kit had to lean right in to catch the whispery chirrup of her voice.

'She needs to grow, the little mite. Like I've been telling my daughter-in-law, you have to feed them whenever they cry.'

Wearily, Dora explained again. 'She's too weak to cry for food. We have to wake her up, or she would simply sleep through her hunger.'

Mo continued as if Dora had not spoken. 'Premature babies need their mothers even more. You'll be breastfeeding on demand, I'm sure. Although, if you're drinking . . .' She eyed Dora's large glass of wine disapprovingly.

It was pointless, but Dora pressed on, anyway. 'Beatrice was born before she had a sucking reflex. If I'd tried to breastfeed, she would have starved. We're following what the paediatrician said. She's doing very well.'

Terrence said, 'You could learn a lot from Mo, Dora. She's a wonderful mother.'

Mo's eyes suddenly filled with tears and the little island mole on her forehead wrinkled into tiny mountains.

'What is it, dear?' asked Terrence.

'I am just so excited about our grandchild.'

Terrence put a comforting hand on her knee. Dora glugged her wine and filled up her glass again. Kit had picked up a book and was turning it over absently. He did this when he couldn't hear a conversation or was bored.

'That's quite a boat you have out there,' said Dora.

'Oh, yes,' said Terrence, with a tremor in his voice. 'That boat is my pride and joy.' His eyes looked ready to brim, themselves, at the thought of the *Lady Maureen*. 'We've had her how long, Mo?'

'Twenty-five years,' said Mo. 'Remember, we got her so we could go sailing with Theodore?'

'We don't take her out that much anymore,' said Terrence. 'She's an old girl now. We let our friends' kids camp in her.'

'She needs a lot of space . . .' said Dora, carefully.

'Felicity and Matthew loved *Maureen*,' Terrence said firmly. 'We all just got along, you know? You have to learn to share in a shared house.'

Kit took a long, thoughtful sip of his drink. 'Dora says you've been here for fifteen years; is that right?'

'Oh, yes,' said Mo, her cheeks a little flushed. 'We've seen lots of neighbours come and go.'

'And your son lives nearby?'

'Not Helensburgh – he couldn't afford it. He lives in a flat in Dumbarton. We were supposed to all live together . . . but we were cheated out of that.' She trailed off, looking at the cornicing and the mantelpiece.

'What do you mean, "cheated"?' said Kit.

Mo adjusted her hair and, for once, spoke clearly. 'Felicity promised us this house.'

'This house? *Our* house?' asked Dora.

'We were meant to have it.'

'But it went out for bids in the normal way,' said Kit. 'We bid for it, through the estate agent.'

'Well, something happened, because she promised it to us,' said Terrence.

'I hope you're not accusing us of something. That would be very unfortunate. We saw the house and bid for it. A large bid, I should add, because of the lawn.'

'I never liked that Felicity,' said Mo to her husband. 'We never should have trusted her.'

'Hang on a minute; I think we need to clear up that we haven't cheated you,' said Kit.

Mo ignored him and looked sadly round the room. Finally, she said, 'We longed to have Theodore with us all these years, and finally it was going to happen. And then . . .' She looked as if she were going to cry again.

'The members of our church have been a great support to us through what's been a very difficult time,' said Terrence, handing his wife an immaculately folded handkerchief. Mo dabbed her eyes.

Terrence shifted in his seat and said, as if he had given up searching for the right moment to say something and just had to get it out, 'The drive is communal, you know. I can put *Lady Maureen* where I like. And park where I like.'

Kit shook his head. 'I'm afraid not, Terrence. We own the drive and you have a right of way to get to your door.'

'No, no — it's communal. We've always done it this way.'

'Shall we get the lease out and have a look together? We can clarify that the lawn is ours as well,' said Kit, pleasantly.

'We've been here for years, and we have parked where we like. *Precedent*, I think you'll find,' said Mo triumphantly.

'I don't know why you don't just turn one of the flower beds into parking,' Terrence said. 'I mean, that bit down the end, you could get a car down there. Just a lot of shrubs. I don't see the point of all these plants.'

'We won't be turning the flower bed into a parking place,' Kit said gently. 'And I'd like to ask you to show some consideration when you and your guests are parking; you know, not blocking our windows and so forth. Since it is actually our drive. And we do live here.'

'There's no law of trespass in Scotland,' said Mo. 'The children can play where they like.'

Kit sighed. 'Let me get this straight, Mo. You tried to buy our house . . . and failed, but think you're entitled to it anyway?' He gave a bewildered laugh. 'Tell me, are you planning to use the inside as well? You know, it would be useful to know. In case we need to tidy the place up for you.'

'You can't talk to us like that!'

'Like what?'

'We're *good people*!' Mo had turned quite red.

Terrence frowned. 'You've upset her, now,' he said. 'Mo is very sensitive.'

Mo clasped her husband's hand. 'We'll be talking to our solicitor,' she said.

'I think that is a very good idea,' said Dora.

Mo turned on her in fury. 'I don't understand why you've come here! You don't belong; you don't know how to share. We were all *just fine* before you came along, making your land grab.'

With unexpected nimbleness, Terrence jumped to his feet and took his wife's hand, lifting her to her feet.

Dora looked round for Kit, but he was already holding open the door for them, stooping slightly, like a weary butler.

'God bless the wee one . . .' said Terrence, awkwardly, as he ushered his wife out.

'Wow,' Kit said when they had gone. Footsteps creaked overhead. Voices blurred and bloomed.

'Did you hear that?' Dora said. Even the drunk bag-lady who shouted at everyone on the corner of her street in Oxford had never directed anything at her so personally.

'We need to calm it all down,' Kit said. 'They're disappointed in life, that's all.'

Kit followed his wife into Beatrice's room, where the baby was still sleeping deeply. The little clock with a fairy on it showed nine o'clock. It was time to wake her up for a feed. Slowly, soothingly, with her heart pounding, Dora gathered the baby into her arms.

'Is she right? Can they do what they like?' Dora asked.

Kit didn't say anything, turning it over in his mind.

ELEVEN

Wystan

IS THERE ANY CHANCE you could visit? Or send someone to visit me? I know absolutely no one here! This is to Christopher Isherwood, still in Berlin. The summer term yawns ahead of him, the days are blazing and full of thunder. *I'm coming over in the holidays.* Letters are Wystan's lifeline. Every day, he writes letters, making an entertainment for his friends out of his loneliness.

He will write, one day, that he has come to like teaching, but at the moment it is an exercise full of terror. The only thing to be thankful for is that no one observes his classes. He is left entirely to his own devices.

He starts them on *Romeo and Juliet*, believing it to be the easy one, and he giggles inwardly at their Scottish accents mangling the exchanges. But the boys soon grow bored of declaring undying love and enmity in incomprehensible language, and start to misbehave, so he switches to *Macbeth*, where the accents suddenly make sense. McLeod, with his head of curls and pretty face, is woefully miscast as Macbeth, but Wystan loves to hear him stuttering and stumbling over the soliloquies, and Wystan himself reads Lady Macbeth alongside, creating an odd but beautiful conversation between them.

But McLeod is bored. They are all bored and Wystan does not know how to entertain them. He is not a great lover of the classics himself; he is drawn to Lawrence, who is talking about things he's interested in: heroism, masculinity, sex. But always the classes are full of giggling and whispering, and McLeod's smiling face, like a beacon, distracting him.

When he approaches the classroom, from where he can hear shouts and scuffles and laughter, they always hear his step. Someone shouts, 'He's coming!' and there is scraping and more laughter, and when he opens the door, they are all sitting down at their desks, but usually they are at the wrong desks and ten minutes must be taken up rearranging them. Or they are sitting, as if nothing were wrong, on top of the desks, or under them. He never shouts at the boys to tell them off, for he cannot bring himself to believe they are not on the same side. After all, there are only twelve years between Wystan and the eldest of them. They exploit this mercilessly, sensing his desire to be liked by them above all else.

And then the classes end and he is released, to his bare room and the silent avenues of Upper Helensburgh, with nothing to do and no one to do it with. He can work – nothing stops his working – but there are many hours, especially in the long evenings, when he fears his loneliness may get the better of him, may cause him to be reckless.

Wystan thinks often of Oxford, of the way that the person he was, while an oddity, fitted in naturally. He remembers the late nights with his friends, the society, the meeting of minds and ideas. Apart from the exasperated exchanges he has with the boys, he goes almost the whole day without conversation.

The bell rings below, searing into his room as if there are much greater depths and heights to be alerted. He hears nothing more until a gentle footstep and a knock on his door.

'Come in!'

Like everyone here, Olive, the maid, behaves as though there is a pall over the school, as if everyone should be whispering. 'Mr Wallace is here to see you, Mr Auden. He asks if you would care to join him for a drink. He's waiting downstairs.'

'Tell him I shall be down right away.'

Auden excitedly pulls on his shoes. The evening outside is bright and warm, the sort of evening that's a torture if one is confined alone to one's room, but a joy to share with someone. He hopes Wallace will not be too dull, nor too drunk, but in truth he doesn't care that much. He almost skips down the staircase and enters the tiny parlour.

A man dressed comfortably in tweed, as if ready for a country pursuit, stands to greet him. He has the soft, clean-shaven skin of the well-bred. Close up, his rosy cheeks are threaded with broken veins.

'Mr Auden, what a pleasure!' says Wallace. If he has a Scottish accent, Wystan cannot discern it. This man is the first Wystan has met in Helensburgh who seems not to be foreign. He's a posh Scot, Wystan realises, for whom Scotland is both home and playground. Wystan's hand vanishes into Wallace's grip, as if into a warm rabbit hole. 'We all warmed to Cecil and Mary; how is he getting along down south?'

'Very well, I think. The school is a bigger one, more of a challenge and so forth.'

'I apologise for the lack of advance warning – my son is back from university and, what with my daughter and wife, so many demands are made on my time that I never know until the last minute if I can escape!' He takes out a large red handkerchief and blows his nose. 'I took a punt on you not being otherwise engaged, and perhaps free to come and have a drink with me. I'm Pop Wallace, by the way.'

'How do you do,' says Wystan. It is a relief to understand English without effort, and soothing to be in the company of someone who looks like an English gentleman. Wystan can place himself, at least in class terms, and that, after many bewildering days, is a relief.

'Well then, let me show you one or two of my favourite places,' says Wallace, striding out into the sunshine as if he owns the school and everyone in it. 'I thought we'd have a drive first; what do you say? You can have a go at the wheel.'

'It's been a few months since I've driven . . .' The roof of the car is pulled back and the wood is warm to the touch. Wystan climbs into the driver's side and runs his fingers over the wheel.

'You have a car at home?' Wallace asks. The vehicle bounces as he settles himself.

'My father has one. He taught me to drive.'

'You're just down from Oxford, aren't you? Here's the key. She starts like a dream – usually.'

'I came down a little over a year ago.' Wystan is coiled like a spider. His toes reach to ascertain brake, accelerator and clutch, and he turns the key. The starter motor whines and grumbles into life.

'They've abolished the speed limits, you know,' says Wallace. 'But I think we'll keep to thirty in town, seeing as you're new.'

Wystan would have greatly preferred Wallace to drive. He can do it, it's true, but, like many poets, he would sooner be a passenger; he enjoys entrusting his journey to someone else, so that he can take in the view and think. But his new friend is clearly thrilled with his own generosity, and Wystan doesn't like to disappoint. He cranes to see behind them and grinds the car into reverse. It shoots backwards and, when he slams the brake, jolts forwards and stalls.

'Watch out!'

Wystan sighs and, as he did with the rugby ball, focuses his entire attention on getting the car started. His arms are already aching – whether from tension or hauling the wheel, he is not sure. The sun beats the back of his head and he wishes he had brought his hat. At last, they move forward through the Larchfield gates.

'My son says they still talk about you there . . . in Oxford,' says Wallace. His voice carries over the wind as they bowl up the hill past Hermitage Park.

'That's very generous of him, your son, though I can't think why they would. What's his name?'

'Callum. He has come back with a lot of peculiar ideas and a head full of socialism.' Wallace looks sideways at Wystan, the breeze blowing his greying hair out of place. 'Are you a secret Russian also?'

'I'm from Birmingham,' gasps Wystan. 'My father is a doctor. We are not revolutionaries.'

They have reached the open road, necessitating no gear changes. Wystan relaxes a little and looks across at the hills beginning to bunch towards Loch Lomond.

'I don't know how such nonsense got in his head. He's a sensible young man, with an expensive education. Perhaps you can explain . . . ?'

'Young men are trying to think of ways out of the mess we're in. Russia has an interesting model. I don't know exactly what I think about it. But I do think about it. I'm pleased Callum is thinking about these things too. He sounds like a most interesting young man.'

Pop Wallace says nothing for a few moments. He indicates that Wystan should turn right to head back towards the front.

'It seems to me that Oxford, these days, is nothing but a festering pit of communism and perversion. My boy is unrecognisable. I see I shall have to pack him off, for his own good.'

Wystan slams the brake, making them heave and jolt again. He puts out a hand to steady himself and presses the horn by mistake, giving a blast that shakes them both.

'Careful, man!' Wallace says, his arm now hovering beside the steering wheel in case he needs to intervene. 'The school is crumbling, you know. Bloody Perkins – he really is the most miserable creature.'

'Mrs Perkins has been very kind,' says Wystan.

'Yes. Daphne – lovely person. Very sad.'

These are the outskirts of Lower Helensburgh, where the town reaches a silvery finger towards Dumbarton. Wystan cannot help but notice the change from Upper Helensburgh. Though the sun is shining and the sea is twinkling, the shop awnings that are still out are tattered and there's an eerie quiet. There are men standing on the corners, playing ha'penny toss. They gaze at the car roaring by. It is hard to tell their ages, for their faces are lined and their teeth blackened, their clothes shabby. Today is Thursday; tomorrow is the day for picking up dole money, or whatever wages may be coming to them for a three-day week at the ship-breaking yard, so they have no money left. They are sober, idle and not a little intimidating as they stop what they are doing and stare quite openly, as if he and Wallace were a visitation from another world.

A familiar shape moves in the corner of Wystan's vision. His hands jerk and the car swerves perilously close to the pavement. Wallace grabs the wheel. 'Keep your eyes on the road, boy!'

Wystan's mouth hangs open. The man on the train – his vision, Florid – slips round the corner and into the railway station. The man turns, just as he disappears from view, his face breaking into a stubbly grin.

'I'm sorry.' He shakes his head to dispel the sight.

The shorefront is upon them now, crowded with people. Couples stroll along the promenade and a long queue snakes away from the ice-cream stand. A crowd bursts into applause as someone putts a hole on the putting green. But Wystan's attention is drawn to the lido, some fifty yards away. Young men and women jump and splash, their shouts and challenges ringing in the air. Although it is warm for an evening in early summer, Wystan imagines the water must be frigid. The young people seem oblivious and Wystan suddenly longs to join them, to be carefree.

Perhaps the boy who was smoking at the station is there . . . If only he could see him again; Wystan imagines he sees him in every lean youth he encounters.

Pop Wallace turns to face the disappointing creature beside him. 'I hear you acquitted yourself on the rugby pitch. The school needs a sportsman. Poetry is all very well, but these boys need physical leadership.'

'Do you know about poetry, Mr Wallace?'

'I know enough to know that rugby is more important.'

Wystan gazes hopefully around. Perhaps, in the crowds milling by, he will see someone even a little like himself. But he is surrounded by couples and families and tantalising young people who look at him a little sideways, as if they know what is wrong with him.

'You did quite well, Wystan!' Wallace gives him a semi-playful punch on the arm as they pull in. 'We'll toughen you up, don't you worry.'

Wystan follows his companion through a doorway and into a hotel snug. A few men look up from newspapers and a fat bartender lays down the glasses, greeting Pop by name.

'This young man is from Oxford, and I don't believe he's ever had a proper drink,' grins Pop. 'We should show him a few malts, don't you think, William?'

Wystan looks wistfully at the square of lido that can be seen through the window. The water glitters and young skin flickers with life. A glass appears before him, containing a liquid the colour of his polished dining table at home. As he raises it to his lips, he gives an involuntary cough at the fumes lifting from it. An image of his mother sitting at the table swims into his vision.

Pop and William are both laughing at his hesitation. The liquid burns his mouth, like soft embers in the grate at home against his fingertips. He hears his mother call, *Wystan, don't put your fingers in the fire!* and he turns and runs to her, and buries his face in the rough lace of her dress, and feels her warmth in his throat, in his belly.

Every time he finishes one of these brown drinks, another appears. Wallace is in earnest conversation with someone. His eyes have the melancholic gleam of the person making his confession for the hundredth time, still not comprehending how he had anything to do with it. Wystan realises that he is the other person in the conversation and he tries to steady his mind, which is wobbling free of his brain.

'I'm a disappointed man, Auden,' Wallace is saying. 'My son . . . I had hopes of his becoming an MP. Or a bishop. But he's been reading God knows what – poetry, mostly, I think – no offence – and he's lost to me. Lost to me, do you understand? It's as if he's on some island and I'm waving from a boat . . .' He trails off. He pulls out his handkerchief and blows his nose noisily again. Another thought fights itself free of the white water in his mind. 'That boy, Jessop. What do you think of him?'

'Oh, I don't think he likes me,' says Wystan.

Wallace frowns. 'I think he's a good boy. Steady, bright, hard-working. Why doesn't he like you?'

'Something about me having no Helensburgh connections.'

Wallace gives a great spittle-filled laugh. 'He said that, did he? Plucky little sod. You know, he's madly in love with my daughter. And I'm not against it. No, not at all. His background isn't quite what we'd have hoped for, but his qualities . . .' Jessop's qualities are so marvellous, they seem to drift clear of Wallace's memory altogether; then, as can only happen when someone is incredibly drunk, Wallace snaps forward with breathtaking lucidity. 'He's a man – a man, d'you hear? I can make something of him. He's a Good Thing. Yes, rough round the edges, but a Good Thing.' A yawn invades his whole face. 'Auden, I will take you home. William! Thank you!'

Wallace climbs unsteadily to his feet and sets off for the door. Wystan stands too; at least, he imagines he does; his mind is upright, but he is not completely certain his body has followed. Christ, who is going to drive? He hopes it will be Wallace. There is no chance Wystan can operate any pedals, any more that he could at this moment pat his head and rub his stomach at the same time, or indeed formulate a coherent sentence. The whisky he has consumed – which kinds and how many he has forgotten – has smoothed away some critical element of his machinery. He need not have worried; Wallace is in the driver's seat, revving up. Busy talking to himself, he does not look up as Wystan clambers in.

The moon is out over the sea as they hare along the front. There is silence from Wallace, who has slumped over the wheel. Wystan gives him an almighty poke in the arm – 'Mr Wallace, sir!' – and the older man coughs awake, grabbing the wheel as they swerve into the middle of the road and back. 'Don't poke me, lad. Don't poke me!' They speed up Sinclair Street, the night completely deserted, the gas lamps and the moon the only lights. Wallace is clearly going to drive right past Larchfield unless Wystan stops him, so, as they near the gates, Wystan yells as if stopping a taxi – 'My stop, here!' – and Wallace slams the brakes on.

The benefactor turns to him as he struggles with the door. His face is wet with tears. 'Auden, dear boy, do I seem like a tyrant to you?' He hangs on to Wystan's sleeve. 'Callum says that's what I am. He hates me, you know. My own son. All that money on his education, and that is all it's taught him.' He sobs into Wystan's arm, and, even though Wystan is so drunk he can hardly move, he knows that on no account must Wallace remember this end to the evening. The humiliation will ensure Wystan's absolute doom.

91

He takes a huge breath and slurs, as if Wallace had not spoken, 'What a wonderful evening, Mr Wallace! Cecil said you were the greatest company in Helensburgh, and how right he was! A good go on the rugby field tomorrow will clear my head!' He bows clumsily and pours himself out of the car, waving as he stumbles to the gates. He prays silently that Wallace will just go, and – thank God – he hears the engine roar and the car depart, a final 'Goodbye, Auden!' ringing through the night.

TWELVE

Dora

SCATTERED AROUND THE HOUSE, there was evidence of Dora's former self, if you knew what to look for. Her boxes, still not unpacked, were piled haphazardly around the spare room. On the shelves were her paperbacks, novels and poetry collections, as well as the critical books that she had used in her university career. Her prized leather-bound edition of the full Oxford English Dictionary – all twenty volumes – was in the sitting room, where any beautiful books they each owned were housed. In the spare room, too, was her own poetry book, a slim paperback occupying about an eighth of an inch of shelf space beside some thrillers.

There were also photographs of her as, it seemed, a much younger woman. She was dressed up in these photos. They were from various events and prize-givings. The names of these events sounded foreign on her tongue now – laughably old-fashioned.

On the dressing table was a laptop, neatly closed, and a notebook. She wrote only in pencil these days, feeling that her words looked wrong in ink. She could not see herself anymore in what she wrote, even when she had time to do it. Writing was a genie that appeared only in order to torment her with her own inability to speak.

Kit left early for work every morning now, and it was just Dora and Beatrice, and the cacophony of noise from above, all day. But that was okay; Dora felt that it was okay. She was used to solitude – though, admittedly, it had never been so surrounded as this, nor so noisy. She was quite good at keeping herself and the baby busy, going for a walk every day, keeping to the sleeping and feeding routine, so that when Kit came home about six it was bath time and bedtime, and they had the semblance of some time alone. She had read this was good for your relationship, to find time to be alone – although all they did was collapse in front of the television and occasionally argue about the apparent disappearance of Dora's life. She felt okay about most things, as long as she did not think about them too hard . . . and she was so tired that not thinking came easily.

Dora took Beatrice to the nursery for a nappy change. Bea's now-blue eyes stared around and small mews emerged from her lips. She had returned to a kind of guinea pig/squirrel state, in that Dora found that mother-love was all in the doing. This cleaning, soothing, maintaining of body weight and sleep patterns was more like the caring she had done for small animals than it was a behaviour peculiarly human. Never had she felt so close to the animal world – its wordlessness, its needs, its smells and vulnerability. Though surprised at her lack of feeling, she was comfortable in this space. She knew how to be, when she was doing, doing, doing.

She wrestled the last nappy out of the bag, fluffed it out – and then was startled by a tiny noise from Bea. Looking down, she saw that Bea's mouth was open, and her little face was turning, first, deep pink, then purple. The baby was straining silently for breath.

Was she choking? On what? Frantically, Dora searched the baby's mouth. Nothing. Bea, the tiny, mute animal who still could not smile, who was still lost in her amniotic life, turned her tiny head and fixed her bulging eyes on her mother.

OhmyGod. OhmyGod.

Dora scooped the infant, belly down, into her palm – Bea was still small enough to lay in a hand. Then Dora tapped her on the back between the shoulder blades while she walked quickly from room to room. Her baby was dying in her hands, and there was no one here, no one to help. She walked and tapped, round in circles – OhmyGod, ohmyGod – out into the sitting room, where the sky beyond the window had melted into the rain and the sea, making one huge ocean of grey. She knew that there were only a few minutes available now. Could this be possible? Was the lonely, enveloping grey a signal – perhaps that it had already taken place? She tapped and scurried, desperate animal mother with tiny dying baby, with no idea what she was doing.

Then a sudden gasp, like a fully-grown man's gasp, or a door blown open in a storm, and air rushing in to inflate her tiny chest. Dora swept the baby round and held her to her breast, and the gasp turned to sobs – enormous, beautiful sobs. The baby was alive! Was she all right? Dora cradled her, tears falling now.

'Little Bea, my little Bea,' she said. 'Don't you worry. Everything is all right now.' Slowly, as Dora stood in the hallway, cradling and whispering to her child, Bea returned to a normal colour, her crying eased and she snuggled into her mother.

When she related this story to Kit, later, Dora would downplay her terror, her certainty that the baby was dying. She would also downplay her bewilderment that she had instinctively done something to save Bea's life. It seemed too improbable, and also too terrible. Her responsibility for keeping this baby alive was now as clear and awesome as if a blizzard had blown itself out, revealing that she and Bea were on a tiny ledge together, and one false move on Dora's part would see them both plummet to their deaths.

Later, Dora would discover that new mothers had many such near misses. They never told anyone how they, on the off-chance, checked their baby in the night and found them not breathing and brought them back, or encountered fevers, or babies about to fall, or with something fatal stuffed into their mouth and saved them without thinking.

Strangest of all, these mothers, as Dora had, saved the baby's life and then *got on with their day*. For the daily routine of a baby is remorseless and relentless, and what else is there to do, if your baby is in fact alive, than to do as Dora did, which was to pick up where she left off and proceed with her walk.

She wrapped the baby up warmly, the incident already fading into a trembling past, and laid her in the pram. They would walk, as they did almost every day, mile upon mile in the freezing winter, trying somehow to escape the vast open skies, the hungry ocean and the impossible light.

She manoeuvred the pram out of the door and through the cars – unmoved since the altercation with the Divines. A car had just arrived and there was a little welcoming group on the drive, Mo's laughter cracking through the damp air. Dora pressed on, out of the gate and on to the pavement running alongside the narrow road – beyond which was the sea.

Their part of Helensburgh was some distance from the town centre; it was an extension of Lower Hel that became a rocky spit of land poking out to sea. To reach the shops and cafés entailed a walk of almost three miles along the twisting coastal road. Dora usually walked the other way, up into the Duchess Woods or down on to the beaches. If one was going into the town centre, it was better to drive.

But today she wanted to exhaust herself. She wanted to walk away her isolation and lose herself gradually in the slow appearance of habitation. She passed the long lines of mansions she was so familiar with, all with their façades ruthlessly intact. It was impossible to tell if, behind the grand exteriors, people were living as she did. No one came out. The gardens were deserted. Cars whizzed by, and the bus – which took such a circuitous route to the centre that it seemed to take even longer than walking – swept round the corner with a penetrating beep of the horn. No one was out on the pavement. This wasn't completely unwelcome, as it was very narrow and impossible for her to move out of the way.

As she passed the entrance to a lane, she heard voices, and out stepped a group of elderly men wrapped in long black coats, expensive scarves and gloves: the uniform of the elders. When they saw Dora, their chatter died. Dora thought she recognised one of them; in fact, if she wasn't mistaken, hadn't he been at the party on the lawn? They must have walked down the lane from the church.

'Hello,' she said, smiling and coming to a stop because they were blocking the pavement.

The men did not say anything for a moment. Recognition moved slowly over their faces.

'We've been hearing about you from Mo,' said one, pointing with a black-gloved finger. 'Such unkindness to two old people!' The men all looked the same, like a clump of angry angels.

'What?' she asked, but they were sweeping past her now, stepping into the road reluctantly, as if she were a rock and they were an eddy of clean, bright water. And then their chatter resumed and, when she looked behind her, their coats were swaying together like curtains closed after a definitive final scene.

Dora stopped dead, her face burning with shame. What did they mean? Thank God that Beatrice was asleep, or she might have heard her mother spoken to in that way. Never mind that she was a baby and could not understand the words – it was contempt that did not need words.

'On we go,' Dora said brightly, and on they pressed, though Dora's legs trembled. The rhythm of her trainers on the ground and the regular creak of the wheels soothed her, and she found her mind drifting to Larchfield and everything Lois had said about W. H. Auden living in Helensburgh. Why not go and see it? Now – today! And then . . . she could write about Auden! She picked up her pace a little, feeling a welcome flicker of interest in something.

At last, the winding coast gave way to a promenade, where old people perambulated in neatly organised pairs. At this point, Dora turned away from the sea, taking a road towards Upper Helensburgh. She passed the old cinema, La Scala, which was being refurbished and turned into a restaurant and arts centre. This was where Kit worked. He was the architect for the project and would be busy inside, project-managing the build. Scaffolding covered the art deco frontage.

She could visit him! She could tell him that she'd saved their baby's life that morning. Perhaps they could have lunch together, perhaps visit Larchfield together! Dora paused on the other side of the road and looked up at the windows. Her husband was behind one of those windows, probably with a coffee in his hand, poring over some plans with one of the assistants – all women Dora's age. She longed to see him.

But she continued past the building for much the same reason as she wrote in pencil in her notebook, not pen. Her existence, her visibility was uncertain, even to her husband. She knew what would happen if she visited unexpectedly. He would look up genially and a shadow of non-recognition would momentarily cross his features, for Dora was out of place. She only really existed in her old clothes in the confines of Paradise.

Then he would fly out from behind the desk, for, if she had chosen to manifest here, three miles away, was there something wrong with the baby? He would rush to the pram, trying not to look as though he was rushing, and say, 'Everything okay?' The other members of staff barely knew her and would look at her with a confused mixture of pity and impatience. What was she doing here?

Indeed, what *was* she doing here? So she kept walking, padding by in her trainers. La Scala could be another world, for all she belonged there. Her husband was a different person, important and busy in the kingdom of work.

It wasn't too far now. Lois had explained that Larchfield was on the corner of Montrose Street and Colquhoun Street. Helensburgh was laid out as a grid (having been designed and built all in one go, as a gift from the laird to his wife, Helen, some 200 years previously) and so was easy to navigate, even though the hill was steep. She stopped in Costa on the way and bought coffee, almost tempted to sit down and forget the mission, but her restlessness kept her moving. If she stopped, she might begin to cry or blurt out to a fellow customer that her baby had almost died that morning, and did they know about W. H. Auden? No, she could take the coffee with her. Bea's cheek was pink, her tiny mouth slightly open. Dora wondered what she was dreaming of, if she had forgotten her brush with death that morning. She said to the little shape, 'You're safe, my sweetie,' and this thought almost made her cry again, for it was, in truth, what she wished that someone – a mother, a husband, a friend – would say to her.

Just Montrose Street to cross now. It was a wide, leafy avenue that divided Upper Helensburgh from Lower. Above Montrose Street the houses got steadily bigger, and fewer and fewer were converted. The seriously rich lived up here and it seemed almost a different town from its lower counterpart.

Larchfield was behind a tall hedge. She could just see the upper floors. The whole façade, Lois had told her, was completely preserved and exactly as it had been in Auden's day. How amazing this was. Her tiredness forgotten, Dora stepped across the road and wheeled the pram to the entrance on the Colquhoun Street side.

The gate was tall and wrought-iron, with the name *Larchfield* looped in gold. Ivy crept along the front of the building, and the tall windows looked out over a Helensburgh that was essentially unchanged in appearance since his time. She could imagine the poet emerging from the stone porch, the sounds of children.

Bea was starting to stir. Dora picked her out of the pram and held her close. And when she looked again at the porch, it seemed that she met the gaze of the young Auden through the iron gate. The poet was rather shabby, but his clothes were good. It was as if he were looking out from the fine drive on to a pauper come for alms and he was stuck in the moment, unable to traverse whatever distance it was to press a coin into her palm and smile at her dirty brat, but also unable to turn away.

Part Two

THIRTEEN

Wystan

AFTER A CHASTE AND sobering term at Larchfield, Wystan is desperate for escape. The summer holidays are just days away. He reports to Christopher that he has made two friends, Callum and Daphne, but it isn't enough to ward off the corrosive loneliness. In a flurry of letters, he arranges a trip to Berlin, where Isherwood is living and, by his own account, having the time of his life.

Not long after his night out with Wallace, the benefactor's son turned up to see him. Callum has a common face, plain as an urn, with ears like handles. It is not a face that suggests a hunger for knowledge, but when Wystan invited him up to his room and showed him his books, Callum seemed on the verge of tears. He pulled out one volume after another, grasped each of Wystan's suggestions as if it were food.

'We have no books at home; well, we have a leather-bound Scott and Fielding, but we're not supposed to read them. They're valuable. I envy you so, Auden. It is callous of my father to send me to

Oxford and then shut me back in the cage as though I'd never had an intelligent conversation. I miss it so, don't you?'

'I know what you mean. Indeed, I do.'

'My father is very angry about it. He called you a bad influence.'

'Oh dear.' Wystan sighed. 'I did try very hard when we met, but if a man feels that strongly that rugby is more important than poetry, well, the odds are rather stacked against me. But should you be here? If I am a bad influence?'

'He doesn't know. Please don't tell him. He thinks I'm here to see Jessop.'

'Well, Callum, you are welcome to come here whenever you want. I don't lock my room. You can borrow any book you like; I don't have to be here, and, if I am and not busy, well, we can talk about the books.'

Callum's face had split into an extraordinary smile. 'Thank you, Mr Auden, thank you.'

'Call me Wystan.'

'Of course, Mr Auden. Wystan. Thank you!'

And thus had begun Callum's visits to his room, often when Wystan was teaching, and there would simply be a book missing and a neatly written note detailing what had gone. But sometimes, as today, Callum visits when the poet is in his room. Wystan is packing for his trip when there is a timid knock on the door and his new friend peeps round.

'Come in, Callum!'

The young man has a book in his hands.

'Ah! Cecil will be delighted!' Wystan smiles at the sight of his old friend's poetry collection. 'But that's pretty incendiary stuff to have round your way, isn't it?'

'It's perfect subversive material,' grins Callum. 'See, not too big, not too small: slides perfectly into my jacket pocket, like so –' he demonstrates – 'and Father never knows I am carrying poetry around with me.'

'Well, I'm pleased to hear it. Now – I am leaving my key on the lintel above the door, like so, and the library will be open for you in the holidays.'

'Are you going away?'

'I'm off to . . . Europe. A bit of a tour around, that sort of thing. With some old friends. From university. And you? What shall you do?'

Callum's face falls. 'Well, Father is bashing every acquaintance he has to get me a position at the bank. So I suppose I will be going to interviews with boring old men.'

'Oh dear. The plans to be an MP or a bishop have not worked out, then?'

Callum snorts with laughter. 'Really, Wystan, can you see that? Anyway, my degree is terrible, I'm very shy and I'm also agnostic. Though I fear that may qualify me for the bank.'

They both laugh at this, and another half hour is pleasantly passed selecting more books for Callum, until the clock downstairs chimes and Wystan exclaims, 'I'm afraid I have to finish packing for my European tour! I will see you in a few weeks. Good luck with your job search.'

Daphne Perkins' eyes brim with tears when Wystan breaks the news to her about where he is going. He is able to be truthful to Daphne; for one so frail, she is robust when it comes to gossip. 'Oh, how I hate the holidays!' she exclaims. 'Day after day with nothing to do and, of course, we don't go anywhere. The sea air of Helensburgh is supposed to be my cure.'

They are in Daphne's room in the cool of his last evening. Apart from occasionally encountering Callum, Daphne has been Wystan's only diversion. He is suffocating in the leafy properness of Upper Helensburgh and has found no distraction in the down-at-heel alleyways of Lower Helensburgh. Sometimes, he wanders down to the lido to watch the young men, but knowing none of them has made his loneliness worse. It seems there is nowhere where men like him go to meet. But he can forget all that in Berlin.

'Maybe you should come with me,' Wystan says.

Daphne giggles in spite of herself. 'I don't think you will want a sick old lady round your neck while you're having fun with your friends. I hear Berlin is very . . . free.'

'Free is exactly what it is.'

'I imagine you need a bit of that after a term here . . . What shall you do there? A lot of drinking and dancing, I expect. Perhaps you will come back quite dissolute.'

'I shall come back with a broken heart. One always falls in love in Berlin. Or I do, at any rate.'

She smiles at him and pats his hand. 'You must come here straight away when you're back and tell me of all your adventures.' Her eyes are full of something. She says, 'And send me postcards. But send them poste restante and I will pick them up from the post office myself. It will mean I go out, and give me a little intrigue over the summer.'

'I'll do that,' says Wystan. He is restless and yet exhausted.

'Shall we?' Daphne reaches up to the shelf and brings out her gin. As she stands to pour out a couple of glasses, she is overtaken by a terrible wheezing coughing fit. Wystan clasps her arm and helplessly pats her back. Daphne signals to a drawer. 'My inhaler!' she gasps.

Wystan pulls the drawer open and finds the contraption, which she grabs from him and sucks on as if her life depends on it. She slumps into the chair as her breathing calms a little and the coughs become regular and shallow. From her pocket, she takes out a lacy handkerchief and wipes her lips. There are spots of blood on it when she takes it away. Wystan says, 'Shall we call the doctor, Daphne?'

'Oh, good heavens, no. He knows all about it. As long as I keep up with the inhaler, I am all right.' She picks up one of the little glasses and takes a large gulp before raising the glass to him. 'Thriving, in fact!' She grins, and a little colour surges into her cheeks.

'The inhaler is rather magical,' she continues. 'You know, I think you could use a little puff of it. You look far too exhausted for a young man of twenty-four.'

'I'm not asthmatic anymore . . .'

'I'll let you into a wee secret.' Daphne is quite lively now, passing Wystan his drink and topping hers up. 'My inhaler is quite a *stimulant*. I often take it, even when I don't have an attack, because it clears my mind. I spend my days in a terrible fog without it.'

'What is it?' He takes the inhaler from her. *Benzedrine*, he reads.

'Go on, have a wee go, dear. I think you'll be surprised.'

Wystan rather awkwardly puts the instrument in his mouth.

'Now breathe, short and sharp,' she says.

When he does, he feels a powder spray all over the back of his throat and he erupts into coughing.

'Daphne, what are you doing to me?' he says, doubling over, half with coughing, half with laughter.

'Now, sit back and have your drink,' Daphne instructs.

Wystan's heart is beating a little faster and a bright clarity is indeed opening in his mind. The weariness of the last weeks is receding. An involuntary grin creeps across his face.

'Good heavens . . .' he says, wonderingly.

'I told you, didn't I? I find I can do my writing much better after a little puff on that.' She indicates the bookshelf filled with jotters.

Wystan nods, considering. He feels, now, that he could go to his desk and work late into the night. In later years, he will come to depend on drugs like this one; he will have a 'chemical life'. But, this first time, the energy is an unadulterated good.

Daphne shyly hands him a jotter from the end of the bookshelf. 'Take it with you to Berlin. Read it on a quiet morning after sleeping off your excess.'

'Why, thank you.' Wystan's mind is moving very quickly. He really does want to go and work. 'I must go . . . It's most peculiar . . . this energy.'

'Isn't it just!'

'Goodbye, then. And see you in a couple of months.' He takes her hand, brushes it with his lips.

'Goodbye, Wystan, dear. Take care of yourself.'

And Wystan almost skips to his little room, and, instead of packing, he sits at his desk and gets more written in the next two hours than he has all week. When he finally does get round to finishing his packing, in the early hours, he presses the jotter into an inside pocket. He will read it during the channel crossing and he will find something encouraging to tell his dearest Helensburgh friend.

WYSTAN HAS NOT SEEN Christopher Isherwood since the previous summer, when they discovered Berlin together, and Christopher was so taken with it that he decided to stay for good. They embrace on the platform, Christopher's grinning face bumping at Wystan's cheek. Then a taxi to Nordstrasse and the Institute of Sexual Science.

'It seems I've got the most expensive room in the whole of Berlin,' Christopher says. 'But it's clean and quiet and I can do what I like.'

The Institute is sooty and grand, with a complex of apartments and library storage rooms behind it. There is another room in Christopher's apartment whose occupant is gone for the summer, and Christopher has arranged for Wystan to sublet it. The rooms are bright and clean, with framed explicit drawings and posters on the walls, advertising shows long gone. Wystan flings open his window to enjoy the traffic and voices outside. Civilisation! The air, full of exhaust fumes and coal dust, tastes fresh to him after the sultry ether of Helensburgh. How far away all that is; how far away his shrivelled, inauthentic self.

That first night, they head for the familiar Berlin side street. The façades of the buildings are ornate and pleasing beneath their grubby layers. Shadows from the evening sun pool on the pavement. Wystan begins to unlock a little; he and Christopher joke and smoke as they make their way to their favourite boy bar, the Cosy Corner.

Once found, the Cosy supplies almost every need of the young, bright homosexual in Berlin. It has no sign, no polished window to show off those inside. A few young men are loitering around a nondescript door. The windows are boarded up. Christopher presses a bell, which makes no sound, and, after a time, a door inside opens and music and voices can be heard briefly before being shut away again. Then the nondescript door opens, a leather curtain is pulled to one side and a beefy man looks them up and down.

Two of the boys at the door attach themselves to Wystan and Christopher and follow them in. Wystan's companion wears tattered trousers and his hands are white with dust. Dirty blond hair drifts over his face. His eyes meet Wystan's with an arousing mixture of appeal and arrogance. He smells of sweat and fresh air, as if he has been walking a long time.

Heavy boots and well-made British shoes clatter down a wooden staircase into the fug of the Cosy. It's a dim room the size of his classroom at Larchfield, with a bar down one wall. A chandelier hangs from the ceiling, giving out a sparkling, shadowy glow. Along another wall is a stove, which is lit, pouring even more heat into the crowded space. All the rent boys have stripped down to the waist in the heat, their torsos gleaming with sweat.

The clientele is a mix of ordinary-looking local men, interspersed with foreigners, like Wystan and Christopher, and all manner of boys from the surrounding areas. Most of all, there is laughter. The four of them squeeze on to a table; Christopher orders beer and sandwiches at the bar. Wystan is pressed close to the blond boy, who has opened his shirt to the waist and rolled up his sleeves. His youthful cheeks are flushed in the heat. Wystan smiles down at him. 'Hungry?' he says, knowing the boy won't understand. The other boy has scrubbed a clean patch over his face and neck. He is dark, where the other is blond, and has an arresting, strong face that would suit an intellectual woman, Wystan thinks. He wears dungarees, with a thin shirt, which he proceeds to remove without dislodging the dungarees, the whole ensemble greyed with – what? Soil? But his teeth are all present and white. Both of these boys are vigorous and handsome, and they know it.

Christopher appears very pleased with his acquisition, though he casts long glances at Wystan's boy, whose name is Erich.

A saxophone starts up, a long, piercing melody that seems to vibrate through the tables and the floors, setting the very air trembling as it enters their lungs. Wystan hands Erich a cigarette and lights it for him. He whispers in his ear one of the many obscenities he knows in German and the boy nods and grins. Wystan pushes the boy's fringe from his eyes and slides his hand into the boy's hand. As he leans back, the smoke and music and alcohol smooth out his anxieties, and he finds Helensburgh and Larchfield fading from his mind, like an incomprehensible dream.

Later, when they stumble out of the Cosy, laughing and throwing German and English words at each other, Wystan is filled with pure delight. Christopher is going on to the El Dorado with his companion, called Otto; they wave and part in the street and Erich walks by Wystan's side, back to the Institute. He is quite the most thrilling person Wystan has stood beside in his whole life. His strong body has all the perfection that Wystan himself lacks.

When they reach the apartment, Wystan indicates the bed and sits at Erich's feet to remove his boots. Erich says, 'Five marks, Herr Odden.' Wystan riffles in his wallet, pulls out the five marks and places it on the bedside table. Erich reaches over with lightning speed and whips the note into his trouser pocket.

When Wystan removes the boy's boots, he is shocked to see the blisters and blood that cover his heels. 'You walked a long way tonight?' he asks, to Erich's blank expression. 'Work?' he asks, making a sort of digging motion with his arms.

Erich shakes his head. 'You . . . my work.' He smiles his angelic smile.

Wystan goes to the washstand and wets his facecloth and dabs it on the injuries. The boots are cheap, made of almost immoveable leather, and the boy wears no socks. Looking up at Erich, he says urgently, 'We must get you new boots, Erich. This won't do at all.' The boy nods and smiles, uncomprehending. Tiredness gathers in his expression and he falls back on the bed. 'We fuck now,' he says, sleepily, from the pillow.

A commotion beneath his window wakes Wystan. It is early morning and the curtains are breathing gently in the breeze. 'Otto!' Christopher is screaming. 'Come back here!' Wystan looks down at his friend, who is topless, clutching the waist of his trousers.

'What's going on?'

Christopher shakes his head. 'Only ran off with all my fucking rent.'

Wystan checks his own bed, but the sleeping form of Erich is still there. 'Unlucky!' he calls down, not able to suppress a laugh. 'Come on, let's get some breakfast.'

When the three of them head off, back to the Cosy, for breakfast, Erich enquires after Otto in his mangled English. Christopher makes a neck-wringing motion with his hands. 'Your friend stole my money.

When you see him, tell him I'm looking for him.' Erich's eyes widen and then he grins.

At the Cosy, Erich tucks into sausages and sauerkraut like a boy at prep school. Wystan and he have a blurred quality, hair and clothes askew, and Wystan is already, his friend knows, in love. His long fingers tap close to the boy's plate as he watches him eat. As the beer glass empties, Wystan looks around for the barman and indicates that it should be filled. They say nothing to one another, but Wystan's face has the solemn, appreciative expression it takes on when he has fallen.

From time to time, the boy looks up at Christopher and grins over his food. Of the two boys, he was the lovelier, and probably the cleverer, too, as he knows Wystan is a good bet over the medium term. Otto was stupid to run out with a bit of cash on the first day. Christopher sighs, sips his coffee and meets the boy's gaze with a smile. Otto might be a thief, but this little imp is going wreak havoc.

FOURTEEN

Dora

Into her cloistered, claustrophobic life, emails came, still addressed to RJ. This was the name she wrote under, having had, in her youth, the notion that initials made one appear more serious and took away the baggage of identity. It worked for many writers: T. S. Eliot, W. H. Auden, J. K. Rowling . . . In her case, the initials – which stood alone and did not refer to actual names – had stuck as a name in themselves, and it was this by which her friends in her professional life came to know her.

Dora looked at the emails on the screen, unsure if she was legitimately entitled, anymore, to respond. *Dear RJ*, they said. *What are you writing? How are you? How are the maniacs upstairs?*

They've moved into my head, she began to write, then deleted. *And they never sleep.*

It was as Dora that she cared for her baby, trudging dutifully to baby group, walking for miles along the forestry tracks and shores with the warm little body strapped to her chest. It was Dora who waited until the weekend, when Kit was around and would drive them somewhere, anywhere, and she could spend money on useless commodities that reminded her that, as a consumer, at least, she existed.

As the poet W. H. Auden said (Dora was becoming something of an expert on him now), we need the courage to choose ourselves. But it had become clear that either RJ or Dora had chosen, or been compelled to choose, something else. What else is there to do when a woman is all grown up?

Why don't we all come and see you? the emails insisted quietly.

Whom did they want to come and see? Dora could not locate RJ anymore. Her friends would be disappointed. They had never met Dora. And none of them had a baby or was married. Her friends, in fact, were strangers. Perhaps it had always been so. Perhaps they had never known her at all.

She thought of Auden and his tight circle of friends, the letters winging back and forth throughout his time in Helensburgh. His lifelong friendship with Christopher meant that, no matter how isolated he was, there was someone he could refer back to, someone who could remind him of who he was.

So . . . perhaps these people were *her* real friends, trying to reach her. The trouble was she did not know how to articulate what had happened to her in a way that they would understand.

Each day was enormous. It seemed impossible to traverse, so, often, Dora did not try, simply floating into it on the sofa, with her gurgling baby on her knee. And, surrounding her raft, the endless banging and music from upstairs, the revving of cars and slamming of doors, and – what was worse for being indefinable – Mo's hatred seeping through the walls and the ceiling.

Okay, why not? Good to see you, she wrote, finally. What else was there to say? Dora scrutinised the message, over and over; did it sound as nonchalant as she wished it to? Even if she knew she had made some kind of massive mistake, she didn't want her friends to think so – to pity her.

And so they came, driving up together from London, a place so far away in every way that it was another world. Here they were, miraculously unfolding from the car: two women and a man, all immaculately themselves.

'Fuck me,' said Steph, looking out wonderingly over the lawn and the glittering ocean. Dora had known Steph since they were undergraduates together and she was now a successful academic and scholar of the moderns. She turned to Dora and said, 'How are you, gorgeous?'

Steph called almost everyone gorgeous. It was not to be taken seriously. And it bore no relation to how Dora actually looked. She had been waiting for hours. She'd changed her clothes several times, but there was no getting away from it: she looked completely different from the woman they knew. A few months previously, she had thrown out or sold on eBay all her 'RJ' clothes: the dresses and jackets for readings, the nice shoes. She wore anything now; she really wasn't particular.

But they looked just the same. How clean and well groomed they were – had Dora been like that once? How *substantial* they were. She looked at them with terrible longing.

'RJ,' said the other woman, Tracey. She was younger than Dora, and had abandoned poetry to become a successful playwright. Dora didn't react. 'RJ!' She prodded Dora and, with a jolt, Dora realised this was her name. She smiled and they embraced. Dora found herself inhaling the scent of her friend's hair, as she did her baby's. She clung on a fraction longer than the closeness of their friendship warranted, a little afraid of being unable to speak.

'I get it now – I see why you live here,' said the man, Martin. He was the poet of the group, uncompromisingly eking an existence on the fringes of fashionable literary London. He had kept his northern accent (Dora had jettisoned hers at the first opportunity) and was wearing much the same student outfit as he had worn throughout their acquaintance. This had begun when their first books came out with the same publisher. Martin was the one to warn her about all this: her marriage, her move far away and, most of all, her baby. *You know what all that means, don't you?* he'd said. *You'll become a housewife, and no one wants to read housewife poetry.*

But now he was advancing on her, smiling broadly. 'Good to see you, RJ,' he said softly. His body against hers felt electric. No one but Kit or Beatrice had touched her for such a long time.

The Divines were, by a miracle, out, although who knew when they would be back.

Dora said politely, 'It's so lovely you've come,' then she blushed at how weirdly formal she sounded, and pressed on: 'Yes, it's so lovely, isn't it?' (Oh, God. Dora never said the word *lovely*, ever – it was as meaningless as *nice* – and here she had said it twice in the space of five seconds.) But, as they all stood in silence for a moment, looking out at the view, she knew that they all knew it was beyond lovely; it was where that word lost its meaning. It was another world, and Dora had gone there never to return. If she had a sense of humour, she might have joked that she had indeed died and gone to Paradise.

'Come on in and see everyone,' she said. 'You must be dying for a drink after that drive.' With her friends there, jostling, filling the air with friendly noise, Dora wanted to explain about her life, but the words eluded her. Would they even understand?

Kit had an apron on and his sleeves rolled up; he was making dinner and taking care of Beatrice so that Dora could enjoy this visit from her friends. He was quite unconscious of the vision he presented to the urban young people. They stared and Steph said clumsily, 'So . . . busy in the kitchen, Kit?'

Dora's husband grinned happily. 'Well, yes, I am, actually. Whipping something up for you all. Dora . . . Dora is so pleased to see you.' He winked at his wife and disappeared back into the kitchen.

The baby clearly alarmed them. Tracey held her like a bomb and handed her back. The other two made admiring noises and then drifted out of the room to gaze once more over the pulsing sea. So Dora put her back in the bouncer in the kitchen doorway and followed her friends down to the beach, where the sun was staging an incredible wintery show.

They cracked open some beers on the shore and swapped stories of their writing and their times together. Her friends were making a good effort at hiding their pity, but she knew it was there. The other-worldliness of the setting merely decorated the stark truth that she had left intellectual and artistic life behind to have a baby. It was disappointing, she knew. Had she not known that to go to another place, so far from London – instead of doing as they had done, travelling *to* London – was career suicide? That to have a baby was a lifestyle choice that would render her uninteresting?

Martin had indeed tried to warn her, but Dora had dismissed him as jealous. In her arrogance, she had thought that the rule did not apply to her. In so far as she had considered the unspoken rule at all, she had known she was different, that she was a writer first and all that other stuff second. As she liked to quote Charlotte Brontë, privately, in pencil, in her notebook: *I am neither man nor woman, but an Author.*

They filled her in on their lives. Steph had a high-profile position at UCL. She was on the radio quite a lot, talking about poetry. Tracey was getting married to her writer boyfriend next year. They would move into his studio flat. She would be able to work, she was sure, if he kept the TV down. She was teaching a lot, but living in London was so expensive, there was no choice. And Martin was much the same, possibly drinking a little more, definitely looking older. But he was publishing, he was writing. He was definitely in the swim.

Listening to their stories, Dora realised it was not distance that separated them, nor age.

She drained a second bottle and laughed when they did.

Dora had made real, hard choices, and they had not.

Had she lacked courage? Had she, in fact, betrayed herself? Talking with them, she missed her old self – deeply, painfully, like a friend. She felt grief pressing in on the afternoon.

It was growing too cold. She beckoned them in, to where Kit had got the sitting room toasty warm and Beatrice grinned and burbled in her playpen. Dora felt her friends' incomprehension of her life, and it rankled. Did they think she wanted to reverse everything? Did they think she wanted their lives? Beatrice was what Dora had now, instead of participation in the world. Beatrice was her explanation for everything. Unfortunately, it was an explanation that had no words.

Steph enquired politely about her life here. How was married life? How were the neighbours? Dora played it all down. How could she tell them how terrible everything was, and that she could *never* in a million years leave? It made no sense. Dora remembered how, as a younger woman, she had scoffed at *Brief Encounter* and *The Bridges of Madison County* – the heroines who turned their backs on true love for a life crushingly unfulfilled. Feeble, she had thought. *Unrealistic.*

And now she could not see those films again because she understood them completely. The stilted language, the overblown sentiment – they absolutely broke her heart.

While she talked with her friends, answering their questions with superficial cheeriness, her mind stumbled over the rocks of what was now true.

Dora had love in her life where she had not had it before: love that she felt for her tiny family and love that she felt back from them. It was love that rooted her into the world; looking at her friends, she wondered how it was that they did not float away.

This was it.

Her dearest friends knew nothing; what life was really about, what it really cost.

Dora brushed away tears brimming in her eyes. She caught Martin looking at her with a sharp, kind look. *Don't say a fucking thing*, she yelled at him wordlessly. He held her gaze until she broke it and she heard his words in her head: *You're struggling, aren't you?*

NO. Dora Fielding was not struggling. She had a name, though she kept forgetting it, and three people had travelled up from London to see her, which proved she existed. She was becoming aware of the full ramifications of her decision, that was all. She was becoming aware of the rock-hard truth about life.

'It's a relief to be out of all that, in a way,' she managed, in response to a conversation about the unrestrained ruthlessness one writer had shown another. The three of them nodded sagely and completely without conviction.

'I bet it is,' said Steph, though a follow-up to this was beyond her. 'The thing is, I know how it sounds, but I couldn't manage without being able to buy an overpriced, but very good, cappuccino. Go on – call me what you like. But it symbolises the problem.'

'I understand what you mean,' said Dora. 'Though we do have Costa.' They laughed uproariously, but actually Dora was sincere. Thankfully, Kit distracted everyone by coming in to let Dora kiss Beatrice before he took her up to bed.

A short time later, he produced dinner. He sat at the head of the table, like the head of the family, a man among children. Dora's friends paid him polite respect, as they did their own parents.

He said, 'Dora' this and 'Dora' that. So proud of her, he thought they knew her. The name clipped at their ears like a teacher and they exchanged glances.

He tried to tell them a little of what Dora had been doing since she had moved to Helensburgh. 'W. H. Auden was here, you know,' he said. 'Dora is going to write about it.'

'Auden? Here?' Steph sat upright.

'No mistake . . . and Dora is writing about him.'

Steph's expression was a comical mixture of delight at this turn of events and – this pleased Dora immensely – envy. 'RJ! You lucky dog, stumbling on to something like that. And I bet no one has even touched it before. It'll be virgin Auden territory.'

'Yes. I don't think anyone can be bothered to come here.'

'Was it for long? The agape moment was after it, wasn't it?'

'It was two and a half years. He wrote *The Orators* here,' said Dora proudly.

'When you've researched it all, you should come down to the university and talk to us,' said Steph. She was still looking at her with a kind of wonder.

Tracey said, 'I wanted to write a play about Rimbaud and Verlaine, but it was impossible – information overload, and impossible to find something new to say. You're very lucky . . . This wonderful place . . . your delightful husband –' here, she smiled with exaggerated coyness at Kit – 'and now this! Maybe I'll move up here.'

'You'd last five seconds,' said Martin.

'Rubbish! I'm very adaptable.'

'Remember when we went to that weird festival in Dubrovnik? And you couldn't work out how to open the minibar? I thought you were going to have a brain haemorrhage.'

They laughed together, a group of friends to which RJ had now returned. Tracey gave Martin the finger. The conversation moved gaily on. At last, Kit tired of the reminiscing and excused himself to go to bed, and Dora went to get her guitar. As she got up from the table, she saw the lights of the Divines' car glow behind the curtains. They were back.

'Is that the mad neighbours?' Tracey asked.

'Can either of them sing? They could join our band,' said Steph.

At that moment, nothing could disturb Dora's happiness. She was

RJ again with her friends, and Mo and Terrence were just mad old people who were not of significance. She gave the guitar to Steph, who was the best player among them, and the friends decamped to the sitting room for the sing-song they had ended so many evenings with before.

They had run through a couple of their favourite songs when the telephone rang. Dora stopped mid-chorus and rushed out into the hall to intercept the deafening ring.

'Aye, this is Terrence Divine. Stop the racket, please.'

Racket? They were singing a few songs with an acoustic guitar. It was the first time she'd been up past ten since the baby was born.

'It's a few friends I haven't seen for a long while. We're not singing loudly.'

'You've woken us up.'

'You've been out all evening.'

'We're back now.'

She could hear her friends starting up 'I'll Follow the Sun' in the other room. She felt RJ's urge to return to them.

'Terrence, can't you just . . . sod off!' she said and hung up, then left the phone off the hook. Swept up in her friends, she swiftly forgot the exchange. For a little while longer, RJ sang her harmonies until it was time for her friends to head off to the little B & B they had booked. It was an evening that Dora would always remember, bathing her in friendship.

She woke in the morning with new energy. After Bea had been fed and Kit waved off to work and effusive goodbye texts shared with her friends, Dora went into the spare room and took out her poetry collection and read it. While her baby slept, she fell into the world she had created all those years ago, as fully and completely as if she were encountering the poems for the first time. She heard her voice, RJ's voice, reading the poems and she read back through some of the journals in her boxes to remind her of the things RJ had done. It was secret and joyful. She forgot about Dora . . . Dora, with her down-in-the-mouth face, her philosophical confusion about *Brief Encounter*, her social ineptitude, her silence. Dora was RJ again. It might just last.

THERE WAS A KNOCK at the door. On the doorstep was an elderly woman whom Dora did not recognise. She had the brittle elegance of a wealthy churchgoer, and pulled her lips into a glossy smile.

'Hello, Dora. I'm Harriet McGuire. May I come in?'

'Um . . .'

'I am from the church. I have heard about your troubles, and perhaps I can help.'

Bea wriggled in Dora's arms. Dora stepped aside, not knowing quite what else to do, and let Harriet pass, in a waft of sepulchral perfume.

Harriet gave a little exclamation of disappointment as she settled herself in a chair by the window. 'I used to visit my parents' friends here, long ago, when it was a whole house.'

'Oh, yes?'

'They've cut this room in half, haven't they? Oh, it's a disaster for the light, isn't it? We used to push the furniture back against the walls for dancing.' She hauled herself back to the compromised present. 'They are so heavy-handed when they divide the houses, aren't they?'

'We like it . . .' Dora said feebly. Her euphoric feeling of being RJ was shrivelling away as the old lady spoke.

Harriet's knobbly hands clasped in her lap. 'Now, I hear that there is a problem between the Divines and you. I thought that I might be able to help.'

'Help with what?'

'Why don't you tell me what the problem is? Then we can see.'

'There isn't a problem.'

'Mo says there is. She has been crying at the church every Sunday. She says you're the neighbours from Hell.'

'I don't know why she would say that. They have a lot of visitors and block our drive, but . . . it's not something we can't sort out ourselves.'

'Well, that's it, you see. I don't think you realise how things are done here. Mo and Terrence, well, they are—'

'Good people?'

Harriet gave Dora the same look all these women gave her – health visitors, midwives, neighbours – the look she might give the ghastly daughter-in-law, the sort of young woman who must be dealt with, have deference drummed in somehow.

'What I was going to say was . . . they are a good churchgoing couple who do good things for the community. All they want is a peaceful retirement.' She glanced out of the window. 'I gather you had a party last night.'

'No. My friends . . .' Dora's fuzzy brain finally made the connection. Harriet McGuire was not a disinterested observer. She was here to advocate on behalf of Mo and Terrence.

'You know, Helensburgh really isn't the kind of place where we disturb others with wild parties. And you having a wee one, as well.'

At this, Bea gurgled engagingly.

'Although, I suppose, when a house as lovely as this is divided, then a whole other sort of person is attracted to being here.' Harriet sighed and turned once again to the window. 'You can never escape the *element*.'

'I didn't have a wild party,' said Dora, bewildered.

Oblivious to Dora, Harriet continued: 'There used to be croquet, out on the lawn. I loved it so. I have such happy memories of those times. So terrible that it is a site of conflict now.'

'Well, there is no conflict from us,' Dora said, getting to her feet. 'Mo and Terrence keep trespassing on our garden and play Christian pop songs at full volume. They fill the drive with cars and the house with strangers. I have a baby, as you can see. I am too busy for conflict and so I let most of this ride. You might . . . feed that back? To your friends? That I am too busy for this sort of thing?'

'I came to help,' Harriet said. She was clearly unaccustomed to leaving before she was ready, but reluctantly she stood.

Trembling with anger, Dora let the woman pass, observing her angular figure, her shiny shoes and woolly stockings as she left the house without another word. Harriet paused every now and then to survey the garden, and, at the gate, gazed back at the house. Dora had the painful feeling of something being stripped away from her. It was RJ, of course. RJ was gone now.

Mo and Terrence held a loud and blurry discussion above Dora's head.

Exhausted, she travelled back to the sofa with her baby and turned up the volume on the TV. The only feeling she permitted herself was the tiny spark of gladness that her friends had not seen this. They had been and gone without witnessing her complete shame, the death of who she used to be, right before their eyes.

FIFTEEN

Wystan

CECIL DIDN'T MENTION THE rain. Out come the buckets in the corridor and metallic thuds punctuate the classes. A broken gutter outside his window chucks water on to the sill. Wystan lies on his bed, smoking and listening to the pattering, like the tachycardia heartbeat of a failing industrial machine. Outside is grey, even the rhododendrons seem a peculiar shade of grey.

This morning, the author copies of his book arrived. There lies the package, torn open in his excitement, and there is a stack of them, signed and waiting to go out to his friends. Later, he will take one to Mrs Perkins, who he knows will appreciate it. Perkins himself won't care a shit about it. On his lap, as he smokes, is a copy. He has held it all night there, occasionally waking to admire its dusky-blue cover and the simple *Poems by W. H. Auden* of the title.

Holding the book after all the waiting is so perfect a feeling that it almost breaks his sense that he ought to be somewhere else when this happened. Like where? In Berlin, reading extracts to Erich? The silence of this place, and the pounding, terrible rain are a strange reception for such a slim, delicate thing.

He gets up, ash falling all over the bedspread. The air tastes stale and damp, and through the leaky windows he can smell the garden's leaf mould. In the bowels of the house, the boys clatter and yell to the latrine, interrupted by occasional shouts from Jessop. But for the modest pile of blue books, this day has begun like every other.

His excitement is clouded by the troubling events of last night. He was woken by Jamie Taylor's sobbing, audible through the floor. It is not every night; it does not happen, for instance, on the nights when Wystan is on duty. Jamie Taylor cried at night, inconsolably, at least twice a week all through the summer term, and has started up again in the new term. School does this to a boy, Wystan knows, but for it to continue unabated like this? Wystan has shepherded the boy to Mrs Perkins on a number of occasions, but she cannot get much out of him. Unlike the rest of the boys, he appears to have lost weight over the summer rather than gaining it.

Last night, Wystan could bear it no longer. Jessop was obviously going to do nothing about it, though he was on boarder duty. Like Wystan, Jessop had a room in the house within easy reach of the dormitory should there be any problem, though his room was on the ground floor, on the other side of Larchfield. The master on duty was supposed to check on the boys during the night and to listen out for any crisis. There was never any sign of Jessop. Where, in fact, was he on these nights when he was supposed to be looking after the boarders?

When the crying started, Wystan turned on his lamp and consulted his watch. It was 2 a.m. He pulled on his dressing gown, lit a candle and felt his way blearily down the stairs. As he approached the door of the dormitory where Taylor slept, it opened and Jessop emerged, face intent and shadowy. He gave a visible jump as he saw Wystan before him.

'Jessop!' Wystan exclaimed. If his colleague was there, why was the crying continuing? 'Taylor's crying . . .' he said.

'What is it to you?'

'He's right underneath my room.'

'Hopeless baby.' Jessop moved to push past Wystan, but Wystan put out his arm.

'Steady on,' he said. 'He doesn't cry when I'm on duty. It's only when you are.'

The two men glared at each other over the candle flame. And, in that moment, Wystan was transported back to similar stumbling moments of discovery in his school days: prefects inexplicably emerging from dorms at strange times; his old cricket master sidling into the small dorm he shared with three other boys and sitting on the bed of the boy he had picked out from the first day, his hands doing something under the covers until the boy cried quietly. They all knew that it was something that must not be spoken of, that was a mark of specialness little boys both craved and feared, and at any rate endured – and he saw the same expression in Jessop's face, the horrible *shiftiness*.

'I'm going to bed,' Jessop said.

'Jessop, why does Taylor cry every night you're on duty?'

'He's a crybaby. I tried to get him to snap out of it, but he's a hopeless case. Now, Wystan, *dear* –' he leant into Wystan's face – 'let me pass.'

'I hope this isn't what I think it is—'

'And what is it, then, clever boy?' Jessop leant in so close Wystan could feel his hot, stale breath on his face. 'I know what *you're* up to, more's the point. What goes with your fancy friends down south won't be put up with here, do you understand? Don't think I don't know.'

'You don't know anything about me.' Wystan was both angry and frightened now.

'I know enough to know you need to stop insinuating things about me and let me go to bed!' And with that Jessop pushed past him and disappeared to his room below.

Wystan suspected that every ear was straining to catch what was being said. Furious, he climbed the stairs back to his room, and lay, unable to sleep. What should he do? Could he, in fact, do anything at all?

Wystan cast his mind back to his own schooldays and how he had managed to deflect the hostility and bullying that was meted out to boys less strange than he was. He did not radiate whatever it was that attracted bullying. He had become proficient at practical jokes which made even the thickest aggressor laugh – was that what had protected him? He did not fully understand why Jessop disliked him so. But now . . . the feeling was mutual. It sat very uncomfortably with Wystan to have a strong negative feeling about anyone. He prized his detachment; his detachment allowed him to work under any circumstances, favourable or not.

With these thoughts churning in his mind, the night passed, and the new day brought sunlight, a bright space between him and the night's events. It also brought Wystan's books. Olive had carried them in and lingered a little, eager to see what was in the package for Mr Auden.

Now, there is no time left to rejoice in the books because he is late for his class. He dashes along to his classroom and picks up where they left off discussing a Hardy poem yesterday.

'To recap: what is the only legitimate subject for poetry?'

'Love, sir,' says McLeod.

'Correct. And what has this poem taught us is the most important aspect of poetry?'

'Beat, sir?' says Theakston, the spindly little blond with the talent for rugby.

'Yes, and we call that meter. What do we call it, boys?'

'Meter, sir.'

'A poem should be spoken aloud.'

'Sir?' McLeod raises his hand.

'Yes, McLeod.'

'Is it true you write poems, sir?'

'It is.'

'Will you read us one, sir?' The request sounds genuine, but is, of course, accompanied by the smirk that is stuck to every boy over ten.

There are a few minutes left. There is nothing further to say about 'The Darkling Thrush'; the boys are fidgeting. Wystan replies by reciting immediately, in a voice much stronger and clearer than his normal speaking voice, one of his favourite passages in his new book:

'Will you turn a deaf ear
To what they said on the shore,
Interrogate their poises
In their rich houses;

Of stork-legged heaven-reachers
Of the compulsory touchers
The sensitive amusers
And masked amazers——?'

The bell erupts into the silent room. The boys freeze, half out of their chairs, and stare at him.

Wystan smiles indulgently. 'Yes, off you go.' And, in a great muddle of noise and colour, the boys head for the next lesson. Wystan watches them leave, and thinks he may weep at their great friendly mass, pushing and shouting. They do not look back at him. He is forgotten as surely as breakfast.

'McLeod!'

The boy pauses and turns back.

'If you don't all start behaving in class, I'm going to cut my prick off.'

McLeod stares, as do his two friends who have turned at the sound of obscenity.

'What do you mean, sir?'

'You know what I mean.' Wystan appears absolutely serious.

McLeod sniffs and wipes his nose, at a loss as to what to say. 'Don't do that, sir,' he says.

'Reluctantly, of course. I would rather you paid attention.'

'Yes, sir.'

'Off you go.'

They leave, this time, in complete silence, until they are out of the door, when there is an almighty outburst of whispering and disbelieving laughter. He has got their attention, anyway. Wystan sighs. His genius for practical jokes is wasted here.

At lunchtime, he returns to his room and sits again with the dusty-blue cover on his knee. He examines the text once more, wincing at the cracks in the punctuation, at the way the poems in print seem angrier, more like his mother speaking than anything original. In the letter that came with the books, Eliot tells him to send the address of any shops in Helensburgh that would like to stock the book. He says again that he is very proud to be publishing this book, that the work is singular and full of promise, even as it seems, at times, wilfully obscure. Wystan feels like a boy again, holding some treasured gift. His gangly legs are half hauled on the bed; he is utterly unconscious of how he looks or what he is, except that somehow he has produced this beautiful thing. He presses it briefly to his chest, knows that to do so is silly, flicks through the pages again.

That no one is there to share it with him cuts deep. This afternoon he has a couple of hours off and he decides to post copies to Cecil and Isherwood and Spender. He will put some in the bookshop and maybe the tourist office will care to have a copy. This will connect him with the world that knows him, that, through this sheet of rain, seems so far away. The boy at the station slips into his mind again. He shifts uncomfortably on the bed; will this wound never heal?

There is a telephone at the school. No one has rung it to congratulate him, but he supposes they might. Mrs Clyde guards it rather jealously, interrogates anyone who uses it, explaining how costly it is to place and take calls. 'This telephone,' she says darkly, 'will be the ruin of this place.'

Wystan takes a piece of paper and writes in his spidery hand:

I am a young man, with light brown hair and a book of poems.
Telephone Helensburgh 120 and ask for Wystan.

What should he do with the note? There is no one to post it to. He remembered, as a boy, once writing to his father, who was far away in Egypt, and he simply wrote, *Hello, Dr Auden, this is your son, Wystan. I hope you are well. We had toad-in-the-hole for dinner at school.* And he told no one, and simply put the envelope in the postbox on the way to church in the village, with his father's name on and *Egypt*. The postman emptying the box brought it back to the school, guessing a lonely boy had sent it, and Wystan had to suffer the humiliation of a summons to the head and an explanation of both the school postal system and the ills of excessive sentiment in wartime.

After lunch is a dead-end French class, for which he has not properly prepared. Unnerved by the boys' expectant faces, he takes a penny from his pocket and a stamp from his wallet and, with the flamboyance of a magician, he instructs the boys to watch.

'What's important here is a steady hand, and a confident flick. What's important, Douglas?'

'Steady hand, sir. Confident flick.'

'Excellent. And we lick the stamp so –' he sticks his tongue out ostentatiously to lick the stamp – 'then we lay it carefully upon the penny, like so. And we do not breathe, boys. It is imperative we do not breathe – for, if we do, the stamp will flutter away like a butterfly upon the breeze, taking our dreams with it.'

The boys are transfixed. What in God's name is he doing? Wystan has balanced the penny upon his thumb, with the stamp upon it, slightly arched, ready to waft away at the slightest breath. 'Do not sneeze, boys. Hold your breath!' Wystan gives an authoritative flick with his thumb; the penny sails up to the ceiling at rocket speed, hits the ceiling and clatters to the floor.

The boys' gaze drifts around the room, trying to see what has happened, then Davies squeaks, 'It's stuck to the ceiling, sir.'

'Indeed it is. Would anyone like to have a try?'

Enthralled, the boys take the pennies and stamps he hands out to them and chaos ensues as they jostle to find a good spot. 'Remember – don't breathe. And steady hand, confident flick!' Wystan patrols them as if they are practising declensions, or writing about the Revolution, for sticking stamps to the ceiling is not easy. It is, however, great fun.

Wystan tries not to stare at Jamie Taylor, whose white face barely raises from his desk. He goes through the motions of attaching stamp to penny, but there is no confidence whatsoever in his flick. Wystan stands over him and tries to demonstrate, but the boy simply freezes. At last, the bell rings, and, as the boys pour out, Wystan calls Jamie back. A look, quite simply, of terror crosses the boy's face. He will not move from the door.

'Taylor, dear. There's nothing to be afraid of. Come closer; I want to say something to you.'

The boy shuffles forward.

'I know,' says Wystan.

'Know what, sir?' the boy mumbles.

'I want you to know it is going to stop.'

'Don't know what you mean, sir.' The boy shuffles from foot to foot, but a small eye briefly meets Wystan's.

'Of course you don't. Just hear my words.'

'Yes, sir.' Jamie Taylor waits for the command to go, his lip trembling.

'Now, off you go. And don't worry.'

A short while later, Wystan is leaving the school with his books well wrapped in his leather satchel when he sees on the step a newly cleaned milk bottle, and he picks it up and puts it in his bag. Why?

I don't know.

You don't have to know why you do everything.

How he misses Isherwood. How he misses even Sheilagh, not that he will be sending her a copy, as his poems apparently gave her the irrefutable evidence she didn't want of the weakness of his character.

It's still raining, but now it's the thin drizzle that Scotland specialises in, where the air itself seems to be composed of droplets of water. He pulls his cap down and sets off into the wet streets. When he comes home, striding up the shining hill, he will have sent his book to his friends and bought a steak to complete the practical joke he alluded to this morning. He will have a lightness in his step because the note will have found its way into the bottle, and he will have sent his loneliness off into the sea.

And, that night, Jamie Taylor won't cry.

SIXTEEN

Dora

'GOOD MORNING, DARLING.' THE tea went down on the bedside table. If Kit ever left Dora, she would be unable to get up anymore. This tea he made was an elixir.

Exhaustion crept through her, as if her blood were the thin, grey run-off from a watercolour. The baby had fussed in the night. It was dull and raining outside, and so cold. The central heating wafted feebly in the cavernous rooms before shooting up the stairs and through the skylight.

Kit crept in beside Dora and they clung together in the early-morning chill. Kit had warm skin; he was one of those people who was always warm. Dora burrowed into him. She found it almost impossible to express in words the unease that permeated everything.

There was a creak upstairs, as if someone were crouching right over their heads. Kit gently stroked his wife's face. 'You'll be all right?' he asked.

If one is not to admit to being stark staring mad, there is no reply to this except yes. Alone all day with the strange neighbours creaking overhead, playing their insane Jesus music? Fine! Dora had chosen this! Afraid to go out because the looks Mo gave her chilled her to the bone? No problem! No friends? Who needed friends? She had a baby!

'Please . . . stay for a while,' she said, reddening as she did so. It was humiliating to ask for help, to believe she actually needed help.

Kit extricated himself and sat down awkwardly on the bedroom chair. 'I have to go to Edinburgh – for a meeting,' he said.

'Oh. What about?'

'Actually, it's for Susie – to discuss a grant application.'

'Can't she do that?'

'I said I'd go with her.'

Kit looked uncomfortable. Susie was a new member of the La Scala team. She was younger than Dora and also single.

Dora suddenly saw herself from above: an exhausted woman approaching middle age, unkempt, whining and paranoid. She wished she could be like Susie – unencumbered, the sort of woman a man wanted to assist.

'You know,' said Kit, coming back and taking her hand, 'I've been thinking about this. I wonder if you're being too hard on yourself, trying to do too much?' Checking Dora's expression, he pressed on. 'I thought of two things. First of all, why don't we have a Christmas party? To show you off as hostess? To show off Bea? You'd be so good at it . . . And it occurs to me that you might be happier if you eased off on trying to write, just for a little while. It's causing you so much frustration and distress, when what you probably need is just a rest from it. You know, just let life catch up with you a bit?'

He squeezed her hand encouragingly. Dora noticed that he had somehow become dressed; it seemed that he was always dressed and on his way out, and she was always in her nightclothes, or some terrible ensemble of ex-maternity clothes she had hauled on, and in some way always on the back foot, always behind him.

His expression remained calm and kind. 'Yes? What do you say? A lovely party. We could plan it together this evening.'

'A party.' The words came out slowly, wonderingly. It was such an outlandish idea, *so far* from what she wanted that the initial blow of it felt almost pleasurable. Like a slap to the shoulder that, for a moment, seems just vigorous, friendly, and only slowly does the sensation reveal itself to be the dull thud of pain.

'But my idea . . .' Dora said, haltingly. 'This thing about Auden, about him living in Helensburgh? I thought you liked that. I could really do something with it; I mean, no one seems to care much about him – maybe because he's gay, or English or something – but the biography idea is a good one, isn't it? One poet to another, you know?'

Dora shifted in the bed so she was propped up on the pillows. 'It's been giving me something to do, the research and so on . . . I really feel I'm starting to know him . . .' She trailed off.

'Darling, look at you; you're so tired. Why take on such a big project right now? With everything that's going on? Don't take this wrongly, but . . . you're going to snap if you put yourself under more pressure . . . and what if no one wants to publish the book? It would be terrible to do all that work and get nowhere with it. Honestly, darling, I really believe that you need to rest.'

'And have a party?'

'Yes, a party. You and me.'

He smiled encouragingly and got up to leave.

'Wait,' Dora said, holding him back. 'I . . . I don't want you to go to the meeting with Susie. I know it sounds unreasonable, but I don't. I really don't. I want you to stay here with me.'

'She needs me to go. The project needs me to go.' A third of him was out of the room. He said, from the door frame, 'Look, why not just take the day off? You and Bea. Don't try to accomplish anything. Watch some TV, read a book. Go for a walk.'

'Kit, I don't want you to go.'

'I have to. I'm sorry.'

'So, you're going to leave me alone all day with our baby in this freezing house, with these people up above who hate me – while you spend the day in Edinburgh with *Susie*?'

'She doesn't know how to work these meetings.' He was extremely calm.

Dora understood now. She had blinked and her husband had become a different person, one who was not dishevelled, shivering and covered in baby sick and fighting tears all day. He was a person in the world. He was meeting people, forming friendships with Susies. He was escaping Mo and Helensburgh and everything in it. And the part that frightened Dora – that was bringing her out in a sweat as it dawned on her – was that he was strangely untroubled by her distress.

Fury took charge of her tired bones, her chapped lips. She snapped upright and pointed at him and spoke clearly in a wobbling voice.

'You can't go to Edinburgh with Susie and leave me like this.'

He began once more, patiently, 'I have—'

'If you do that . . . if you leave me here, your *wife*, and go to Edinburgh for the day with *Susie*, you are telling me it's the end of our marriage. I will *divorce* you.' Panting, she fell back.

'Divorce me? Don't be ridiculous. It's just a meeting. Susie doesn't know how to do it. It's a kitchen refurbishment at stake.'

'If she doesn't know how to do it, then why did you give her a job? You are not everyone's friend or dad or honorary husband or whatever you think you are. You're *my* husband and you can't leave me like this. I gave up everything for you.'

It was this last statement that penetrated Kit's patient demeanour. The threat of divorce could be written off as mad. But this was an accusation.

'Coming here was a joint decision,' he said, leaning close over her on the bed. 'Don't you put that on me. Remember? Our new start?'

'I haven't had a new start! I'm trapped in a horrible house with nasty people, and I'm all alone.'

'You wouldn't be alone if you made more effort,' he said. 'How are you going to make friends if you lie around all day being so negative?' Kit paced around the bedroom, red with anger. 'I won't be told I can't go to work as I see fit. I won't be.'

Dora said, 'You just don't understand, do you?' She put her head in her hands. 'You want your own way more than you want me. Have you any idea how frightening that is, now that we are married and I have no one else? Nowhere to go?'

Kit sat down heavily on the bed and sighed. 'Okay, okay! If our marriage is on the line, then obviously I can't go. I'll have to ring her up and tell her . . . God knows what I'll say. And she can't possibly go on her own. But, just so you know, darling – this is a *monumental* overreaction. I'm going along with it because I have to. But you're being completely unreasonable.'

They stared at each other, perhaps for the first time, as two individuals with no romantic illusions. Then Dora's husband unpeeled from the bed and looked back at her. Kit had an actor's face: beautiful, and always slightly reminding you of someone else.

He didn't say a word as he left. Dora knew he would be home late that evening and would not ring her all day. Sadness pressed her back against the pillow. The compromise they had reached, unspoken yet clear, was that Dora would be alone all day, but her husband would not be spending the time in a romantic city with another woman.

'Fine. See you later,' she mumbled as the front door slammed.

Exhaustion tugged at her, but it was time for Bea to wake. Dora got out of bed, shivering, and microwaved the bottle. She lit the hob and let the flames push a little warmth into the air. As she did so, the door upstairs opened and the familiar black shoes clopped down the staircase. Dora did not even flinch now. The flagstones ached through her slippers.

Kit worked five days a week, but it was a little architectural company, a start-up, and he often didn't take a full wage. And, of course, Dora had left all sources of income behind in her old life. They couldn't afford to have the heating blazing all day; the house seemed to drink fuel. Worse, the fireplace in the sitting room didn't draw, though Kit had persisted in trying to light it. After she'd collected Bea from her cot, Dora placed the electric fire on the hearth, switched on the lights of the little artificial Christmas tree they'd bought, and wrapped herself and her baby in blankets.

Beatrice wriggled in her fleecy jumpsuit and sucked the warm milk like a hungry calf. Her eyes were closed in bliss.

It was not even eight-thirty. Dora looked out over the front lawn, which was a tangle of mist, overgrown hedging and the sea beyond, all of it shades of the same grey. Her feelings were a similar fog. A little hand crept up to grab her nose.

The CD player started upstairs. The first inspirational tune of the day pounded through the ceiling.

Beatrice needed to be awake for another hour or so, so Dora got out the play mat, with its little meadows of felt, its bells, its rivers of Velcro and lakes of velvet. Bea ran her fingertips over it, gurgling with pleasure, pressing a yellow button that quacked and made her smile.

The simple truth was that Dora had given up one life and started another. The two were unrelated. She used to have an apple, and now she had an orange.

That fucking music! Dora scrambled to the CD player and the Mamas and the Papas rang out. Bea looked startled as Dora turned the music right up.

It was just that Kit had an apple *and* an orange. He had not given anything up. His life was about *more*. Why was hers about less?

Love. Marriage. The words turned over as mother and daughter played. Dora had thought she knew what they meant. Did she even love her husband anymore?

The floorboards creaked right over her head, and Mo's voice warbled like a bird trapped somewhere in the stonework.

'Don't they *ever* go out?' Dora asked her baby. Bea was engrossed in the seashore of sequins on the play mat, and pressed the quacking button time after time.

Dora's idea about the Auden biography . . . How could she have been so stupid? She sensed embarrassment from Kit, as if she were overstepping herself, somehow, in his eyes. Of course . . . she was a lonely, defeated mother, with delusions about her capabilities. He was trying to save her from herself. And yet . . . it would have been *fun*, wouldn't it? To write about a poet, live in his mind a little, even as she couldn't write poems herself?

She was tired. He was right about that.

Dora went to the window and looked out over the thorny tangle of the lawn. Something really needed to be done about it. In another season or two it would envelop the drive and completely enclose the house.

But then she saw it.

Simply because it was the only perfectly black thing in a world composed of grey.

Just outside the window was a small dog. It had enormous ears and an elegant way of sitting, like some kind of Egyptian talisman.

Dora blinked, but it remained. It was young. And thin.

'Bea, look at this!'

Dora ran to open the front door, and the little black dog trotted in, as if he had been living there all along.

SEVENTEEN

Wystan

T HE SUNLIGHT, WHEN IT comes, is horrible.

Wystan likes to remember his Icelandic heritage, but he will never feel comfortable in the northern sun, with its searchlight that asks of him, constantly, *And why are you not working? And why is your skin so useless, blistering?*

He will spend most of his late years in Italy, where the Mediterranean sun pours over the hills like honey. The southern light asks nothing of the man who finds himself in it. *Rest,* it says. *Let me warm you.* There, if he closes his eyes, he feels as if he is in a gentle embrace.

In Helensburgh, there has been so much rainy gloom that the sun is shocking. His room faces south and he cannot work with the sharp light cutting across his attention. He longs for the anonymity of winter, for the fug of darkness in which he can think and be who he really is.

The scareball, as he has privately named the sun, points as if trying to drive out a confession. That is nature, always prodding one, showing one up for what one is: pale, etiolated, inadequate.

Wystan places his small table to face the wall and closes the shutters tight. His room is plunged into a pungent gloom, with knives of light darting through the gaps. He tears some little strips of fabric from his sheet and these he stuffs into his ears; he would prefer to play a record on the gramophone, but he is aware that everyone can hear this, even if it is very quiet, and as what he needs to do is to play the same record over and over, it is impossible.

The only problem now with this strategy is that he can no longer see his own spidery writing. So he lights the candles bought from the twins in the hardware shop and now, in the middle of the day, he can almost persuade himself that it is night-time. Finally, he can concentrate. He will emerge, some hours later, with a headache, blinking like a mole. He coughs and splutters after inhaling his own smoke, several times over, in the tight little space.

In the artificial dark, his thoughts take on a slightly hysterical and hallucinatory quality. He tells Christopher in a letter that his long poem, *The Orators*, will likely destroy the Church.

In the dark cave he has created for himself, he is thinking explosively today. He is thinking of freedom.

He rocks himself, mumbles. His mouth feels full of earth.

A tiny thread of light works its way through the shutters, splits and waves a dim rainbow across the wall. The candle waves back, like someone earthbound to a celestial relation.

He wants to tell the truth about himself.

But the truth is that he is immature and loathsome and will never be loved. How can he set that truth down?

He rubs his eyes. The boy at the station drifts into his mind. The thought of him is a thrill, which, in a second, becomes pain.

No one must ever see this, the hunched young man, making blots on the page about his pathetic secret life. For is his love not pathetic, conducted as it must be either in the dark or in his imagination?

Wystan thinks back to the lovely Erich, his nonchalance and bleeding feet.

How was it that he could seem free?

At this very moment, Erich will probably be out performing some kind of heroic act of survival. He will be out on the farm back in his village, or gambling the money Wystan gave him on some race or other. He'll be dreaming of better days.

How Wystan wishes he could be like Erich, *be* him, instead of the thing that he is.

He can write about a hero, but he cannot be one.

The hero is free of shame, and shame is what cripples Wystan as he bends his white frame over the too-small desk.

Why does God despise him so? Of course, he knows why. He was the brilliant, delightful son of a good mother, who got stuck somehow and became an abomination.

Christopher manages not to feel this cancerous shame. Christopher coexists with his nature – embraces it, even. But then, he does live in Berlin.

There is a price to pay for hiding from the truth.

One can love, but never be loved.

One can describe freedom, but never be free.

It's too much. Wystan throws open the shutters and the light bursts in, as if the glass itself had broken. It is dazzling and awful. He wipes his eyes, lays down his pen and strides out of the room and out of Larchfield, going he is not sure where.

A little after he has gone, Olive knocks and comes into the room to clear up. It reeks of old smoke and sweat. Dirty plates and cups are piled on the floor. A candle is burning dangerously close to a chaotic pile of paper. She blows out the flame and begins to gather up the plates. The room is in semi-darkness; she opens the shutters fully and heaves open the window, letting in a gust of fresh air. Outside, the trees stand newly green, and, beyond them, the sea shimmers. It's going to be a hot one today. Mr Auden must have gone down to the lido. He's a strange one, that's for sure. So alone, and so polite. Her eyes fall on a heap of clothes in the corner.

And going out in his slippers. Really, it's not very Helensburgh. It won't work out well.

She sighs and surveys the room. The filth in there haunts her. Not sure where to start, she straightens his bed, sending a haze of ash into the air. Books slide out of the folds of the blanket; she stacks them neatly by the bed. These sheets have not been washed for weeks; Mr Auden is paying for his keep, is he not?

She pulls the sheets off, used to little boys and their fetid ways, wrinkling her freckled nose. The stained pillowcase is next; when she lifts the pillow, she finds yet more papers. She holds them uncertainly in her hands and her eyes fall on the first line: *Daylight, striking at the eye from far-off roofs, why did you blind us: we who on the snow-line were in love with death . . .*

What does that even mean, anyway?

Is Mr Auden afraid of daylight?

Is he a vampire? Olive has seen *Nosferatu* and did not sleep for days afterwards.

He is awfully pale and funny-looking.

Olive lays the papers with the others on the desk without looking again and runs out of the room with the dirty sheets.

Wystan strides quickly away from the school, down the hill. Immediately, he feels calmer. He shields his eyes, annoyed that he forgot his hat, and almost bangs into a street lamp. Recovering himself, he sees, pasted on to the lamp, a poster: *SIR ALAN COBHAM'S FLYING CIRCUS COMES TO HELENSBURGH* and an illustration of planes wheeling in a blue sky.

His slippered feet seem to be taking him of their own accord towards the kirk on the corner.

The door is closed, but he can hear church organ music from inside. Cool air brushes his lips as he pushes it open. Flagstones chill the soles of his feet.

The congregation is standing, singing a hymn he's not familiar with. It's too late to back out now, so he slips in beside a tall lady in furs, who looks him up and down before giving a thin smile in the direction of her hymnal.

The church is spartan and cold but slightly less so than the kirk further along the road. This is the Scottish Episcopalian church, the Piscy as he heard others call it. At the kirk, there are no kneeling pads; the Scots do not kneel. There are no cushions on the hard benches. The Piscy reminds him a little of the church in Birmingham where the Auden family have marked all their important events. Light, through the massive stained-glass window, illuminates the dust motes.

The last chords of the hymn die away and everyone sits down. A man in plain ecclesiastical dress ascends the pulpit. He has a most fantastic head of auburn hair, out of all proportion to both his physique and his age. Wystan is quite transfixed as it bobs and slides over his forehead. It distracts him from the matter in hand, which is that he has come to church, where he most certainly does not want to be, in his slippers and with nothing of use in his heart or his soul.

But then he remembers. He is here for a reason. His very unconscious has brought him to where he needs to be. For it is the anniversary of Uncle Henry's death.

Every year, on this anniversary, Wystan finds a church and lights a candle. There is never a mention of the date from his parents; Wystan knows his mother loathed Uncle Henry and blames him for the unmentionable way her youngest son has turned out. She fears his attachment to Uncle Henry, dead or no.

Mostly, we are absolutely unknown to our parents. They hover at the edge of our adult consciousness; we are as impenetrable to them as the sea. Wystan does not feel even related to his mother. Whilst he finds himself longing for some kind of tenderness from her, he avoids her as far as he can. Our real ancestors are often someone else entirely; certain characteristics are planted, discovered, created by those other than our parents. Uncle Henry is Wystan's true ancestor, and now, while he waits for the sermon to finish, he bows his head and worships.

Uncle Henry was a chemist; he was *clever*. Even Wystan's mother grudgingly conceded this when trying to come to terms with Henry's interest in her son. Wystan's first memories of his uncle were confused; his appearance made him uneasy. He had protruding eyes which seemed to change colour. On visits to the Auden home in Birmingham, Henry radiated disapproval, which made Wystan feel ashamed. But Wystan liked to run little errands for him, and, when he won a kind word or a sweet as a result, he was delighted for the whole day. Uncle Henry began to write letters to Wystan when he was about thirteen, to send him money and tell him little facts that Wystan hoarded. His mother would hand the letters over with a sniff.

But it was not until Wystan was sixteen that he actually visited Uncle Henry alone. At sixteen, Wystan was a clever blank, full of facts and opinions, but a sea of ignorance to himself. His fumblings with Christopher and other boys were, to his mind, corrosive immaturity, part of the poison that the public school system produced. And yet he had grown to feel comfortable with Uncle Henry, enjoying his snobbery, lascivious smile and extremely funny impressions of the female members of the family. When the invitation to visit came for Wystan, his mother sulked, but how could she articulate the unsayable? That would make it true and in the world.

That was the evening Wystan suddenly had a vision of himself in the future. Uncle Henry was *him*; *he* was Uncle Henry, just thirty years behind: a cigarette in hand with a huge droop of ash; solitary but gregarious; apart from the world.

He would have liked to see himself in his father, but he did not. His mother needed a quite different sort of partner, a Latin Lothario who would have dominated her and treated her badly but ravishingly; his father needed someone simple and happy, who could be *satisfied*. He was gentle and weak, and though Wystan loves his father, he feels forever distant from him.

As he and his uncle sat down to dinner and drank champagne, Wystan knew this was a turning-point. Afterwards, Henry casually showed him his collection of photos of naked choirboys and asked him, did he like them? When Wystan said yes, and embarked on a new glass of champagne, Henry stroked his hair, pulled him on to his lap and asked if he liked that. Wystan's champagne spilt a little, but he gulped and assented. They had remained in this awkward position for a little while. His uncle's breath warmed his cheek, and it was the first time he had felt this, the breath of a grown man upon his face. Henry slid his large hand into Wystan's trousers, and Wystan waited for the question: did he like it? But it didn't come. Anyway, what he felt was not possible to express in a yes or a no.

When he left Uncle Henry's flat, some hours later, he knew that Uncle Henry was his true ancestor. And this was why he remembered him with a candle, for he was grateful to his uncle, who had shown him what he was, and what his life would be.

Now the congregation is filing out, with great rustlings of furs and clacks of heels and wafts of scent and hair cream.

At the back of the church is a small rack of candles and, when everyone is gone, Wystan drops a shilling in the box and takes one, lighting it from one of the others. He plants it carefully in the top row and he bows his head again.

The ancestor must be worshipped for showing him the truth. That he in no way prepared him for love is beside the point. How to face the loneliness, the longing, the sheer overwhelming pain of desire that cannot be fulfilled . . . these are his burdens, as all people who face the truth must carry burdens.

EIGHTEEN

Dora

'HE'S A VIRGIL, DON'T you think?' pronounced Dora of the dog, who was sitting in a shaft of weak sunlight, immaculately positioned and wise-looking. They had expected someone to come and claim him, but no one had, and they had gone on with no name for too long. 'He lives with us in Paradise . . . and I think he knows something.' The dog was slender and agitated, unfamiliar with open spaces, frightened also of the shadows in the large rooms.

Kit nodded thoughtfully. His suggestion had been Ben, for no reason other than his father had had a black dog called Ben, but Virgil was better. And so the dog got his name. Virgil appended himself quickly to Kit, following him everywhere, and this was an excellent survival tactic, for Kit adored him. When the dog revealed his tendency towards hysterical barking at the postman, his unstoppable jumping up at anyone who visited and his foaming terror of any other dog, Kit was already attached to his new companion and forgave him.

Dora was less sure. The dog was not very friendly, and he could, should he turn, devour Beatrice in two gulps. But there was something about him that she recognised, that prevented her from insisting he go. He too was sensitive to what could not be seen, things just on the edge of hearing. He froze when the music upstairs came on, and the banging of feet on the ceiling made him trot up and down the sitting room, nose in the air like a dressage horse, whining, trying to taste or see or smell whatever the invisible disturbance was.

That January day was the inauguration of Barak Obama. Dora had looked forward all day to watching it on the television. Towards evening, she settled herself into her usual place on the sofa, with the baby in her arms, and Beatrice slurped lazily on her bottle while they listened to Obama's speech. Outside, it was glittering dark and cold, but inside it was bright and excited, as if this small family on the Scottish west coast were part of the global audience. Obama's breath crystallised as he spoke.

'Do you think anyone else in Helensburgh is watching this?' Dora asked her husband. Kit was trying again to light a fire in the vast fireplace, unable to accept that it would not draw. He opened the windows to increase the airflow and held some newspaper over the space. He sighed as smoke wafted into the room and the flames refused to grow.

'I know, I know!' he said irritably as Dora glared at him. He retrieved the electric fire and placed it on the hearth, and closed the windows. The dog, who had been shivering by the door, immediately came and slumped in front of the two bars, and Dora's shoulders visibly relaxed.

'Come and sit down,' she said. 'Please.'

Her husband passed her a glass of wine and rested a hand on her shoulder, and her fingers crept up to link with his. At last, she and Kit were part of a wider world where events of significance happened. Neither the footsteps above, nor the cold at the edge of everything could detract from the sense that they were connected, however briefly, to a hopeful, exciting reality that wanted to include them.

Dora sipped her wine and closed her eyes to the lines of Elizabeth Alexander's poem, read into the frosted air:

> . . . Some live by *love thy neighbour as thyself,*
> others by *first do no harm* or *take no more*
> *than you need*. What if the mightiest word is love?

> . . . In today's sharp sparkle, this winter air,
> any thing can be made, any sentence begun.
> On the brink, on the brim, on the cusp,

> praise song for walking forward in that light.

Her fingers crept around the baby's pudgy hand, as if never to let go, and Dora gazed into her eyes. Their lash-framed blue depths seemed full of contentment. How could Bea trust so, when there was so much danger in the world? Especially their tiny corner of it?

A voice spoke clearly in Dora's head as she stroked her baby's cheek. It was her own voice – or was it? It said, *I can win this.*

Dora shook her head, but it came again.

I can win this.

The clarity of the words was confusing, as if they were from outside herself. Dora glanced round, in case Kit had said something.

Again the words came – clear, unmistakeable – confirming, if confirmation were needed, that Dora was strange and possessed by wrong feelings. What kind of mother has voices outside her control in her head?

'Win what?' Dora whispered to herself. She pressed the side of her head, as if to knock the words out of it. She didn't want a voice in her head, certainly not one that spoke like this.

'What did you say, love?' Kit asked. On the television, the crowd was singing the US anthem, the words fogging the air.

To hear voices was crazy.

She knew she wasn't crazy.

The baby was happy and safe.

Nevertheless, Dora passed Beatrice to Kit, who planted a huge kiss on the baby's cheek and held her up above his head; she mouthed and murmured in response. He smiled over at Dora. 'What?' he asked.

'Nothing . . . It just makes me happy to see you like that.'

'I am happy,' said Kit. 'This is all I've ever wanted.'

Perhaps that was her moment to speak, to connect with her husband and bring him back from being a stranger. Joy from the outside world was brimming in their draughty room. The three of them were a cosy, close unit. Perhaps, indeed, this is what the voice meant? Could she win out over the forces against her?

She need only forgive her husband. She need only make a kindly enquiry, as a good friend might, something to open up a dialogue. *Your first wife*, she might say, *your dead wife . . . I know you miss her. It's okay. I understand. I'm lonely too.*

But she could no more do this than she could banish the voice that rose again in her head.

It's over.

'No!' Dora clapped a hand over her mouth.

'What's the matter?' Kit asked.

Shaking her head, Dora got up. 'It's time for her bath now.' She held out her arms and Kit handed the baby over, puzzled. Saying nothing more, Dora carried Beatrice into the Baltic freeze of the hall and through to the huge Victorian bath, big as a swimming pool for the little girl. Soon the room was full of steam. Dora pulled off her own clothes and she and Bea slipped into the gorgeously warm water together. Now, the only voices were Dora's and her baby's. Bea sneezed and gurgled and slapped her tiny hands against the surface, and Dora murmured the lines that came into her head, some lines from Lawrence that she had been reading lately:

> And truly I was afraid, I was most afraid,
> But even so, honoured still more,
> That he should seek my hospitality
> From out the dark door of the secret earth . . .

The words took on the rhythm of a prayer.

Even if Dora feared that something had changed, that she had missed some crucial opportunity to speak, it didn't matter now. Mother and baby were together as they should be, inseparable in the warm amnion of the bath.

Kit left for work the next morning, as briskly and routinely as ever. He and Dora were two arms of a machine that whirred on and on. Dora prepared to take Beatrice to the baby group in the church hall. No one talked to her at the group, but nevertheless she plodded along every week because going to baby group is what you do when you're new to a place and you have a baby.

Dora gently brushed Bea's hair, now a downy auburn, and dressed her in her warmest clothes. She slotted her into the pram and they careened and jolted down the drive towards the narrow pavement. Deep in the house, Virgil yapped his despair at being left.

As she passed along the front of the house, Dora felt the familiar prickling at her neck that denoted Mo's staring presence at the upper window.

Every instinct told her to press on, not to look. No good would come of it. But Dora, that day, could not resist. She wanted to break the deadlock somehow . . . prove its non-existence, even . . . for little Bea. And so, she stopped the pram and looked up.

Dora was stuck to the spot with awe; she had never before looked upon a face so . . . naked in its hate. There was no softening of Mo's expression as her gaze drifted to Beatrice wriggling beneath the straps. The child fell outside Mo's sentimental grouping of 'God's children'. She began to mouth something at Dora, but then Terrence appeared beside her and gently turned her away.

Dora pushed on, her hands and legs shaking. How could she ever explain this to Kit? It made no sense.

At the church hall, the smell of sweaty toys, dust and yoga mats gushed over her. Children's voices combined to create the sense of stepping into a brightly coloured circle of hell. Flabby, exhausted mothers lined the walls, as if at a superannuated school dance. Towering in the middle of a clump of baby-group organisers by the subs table was an unexpected sight: a man. He had highlighted hair, stylish glasses and a small baby strapped to his chest. All the women had their faces turned up to him, listening to an anecdote he was telling in a low voice, then the group broke into laughter. Dora knew who he was immediately. The unexpected handsomeness, the popularity: it could only be Theodore, with the fabled grandchild. He caught her eye and did not smile.

Dora wrestled the pushchair through the door, then stood help-lessly for a moment. She propelled herself to the table, dropped her subs into the jar. 'Morning!' she said brightly, expecting and receiving no reply, then she lifted Beatrice out of the pram and carried her off to find something for them to play with.

She knew that coming to the group did no good at all, but its unpleasantness that day felt right, like a penance for the voice that had spoken yesterday.

I can win this, indeed.

Dora settled on a mat with her baby. She wished only to be invisible and simply rest amongst the muffled echoes of the children's voices, much as she used to enjoy writing in a café, amongst life but not part of it. But she wasn't the lucky sort, the sort who gets to be invisible when she wants to be. In due course, a pair of immense trainers appeared beside her and she looked up into the hard and disconcertingly lovely face of Theodore.

'You upset my mother this morning,' growled the man. He had clearly rehearsed this intervention, and was convinced of its rightness.

'I'm sorry?'

'She's rung me up crying. What did you do to her?'

'I don't know what you're talking about.'

'My mother's a *good person*. You should remember that.'

'Your mother,' said Dora, struggling to her feet, 'is a nasty bitch.'

Theodore's eyes widened behind the expensive frames. He took a step closer.

Shit! The words had come out. Dora had meant only to *think* them, and there they were, out in the world. She put her hand over her mouth again. What was happening? Words were flying unbidden into her head, and flying out of her mouth.

Women now surrounded them, arms folded, eyes gleaming. Dora pressed her lips together to prevent her pronouncing them all a coven of stupid evil witches.

'This one just called my mother a bitch!' said Theodore. He leant over so close that his baby's woolly hat almost brushed Dora's lips.

'I did not!' said Dora. She scooped Beatrice up and held her to her breast. 'My baby isn't safe here. We're leaving.'

The mothers lining the walls raised their drooping heads like desiccated flowers suddenly given a drink. Dora hauled herself across the room, just a step ahead of the silence cresting behind her. She strapped Beatrice back in and headed out. The baby writhed and mewed.

What the hell just happened? Dora bumped roughly along the pavement, going – where? She could not face the long walk up the drive, with Mo glaring at her all the way. Every window she passed seemed to stare out at her now. Should she ring Kit? And say what? That she had inadvertently called Mo a bitch to her son? Kit's patience was wearing thin. And now came the voice that had spoken last night.

It's over.

There was no one to ring and no escape.

And truly I was afraid, I was most afraid . . .

162

Down to the shore. Where else? The sea sparkled in the stark cold.

Bea protested gently at being hauled out of the pram again, then she snuggled in Dora's arms. Dora paused at the top of the bank that led to the little cove near Paradise, dumbstruck at the sight of the ocean and the islands beyond, picked out today in purple and gold. She had found, since arriving in Helensburgh, that she had an eye for sea glass, would see it glinting from far away. She clambered down the bank and scanned the jumble of the shingle.

They were alone on the beach, and, being some way below the road, almost invisible. When Dora found a piece of glass, she showed it to Beatrice, touching its smooth shine against her cheek. She wished she could get the pram down as well, so that no one would know she was here at all. Invisibility was what she craved, or just to be somewhere else, viewed with different eyes.

Then she saw, a little way ahead, a flicker of light. A big piece of sea glass? This was always the quest, to find a large smooth piece of the rarest kind: blue. Dora cooed to her daughter and hurried across the stones to see what it was.

It was a bottle, glinting through its grime. It was still wet, seemingly just deposited carefully by the fingers of the sea. Disappointed, Dora began to turn away, but something made her pause and look at it again.

She pulled away a strand of obscuring seaweed. Inside the bottle was a twisted piece of paper.

'Beatrice! It's a message in a bottle!'

The cork was stuck fast; easing it out was impossible.

Shielding Bea's face against her chest, Dora smacked the top of the bottle on the nearest boulder. It broke immediately, leaving a raw, jagged neck. At her feet was a twig, and she dipped it into the bottle neck, pulling out the neat scroll of paper.

It was unbearably exciting. Dora remembered, as a child, setting free a helium balloon with a card wrapped in plastic on the end of the string, on which was carefully written her name and address. A girl wrote back, some time later, from Yorkshire. She had been riding by a hedge on her pony when she saw the balloon, and she was keen on a correspondence. The two wrote for a while, but the girl in Yorkshire lived a life very different from Dora's, and they received no encouragement from either family to move the friendship from the page to anything more. After an exchange or two, it fizzled out. But it left Dora always with a hunger for pen pals, for the sheer adventure of communication in unexpected places.

The coil was very neat and tied with string. By now, Dora's fingers were freezing and it was impossible to undo the knot. She eased the twine along the scroll with her teeth, gagging slightly as the paper touched the inside of her mouth. A fingernail, at the end, lifted it off.

Dora pressed the soft, yellow paper flat on her jeans. The writing was very spidery, but as black as if it had been newly written:

I am a young man, with light brown hair and a book of poems. Telephone Helensburgh 120 and ask for Wystan.

Wystan? Dora turned the paper over in case there was an address. There was nothing.

There was only one Wystan in the whole of recent history, as far as Dora knew.

Of course, it might be another person with the incredibly rare name of Wystan.

But Helensburgh 120? That was a very old number indeed.

Dora took out her phone and dialled the code for Helensburgh, followed by the number 120. While the line hissed and snored, she squeezed Bea excitedly.

It was miraculous to be holding a note from the great poet!

As she shivered with the phone against her cheek – not expecting anything to happen, but thrilled to be ringing someone, anyway – she thought of how much money the note might be worth. Perhaps it would be enough to escape?

But then, of course, it was just a scruffy piece of paper. It could be all made up.

'Ow!' There was a searing whistle down the line. Dora jumped back from the phone.

'This is Helensburgh 120. Mrs Clyde speaking. Who is calling, please?'

'I'm . . .' Dora dragged her exploded thoughts back into words. 'Pardon? Have I connected? I'm . . . Mrs Fielding. I'd like to speak to . . . Wystan?'

'Mr Auden is teaching at present. Is he expecting you?'

Mr Auden! 'He . . . left a message asking me to call.'

Surely, at any moment, the sounds in her ear would return to the sounds of the sea, as if, instead of a telephone, she was holding a conch shell. She strained to hear every detail, desperate that it should not end.

An irritable sigh. 'In that case, please come to the school and you can wait for him to finish his class. Thank you!' The voice faded sharply as the woman made to hang up.

'Wait!' Dora's voice echoed round the little bay.

'Pardon?'

'Just . . . Can you tell me what school? I mean, your address?'

'Larchfield School. Colquhoun Street. Helensburgh. Goodbye!'

And the voice was gone.

The phone slipped out of Dora's fingers and clinked on to the glossy pebbles. Bea's head wobbled on her neck as she pushed against her mother, trying to get free.

Dora had always believed in miracles. They were an essential of existence; sometimes only a miracle made sense. They happened all the time to lucky people. But now . . . the weight of sadness lifted and she spun round and round with Bea. 'It's going to be all right!' she cried to the sea, to her daughter. Magic was just *right there*, waiting for you to believe in it.

She slid the note into her pocket and clambered back up the bank, one hand still cradling Bea's woolly-capped head. Bea wriggled and her pie-round face broke into a grin. She sensed something exciting had happened, and was *happy*. Dora made a smile back and kissed her cheek.

As they approached the front door, Kit emerged, home unexpectedly for lunch. Dora was dizzy with what had just happened. She composed her face back to its normal impassivity.

She said, 'I need to go and do a bit of shopping. Can you take Bea for an hour or two?' She pushed the pram towards her husband.

'Now? Don't you want some lunch?' Kit looked at his wife peculiarly, as he often did.

'Not hungry, thanks! Do you want anything?' Dora was already walking past him to the road; already her mind was on the school.

Kit hugged Bea, frowning as he followed his wife down the drive. 'Just an hour? I need to get back to work.'

She turned, smiled at her daughter and received a kiss on her lips from her husband.

'No more than two,' she said, normality personified.

Kit was the sort of person to talk her out of a miracle, and that was not going to happen. It was better to smile and not explain.

Dora's little family shrank behind her. Her eyes itched. *It's over.*

What lay ahead was unknown, icy, full of shadows.

There was still time to forget about magic, to turn back up the drive, have some lunch and try to make the best of things.

I can win this.

But, of course, she went.

She'd be mad not to.

NINETEEN

Wystan

TRANSITUS TWO: PERFECT BOYS at the perfect age. Wystan is helpless before them, these beautiful twelve- and thirteen-year-olds, full of arrogance and insecurity in equal measure. Their voices are not yet broken, but now is when they begin to have the first sense of themselves as men; they glimpse the oncoming possibility of power, like a horse cresting a distant hill.

The boys of this age are products of the euphoria after the war, the darling children of reunions after the armistice. They both delight and frighten him, such hope is invested in them. They do not know they embody the attempt to lay unspeakable horror to rest, to send the past away. They crow and strut, sensing their importance, which has nothing to do with who they are. They seem to shine with the future, and yet the future is as uncertain as ever it was.

They pay absolutely no attention and he can hardly blame them. The stuff Perkins told him to teach is as dry as a bone. But still he has to get through at least some of it. After this, some of the boys are going on to the big Scottish schools; others will be packed off to England. There are examinations for them to pass, and, the way things are going, they're not going to pass them.

Larchfield, as he writes to his friends, is a marvellously awful school. Apart from the ragbag of teachers – of whom he counts himself firmly as the worst – it is truly crumbling round their ears. Hamish, the gardener and handyman, seems to spend most of his time on the roof with nails in his mouth, hammering pieces of tarpaper over the gaps in the slate. Woodworm seems to have invaded every beam that is not damp. Tiny piles of wood-dust line the corridors. Wystan writes to Christopher that he spends most of his own time adjusting the water pressure in the boys' urinal with a brass turn-key.

The bell goes and footsteps rattle down the hall. The door flings open and the boys come tumbling in, lethargic and hysterical after a lunch of grey stovies doled out by Mrs Clyde. Wystan says nothing, leaning back with a wry smile on his face. A couple of boys glance up as they shift in their seats, opening and closing the desks, arranging books and hiding contraband of different sorts. On the blackboard behind him is written, *D. H. Lawrence: the hero and the snake.*

'So,' says Wystan, getting to his feet and hovering at the front of the class.

McLeod looks up briefly and his expression freezes. He nudges his companion who also stares, the giggle dying in his throat. The class falls silent as Wystan parades slowly up and down. He has a pained, weary expression on his face and is limping slightly. Eventually, McLeod's hand goes up.

'Sir?'

'Yes, McLeod.'

'Sir, did you do it?'

'Do what, Mcleod?'

The boy's hand moves through the air to point reluctantly at Wystan's crotch. Blood is seeping round his fly.

'Oh, that. No, not quite.' Wystan lifts a knife from the table, opens his fly and partially pulls out a rolled piece of flesh, which he severs with a cry and holds up.

One of the boys gives a strangled scream.

'See, boys!' Wystan gasps. 'See what you've driven me to? I told you I would do it, if you didn't pay attention!' Then he falls to the floor, clutching his crotch, the meat dangling feebly in his fingers.

There is a horrified silence. Then McLeod says, 'He's pretending.'

Wystan pleads into his trousers, 'What shall I do? No children! No wife!'

'Sir, you're fibbing, aren't you?' McLeod comes from behind his desk and stands over his teacher, examining the severed member held aloft.

Whereupon Wystan leaps to his feet, zips his fly and stands in a triumphant pose, like a ballet dancer. 'Now, let us commence today's lesson, attested to, here, on the board behind me. Theakston, can you read it?'

Their teacher is clearly quite mad. Theakston reluctantly drags his eyes to the board and reads the line on it. When he's done, he gazes upon the crumpled piece of flesh on the desk.

'What *is* that, sir?'

'That? That, Theakston, is a prime steak. I shall be eating it tonight. Now. I've decided it is time for Lawrence. Some heroes are needed in this sorry country of ours, and it is, I'm afraid, down to you lot to step up.'

'Sir, if there's another war, you'd be called up.'

'That, Frazer, is true. But I am not made of the stuff of heroes. I'm the kind of man who'd cut his own prick off for attention, and that's really not the calibre of officer our great country is seeking.

'In my view, the stuff I am supposed to teach you will equip you only for another futile war, and for emasculation on a par with my wee joke there.

'What you need to know is how to integrate the body and the mind. You need to know how to be a man – a real man. You need to understand heroism, to think from your . . . *loins*. And we are therefore going to study, for the next few lessons, the pinnacle of the male: D. H. Lawrence.'

He has their attention. It is a giddy feeling.

'McLeod, please read us "Snake".' He hands the book to the boy, his eyes fixed on the class as he does so. He is afraid that, if he breaks eye contact, the spell will be broken and they will all start giggling again.

McLeod takes the book and, in his lovely voice, brimming with childishness and yet cracking a little at that very edge of adulthood, reads:

'The voice of my education said to me
    He must be killed,
    For in Sicily the black, black snakes are innocent, the gold
are venomous.

And voices in me said, If you were a man
    You would take a stick and break him now, and finish him
off . . .

A hush descends on the class, for the boys are listening. What is more, McLeod is listening to his own words, unconscious of reading them aloud.

'Was it cowardice, that I dared not kill him?
Was it perversity, that I longed to talk to him?
Was it humility, to feel so honoured?
I felt so honoured.

And yet those voices:
If you were not afraid, you would kill him!'

This is the moment Wystan will remember; at this moment, he becomes, for however long the magic lasts, a teacher. Even if what he is teaching them is not on the curriculum and he is further jeopardising their chances of passing the examinations, he is teaching them something important. Or letting them learn it themselves.

'And I wished he would come back, my snake.

For he seemed to me again like a king,
Like a king in exile, uncrowned in the underworld,
Now due to be crowned again.

And so, I missed my chance with one of the lords
Of life.
And I have something to expiate:
A pettiness.'

Wystan is so moved by the boy's solemn speaking of the lines, his innocence reverberating through a story of the loss of innocence, that he cannot, at first, speak. Even though some of the words are beyond the boys' vocabulary, they have understood the poem, and they have felt its sadness. McLeod closes the book uncertainly and they all look to Wystan for guidance. He may be a young man only just out of childhood himself, with bloodstained trousers and the curling remains of his practical joke on the desk in front of them, but, in this moment, he has earned their respect, and poetry has touched their undeveloped little hearts.

'Now, isn't that wonderful, boys?' Wystan says quietly. 'And do you see? Do you see how hard it is? To resist the pettiness of the world?'

He will, in later lessons, return to the curriculum; they will trudge through the set texts; he will do his best to liven them up and the boys will pay attention. Wystan has crossed some kind of line drawn in their budding souls. He has reached them, and something has changed.

Despite his misgivings about the school system, he does want them to leave this sorry place equipped, in even a small way, for the rigours of public school. The forward momentum of British education cannot be resisted: a relentless fascist machine that will spit them out the other side as soldiers or sexless governors-general and the like. All he can do is plant some small seeds of independent thought into their minds. He is sorry for them, and what is coming: every rottenness and corruption.

But they will remember this Lawrence lesson, and the ones he slips in after: the Wilfred Owen lesson, and the one on Edward Thomas. Somewhere in their hearts they will carry what he has shown them: that there are many ways to be a man, and many ways to be brave.

TWENTY

Wystan and Dora

H OW COULD IT BE that, when she had been *summoned* (for was that not what the message in the bottle was, a summons?), her destination should vanish?

Sleet howled in her face. The Helensburgh she knew was gone. The cherry trees lining the streets were a forest of twisted branches writhing overhead. Dora focused on the pavement, and the sodden toes of her boots trudging past La Scala. The art deco frontage was swallowed by leaves and creepers and the wind was so fierce that her eyes blurred. She knew she was heading in the right direction only because the road was sloping upwards.

What if Larchfield itself was gone?

It *couldn't* be. She had been *summoned*.

Her ears stung beneath her thin hood. The wind echoed with distorted voices. If she called out herself, the sound would be stretched like that. 'Wystan!' she found herself crying, and no sooner had her mouth opened than the freezing air snatched the name out with a balled icy fist and hurled it away, sending it back to her in the sound of a child's cry.

Should she turn back?

Behind her, the trees closed in further. Only if she looked straight ahead, up the hill, could she see a break in the iron sky. Could she duck into a shopfront to shelter, catch her breath? But everything was sucked away into the shadows.

When she got there, it would be all right. Larchfield would make sense of everything. *Nothing worth having is easy*. Her grandmother, Bea, had said that, long ago.

The last part of Colquhoun Street was very steep. The wind heaved against her and she had to turn her back to it to catch her breath. She moaned in panic as she saw that Helensburgh, the sea, everything, was swallowed in a blizzard of leaves.

Dora shoved one foot in front of the other. It was all a terrible mistake. A mirage. Her sodden clothes chafed against her, as if to remind her of her egotism and stupidity.

She paused to cross an empty Montrose Street near the top of Colquhoun Street. Twigs and old cans sped down it instead of the usual mash of cars. Judging that she would probably collide with all these things no matter what she did, she pressed on. The moment both her feet were on the opposite kerb, something changed. The screech of the wind abated. The sky opened, extending a shaft of light, and she saw that she was standing in front of the gate at Larchfield, her numb fingers once again on the gold lettering.

Larchfield's garden was a twisted mass of rhododendrons laced with frost. The sun bathed the building, making it look both magical and crumbling. The gables were peeling and a blackened chimney at the top pumped smoke out into the crisp air.

There was silence, broken only by sounds from the school: scraping chairs and adult admonishments, a piano, some uncertain singing.

So. She had made it. And what now?

Sodden and shivering, she took a deep breath, as if about to dive underwater, and ran through the gate. Up the front steps . . . Was he here? The hall was empty, so she turned into a little snug off it, with an unlit fire and a bench on which had been placed some lumpy hessian cushions. The room was freezing. A faded watercolour of the *Waverley* hung over the mantelpiece. Lines whirled into her head, those same lines from Lawrence. Why? . . . *That he should seek my hospitality / From out the dark door of the secret earth* . . .

There was a cough. She turned around, and there he stood.

Of course she recognised him. It's a famous face – mostly the older version, with its deep map of folds and lines. The young face was striking in that it held something of the older one, and, at the same time, nothing at all.

'Hello,' said Wystan, standing decorously just out of reach. 'This door! Always drifting open . . .' He disappeared from view for a moment and the front door slammed. 'Are you being . . . attended to?'

Dora said, 'I got your message. In a bottle. Here –' She thrust the note out to him, which he took with his long fingers, glancing briefly, then sliding it into his pocket. Dora continued, 'I'm so very, very glad to meet you. It is you, isn't it? Mr Auden? Wystan?'

Wystan Auden said nothing.

Dora pressed on. 'I mean . . . I am an admirer, a real admirer. I've been reading you, and all about you . . . We studied you at school! And I'm meant to . . . I'm meant to . . .'

Dora's mind's eye was released from its mooring, dismaying her with its revelation. Here was a woman in the middle of her life, lost and clearly desperate. It was perhaps the worst outcome of all for Wystan: hoping for a keen young man, he had simply attracted someone's eccentric mother.

She said, 'I've just realised you were hoping for someone else. I'm sorry.'

'Not at all,' he said. His voice was quite high, but warm. 'I had quite forgotten about it, that's all. How do you do?' And out came the long arm with its big hand, into which Dora's blue-tinged one briefly slid. 'You're very cold,' he said.

Wystan rested an elbow against the doorframe and studied her. 'We should go to my room. Olive will bring us some tea there. The fire is lit, and I'm above the boys' dormitory, so I get some rising heat.'

A bell outside the door exploded into life and Wystan jumped, hands over his ears. 'I will never get used to that din! But it signals my freedom – for fifty minutes, anyway.'

Dora followed him up a multitude of stairways and twisted half landings. His tall frame, ahead of her, loped awkwardly, but there was something solid and certain about him.

The bedroom was a spectacular mess, the bed unmade and the air grizzled with cigarette smoke. Nicotine stained the walls and the fire glowed feebly in the grate. Papers and books were piled on every surface, but there was a reverence to the mess, as if it arose because every single scrap mattered and simply could not be thrown away.

Forgetting herself, Dora went immediately to the swamp of coffee-ringed papers that lay all over the unmade sheets. Some were typed and therefore legible; some were carbon copies and the ink came off on her fingers. Dora laid her hands flat on the pages to feel the gentle warmth that paper always seems to have.

Wystan fished in his jacket pocket for his cigarettes. He held out the box.

'No, thank you.' She sat carefully on the edge of the bed. He nodded and lit up, and then studied her closely.

'What's your name?' he asked.

Dora gave it, and waited.

'And where did my bottle wash up?'

'Down the bottom, there . . . Lower Hel.' Dora waved her arm vaguely down the hill.

'It went a long way in one way . . . and nowhere in another, then.' His eyes travelled over Dora, causing her to glance down at herself. She was wearing a long tweed coat that went almost to the ground, and neat lace-up boots. Her soaked anorak and leaking walking boots were gone. 'How did you come by it?'

'I went down to the beach . . .' Dora began and then stopped. She began again, but her memory had folded in on itself, like a dream on waking, and the words stuttered to a stop.

'I know that I . . .' she began again. 'I . . . have broken some kind of rule . . .' She took a disbelieving breath. 'Hurt someone, maybe . . . ? Oh, God, did I hurt someone?' She stared as if he might have the answer, but he simply nodded inscrutably. She said, hesitantly, at last, 'I'm lost. That is why I am here. I am completely lost.'

Wystan leant in a little and said, 'I can see that. I can see that you are lost. But don't worry. You've come to the right place. I'm sure of it.'

Dora began to cry. 'I'm so tired . . .' she said. 'I took a wrong turning somehow.'

Wystan coughed a ghost of smoke into the air. He said, 'Or a right turning? When you were not guarding against such a thing?' He handed Dora a grubby handkerchief from his pocket. She blew her nose and nodded.

'I've wanted to be here so much. With you. More than anything in the world.'

'And now you are.'

Into the resulting silence he said, 'There's a boy I saw, some time back, and I keep looking for him. I have only seen him once, for two minutes. Daft, don't you think? But I feel there is an answer there, somehow. I just can't work out what it is. I suppose I wondered if, by some magic – do you believe in magic? – he would find my message. But now I realise it was meant to be you. I believe there's purpose in that.' He winced and stood awkwardly.

'I have . . . lower-back pain. It's excruciating. I either have to stay on my feet, which is exhausting, or I recline . . . like so.' He arranged his pillow and what looked to be an overcoat wrapped in a blanket on the floor. He then lay on his side, slightly propped, like a weary lady of the house. 'I need a chaise, really,' he sighed. 'But one doesn't come with the job.'

The sun poured through the windows, creating a plank of warmth against which Dora's face pressed.

Wystan stubbed his cigarette out in a little enamelled ashtray. 'Do you know about Emile Coué?'

'A little . . .' Dora lied.

'It's the philosophy I live by. You will become what you believe you will become. Can you subscribe to that, do you think?'

'I can try . . .'

'Because everything is going to get worse before it gets better. That is how things are.'

'I see.'

He looked at her thoughtfully. Here—' He picked up a notebook from a little pile beside him. It was a beautiful hardback notebook, with a swirly design on the cover and thick creamy paper inside.

'This is for you . . .' he said.

Dora took it from him with a gasp. 'Really?' She ran her fingers over the cover and rubbed the paper between thumb and forefinger to check its thickness.

'I knew it! You're a stationery lover!' He smiled. 'I get these from the hardware store on the seafront. The twins. Who'd have expected they would stock the finest notebooks in Britain? Have this too.' Out of his jacket pocket, he handed Dora an ink pen. It was made of hard rubber and grew warm in her hand.

'*Thank you*,' Dora whispered.

'You know, Dora, I have two brothers. We're not close. I was always an oddity. The thing is . . . I always felt as if I carried a feminine self, sort of like a sister . . . inside me.' He looked at her shyly, clearly never having articulated this before. 'And now . . . here you are.'

They smiled at one another.

'Well, now that you are here, how about you help me with this? McLeod's design for the cover of the *Larchfieldian*. I'm resurrecting the school magazine. Encouraging the boys to write a bit of poetry, perhaps a play, with me.' He turned the picture back round to himself and considered it. 'A bit militaristic?'

'It's good. How old is he?'

'Ten. Destined for the army, like a lot of these boys. Hmmm. Not sure.'

'It's very colourful . . .'

Wystan peered at the figure. 'Maybe.' Then he picked up another sheet from beside him and gave a great bark of a laugh. 'This is from a little lad . . . Jamie . . .'

Jamie had submitted a poem to the *Larchfieldian*:

UNCLE WIZ

Uncle Wiz is a very fun chap

Teaches Eng/Fr and wears a cap

Rugby's boring, says Uncle Wiz

D. H. is best and school a swiz.

'Well, that's definitely going in!' Wystan placed it on the growing 'yes' pile on the bed. There was a silence between them, then Wystan said, casually, 'I suppose this is where we can test Coué's method. Am I any good? Or am I . . . *going* to be any good? In the future?'

'Yes!' Dora said without hesitation. A beam of boyish pleasure spread across Wystan's face. Dora thought how wonderful it was that a genuine smile transformed a face, any face, and created beauty. Despite his façades and pretentions and his ostensible indifference to his success, underneath, Wystan was a delighted little boy that all his efforts were not going to be in vain. It made Dora pleased to be the messenger.

Olive rattled in with a tray on which was a single teacup, a teapot and a plate with two fat slices of raisin cake. She looked for somewhere to lay the tray, but Wystan held out his hands. 'Just leave it with me, Olive. Thank you.' She nodded, and hesitated, observing the renewed squalor, but he waved her away. 'Don't worry about me, Olive. There's a purpose behind it all . . .'

'You look most uncomfortable, Mr Auden. Don't you want to sit on the chair?'

'Thank you, no, Olive. You're very thoughtful.'

She frowned and closed the door behind her.

Wystan placed the tray on the floor between them and filled the cup. 'You have this – I have a tooth-mug over here.' The giant arm uncurled and lifted a cracked mug from the basin. He wiped it on his shirt and filled it too. Then he held out the plate with the cake and Dora took a slice.

As the poet gulped his tea and gobbled his cake, something came to Dora.

'It's so peaceful here,' she said.

'An illusion,' he said. 'It's quite mad. I wonder, every day, how long I am going to last. I'm working on something very odd, a sort of mess of poems and speeches . . . in response to the madness. I'm going to call it *The Orators*. It's got an airman in it. A very handsome balls-up.'

'Can I see?' Dora said, excitedly.

He laid the *Larchfieldian* papers to one side and, with a wince, went to sit at the desk. 'I've been working on the beginning. It's a kind of spoof speech. I'm modelling it on Larchfield, the boys getting their prize-day speech. But this one is all about destroying that part of themselves that will destroy them if they don't.' He handed her a sheaf of papers.

The writing was minuscule and spidery. She stared at it for some minutes, taking in the extra scribbles in the margins, the lines leading off to new scribbles. His words were virtually illegible, but the paper seemed to give off an energy all its own. She could feel his youth and the sheer torrential vigour of his ideas.

Dora laid her hands on the pages. They were tired hands. She turned them over, taking in the wrinkling of the skin at the knuckles and the bitten nails. Whatever these hands had been doing, it wasn't writing poetry. And yet, looking at Wystan's scribbles, trying to decode them, latching on to a sparkling phrase here and there . . . it felt familiar. It felt *fun*.

Just then, the door flew open and a little boy ran into the room. He hovered uncertainly.

Wystan shrugged. 'Bit of an open-door policy, here. Come on, then, Jamie. I've got cake!'

The little boy came in cautiously, looking back at the door to make sure he still had an escape.

He looked up at Wystan and said, 'Can I—?'

'Draw? Why not? You know where everything is.'

Jamie grabbed some paper from a pile at the window, and a pencil from the desk, then curled up near Wystan's feet and began drawing.

The child made Dora nervous. Children were so much bigger than their size. They radiated – what was it? *Need*. They broke all kinds of rules, all the time, just by being alive. It was impossible to know how to be around a child, especially one like Jamie, so fragile-looking and so vulnerable.

Wystan absently wiggled his toes against Jamie's tummy as he returned to the papers on the bed. The little boy giggled and pushed the toes away. Wystan began to read a page, but his attention kept drifting to the child on the floor.

'You are ticklish!' he said. 'This is just too easy!'

Jamie held up a picture of a house with three people standing outside.

'Ah, a family scene!' Wystan beamed. 'Very good, Jamie! You know,' he said to Dora, 'it's really very sad the way they spend so much time drawing pictures of home, or writing tragic love poems about their sisters. This environment is terrible for a boy. Dragged from home, all alone with a bunch of other savages. Really, it's a miracle we're not all stark staring mad. Or maybe we are. What do you think, Jamie? Are we all dotty?'

The little boy's hair was sticking up. 'You're a bit mad, sir,' he said in a small voice. 'Talking to yourself and all.' Wystan clapped his hands in delight.

'Jamie, you're not wrong there. Now –' he looked at the clock ticking loudly on the mantelpiece and ruffled the boy's hair – 'off you go. That bell is going to explode in a moment and you need to be in my French class.' Jamie pushed the picture into Wystan's lap and ran out of the door.

'Here, have this,' Wystan handed it to Dora. It was a simple, very cheerful drawing. A big U-shaped smile was on each round face.

'But he gave it to you.'

'Truthfully? I have dozens of them. Keep it as a memento.'

Dora took the paper and folded it carefully, slipping it into a pocket of her coat.

'I don't know how people can send their boys here, really,' Wystan said. 'I see Jamie and I think of myself – lonely, missing my parents.'

He took a final swig from his tooth-mug and set it down. 'Dora,' he said, 'I am so glad you've come . . . Why don't you stay here, make yourself at home? I must go and teach these little boys some French.' He paused at the door and gave Dora a wink.

Dora was alone, among W. H. Auden's papers. Delight filled her as she surveyed the room with its glorious mess. Now that Wystan was not here, with the force of his presence, it was easier to study the interior, to think about her place in it, to enjoy herself.

She turned to the desk, laid out the notebook on top of the scribbled sheets, and her pen slid smoothly over the page.

She wrote her name, turned the page and hesitated. Then she began to write, filling the page with neat, frenzied handwriting. She wrote with breathless speed, trying to preserve what had just happened, this meeting that changed everything, before her faulty mind took it away.

TWENTY-ONE

Wystan

WYSTAN EXAMINES THE EMBOSSED invitation with a sinking heart.

Mrs M. Wallace requests the honour of the company of

Mr W. H. Auden

for

An Easter Party

at

Dunluin

Smart attire.

Did Cecil go to these things?

Christ. It is everything he despises and his pen pauses over the RSVP note. *Mr Auden regrets* (does he hell) *that he is unable to attend your* (life-extinguishing) *delightful party* (for liars and spies). Oh, how he would love to refuse. Christopher would do it, without a blink.

The gathering will take him from his work, leave him hungover and anxious, and drain him for days to come. But Wystan knows that he cannot say no. These invitations are polite commands. Helensburgh society would like to meet him. He must pay his respects to the ladies of Helensburgh society. Wallace is a benefactor of the school and the invitation to the Wallace Easter Party is both sought after and cannot be refused.

In later years, he will simply say, *Sorry. No.* But he is only twenty-four and a hired hand, and it would cause consternation. And, here, what people think carries real weight. Other people hold the power over his job, over his freedom. He decides, instead, with new confidence, that he will simply sail through it. They cannot touch him, not really. Wystan is whole, he is solid and, most important of all, he believes that *magic happens*.

On the appointed day, he pulls out his suit. It's not very clean, but there's no time to do anything about it. He half-heartedly asks Olive to give it a brush-down. He's going to wear his bow tie, which is yellow, and his fedora, and they can fuck off.

The Wallace house is one of the largest mansions in Upper Helensburgh. In the lamplit garden, newly opened camellias sprawl over a pergola. It is a warm, slightly damp spring evening. Opening the iron gate sets off a chorus of yapping from inside. Tiny dogs with fat eyes are bouncing in the window. He presses the bell and, to his surprise, McLeod answers the door, dressed in a footman's livery, grinning shyly. This is another tradition of the Easter Party: the eldest boys get to dress up and serve the guests, receiving payment for their efforts.

The dogs fly out to his ankles. Pekingese? Chihuahuas? Animals do not intrigue him, and tiny ones even less so. He steps high, taking care not to crush them, and follows McLeod to the drawing room.

Mrs Wallace – 'Call me Marilyn, dear, everyone does' – speeds across to him, assesses him, from her low height, as if he were a relative who has grown. She is much as he expected: thin, where Pop is thick, with the nervous, slightly starved quality that the wives of unpredictable husbands often have. 'Am I late?' he asks her.

'Oh, no, dear. Everything is early in Helensburgh.' She leads him into the room, where Wystan's heart plummets to see Jessop leaning against the mantelpiece, deep in conversation with a sensible-looking young woman with flowers in her hair.

'You know Mr Jessop, of course?' says Marilyn, leading him inexorably towards Jessop's sneer. His colleague nods. Every face is turned towards Wystan, and it feels as though there is not quite enough oxygen to go round. Thankfully, Wystan is intercepted by Wallace himself, who pumps his hand and indicates an array of whisky bottles lined up on the sideboard. 'We've decided to further your education,' he grins. Wystan can see the memory of their previous conversation etched beneath the cheerful expression. Pop Wallace drops his hand and turns away. 'What would you like?'

The rugs have been taken away and all the furniture pushed to the edge of the room to make space for dancing. The interior is immaculately decorated in a pale yellow, with trompe l'œil panelling. A huge chandelier in the middle of the ceiling casts a sparkling glow over the party. In the corner, a young woman in a gold dress is playing a harp. About thirty or forty people are gathered, glasses in hand, immaculate in their smart attire, the ladies in long, unostentatious dresses. No flappers here. Nobody has knees in Upper Helensburgh.

Marilyn appears with an etiolated brown-haired girl in spectacles. 'This is Anne,' she says, and the girl smiles. 'I thought you would both have lots to talk about. Anne is a teacher as well. And she has lots of unusual notions, the sort of thing young people have.'

Anne is Anne Fremantle, a young woman of adventurous ideas which are going to fall on stony ground in Helensburgh. She is very excited to meet Wystan and she presents him with a copy of his poetry book, which she has bought from the tourist office on the shorefront. Her height marks her out in the room. 'Would you sign it for me?' she asks. She even has a pen.

'Of course.' He scrawls his name and adds, after a hesitation, *for Anne, with warmest regards*. She peeps around his arm as he writes and holds the book to her breast when he has finished.

A tumbler with a dark amber liquid appears. 'Here we are; this is Talisker. Have a go at that,' Pop says.

Wystan does have a go. The liquid burns a track down his gullet and he tries not to cough. But as it reaches his stomach, a pleasurable warm glow spreads through his body and causes a click of confidence in his mind – a click that says, *I can win this.*

Pop is tapping his glass with a fork and the talk dies down, along with the soft notes of the harp. 'Ladies and gentlemen, Marilyn and I are delighted you're all here for our Easter Party once more. We have a small announcement to make.' Marilyn nestles at his side and slips her arm through his.

'Our beautiful daughter, Amy, whom I know you all know . . .' He indicates the sensible-looking girl next to Jessop. 'Well, I'm delighted to tell you that the young man standing next to her, Mr Jessop, came to me earlier today to ask for her hand in marriage.

Arthur is a fine young man, and, of course, I gave my blessing, and so these two young ones are now engaged.'

Sighs ripple through the party, and then applause. Some of the women go to embrace Amy; some of the older ones embrace Marilyn. Jessop is surrounded by men slapping his back, guffawing congratulations. Wystan stands very still with his glass in his hand.

'I enjoyed your book,' whispers Anne. 'I've been wanting to meet you so I could ask you about it.' She takes a delicate sip of sherry. Wystan nods and smiles at her. Theakston and McLeod appear with champagne, and now Wystan's whisky has been replaced by a glass for a toast.

'To Amy and Arthur!' says Pop Wallace, beaming proudly.

'To Amy and Arthur!' repeats the party, like an amen.

Wystan throws down the champagne, noting that the sensation is not a warm one, the bubbles ricocheting their way upwards to his brain, making him dizzy for a moment.

Anne is still by his side, face turned to his. How quickly men and women take on the appearance of their adult roles, Wystan thinks. She stands demurely, trying not to emphasise her height, which would put her taller than him. She holds her drink, which she plainly does not like, in the way she has been taught. And she grasps the reins of conversation, though it seems to him that she would like to be giggling, or running about outside. And he, too, is standing now as he ought, dipping his ear to catch her not-too-loud voice, positioning himself at a slightly protective angle, as men do with women, an indulgent smile upon his face. She is about his age, but here they are, new gentleman in town and young provincial girl, already moulding themselves into something like their parents.

'I don't know how to put this exactly, but your poems seem

unchristian.' She has clearly rehearsed this statement. A frown appears behind the spectacles; she does not want to be rude. 'But big-hearted.'

Wystan does not know quite how to reply. He takes a fortifying sip of his drink, raises his glass slightly to Pop Wallace, who is across the room, watching him. He says, 'I've rather fallen out with organised religion. I find myself much more interested in people.'

'Do you go to church?'

Wystan shakes his head. 'I've no direct aversion. It's just . . . you know.'

'And are you a Christian?'

'Well, if you're putting a gun to my head . . .'

She blushes. 'Oh, no! I'm just trying to fathom . . . Oh dear. I've been rude. I'm not accustomed to talking to the author about their work. You seem very spiritual, that's all, in your work. But there's no God.'

'I believe in God. But, *possibly* . . .' And, here, he pauses. 'Possibly he has ceased to believe in me. I'm sure it's only temporary.'

'What I think Anne is getting at,' says the widow Laithwaite, who has appeared in full rustling skirts between them, 'is that your book is rather *eccentric* – for us poor types far away from London.'

Anne looks at him with appeal in her eyes. 'I didn't say that,' she says.

'What I personally hope for in a poem,' continues Mrs Laithwaite, 'is beauty and joy. An uplift of the spirits. Those of us who've suffered loss in the war . . . well, we turn to poetry for solace, don't we?'

McLeod appears at his elbow bearing a silver tray on which are piled oysters. 'An oyster, sir?' Beside him, Theakston brings china plates with tiny silver forks.

Wystan has never had an oyster before, and doesn't like the look of them, with their snot-like appearance and their briny undertow, like a woman's knickers. How he wishes Christopher were here – or, more to the point, that he was with Christopher. His friend would not set foot in such a gathering as this, knowing it for what it was.

'Well done, you two,' says Wystan to the boys, and, with a shudder, lifts an oyster on to the plate Theakston is holding.

'Only one?' says Marilyn. 'You need feeding up, Mr Auden.'

'Oh, I'm fine just now. I'm a slow eater of fish.' Auden lays his drink down and tackles the oyster. It slips down his throat in a buttery mass and he stifles a retch.

Plates come and go, McLeod appearing like a sprite at his elbow. More oysters. Funny biscuits with pâté. Pineapple pieces, which he really can't stand. Under Marilyn's watchful eye, he takes some of everything he is offered.

Then a commotion behind him and a large roast of pork is brought in, which the cook shreds before their eyes and heaps on yet more trays, with an arrangement of greens.

Wystan likes this more and, indeed, calls McLeod over to top up his plate. He's just got his mouth full of delicious melting pork when Pop Wallace announces loudly, 'We have another special guest tonight: Mr Wystan Auden. Mr Auden is a poet, a real poet, who has published a book.' More sighs, more faces turning to study him. Wystan feels their eyes scraping up and down his clothes. Pop goes on, 'Perhaps Mr Auden would care to read us one of his poems?' An ocean of silence swells through the room. Fearing the guests can hear him eating, Wystan gulps his mouthful unchewed.

'Mr Auden's reputation precedes him,' pipes up the nervous voice of Callum Wallace. He gives a friendly admiring smile to his mentor. 'People still talk about you at Oxford. In Helensburgh, we may be finding your work unusual, but there they have been talking about this book all year!'

'Oh, yes, do read us something,' says Anne eagerly, offering him her copy of his book. Callum's bright, bony face is full of encouragement and Wystan decides he can simply speak the poem to Callum and Anne: the two young people can be his audience. So, he takes the book from Anne's proffered hand, closes it, because he does not need to read his own poems from the page, crosses his hands in front of him and closes his eyes, as if he is praying. The silence goes on for long enough to cause Pop Wallace to cough uncertainly.

After an agonising forty-five seconds or so, Wystan raises his head and begins to recite:

> 'It is time for the destruction of error.
> The chairs are being brought in from the garden,
> The summer talk stopped on that savage coast
> Before the storms, after the guests and birds:
> In sanatoriums they laugh less and less,
> Less certain of cure; and the loud madman
> Sinks now into a more terrible calm . . .'

A long silence greets this, the audience being neither sure whether the poem has finished, nor what it is about. Then there is a cough from someone by the window, and a 'Bravo, Mr Auden.' A single clap.

Pop Wallace mutters into his drink, 'Doesn't sound like poetry to me.'

'Father!' hisses Callum.

'Thank you, Mr Auden. I wonder . . . Do you have any poems *not* about sanatoriums?' asks Mrs Laithwaite.

Anne takes the book back, gently, from Wystan. 'I think the poem is profound,' she says from her great height. 'And we haven't heard it all, anyway – just a few lines. Mr Auden is telling us about the decay of the nation.'

Pop Wallace frowns, trying to work out right from wrong. These young people seem to like bad verse and to enjoy its subversive message.

'Mr Auden, I can't work out if you are insulting the company or not. What's the "savage coast" if it's not here? There's no coast in Birmingham, or Oxford! What is the "destruction of error" if it's not a call for revolution!'

Mrs Laithwaite draws a little closer. 'You seem awfully nice in person, and I am sure your next book will be much better.'

It is Jessop's wicked smirk that enrages him the most.

Wystan gives a slight bow to Mrs Wallace. 'I'm afraid I was not prepared to read a poem. I apologise if it was the wrong one. It was the only one to come to mind on the spot.'

'Oh, but Mr Auden, we are just trying to talk!' cries Marilyn. 'Please don't take offence. It's our way of, well, taking part.'

Just then, the liveried boys come in and take away all the plates. They are followed by a quartet of musicians, who immediately start up a bouncy tune for dancing. Wystan is forgotten as the men take their partners and begin the Lindy Hop.

Anne is standing hopefully by his side. He knows what he has to do.

'Would you do me the pleasure . . . ?' he asks her, offering his hand.

'Oh, thank you! Yes!' says Anne, and her hand slides into his.

And Wystan's mortification is complete as he shuffles through a poorly executed Lindy Hop, grateful only for the fact that Anne is almost as clumsy as he.

Why would anyone do this?

This is Hell, to be sure. Couples laced together in conformity, dancing a dance that looks as though it is trying to break them free, but is just more of the awful same.

When I go to Hell, Wystan muses, it will look like this: eternal Lindy Hop in a Helensburgh drawing room.

When the tune finally ends, Wystan says to Anne, 'I'm very tired. Please, will you excuse me? I must go.'

A goodbye to the disappointed hostess. McLeod appears from the shadows and escorts Wystan out of the room. His footsteps sound like gunfire on the parquet floor.

The air outside is soft and thick, with a taste of rain to come. Then there is a hand on his arm. 'Mr Auden, *Wystan*,' says Callum. 'I loved your poem, and I do hope that tonight won't make you break off our acquaintance.'

'Of course not! Although, clearly, your father would be no more pleased about it, if he knew.' They share a secret grin. 'I don't want to be someone who corrupts an idealistic young man, but, well, it pleases me greatly that you borrow my books. And take my eccentric opinions seriously.'

'I will always come,' says Callum, and he slips back behind the door. Wystan feels a wave of relief wash over him that he has escaped. What did he expect from a gathering like this? To be understood?

It's no time to go home, though. Night has fallen and it is the perfect time to enjoy a walk. Wystan sets off, not quite sure why he is heading with such a decisive step towards the railway station. Except that he longs to see something, someone else. He longs to see that boy.

Wishing can make all kinds of things come true. He firmly believes this. The world is a place of magic – and longing is the greatest magic of all. It is the stuff of which we are all made, the simple force of love trying to exist.

The station is lit with a dim glow. People are milling in and out, on and off the trains into Glasgow. It is comforting to sit on a bench and watch people with other, bigger, lives passing him, bringing gulps of city air his way. He lets the patterns of people and voices swim across his eyes and his brain.

And then he sees him.

Him.

The boy with the pocked face and the frame as lean as a cane. He's with no one, and he looks different. Thinner. Paler. The shirt is patched at the elbows and lifts out of his trousers where the material has been cut off to make the patch. He's not smoking this time, just watching, much as Wystan is simply watching.

He hasn't seen Wystan yet, which gives the poet time simply to enjoy the unutterable thrill of seeing him again. Then the boy's eyes meet his, and they are locked together in a moment of shocked recognition. Wystan will never forget as long as he lives the moment when the young man recognises him, though they have never met, and raises his hand in greeting. In that gesture is the validation of all that he is; it is the gesture of a comrade in loneliness. Who knew that sometimes love comes to get you, drags you from the ashes of your life, the terrible empty heart of everyday life?

TWENTY-TWO

Dora

T HE WINTER WAS A cruel, endless cold that seemed to defeat even the house. Something had happened to the earth beneath the drive, a brimming of water whose origin Dora and Kit could not find, there being, apparently, no burst pipe, but water that had turned the outside to slurry for weeks now froze into a solid, filthy lake. It was lethally slippery and thick.

Every day, they took a jar of salt and sprinkled it uselessly over the expanse of ice. Inside, the house was perishing. Paradise was built in a time of servants; even divided, the rooms were overpowering spaces, sucking warmth away. The fireplace in the sitting room remained a decorative hole into which the wisps of warm air produced by the radiators flew.

Beatrice had a constant snuffle because of the cold, but was otherwise thriving. She wriggled herself around her playpen and grinned up at her parents, covered in whatever she had found: cobwebs, dust, dead insects. The house was too big to clean effectively. It needed a small army of people and tools: telescopic feather dusters for the cornicing; the patience and *time* to wipe the carved skirting boards. The old vacuum cleaner collapsed under the strain and they had no money to buy a new one, so dust and dog hair evolved into new ecosystems in the corners.

Did it look as if Dora wasn't coping? She was. In fact, she was coping vigorously. With unbroken regularity, their child was fed and laid down to sleep. She was the hungriest creature Dora had ever encountered, slurping her way through bottle after bottle, and gobbling her way through pureed fruit and rice. The hours when she slept passed in an instant. Dora washed nappies (Bea was now big enough to wear them), or pureed food, or did nothing at all, simply staring at the shadows crossing the walls. At bedtime, she and Kit sang to the baby, or read her a story, side by side, with the baby between them.

While coping vigorously, Dora wore a peculiar concoction of what was left now she had thrown out RJ's smart jackets and boots. Photographs captured a woman dishevelled and overwhelmingly dressed in brown maternity tops and paint-stained jogging bottoms, her face always turned away, staring at the baby to the side of her.

Into this ensemble of ice and determination, the health visitor arrived. Dora had never been sure what Sorcha would be able to do to help, but the small flame of hope that she would be able to help in some way persisted. Someone kind to talk to, perhaps. Someone to reassure Dora she was doing well.

Sorcha slithered up the drive in her purple Beetle, setting Virgil off into his usual yapping frenzy. She was a woman in late middle age who had taken the road some women do at that point, of becoming girlish. So, a teddy bear hung from her windscreen and sparkly brooches adorned her coat. Her scarf was Scooby-Doo themed. Her nails were painted bright red and she was immaculately made up.

'Helloooo!' Sorcha called from the doorstep, rubbing her hands together. 'Quite an ice rink you've got out here! I nearly crashed into your car.' Her breath clouded round her. It was 8.30 a.m., Kit was about to leave for work, and Dora had, by Herculean effort, got dressed. All Sorcha's visits were at odd times that suited her, not Dora or Beatrice. Dora soon gave up trying to get appointments that fitted in with the sleep routine she was following for Bea, started at the hospital to help her growth. A sigh would greet Dora's attempt to negotiate around Sorcha's schedule and an edge would appear in her otherwise cheery manner. Latterly, Dora had begun to think the visits were random on purpose, to catch her out in her bad mothering.

Beatrice was fast asleep, having just been fed. After leaping round the visitor, Virgil retreated to the kitchen. The knowledge of what was coming filled Dora with dread. First, there would be the gaze upon her baby's sleeping form. 'Ah! So small!' Then the hands going into the cot, grabbing the little girl, who would still be so deeply asleep she would not stir. Bea would be lifted on to the floor next to the scales, where Sorcha would undo her clothes. The baby would wake, then, sleepy indignation would come over her features, and then – *plop!* – naked, she would be placed into the freezing weighing pan. Sorcha would observe pitilessly as Bea began to writhe and cry.

After an eternity, she would finally take her out, but the torment wouldn't be over yet. Dora's baby now completely awake and purple with distress, Sorcha would embark on a battery of tests for reflexes, hearing and percentile measurements. The visit would last forty-five minutes or more and Dora and Bea would spend the whole day recovering.

'Hello,' Dora mumbled. 'She's asleep, just gone off.'

'Oh, well, we'll soon sort that out!' Sorcha breezed into the nursery and leant over the cot. Out came her greedy hands.

'She looks well,' she said. 'I assume you've gone back to demand feeding.'

Dora was too tired to dissemble; exhaustion made her blunt. And, anyway, she was *proud* of how she'd made her baby grow. 'No, she looks well because we're feeding her every four hours, no matter what. The paediatrician is very happy with her.'

Sorcha stared, uncomprehending, just as Mo had done, and scooped Bea up with a defiant air.

'Put her down, please,' Dora said. 'There's no need to weigh her today. I'm sorry it's a wasted journey for you, but it's more important that she sleeps.'

'What?' Sorcha paused, half way through unbuttoning Bea's cardigan.

'And, actually, I don't need any more visits. You can see she's doing really well. I don't care about her percentiles, and, as I said, the paediatrician is very happy with her.'

Dora had not known she was going to say this, and was almost as taken aback as Sorcha. Her heart pounded at her own defiance. She had loathed these visits from the very first one, when Dora and Kit had given Sorcha a cup of tea and then sat gingerly with Bea on the sofa, as if it were a kind of interview to decide if they could keep her or not. Sorcha had eyed the books on the table. 'Books! Don't waste your money! Throw them out and just ask me anything

201

you want to know!' She had laughed, but it was clear that she meant it.

Sorcha was staring blankly. Clearly, no one had ever refused her visits, or her advice. Very reluctantly, she stopped unbuttoning Bea's cardigan, but her hand continued to hover, in case she had misheard.

There was now an unstoppable momentum to this meeting. Having surprised herself, Dora was more clear-headed than she had been in weeks. It was time to play her trump card. She called for Kit and he came into the room, smiling affably, but unmistakeably there to back her up. Since the matter of Susie and the Edinburgh trip, he had been making an effort to be around a bit more. He had started cooking dinner more often and coming home early to bathe Bea and put her to bed. This was on top of taking over the last feed of the day.

'Everything okay?' he said, wandering over to stand next to his wife.

'Well, your daughter does seem to be healthy. But –' and here Sorcha leant in close to Dora, so close that it was clear Dora was the one to whom she was speaking – 'this baby is your priority now. Do you understand?'

Dora visualised for a long moment the smack in Sorcha's face that was the only adequate counter to this remark. Then she lifted the baby into her arms and left the room. A silence hung behind her. Sorcha didn't know what to say to Kit, nor he to her. In this new world of women, men were satellites that simply circled, occasionally landing for meals or special events. They didn't really know anything. And babies were not their priority.

Sorcha sulkily packed away her scales and emerged. 'I have to report this as a failure to engage with the service. You know that, don't you?' she said to Dora.

'Go ahead,' said Dora, turning away. She rocked her baby and sang, 'Go to sleep, Bea; close your pretty eyes . . .' until the front door closed and Sorcha was gone.

Kit appeared. 'I have to get to work now,' he said, carefully. Dora nodded.

'It's just that . . . however clumsy they are, darling, I think these people are trying to help.'

'They know better than me, then, do they? All that waking Bea up and putting her in a freezing basin whenever she likes. And being nasty . . . that's all for my own good, is it?'

'Is it really doing Bea any harm? To have a visit from a silly bat like Sorcha?'

Dora stared at him.

'I just think . . . we should try not to antagonise people. If we can help it. Though, I agree; I'd like a pint of what Sorcha's on, that's for sure.'

'I'm curious, Kit,' said Dora. 'What about Mo, then? Should we be appeasing her too?'

'No . . . Although it wouldn't hurt to humour her a bit, would it? Another old bat. She can't hurt us.'

'I didn't know I had married Neville Chamberlain.'

'What do you mean?' He followed her into the sitting room. 'I stood up for you in there, with that silly woman. I'm just trying to tell you that I am sick of you hating everyone!'

'We're all silly women to you, aren't we?' Dora snarled. 'It doesn't matter to you who is right or wrong.' She turned away from him and steeled herself against the slam of the front door.

Bea and Dora were alone again, with the day stretching ahead, tight as a wire, dragging the two of them behind.

Dora's *priority*? How dare she? Fucking bitch.

It was down to Dora to protect their daughter. No one else was going to.

Dora kissed her little girl and rocked her. The baby's eyes grew heavy and she fell back to sleep in Dora's arms.

Would there be consequences to sacking the health visitor? Dora felt only relief that she had succeeded in protecting her baby, and her way of mothering, from interference. She pressed a kiss to her cheek and laid the child back in her cot.

Something opened in her mind, then. While Bea slept, Dora hunted for and found Dante's *Inferno* in a pile awaiting a space on the shelf. It was one of Auden's favourite texts, and he had read it whilst in Helensburgh. Normally, Dora's concentration was so broken that ploughing through the cantos would have been impossible. But now, something was fuelling the synapses in her brain. Now, she felt as if she could read and understand anything. And there was no one here to stop her, to tell her she was straining herself or doing something damaging. She poured herself a strong coffee, wrapped herself up, back in bed, and began to read. She knew that this book had something important to tell her, that there was a message it was important for her to receive. Her years of study would pay off now. She was diligent and determined and would be successful.

Part Three

TWENTY-THREE

Wystan and Dora

WHEN DORA OPENED HER eyes, she was sitting beside Wystan at the edge of a sloping field, high above Helensburgh. This was where Upper Helensburgh ended and the woods and open moorland began. Some way down to their left was the reservoir, shimmering in the heat haze, and, far below, the Clyde. This was a spot Wystan would grow to love, and would be a setting for his poem, 'A Happy New Year'. Today, the smell of aviation fuel drifted on the breeze and the sky above them buzzed with distant planes. Cobham's Flying Circus had come to Helensburgh, making use of the surplus of planes and RAF pilots left after the war. The public could pay to go up in an aircraft, or do as Wystan was doing: simply find a spot nearby and watch the formations in the sky for free.

'How fantastic to be a pilot,' Wystan mused. 'Flying so close to the sun, and coming back.'

'You didn't want to take a trip?'

'Lord, no! I like to admire and observe. It's research for my long poem.'

They were shaded by a tree and Dora shifted her position against its knobbly bark. Her bare arm brushed something poking out of a hollow in the tree. It was a forgotten *Courier*, folded and shoved into the space. The headline, from a couple of days previously, caught Dora's eye: *MAN, 18, WALKS INTO THE SEA AT CRAIGENDORAN*.

'Seen this?'

Wystan tore his attention away from the sky to look at the short, sensational article. His expression saddened. 'Silly boy,' he said, and indicated to Dora the section where the paper posited reasons for the young man to take his own life. He had struggled to get over the loss of a close friendship with another man in Cardross. The friend had recently got married and moved away. The victim had always been something of a misfit and the other men in his family, his father and older brother, had been killed in the war. The piece insinuated that a weakness of character and lack of male leadership in the family had resulted in this tragedy. Police had found a collection of dried flowers in the young man's bedroom afterwards, many of them pressed into fond letters written to his friend, none of which had been posted. His family was quite well-to-do, with naval connections, which was perhaps why the article writhed beneath its twin compulsions to shame and not to upset further an influential local. It ended by expressing surprise that such a tragedy would happen in Helensburgh, with its tough shipbuilding history, its military heritage.

Wystan sighed and looked away. 'At least it's not Gregory,' he said.

'Your friend?'

'Yes, my new Helensburgh friend. I met him at the station. It was as if . . . he was waiting for me to come here. I'm very fond of him.'

The boy in the paper had tied stones to his wrists and ankles, and he had picked a high tide on a windy night. Had there been a moon? Dora wondered. Had he been afraid? Or had he numbed himself in some way before he set off on his last walk? Alcohol?

Or had his sadness been enough to keep him walking into the freezing black water?

Had he changed his mind when finally submerged, and struggled to remove the rocks around his feet and hands? Or did peace descend, the waters closing over his image of his friend in his mind's eye?

Dora said, 'His mother must be beside herself.'

'Oh, no,' Wystan said firmly. 'She will be relieved that at last it is over. The shame will have destroyed her.'

'Really? His own mother?' Dora found she could not stop imagining the boy and the deepening water. There was something seductive about it, as well as shocking. How cold and terrible the world was to those who were in despair. Dora could almost feel the water around her own body, lapping in a way that was both painfully cold and soothing. Would she be brave enough to keep walking?

'You mustn't worry,' said Wystan, looking up at a toy-sized Gypsy Moth glittering as it dipped to make a turn. The heads of the pilot and his passenger behind shone like beads.

'Why not?'

'Because you have found me.'

Wystan was so solid, so young, squinting in the sunshine. The tree was rough against Dora's dress, and the sky was the blue of a child's drawing: high and cut with vapour trails, as if the white of the paper were showing through the crayon strokes. Aeroplanes were such audacious, optimistic machines. Pilots and their passengers were audacious, optimistic people, conquering a new element, flying high above ordinary mortal lives.

And at the same time, a person walked into an opposite element, to be dragged down into darkness, weighted. There was no flash, no show, just a different kind of audacity . . . the determination never to return.

And here she and Wystan were, in the middle, neither dragged down, nor set free. She opened her mouth to articulate this thought and instead her eyes fell on her friend.

He turned to her and said, with a smile, 'Don't you think it's perfect, that we are here? In a place divided into Upper and Lower Hel? Hasn't it struck you as completely marvellous? Who'd have thought the Wimbledon of the North would turn out to be the New Jerusalem!'

The breeze rustled the leaves above them. Birds cheeped invisibly in the branches. When Dora peered into the depths of the tree, she could see the dark outline of a nest, then a magpie pushed itself out of the foliage and launched itself on to the air, a wonderful noisy tumult of black and white.

'And which direction are we going?'

Wystan laughed, pointed down to the estuary glinting far below. 'Well, I'm off down there, with the lustful and the gluttonous. Our young friend in the paper galloped on ahead to the wood of suicides.'

'No . . . No, I can't imagine that.'

'Of course, you know that between Heaven and Upper Hell is Limbo.' He leant in closer, studied her face. 'I think you're staying here. I don't know . . . Limbo suits you. You look . . . rested.'

Her fingers went to her face, as if she might be able to feel what he could see. Wystan took out a cigarette – not offering her one, as he knew now she did not smoke – and exhaled some smoke with a sigh.

It was suddenly very important to bring him back from whatever train of thought was taking him away. As if she were tugging at his sleeve to distract him from a dangerous conversation, she pulled her notebook from her bag. 'I've been writing,' she said. 'Just like you said I would.'

'Of course you have!' Wystan said, and looked at her expectantly. 'And may I see?'

She passed him the notebook, with its frenzied but neat hand. She flipped through the ramblings that were more of a diary and pointed to the places where she had begun to form her ideas into lines.

As he read, Dora gazed out to the west, glimpsing a tiny jigsaw of streets far away, and beyond, the deep sapphire sea with its crust of shore. And there, the spit of land at the furthest reach of Lower Hel, where the houses grew more separate, picked out like a train-set landscape . . . She shivered with an apprehension of how far away it was, and how far down.

Wystan spoke, his voice possessing the words. How strange it was to hear someone else's voice speaking your most private, perfect thoughts.

'All the sadness of the hills
was on fire. The swan-galleons
set sail across the grey.
And I ran the length of the loch
to press into your hand this –
for the shining silver of my life.

'Interesting . . .' he said. 'Of course, the silver . . . ambivalent, is it not? As much about betrayal as it is about thanks. Pieces of silver?'

Dora nodded uncertainly.

'Dora, darling, this is a poem about limbo. Neither happiness nor sadness, but actually both at the same time. That is what limbo is to you: two things at once. And whether you know it or not quite yet, that is your subject. It may make you desperately unhappy, but this, here, is where you belong. And we are all, always, drawn inexorably to where we belong.'

'And you? Where do you belong?'

Wystan finished his cigarette and flicked it into the grass.

'Well, I don't know. But it's not looking good, is it?'

TWENTY-FOUR

Dora

WEDNESDAY, 11 A.M.

I have found the third wormhole – the cupboard at the top of the stairs. My notebook rests on my knees and I am curled up among paint tins and mouse poison. This does not trouble me, for the wormhole is my salvation.

Expert in not sneezing, I have almost learnt to breathe through my skin. Aches and pins and needles do not trouble me.

They do not know about this wormhole.

The space adjoins their hall and often they talk here before one or other is leaving the house. When Mo is away, Terrence often sits in the hall, barely eighteen inches from my face. He chats on the phone.

Today could be the day. Today there will be something to tell Kit, something that means the world will make sense again.

I have been here for nearly two hours, for the whole of Bea's lunchtime nap. It has passed slowly, with a constant pain in my chest.

I see myself for what I am – a woman, a mother, hiding in a cupboard, eavesdropping. It is shameful. No wonder my husband treads carefully around me; no wonder officials are circling my child. And yet I remain convinced that somewhere in the endless indecipherable noise lies the answer, the explanation for why my life has come to this.

THE CONVERSION OF PARADISE included many invisible gaps in the insulation which let all kinds of sounds through. It was a feature of Dora's life there that she spent a lot of time listening. There is something maddening about a sound that can be heard but never quite resolved. It never becomes language, but nonetheless promises it will.

In the early days, Terrence and Mo did a lot of talking – at first, mostly in their sitting room, directly above Dora's. Terrence's gravelly voice was the dominant one. Mo's was much fainter and danced around his, clearly laying down some law or other. Their discussions would often be quite heated in those early days, their dialogue so often on the verge of meaning something and revealing something that Kit and Dora would turn down the television and strain to hear.

One evening, Terrence and Mo and some of their family were in their sitting room having a heated discussion. It was so boomingly loud that Dora and Kit could do nothing in the room below, yet, of course, it was too muffled to make out the words. Kit said he had an idea and went out to the tool shed, appearing a few minutes later with a plastic pipe about ten feet long. Laughing so much they didn't think they could see it through, Kit pressed one end of the pipe against the ceiling and held it so that Dora could listen at the other end. But the pipe was so thin and the ceiling so high that it wouldn't stay steady. Kit got the stepladder and they tried again, Dora hefting her bump to the ground to press her ear to the listening end.

But it just made the edges of the language sharper and louder, and, as they were getting comfortable, footsteps signalled the guests were leaving. If they walked past the window, it was quite a sight that would greet them. So they gave up and took the failed device back into the tool shed.

It had been funny then. Dora was in the I-can't-believe-it stage, which lies quite a way before the no-one-believes-me stage.

Another day, Dora was clearing up in the hallway when she suddenly heard Terrence say, 'Aye, well, she said she'll be over later,' as clearly as if he were standing behind her. Dora froze, the disembodied voice seeming to speak directly to her. There was frenzied muttering from Mo, and Terrence said, 'What?' Then more muttering and the closing of a door and the voices returned to being indistinct. This was the first 'wormhole', as Dora christened these odd gaps in the conversion's soundproofing. Were there others? Where were they?

Dora tried to work out where exactly the gap was behind the wall, but it had vanished as perfectly as it had appeared. Refusing, from then on, to have any conversation of importance in the hall, Dora started whispering whenever they were in it, and insisted they cross the garden to the tool shed to say anything that might be of interest to the neighbours. Kit resisted this, especially when it was raining and cold, and so the conversations were hissed in the spare room, or, gradually, not had at all.

Surveillance, both as an idea and an explanation, began to take over Dora's mind. When Kit returned from work one day, she presented him with printouts, from the internet, of easily obtained bugs and cameras. They discussed drilling a tiny hole from their sitting-room ceiling into the upstairs and popping a microphone into it, or installing CCTV outside to record who was coming in and out. Kit was willing to have the conversations, but did not appreciate that his wife was deadly serious. All day, Dora was surrounded by half-formed noise, the strangers driving in and out, and the sense of them listening at this wall or that. Yet, when she stepped out of the door and encountered any one of them, they ignored her as surely as if she were invisible.

Meeting Mo on her drive, she screwed up all her courage and said, 'Hello, Mo!' But, even then, Mo never met her eye, scuttling away like a spider.

Turning once more to the internet, Dora found Nightmare Neighbours, a site for the victims of anti-social neighbours (was this what she was? A victim?), and she tried to articulate her story in the hope of finding some reassurance or comfort.

But then she became certain that Mo and Terrence, or their children, had already found the site and knew who was posting. Inhibited and censored all the way through her mind, like a stick of rock, Dora began to find words difficult to form at all. Instead, she scoured the site for advice on what to do to survive.

Ignore your nightmare neighbour, the site advised. *You may find this difficult. If necessary, wear sunglasses.* This brought brief relief, but the problem with the advice was the grey weather: it was impossible to see in sunglasses. And, worse, catching sight of herself in a window, she looked completely mad.

THE WALLS AND CEILINGS *confirm with their reverberations that something is up; something is going to happen. The urgency of the* conversations increases, interspersed with odd creaking silences, which can only mean Mo and Terrence, and whoever is with them, are listening at one of the wormholes.

Only this one has remained a secret. The hours my baby sleeps are spent patching together, as best I can, the snatches of conversations held in their hall, usually with someone far in the house, whose reply cannot be heard.

Madness is brushing my skin already, with seductive softness. As I sit, I feel something in my pocket – a folded edge. I take the paper out, unfold it silently.

It's a child's drawing: three people, man, woman and child, with a house behind them. Jamie's drawing . . .

I run my fingers over it, momentarily transported back to the little room. I know who he has drawn, of course. It is Wystan, and me, and our child, Jamie. We are so happy.

When it is time for Beatrice to wake, I extricate myself and carry her into the sitting room and try Kit on his phone. No answer. I hold Bea in one arm, the silent phone in the other, and run Friends back-to-back on the television. Virgil trots up and down, whining, the only one able to hear as I do.

TWENTY-FIVE

Wystan

L OCH LONG IS REACHABLE by ferry from Helensburgh pier, disembarking at Coulport. It takes less time than one might think, because travel on the Clyde is direct, unlike the road, which twists along the contours of the shore. But Loch Long feels far away, and Wystan and his new friend Gregory need to be far away. Helensburgh is closing in on them; its eyes are everywhere.

So this they do one Saturday, Gregory wrapped in the sweater Wystan's mother sent for her son. It's thick wool, beautifully knitted and stitched. She must have gone to London and ordered it specially, not knowing that he could get a sweater much more cheaply here, and one more directly suited to the weather. On Gregory's body, it becomes splendid. Over it, he wears a dirty oilskin jacket. He grins, happy.

Mrs Clyde has prepared Wystan some tongue sandwiches, and he has a hipflask of wine for them to share.

The newly docked ferry at Helensburgh disgorges dozens of people, all come to town from the surrounding villages for shopping or entertainment. Wystan and Gregory walk the wobbly gangplank;

Wystan buys the tickets from the man behind the counter and they descend to the lower level. The pier master and the boatman exchange banter, then the rope is cast. The *Julianne* churns away from the pier's barnacled pillars into the Clyde, towards the open sea.

Alongside them all the way are the dramatic frontages of the villas bought by wealthy shipbuilders of the past, which make Helensburgh what it is. But, now that work on 'Ship No. 534' has stopped, leaving hundreds out of work, there is something poignant about the houses' splendour. These houses are going to be sold, split off, divided, their gardens partitioned and sold off as lots. The road will become a row of grand façades, behind which lies the struggle to make ends meet. As the ferry sails alongside Lower Hel, Gregory nods at the glamorous ribbon of dwellings. 'These rich folk,' he says. 'I don't think they're hurting.'

'They will be soon,' Wystan says. 'There's no one can escape what's coming. Unless . . . unless we all try Russia's model.'

'What's that?'

Wystan's face softens as he regards his friend. 'We must find a way to get you up to my room. I have a lot of books I think you would like. A lot of people are thinking about these questions, you know. A lot of people, my friends down in England, for instance, are thinking of how we can get out of this mess.'

Gregory says, looking at his hands, 'There's no point in all that talk. One day, I'd like . . .'

'What?'

'To have a girl of my own. A house. A family. I'm stuck at home with my ma and da. Pawnshop and breaker's yard – that's what I've got to look forward to. Until you, that is.'

'I'd like the same, you know. Family. Marriage. I can't have it, either, but for different reasons.'

They are silent for a few moments. The pier at Coulport chugs into view. The pebbled beaches glitter; torrents of rainwater from the hills clatter down the shingle.

Gregory says, 'A rich man like you, from down south. When you're tired of me, you can have a lassie of your own and weans.'

Wystan says, 'I was engaged. She found out about me. And I was sad about it, but also relieved. It's you who will grow tired of me . . . You'll find your lassie and our time together will be something you never talk about.'

Gregory, though unworldly, is not stupid. Everything that is wrong in his life is for want of cash, of employment. Wystan has both of these – how can he not be the happiest man on earth?

The ferry pulls into Coulport pier, performing a nimble turn on the spot and unsteadying the boatman as he gets into position to throw the rope.

The shore of Loch Long is an unspoilt series of inlets and bays, and soon they find themselves in a deserted spot, where Wystan lays down his jacket and gets out the hipflask and sandwiches.

When they have finished eating and passed the flask between them, Wystan stretches and lays his hat over his pale face. Gregory says, 'Let's have a swim!'

'It'll be bloody freezing!' Wystan protests, but Gregory is already hoicking off his shoes and trousers. 'Come on, Wiz!'

Wystan wants simply to sit and watch his friend cavorting in the shallows, but there is something about the boy's enthusiasm which cuts away at his inhibitions. He stands and removes his clothes, then thinks, 'Oh, fuck it,' and runs into the sea himself, the cold sending aching shocks up his legs. He giggles and screams at the same time. 'It's the frozen fjord!' he cries as Gregory splashes him. There is no one to see them playing beneath the hot, welcoming sun.

Then, Wystan notices a kind of cloudiness in the water, blurred circles advancing towards them. 'What's that?' he asks, pointing, but it is too late, the ache of the cold water is replaced by the searing agony of a jellyfish sting. Not one, but three, four, all down his thighs.

Wystan screams for real and hares out of the water, not noticing the mussel shells and barnacled stones that cut his feet. He crumples on the beach, clutching his leg and sobbing with the pain.

'Jesus, Greg! It's jellyfish!'

Gregory is already by his side, and strikingly calm. He bends over his writhing friend and winces as he examines the angry stings.

'That's a bad one, Wiz,' he says. 'Look, I know what to do. Stretch your leg out.'

Wystan tries to do so, partially accomplishes it, retches from the pain. His naked friend stands near, and, after a moment of concentration, urinates a vast, steaming jet all over Wystan's leg.

Wystan shrieks.

'It's what you do! Piss over a jellyfish sting. Cancels it out. Any fool knows that.' Gregory starts to laugh, sending the jet in spurts, which miss their target.

'You bloody maniac!' Wystan cries, but it's true, the pain is subsiding slightly, or at least the angry, scraping part of the pain. The mass of redness is differentiating into four red points.

'Aye, you'll live!' Gregory says, and, giving himself a shake, turns and starts getting dressed.

'What do I do now? Put my clothes on, stinking of piss?'

Gregory shrugs, still laughing. 'Rinse it off! You're wailing like a girl!'

Wystan hobbles to the edge and flicks cold water over his leg. His teeth chatter. The water soothes, like ice on a burn. When he turns, limping like a hurt child, Greg is there with his arm out for him to lean on, and he takes it and pulls his friend close. Wystan feels suddenly reckless – perhaps the pain has seared away any inhibition – and, without checking first, he kisses Gregory, feels the warm damp of his mouth on his own. For a moment, Gregory's response is complete, and Wystan forgets the pain in his leg, he forgets everything except their breathing and kissing, their chilled skin pressing together. But it lasts just a moment before he snaps instinctively away, for it is daylight and, never mind that they are apparently in the middle of nowhere, a fishing boat could go by, a person could bring their dog on to the beach. The hard fact of daylight turns the thrill into an ache of unsatisfied longing.

As Wystan gingerly pulls on his clothes, the sun vanishes behind a cloud. A fat drop lands on the back of his neck; when he looks up, he receives a face full of rain. It comes from nowhere, as instantaneous as a tropical fall. When they had set off, the sky was cloudless, and, of course, Wystan has not brought anything waterproof. He has not been on the west coast long enough to understand that there are often four seasons in one day, and the unsettled weather is amplified by the Gulf Stream running nearby.

Just ahead of them on the road is a tiny church made of tin, barely larger than his bedroom at Larchfield. It has a small steeple, and light glints on the corrugated roof as if it were solid silver.

Around it, the weeds have been cleared and a neat path leads to the door.

'I don't go to church no more. I've got no Sunday best,' says Gregory.

'Never mind that. I'm soaked!' And Wystan pulls his friend by the hand, up the path to the door, which opens beneath his touch. The rain clattering on the roof is deafening. A fly drifts by the east-facing window.

The church can accommodate perhaps twenty people. A plain altar stands at one end. Gregory and Wystan sit down on a pew. 'Come here, my dear chum,' Wystan says, and he eases Gregory on to his lap and wraps his arms around him. Gregory sits a little awkwardly, a giant boy atop another. There is no room for both sets of legs and so Gregory rests his on the pew in front. They sit like this for several minutes, while Wystan tries to brand upon his memory the boy's warmth and the peace that he feels with his head buried against his side. Gregory's hand creeps over his, and Wystan lets it sit there, even as he feels a throb of fear in this little house of God, where, more than anywhere, he wants to feel right. Does God not see the love between them? Is God angry?

The door opens. Voices: two women. Wystan pushes Gregory off him; he tumbles heavily into a seated position beside him and their faces flame.

'Who are you?' one of the women calls from the door. The boys turn to see a small, swarthy woman with her hair in a straggly bun. A long, flour-stained apron reaches almost to the floor. Her companion is a beefy woman with strong arms. She is carrying a mop and bucket.

Wystan jumps to his feet. 'Wystan Auden, madam,' he says. 'And this is my friend, Gregory. We are visiting from Helensburgh and happened upon this church. Tell me, are you having a service soon?'

Gregory is looking resolutely at the flagged floor. A blush gleams at his ears.

'Yes, we are.' The woman with the mop gawps at Wystan. 'Are you stopping?'

'No,' says Gregory.

'Well, the rain's stopped now,' she says. 'We've a lot of work to do here before the service.'

'Of course, madam.' Wystan bows slightly and backs away. Gregory scuttles behind him. The wispy woman in the apron calls, 'Hey, you, young man.'

Gregory stops but does not turn.

'I'm sure I've seen ye. Are you Vance's boy?'

'No,' says Gregory and keeps walking.

'Ah'm sure I've seen ye. You're a long way frae home.'

'I'm no Vance's boy!' says Gregory, overtaking Wystan. He runs out.

The women exchange glances. The beefy one nods at Wystan. 'We don't see many strangers here. What are you doing with our lad Vance?'

'He's showing me round,' says Wystan.

Her companion shoos at Wystan as if he were an unruly dog. 'Off with you. No respect!' She calls out after Gregory: 'Now, you get home right away to your father.'

Wystan manages to exit the church without running – though, in truth, the women scare him. He catches Gregory up. 'I don't think they saw anything,' he says, putting his hand on his friend's arm, but Gregory brushes him off.

'They recognised me!' he hisses.

Wystan can think of nothing to say as they wait for the ferry. When at last they board, Gregory stands at the bow, his face rigid with shame.

The pass the return journey in awkward silence. Back in Helensburgh, Gregory mumbles a goodbye and strides away, and Wystan feels every soreness in his body and in his heart. How could he have been so stupid?

He goes straight to his room and writes to Christopher, this being the only thing that will make sense of what has happened.

TWENTY-SIX

Dora

'VIRGIL!' DORA CALLED FROM the front door to the dog. Let out for his morning pee on to the lawn, he often got lost in some smell or other, taking ages to return. Dora scanned the shadows of the garden for him.

Before coming to Paradise, Dora could not have identified a rhododendron. Now her garden was being swallowed by *ponticum*, the greedy invader. The hedge at the bottom of the lawn was closing fifteen feet high now, its fronds obscuring the horizon. The fat pink blossoms, which had seemed so exotic when she first saw them, were, she now knew, the hallmark of the feral plant. They indicated that, unchecked, the advance across the garden would proceed at more than a metre a year. More of them, meant to line the lawn, had sprouted into straggly trees, which cast a dead shade over the lawn. All that growth did nothing to screen Dora from the Divines, however; it seems to draw them in closer.

'Virgil! Come on, boy!' Dora called again.

Kit was in the kitchen, standing over the paper with a coffee. He was wonderfully rumpled; neither of them could face ironing, and he pulled his shirts out of the tumbler and put them on as they were. The lambswool jumper which Dora had bought him for their first Christmas had developed small holes. They had come to the conclusion that there was some kind of moth infestation in the chest of drawers. But Kit liked the jumper and wore it anyway.

A yelp, and Virgil came belting round the side of the house, tail between his legs. He flew past Dora and cowered in the corner of the kitchen.

'What the——?' Dora stepped out into the garden, better to see what had happened. She glimpsed Mo disappearing round the side of the house, clearly on her way back to her staircase. She was fully dressed and carrying a walking stick.

'What just happened to Virgil?' Kit had joined her on the door-step. 'He cries if I touch his side.'

'It was Mo!' said Dora. 'I just saw her with a stick. She must have hit him.'

'What?' Kit stepped outside and looked round the deserted garden.

Dora ran back through the house to the kitchen, just in time to see Mo's feet vanish at the top of the staircase. Triumphantly she returned to the hall. 'I just saw her go back up. It was her, definitely.'

Kit shook his head and knelt by the dog in the hall, gently stroking his ribs. Virgil had recovered a little and licked his hand, flinching when his side was touched.

'Poor boy . . . Nothing broken, eh?' He looked up at Dora. 'I think, from now on, we've got to take him out on a lead for a pee.'

'What are you talking about?'

'He's going to get himself into trouble if he's left to his own devices. Do you think he got stuck somewhere?'

Dora stared at him, dumbfounded. 'I just told you what happened. Mo was out there!'

'Did you see her hit him?'

'Well, no . . . but she definitely did something! Can't you see what she's doing? Controlling the garden. Trapping me in a smaller and smaller space.'

'No one can control us, darling. But we do need to be above reproach.' Kit looked at his watch. 'Got to go. I won't be late home.' He kissed her forehead. Dora accepted the kiss dully, only the white of her knuckles showing the rage which now gripped her.

There was movement upstairs and blurred voices. Terrence's, for once, had some volume. Perhaps he was questioning Mo.

Kit picked up his briefcase and, with a stroke to Virgil's head, was gone.

The morning continued to unfold, as every morning did, no matter what happened. Dora was feeding the baby in her arms, rocking her gently near the sitting-room window, while she looked out over the lawn. The rhododendrons were malign in some way, she was sure of it – they were the type of plant to surround a fairytale castle with an impenetrable barrier, while those inside slumbered their lives away, forgotten by the real world.

Virgil wheeled away from the window, where he'd had his paws up on the sill. He had returned to his usual activity of trying to connect the noise from upstairs to something he could see. It was slowly driving him mad that he could not. He trotted to Dora and pressed his nose into her lap, whining.

'Oh, Virgil, what are we going to do with you?' she murmured. The dog's distress was amplifying her own. Not only could he not come to terms with the noise from upstairs, but the procession of cars and strangers passing the windows and ambling down the drive completely confused him. He yapped at anyone who passed the window. In his hopeless way, he was trying to be a guard dog.

There was movement out in the garden: children were running on to the lawn. Dora blinked, wondering if they would disappear when she opened her eyes. They were still there. These must be the children of the Divines's friends; she had heard their voices and endured their pounding feet on her ceiling, but this was the first time she had seen them in person. Virgil rushed back to the window with an explosion of yapping, like the clashing of bin lids.

The scene on her lawn unfurled like a film with the sound down and her dog's barks replacing the soundtrack. There were *so many* children on the grass. Was it all the neighbourhood children as well? Two older girls – one with a cropped T-shirt that revealed her child's rounded belly, and one with a high ponytail around which was wrapped something like tinsel – started doing cartwheels towards each other. An overweight boy with hair clipped to an army fuzz kicked a football towards them. Behind them were the forms of many more children, climbing the straggly trees. The youngest was a toddler in pink frills and a hairband with bunny ears. She wobbled in the space, sucking her thumb and looking round uneasily. Then she burst into tears and ran off to the side.

What on earth were they doing?

'Virgil!' she said sharply, but he ignored her. Dora dragged herself to her feet and, with the baby in one arm, she grabbed the dog's collar and pulled him away from the window and off to the kitchen, where she locked him in. Returning to her chair, the barks, which were now the grief-stricken cries of an abandoned dog, seared through her bones.

Beatrice resumed drinking from her bottle. Could she feel her mother's heart pounding right next to her ear? For Dora was in the grip of a physical tumult in response to the sight of the children. Now, they were swarming on to the *Lady Maureen*, climbing up the sides and hauling each other up and running, squealing, up and down the deck. Then one of them yelled some kind of command and off they poured again, sweeping on to the lawn, filling the air with shrieks. Dora was paralysed: there was nowhere in the house where she could go to escape them. She was pinned to the spot, obliged to watch the children – and a voice in her head reminded her sternly that it is never the fault of the little children – trampling her lawn with complete contempt – although, every child is a child of God and we should be more like the children – how can she blame the children? But she did blame the children! Why did she have to care about the children? They did not care about her.

And that lawn was hers. It was the only space she had to look out at.

It was the only thing on earth that she owned.

Mo lumbered out. 'Time for a snack, kids!' she called and turned back with a smile at Dora through the window.

The children scampered down the lawn and round the side of the house and up the staircase, their countless shoes clanging on the metal.

Dora paced the sitting room, weeping, scratching again at the skin on her arms. Virgil circled and cried at her feet. He unequivocally concurred that there was danger infusing the very atmosphere. This was corroboration . . . but it was making everything worse, not better.

Dora took Beatrice into the master bedroom, whose single window was on the side of the house and offered no view of the lawn. She turned the stereo on loud to drown out the noise from upstairs and danced with the baby. She built a little tower of blocks to entertain her, which Bea toppled with a plump fist, cackling with delight. When it was time for Beatrice's midday nap, Dora checked the sitting-room windows and saw that all the children and Mo had gone.

She tucked the baby in to sleep and made a proper bed for Virgil in the kitchen. He curled up in the basket and seemed relieved to be shut away from the front of the house. Dora pulled on her boots and went out of the front door. She didn't know quite what she was going to do, but it was going to be something. She went into the tool shed. As she stepped into its mossy gloom, she felt suddenly very focused.

Amongst the tools that she and Kit had accumulated was an old handsaw. Beneath Dora's finger, the serrations were blunt. She would have had to press very hard to break the skin, and, for a moment or two, she stood fascinated as the little triangle of metal dipped into her fingertip, creating a dimple of pink. It was tempting to stay there and simply press harder, and observe what happened when the blade did break the skin. An hour or two might pass easily that way, and she would find out if she was squeamish or not; this was one of many things she did not know about herself anymore.

Dora carried the saw down the lawn to the hedge at the very end of the front garden. The hedge muffled the sea and obscured everything beyond the garden. She squinted at the branches, a crazed mixture of rhododendron and hawthorn, with trunks some four inches across. Her neck ached as she craned back far enough to see the tops, which leaned over in massive, neglected bulk.

Right in front of her was a rhodie trunk. Dora stuck the saw into a gap next to it and began to pull back and forth. The saw was blunt, but the action nevertheless tore into the bark. Dora's arms began to ache and it was soon a two-handed job. Cramp invaded her fingers. But she was halfway through the trunk, now, and it creaked and wobbled. Being so close to felling this first trunk gave Dora energy and she sawed harder, sweat breaking out beneath her T-shirt and on her face. When there was just an inch or so left, she grabbed the trunk and pulled it towards her, splintering it from its stump, tearing it free from the hedge with an almighty flurry of leaves.

Light gushed through the gap. The sea was visible, and briny air swept across Dora's cheeks. For a moment, she forgot her troubles as she realised the potential. The hedge was some sixty feet long, with perhaps forty trunks to be sawn. If she did this, and reduced the height to the normal six feet all the way along, they would be able to see out. They would have light. Dora would have a view!

It did not occur to Dora that this was a job of gargantuan proportions, one that needed several people, motorised saws and some kind of exit strategy for all the branches. All Dora saw was light. Escape.

She dragged the rhododendron trunk to the middle of the lawn, glancing at the trees lining the drive. If she cut those too, the garden would come alive. They were much bigger, though; they would require her to climb up into their branches like a tree surgeon and slice her way down.

But that was possible. Suddenly, things were *possible*.

Dora was excited now. She picked up her new friend, the blunt saw, and selected her next target. There were two hours until Beatrice would need to be woken. She paused and strained her ears to hear a cry, but there was nothing. Knowing that the only thing between her and relief was the constraint of her own body galvanised Dora like nothing else.

Glancing up at the house, she saw Mo at the window. The old lady was watching with binoculars. Normally, this would have frightened or enraged Dora, but now, strangely, it was encouraging. Dora started on the next branch, and then the next, and in two hours she had cleared fifteen feet, and created an enormous pile of trunks and branches.

Dora's legs and arms burned with scratches. Leaves and thorns filled her hair. She made the long trek back to the house, forgetting, for once, to check the upstairs window. Beatrice was still deeply asleep, and Dora lifted her warm shape to kiss the little cap on her head. 'Sorry, my love, for not checking you,' she whispered. 'But Mummy has made light in the garden!' Dora's skin was smeared with dirt and blood and smelled of the earth. Her baby smelled of sleep and milk. It was a delicious mixture, which suddenly felt right, strong. Dora released Virgil from the kitchen and he followed them to the sitting-room window. She slipped the teat into Bea's mouth, and, with the dog at her feet, gazed at the rectangle of dazzling light she had made.

A little later, Dora took the baby out to admire her handiwork. Close up, the pile of branches was unbelievable, as if some kind of miracle had taken place and something, some*one* had been vanquished.

Perhaps some red shoes might be poking out from under the branches. Anything was possible.

Dora and Beatrice were still outside when Kit drove in from work. He saw his wife sitting on the lawn with his daughter, the saw glinting in the sunlight, and he brought the old Volvo to a sharp halt. Clambering out, his gaze travelled from the hole in the hedge, to the massive pile of logs, like a pyre, then to Dora.

'Oh my God,' he said.

She would have preferred congratulation, an embrace, some recognition of the superhuman achievement that had taken place in their garden. But, perhaps, if you come home from a normal day at work and find your wife streaked with blood, a saw by her side and the jagged devastation of your garden's trees, you are more likely to do as he did, which was to approach Dora carefully and say, 'Is Beatrice all right?'

TWENTY-SEVEN

Wystan

IT IS JUST EIGHTEEN months since the Paisley cinema disaster took the lives of seventy children, causing a pall to fall over the whole area and the Prime Minister to offer his condolences and new regulations to be put in place for all cinemas. Children go to the cinema alone in the early 1930s, to the early-morning showings, for a penny or two, piling in and shuffling and giggling in the comparative warmth. The Paisley cinema held 500 children; when the gelatine in the film caught fire, most of them were trapped in the ensuing inferno.

Wystan's idea for the boys to go to the cinema on a Saturday morning in the summer term is met with frowns and the shaking of heads. 'They can't go alone, you see,' says Mr Perkins, with a sigh. 'You'd have to take them. And, of course, then we should have to bill the parents for the cost, and they probably won't settle up, like always, so it ends up being a tremendous danger and expense.'

'I don't mind taking them, sir. They are showing *Dawn Patrol*. Douglas Fairbanks. They will love it. And, if we go to the early showing, it is just tuppence.'

'Hmm. They'll be wanting all those lemonades and sweets as well.'

'It's nearly the summer holiday, sir.'

Mr Perkins sighs. 'I hope you are devoting as much energy to their lessons as you are to their entertainment.' He rubs his rheumy eyes. Wystan takes this as a yes, and gives a small bow as he leaves the office.

He tells the boys at assembly the next morning that there will be a trip to Helensburgh's cinema, La Scala, the following Saturday. Day boys are welcome to come, if their parents will allow. Mr Auden will be looking after the party and everyone should assemble at the Larchfield gates at 9.30 a.m. sharp. The film is *Dawn Patrol*.

There is excited murmuring and a couple of muted cheers. Wystan notices his standing in the classroom has increased with immediate effect. Uncle Wiz may be weird, but he has an appreciation of amusement.

Later that day, on his afternoon off, he meets Gregory at their usual place at the railway station. It's a sultry afternoon and, as ever, there is nowhere for them to go, so they set off along the promenade, as they often do, a suitable distance between them. 'How about the cinema on Saturday?' Wystan asks.

Gregory glances down at his threadbare clothes. 'Will they let me in?' he says.

Gregory is very lean – leaner, Wystan thinks, than when they met – but still has the strong physique of the burgeoning working man. In particular, his legs are beautiful, pushing at the thin fabric of his clothes. He has an earthy sort of anger about him too, as if he wants to hit someone, but can't really be bothered.

'Wait in here.' Wystan pushes open the door of Marcello's

ice-cream parlour and coffee shop. He puts a note in Gregory's hand. 'Have what you want and I will be back shortly. And make sure you keep the change.'

Mr Marcello looks doubtfully at the pair from behind the counter, until Wystan says, 'This is my cousin. Give him whatever he wants.'

What Gregory wants, it turns out, is waffles with ice cream, syrup and sugar, followed by cocoa with cream and a long spoon. He is nearing the bottom of the glass when Wystan reappears, flushed and out of breath, carrying a small suitcase.

'Take this into the men's room.'

The owner wipes his hands on his apron. 'What you doing with that case?'

'My cousin's been working and needs to change.' Wystan turns to face the baggy-eyed Italian and says, with icy politeness, 'Is that all right?'

'We're not a changing room,' mutters Mr Marcello. 'This is family place.'

'There's no one here,' Wystan points out. 'Can I have a cup of coffee, please? While I'm waiting?'

The coffee machine whirs and spits, and Wystan settles himself into one of the booths. He has just taken his first gulp when the door opens and Gregory emerges, transformed. The clothes hang a little on his hungry frame, but he and Wystan are the same height and the brown wool suits Gregory. With a shirt, he looks like a professional of some kind. He has run water through his hair and slicked it back.

Wystan will have to send home for more clothes, but it doesn't matter. Gregory smiles shyly and sits down, rather uncomfortably. He has clearly never worn a proper suit in all his life.

Sipping his coffee, acutely conscious of Mr Marcello, barely ten feet away and studying them intently, Wystan says, 'I'm taking the boys to the 10 a.m. showing of *Dawn Patrol* on Saturday. Now you can come.'

Gregory runs his fingers over the wool jacket. He nods in agreement, and the two young men finish their drinks in awkward silence.

As he walks home, Greg scans the busy street, in case there is someone he knows. They would wonder how he got such clothes. His parents will ask. He will say he was given them by a master at the school, in return for some labour about the garden. Gregory swings the suitcase a little, as though it held more of the same items and not his tattered rags.

On Saturday, Gregory presents himself at La Scala, pays his money and slips into the gloom. He is early, but he knows Wystan will be along very soon, as he too likes to be punctual. It is already quite full. Gregory seats himself in the middle of a swathe of empty seats, ready to move to wherever Wystan decides. As he does so, there is loud shushing. Here they come, the Larchfield boys, all done up in their uniforms and caps, their voices loud and entitled in the tiny space. Boys shove other boys; there is sniggering. Gregory searches for the towering figure of Wystan, willing his friend to see him.

'Over that side, boys. Take up those rows.' The boys fill the rows in front, not noticing the extra man sitting next to their master. Soon, there will be more piling in: local children, the unemployed, with just a few pence to spend. A young couple settle themselves beside Wystan and are soon completely absorbed in each other, waiting for the lights to go down so they can start necking. By the time the film starts, the little provincial theatre will be jammed.

Miss Greenhalgh is pounding the piano at the front. She plays for the theatre and the church in her spare time. At last, the boys jumping about like squirrels, the lights go down completely and Miss Greenhalgh slips away. The velvet curtains slide open and the newsreel commences.

At the interval, the boys clamber over each other to buy sweets from the lady with her tray, standing in the gloom at the front. Wystan buys a large packet of bonbons to share with Gregory.

Wystan tries to relax into the film; surely it should be easy with Douglas Fairbanks fifty times his normal size on the screen. Gregory sits rigidly beside him in Wystan's suit and Wystan yearns to touch him, to abandon all thoughts of being in a public place and simply follow his feelings. It is strange to see his clothes inhabited by a body so much lovelier than his own. It is as if the clothes were made for Gregory, and Wystan has been occupying them, like some kind of invading force.

Heroic act upon heroic act unfolds on the screen. The hated flight commander tries desperately to stop the suicide missions. The hard-bitten pilots dull their fear with drink and attempt flight after flight. Finally, Douglas Fairbanks' friend, Courtenay, takes his place on a flight to save him. When Courtenay is killed, the camera lingers on Fairbanks' handsome face as it resists overwhelming grief. And, throughout, the planes roar in the skies – tiny, skittish things that can transport one into forbidden worlds as surely as words can.

Wystan is transfixed by the glamour, the bravery and the sheer dizzying freedom. From time to time, Gregory's hand slides into the packet of bonbons between the seats. A sideways glance reveals that Gregory, too, is enraptured by the film. Wystan leans in a little against him. When the hands of the couple beside him slide towards each other, Wystan lets his own hand slide down beside Gregory's thigh, where it cannot be seen, but can feel his warmth. Gregory does not move away. He chews and stares at the film, bovine in his absorption.

Wystan's venture has gone perfectly; here is his friend, beautifully dressed and devastatingly handsome, right beside him. There are the boys, entertained as they rarely are. It is a memory to turn over forever.

However, a feeling has taken stronger hold over him lately: in comparison to these men in the film, he is a coward. He has saved no one and can imagine dying for no one. All he can do is this: feed bonbons, in the dark, to a boy dressed as himself.

It's disgusting.

Then Gregory turns to him and smiles in the silvery darkness.

Wystan is as close to him as the boy and girl on his other side are to each other. The couple are slurping and rustling, and he longs to put his hands over his ears.

Helensburgh has eyes everywhere. It is a policeman. It is full of spies.

Why should he be stuck in this prison of immaturity, of secret touches and meaningful glances?

Please help me, Uncle Harry, he asks of the darkness.

As the lights go up, he bids goodbye to Gregory as if they were strangers, and motions to the boys to form an orderly line. He does not look back at his friend, the lovely version of himself he has abandoned in the cinema.

It has been a thrilling experience for the boys. They chatter all the way up the hill. 'Thank you, sir. Terrific, sir,' they say as they stream in for lunch.

Back at the school, Olive delivers a message that Mrs Perkins would be extremely grateful if Mr Auden would go up to her room for a moment. When Wystan arrives, ready to tell her all about the film, he finds her waiting at the window, rather subdued.

She offers him a measure of gin and he sits in his usual spot. The daybed creaks and puffs dust into the air.

Daphne wastes no time. 'Wystan, dear, I've got something to tell you. I'm getting to you first, as it were. There's been a complaint.'

This is not what he was expecting. 'Complaint?'

'Yes. It has gone straight to Mr Perkins and he's taking it very seriously. I'm hoping we – you and I – can come up with some sort of mitigation before he calls you in.'

'Good Lord. What is it?'

'It's, ah . . . It's about the young man you went on a trip with . . . Mr Perkins has received a letter from the minister of the church out near Coulport, complaining that the two of you were . . . behaving in a suspicious manner there.' Daphne sips her drink. Her hand is trembling.

'It was raining! We took shelter!' Flushed, Wystan gabbles in a way he never normally does, being very considered in his speech. He takes a breath, endeavouring to slow down. 'Gregory is a friend of mine from the town. He has been showing me round the area; he's born and bred here, you know. It rained and we took shelter in the tin church. Delightful place. I don't understand how that is in any way suspicious.'

'Wystan, darling . . .' Daphne reaches out and pats his knee. 'We all know what people are like, especially those lot, out in the villages. But, the fact is, Mr Perkins has to take any allegation of impropriety very seriously. The rolls are falling, as you know. We can't have even a whiff of scandal.'

'I cannot help it if people are determined to make up a scandal.'

'Indeed. Nevertheless, when we're in charge of other people's children, whose parents are paying – supposedly – there can be no impropriety, or even perception of it.'

'It was raining,' Wystan repeats dully.

'Of course. Of course,' says Daphne. 'The reason I've asked you up here is to try and find a plan. A way out. I'm the last person who wants to see you go.'

'Go?'

'Well, yes. Any misconduct means immediate termination of employment, dear. Really, I'm very worried.'

Wystan lays down his glass on the table. 'I am open to suggestions, of course,' he says.

Daphne claps her hands and leans over, excitedly. 'I already have a plan!' she says. 'We need a gardener here – the place is going to rack and ruin, and Hamish can't keep on top of it. But, of course, we can't pay much. I thought your friend could be an apprentice gardener, see how he likes it. If he's on the staff – well, everything makes more sense, doesn't it?'

'Will Mr Perkins accept that?'

'He already has. Jobs are so scarce that Mr Vance's parents were immediately in favour and no one wants to see a local boy with nothing.'

'That is a good plan. I think he will be very keen.'

'I am so glad you think so. I thought you might suggest he comes to see me and I will make him the offer.'

'So, he would be here every day?' Wystan's delight threatens to betray itself. To see Gregory every day; to look down from the window and see him in the garden. To share lunch with him.

'Well, no; everything is short time, as you know. But I think we can have him here three days a week and he will learn such a lot from Hamish.'

There is a pause. Wystan says, quietly, 'Thank you.'

Daphne leans forward, her dress rustling against her thin frame. 'But Wystan, dear, it is I who should thank you. You've no idea how I have been left up here, for years and years. They all laugh at me, I know: "If she's so ill, why hasn't she died already?" and so on . . . But you have taken an interest in me from the start. You are alone too . . . solitary.'

'You've been a very good friend to me, Daphne.'

'Now, of course, you must be very good while Gregory is here. You know that, don't you?'

'There will be nothing to observe,' says Wystan gravely. He hates himself for being so accepting, even while he is grateful to Daphne. To be scolded like a dirty child – it is unbearable.

'Mr Perkins and I are very tired. It is difficult to run the school under these circumstances, as you can imagine.' Daphne gives a rasping cough. Her eyes wander round the room as if she has forgotten her train of thought. She brightens. 'So, Wystan, we know what we're doing?'

'We do.'

'Little puff on my inhaler?'

Daphne hands him the machine and he takes a deep breath. His anger vanishes in a flash of clarity, and he takes his leave from Daphne in a much better humour.

On the stairs, he passes Jessop, who says nothing but gives a little smile to himself. How much does he know?

Wystan gets past him as quickly as possible and locks himself in his room.

TWENTY-EIGHT

Dora

Dora had made a wonderful discovery: the garden needed all the energy she had. It absorbed all her ideas, her creativity, her fears and more. She could exhaust herself in forcing order upon it. And, most importantly, her efforts made a difference.

The gap of light in the hedge had grown, as had the pile of branches on the lawn. For the last few days, the weather had cleared sufficiently for her to see where else she might tackle. There was a new hazard, something that the postman had spotted. He thrust out an arm in horror: 'Knotweed!'

Knotweed? Dora knew the name. It cast dread into the hearts of homeowners and mortgage companies. It was the most successful invasive species in Britain. It was almost impossible to eradicate and could grow through concrete. Her own specimen had recently flowered, and trailed downy chains of white blossoms from – oh, God, now she realised the full enormity – eight feet high.

The postman shook his head in pity. 'I don't know how you'll ever get rid of that,' he said. 'My parents couldn't sell their house when they found knotweed in it.'

But Dora had secateurs and gloves and the most powerful domestic liquid weed killer available. It wasn't going to get the better of her. She was on her knees, having hacked off the branches, and was now delicately pouring highly concentrated weed killer into the open necks of the stems. So, when the gate opened and a car slid unobtrusively along the drive, she was so absorbed, she barely noticed.

The car door slammed, making Dora jump. Out stepped two women – one, a chubby blonde in a beanie hat, the other with a trench coat that drifted from her shoulders as if from a coat hanger. They gazed around the garden and then rang the bell. The dog barked frenziedly and Dora downed her tools quickly, because she didn't want him to wake Beatrice from her two-hour nap in the middle of the day.

'Hello,' she said, walking towards them, rubbing the worst of the mud from her hands. 'Can I help you?'

The angular one had pink lipstick, which bled into the lines round her mouth. She seemed to be in charge. She said, 'Mrs Fielding?'

'Yes?'

'Can we come in?'

'And you are . . . ?'

The beanie-hatted woman pointed at the wisteria enthusiastically. 'Oh, wisteria! I've tried to grow it round my door for years. But the wind . . . it just rips it off! You'll have to tell me your secret!'

'We're from the child protection department of the local authority,' said the older woman, over the dog's frenzied barking. 'I'm Naomi

Haggith, and this is Lavender McCallum.' As she said this, she winced, as if she was accustomed to the blast of incomprehension which followed.

'Are you looking for Mrs Divine?' Dora said. Mo had worked with children, so perhaps these people were friends of hers.

'No, we've come to see you.'

'Oh.'

As Dora opened the door, Virgil stopped barking and instead rushed out at the new guests, bouncing all over them.

'He's harmless,' Dora said, for the millionth time. 'But I'm sorry about the jumping.' Lavender bent to pat him, which excited him even more. 'Get down!' Dora shouted. She was so used to screaming at the dog, she forgot that it was quite terrifying to the uninitiated. Even more terrifying was when Kit shouted at him. It hardly ever happened, but when it did, it felt like the world freezing. Except to Virgil, who mostly ignored it.

'So, where is Beatrice today?' asked Naomi Haggith, looking round the hallway.

It startled Dora that they even knew she had a baby, let alone her name, and, rather irritably, she said, 'She's having her nap.'

'Alone with the dog? While you're out in the garden?'

Dora tried to ignore her alarmed tone. 'She's in her nursery. In a cot,' she said. She indicated the sofa for them to sit down. Lavender adjusted the cushions to make a sort of nest and curled her legs under her.

'Shouldn't we check on Beatrice?' Naomi said, not sitting down.

'Why? She's asleep. She has about twenty minutes left.'

'Mrs Fielding, we have had a report – well, an expression of *concern* – about your baby.' Naomi rocked back on her neat little heels. She didn't want to waste any time.

'From Mrs Divine, I assume.' Dora rolled her eyes up towards the ceiling. 'She hates me.' Dora's heart leapt slightly – would this be the chance to show the truth about Mo? After all, an accusation like this levelled at them was ludicrous and any fool could see the motivation. They seemed like intelligent women. Dora said, 'My neighbours are trying to drive me out. I think they want our house.'

Naomi said, 'All concerns are passed on anonymously. That's so we can act on them safely. Now, the concern has been expressed about neglect of your baby.'

'What do you mean?'

'Can we go and check on Beatrice, please?' Naomi moved towards the door. Lavender placed a plump hand on Dora's shoulder. 'Sorry about this,' she said.

'Did Mo ring you up? Do you know her?' Dora followed them – followed them, in her own house! – towards the nursery. Naomi's bony body moved authoritatively beneath her coat. Was this something to do with that health visitor?

'As I said, all calls are anonymous. I'm sure you understand why.'

'No, I'm not sure I do understand why.' Dora scurried after Naomi's retreating figure and opened the nursery door.

Lavender, clearly in training and not entirely comfortable with this visit, said, 'Mo goes to our church. Lovely woman. Works tirelessly for the Sunday school, you know?'

No one was going to reach Dora's baby before she did. She overtook Naomi, who was approaching the cot. Just as Sorcha had done,

Naomi leant possessively over the side, and then, without a word, reached in and lifted the sleeping baby from her blankets.

'What are you *doing*?' Dora fluttered round her uselessly.

Naomi was muttering soothing noises into Bea's ear, which was waking her. Naturally enough, she began to cry.

'Give me my baby,' Dora said, forcing her fingers round Beatrice and taking her from the social worker. Naomi's lips parted in disbelief.

'The report we received is that you leave her alone a lot with a dog wandering around – a dog which bites. And the baby cries a lot, seemingly in great distress, and you and your husband shout a lot.'

'Is this about Sorcha? She upset the baby! In front of my husband – so there's a witness!'

Naomi folded her arms and said nothing.

'I've got a dog,' Lavender said, to fill the frozen silence. 'A Labrador.'

'And my dog does not bite!' Dora knew her face was red, her voice stretched. 'He's a stray and has no manners, but he has never bitten anyone in his life.' Virgil had wandered in and was sitting next to Lavender, gazing up at her with his liquid, stray-dog eyes.

Naomi studied the nursery. Because Beatrice had come so early, Dora and Kit had had to prepare it in one day. It was bright and cheerful, but very badly painted. On a bookshelf were dozens of baby-care books. Naomi waved her arm in front of them. 'You know everything in these books has been discredited? You know it's cruel to leave a baby to cry? Our policy is on the GP's wall – we support mothers with demand-led breastfeeding.'

'But she's premature! She couldn't demand feed – or breastfeed!'

Dora couldn't believe she was having this argument again. Was she – the thought whirled in her brain – was she not a mother, after all? Did Beatrice not actually belong to her, as her house did not seem to belong to her? Dora blinked heavily. Fear was making her dull.

'Let me call my husband.' Clasping the baby, she went out into the hall and rang Kit at work. The phone went to voicemail. Beatrice mumbled in her ear. Dora could smell her sleepy warmth. 'He's not answering!'

Naomi's tone was very calm, as if she sensed victory over a frightened animal. 'No matter. I'm only here to make my report, at this time. You know, you mustn't leave a baby alone like this, especially with a dog. And your refusal to engage with the health visitor's services is very concerning.'

'Sorcha? I didn't need her anymore. I'm fine – we are fine. Look at her – she's in perfect health.'

'She is a premature baby, extremely vulnerable. She needs these support services, people looking out for her.' Naomi looked at her watch. 'Now, I need to examine her.' She held out her arms expectantly.

'No,' Dora said. 'She's half asleep and completely fine. I know what is happening here. I want you to leave.'

Naomi tilted her head and regarded Dora gravely, while Lavender absented herself back into the sitting room. 'Am I to understand you have refused to allow me to examine the child?'

'Absolutely. And I have asked you to leave.'

'You realise all this goes into my report and feeds into my recommendations. You have to see, Mrs Fielding – it doesn't inspire confidence that you are so aggressive and unwilling to engage. If there is nothing wrong, why won't you let me examine Beatrice?'

'It's a malicious report! You know it is.'

'I know no such thing. We try very hard to protect children, and we take all reports from concerned people very seriously. We are lucky to have many good people around here who take it upon themselves to look out for little children. And, I have to say, your attitude does worry me a great deal.'

There was a creak upstairs. Of course, they were in the hall, where everything could be heard by the neighbours. Beatrice reached out to Naomi with a fat hand and chattered gamely to her. Naomi stroked the child's cheek, then returned to her point. 'I think you are under great mental strain and this is impacting on your ability to care properly for your baby. I personally believe that your child does need protection.'

'From who?'

'I am going to recommend a care plan for your family. And you will need to go on the register.'

'What register?'

'The child protection register.'

Lavender shuffled into view. 'Naomi,' she said, 'the baby does seem perfectly okay.'

Beatrice was jiggling in Dora's arms now, wanting to get down and play with the new friends.

Dora clutched Beatrice, too tightly. The baby gurgled and mewed. 'We are not going on any register. We are absolutely fine. Except for my neighbour trying to drive me out of my home! Ask my husband!'

It was as if she had not spoken. This was what happened every time she tried to protest about Mo, or indeed protest about anything.

'We know, don't we, Lavender, how children can hide their pain.

Many in our profession have learnt that to their cost.' Naomi laid a hand on Beatrice's head, and then strode out, her coat swaying like a cape.

Lavender tickled Beatrice under the chin. 'Aren't you a bonnie one?' she cooed, and then they were climbing into the black car and grinding down the drive. Not knowing what she was doing, Dora ran out into the garden with Beatrice in her arms. The car had gone and she stood alone with her child in the centre of the lawn. When she looked up, Mo was standing in the window, gazing down at her and smiling.

TWENTY-NINE

Wystan and Dora

IT WAS NOT EASY to find a good open spot in the garden. Olive wandered round the sprawling rhododendrons, looking for a clearing, while Wystan paced the gravel in front of Larchfield, waiting for Gregory to appear. He was overdressed in a shirt, bow tie, fedora and jacket. Overdressed in the sense that it was warm, not in a smartness sense, for everything was worn or stained.

Olive called that she had found the right place. They were to have their picnic beneath the monkey puzzle tree, which cast a spiky, incomplete shade. Rhododendrons tumbled everywhere; how wonderful they must have been once. Gregory would have his work cut out for him, that was for sure. Dora craned round to see the new apprentice, not knowing quite what to expect.

The gardener, Hamish, hobbled over and exchanged a few words with Wystan. He was slight and wiry and, when he lifted one hand to swat a fly from his face, Dora saw he was missing two fingers.

She was distracted from wondering what had happened to Hamish by the frisson that accompanied the arrival of Gregory. Wystan quivered like a giddy young girl. The boy was quite ordinary, it seemed to Dora, but in that ordinariness she could see something of what Wystan saw. Gregory was a perfect example of the young, energetic unemployed one saw around the town, with a kind of rough charisma, burnished by his being out of his element. Down on Clyde Street, idling the day away with ha'penny toss and his friends, he would have seemed much less exciting.

The three of them stood talking for a few moments, though it was clear that the only one who really existed for Wystan was Gregory. Longing filled his expression; first, one hand came out to touch Gregory's arm, then another. Wystan's head bobbed this way and that so as not to lose eye contact with his friend, whose own gaze moved from the ground to the trees, hardly ever settling on Wystan. It was both exciting and pitiful to see the young poet so enslaved. The moment when Gregory responded, and, for a brief second, brushed Wystan's fingers with his own, sent a shock through Dora as it did Wystan.

At last, the conversation having been stretched for as long as it could be, Hamish took his new worker off to start his duties and Wystan reluctantly left to collect Daphne from her room.

Daphne had grown very thin and had a stoop. A plait was untidily coiled on her head and wisps drifted round her long face. As the party reached the spread tablecloth, Wystan winked at Dora.

At their feet was a wicker basket with sandwiches, pickles, fruit and cake. There was some stout for Daphne, as it was meant to fortify her, and some lemonade for Wystan. Olive unpacked everything and laid it out, then left them to it. This whole venture was ostensibly for Daphne. For Wystan, it was an opportunity to be with Gregory in the garden whilst remaining above suspicion.

'So, I'm chaperone,' said Daphne, leaning back in her folding chair, exhaustion all over her face.

'Indeed,' sighed Wystan, combing the garden for a glimpse.

Bursting out from a group of weeds was a knotweed plant. Dora couldn't believe she had not seen it before. It was huge, perhaps eight feet high and with a spread of nearly twice that. She noticed among their shoes the beginnings of new shoots. Knotweed propagates with shoots under the earth, and from broken stems. All the plants in Britain are female, and so the seeds are infertile – only this stopped knotweed from taking over completely.

Dora was about to point this out to Wystan when Gregory appeared, stripped to the waist and bearing some shears. Hamish pushed the wheelbarrow with more tools: a scythe, spade, some large garden knives. Beside the young man, Hamish seemed even older.

'We're over here, Gregory,' Wystan said, pointing to the picnic gathering. 'Would you like a sandwich?'

'No, sir,' said Gregory, his freckled shoulders pearly in the sun. 'I have my piece in my bag.'

'Right-ho,' said Wystan, reluctantly. He turned to Daphne. 'You know the story of Hamish's hands?'

'His fingers?' asked Daphne.

'Yes – he cut them off himself! He got rheumatism so badly that he decided the only ones he really needed were the thumb and the first two, so he just cut the others off. Just like that!' Wystan made a chopping motion with his hands.

'Good Lord! He should have told us; we'd have had Dr Boyce look him over.'

'Said he didn't see the point of a doctor charging to tell him what he already knew. They couldn't be saved. Amazing, eh?'

Daphne shook her head. 'Poor Hamish.'

'Oh, he's fine. What is he? Sixty?'

'Seventy-five!' said Daphne.

Hamish had an enormous pair of loppers and was trimming some tall branches overhanging the wall.

They all sat in admiration of Hamish's wispy figure. Bees hummed around them, bumping into the blossoms. Dora dragged her attention back to the enormous invasive species she had just noticed.

'That's knotweed,' she said to Wystan. 'You've got to kill it or it will take over.' Dora pointed to the plant.

'Did you know that, Daphne?' Wystan asked. 'That's Japanese knotweed – an invasive species. We should kill it, or it will take over.'

'Nonsense,' said Daphne, sipping her stout. 'That's a very valuable ornamental. The original owners of the house put it in about twenty years ago, I think. We need to prune it a bit, to show it off.' She glanced hopefully at Gregory. 'Same with the rhodies. They are the best type, but Mr Perkins has not been concerned about the garden.'

'There's only one way to kill it,' Dora continued to Wystan. 'You have to break open the stems and pour poison down them.'

Gregory approached the knotweed with his shears and began to cut savagely at the purple stems. He tossed them behind him on a growing pile of vegetation. Wystan could not take his eyes off him.

And, actually, neither could Dora, for Gregory was, she realised now, beautiful. His paleness gave an air of vulnerability that contrasted with the sheer lean muscle of him. His hair caught the light and glowed a deep red as he worked. As Dora sat demurely on the blanket, she could not stop staring. She glanced at Daphne, who, even though probably dying, was also transfixed by the young man moving among the stems.

Silence fell over the party as Gregory paused to wipe his brow and then take up the scythe. Turning to a thicket to cut the worst of the growth, he glanced up and saw that everyone was staring at him, their sandwiches untouched. He grinned uncertainly before carrying on.

Dora unbuttoned her coat and a soft summer dress drifted out across her knees. Her notebook slipped from her pocket on to the grass. It fell open, revealing pages and pages of notes and lines. It was almost full. Words and ideas had been tumbling out since Wystan had given it to her.

Gregory's presence had unsettled something in Dora. Why did he have to come and disturb her feelings?

She must have said the words aloud, for Wystan turned to her and said, 'I have asked myself the same question every day since I saw him.'

'I see why you like him.'

Daphne took a fan out of her skirt and waved it gently in front of her face.

'A clever plan of mine, don't you think, Wystan?'

'I'm pleased the plan has benefits for others beyond myself.'

Daphne sighed. 'But we can only look, dear. You know, like a shop window.'

'Stout?' Wystan asked, and poured some out into Daphne's cup.

Dora took her notebook on to her lap, considering how she might encapsulate Gregory in it. This was the strange effect that the young man was having on Dora: his beauty was the sort that demanded to be expressed and distilled into words. Her eyes explored him minutely as she prepared in her imagination some kind of phrase that would bring him to life on the page. Dora was completely spellbound in this activity when she was brought back to the scene by a cough from Wystan.

'What?'

'You need to watch that tendency . . . writing instead of living.' He was studying her.

'But I want to get it down on paper. I *am* living. *This* is living.'

Wystan looked at her sadly. 'No, it isn't.'

The air was sweet and warm and she could hear birds in the sky. Why was Wystan spoiling it all?

Wystan chatted with Daphne. Their voices tinkled through the shade.

'Our heads are full of *so much*. And then it all gets swept away by the sight of a nice bit of flesh. Shop window, indeed! What am I to do with my feelings, if not act on them?'

Dora's thoughts were fuzzy, perhaps from the heat. Boys were streaming out for their break and laughter filled the garden. There was clattering in the undergrowth and Jamie appeared, red-faced and panting.

'Wasp, sir, miss; sorry, sir, miss – WASP!' and he pointed at Daphne's dress, on which a large wasp had settled. Wystan immediately removed his hat and thwacked it across Daphne's dress, sending the insect sailing off into the undergrowth. Daphne squealed and clutched her bosom.

'Jamie! Thank you! I mustn't be stung by a wasp. Dr Boyce said it could make me very ill indeed. Wystan, what quick reactions! Thank you.' She was quite breathless and Wystan topped up her cup with stout.

'Take your time,' he said. 'And why didn't you tell me about the wasp thing? Should we even be outside?'

'Well, that's just it! I never go out anywhere. I knew I wouldn't even get to have a wee picnic in the garden, if I told you.' She looked suddenly petulant, and Dora glimpsed the lovely, slightly spoilt young girl she must once have been.

'Come here, Jamie, lad. Have some cake.' And Wystan lifted the little boy on to his knee and hugged him with spontaneous joy. Jamie smiled shyly and wriggled into a comfortable position, from where he received a slice of cake and leant against the teacher's shoulder while he ate.

Contentment softened Wystan's features. He brought out his pocket watch and showed it to the boy, asked him the time and, when the boy got it right, made a big fuss of him. 'You know, he draws the most wonderful pictures, Daphne. I'm thinking he can design the cover of the next copy of the *Larchfieldian*. What do you say, Jamie?'

The boy nodded, his legs swinging happily. How good the poet was with the boy, Dora thought. Such easy kindness. When he had finished his cake, Jamie slithered down and headed off to play. Sadness flickered across Wystan's face, and his eyes, this time, followed not Gregory, but the little boy. And Dora felt it then, some great feeling in her gut that did not clamour to be written down, but simply revealed its existence: an emptiness, a nameless grief. She reached for Wystan's hand, for she was suddenly terribly afraid. Had she, as she feared before, done something, lost something? Someone?

Jamie was playing some complicated jumping game with another child, who, when she looked now, was a *girl*. She was about his age, with long red hair. She was wearing a school uniform, with a kilt and a blazer, not unlike his. How could there be a girl here?

The thing was, the girl seemed to know her. She turned to face Dora and waved.

'Wystan – who is that girl?'

But, when Dora looked again, Jamie was playing alone.

THIRTY

Dora

CREAMING. DIZZY, GIRLISH; IT could have been a man shot, or a rabbit in a trap. It scraped Dora's shoulder blades like a hook, yanking her from deep sleep.

A shriek beyond words; pure urgency.

Was it Dora herself?

Was it Beatrice?

Dora's eyes broke open. The room was black and dazzling. Dora's arm went out instinctively to Kit. His slumbering form was there, warm and still. The other hand went to her mouth, which was slammed shut.

Dora rolled out of bed, her head bearing the scream as if it were icy water. 'Beatrice!' she cried, bursting into the nursery. The cot lay in a pool of warm night-light. Dora fell towards it, in her blindness not realising that the screaming was not growing louder now; in fact, it was behind her. She had already seen, in her mind, the crib and her baby in it, screaming its last helpless defence, screaming for its mother, its useless mother, always asleep, always late . . .

Bea was a bump under the bedclothes, one chubby arm thrown back. A pink cheek rose above the blanket, then a fat, sleeping eye. Dora reached a trembling hand to the baby's face. It was warm.

She's asleep!

Dora sobbed in gratitude. Thank you . . . thank you, God . . .

But the screaming had not stopped.

Fucking hell. Now Dora was stumbling through the house, pulling wellies on to her bare feet in the gloom of the hall, fumbling for a torch. Virgil agitated at her side.

'What the hell is that noise?' asked Kit. He stood, rubbing his eyes, in the hallway.

'It's coming from outside.'

'Where's Bea?'

'Still asleep. I thought it was her, for a moment.'

Kit eased Virgil out of the way and pulled on his boots. 'Sweetie, I should go. You stay here.'

'No . . . I'm awake now.'

'Virgil – you're not coming!' The dog whimpered in frustration and scrabbled at the door behind them. Now Dora had risen above bare instinct into fear. Was someone being murdered? Was an animal trapped? Was it some kind of domestic dispute in the house next door?

Carefully, they walked out of the house, crossing the forecourt towards the noise, the wobbly beam of the torch pushing through the cool night.

The sound was coming from beyond the tool shed. Dora wished she had stayed indoors and rung the police; the sound was so visceral that it signalled a situation beyond ordinary help. Why was no one else awake? Why were no lights on upstairs?

Now the scream had an undertone: an angry vibration, like a saw. Jesus. The torch wavered.

Behind the tool shed was Virgil's favourite spot to pee and scruffle about. Kit reached round the doorframe and turned on the light. A weak bluish glow bathed the gravel and Dora dropped the torch.

It was Mo, twisting in the light, emitting an inhuman sound. The screams were coming from inside a pulsating black mass that was her head. Her arms were flailing beneath sleeves of – wasps? She could not see Dora, or Kit. She could not see anything.

More screams – Dora's, this time.

'Stay back here,' said Kit. In his hand was his phone. 'Call the ambulance, and shine the torch so I can see what I'm doing.' He pulled his dressing gown hood as far as possible over his head and approached Mo's stumbling figure.

Mo had long since abandoned any attempt to clear the wasps from herself. Kit dragged at the hissing treacle of them on her face. 'Roll on the ground!' he cried. 'Like it's a fire!' He pulled her on to the lawn and began to roll her from side to side. The wasps transferred to Kit like smoke, flowing up his hands and into the sleeves of his dressing gown.

'Which service do you require?'

'Ambulance! Paradise, Helensburgh! My neighbour has been attacked by wasps. My husband is—'

'What is your address, please?'

'Please, hurry. Please!'

Mo howled. Dora grabbed the torch from the ground and shone it on her husband, bent over the writhing neighbour, vainly scooping insects from her and throwing them to the ground. Mo's bare arm rose in the beam and was quickly submerged again.

Dora held the torch in two hands to keep the beam steady. Kit was crushing every insect his hands encountered, wiping them off like an oil slick and pressing their buzzing fury into the grass. Wasps seethed under his hood.

'Keep the light on me!' he cried hoarsely. The grass was glistening, a glistening that moved, for the wasps continued to drag themselves back to the swarm, even half dead. Mo had stopped moving now; only her guttural moans still indicated her suffering. Her eyes rolled white, like an animal's. Wasps buzzed in and out of her mouth. Kit reached inside and pulled them out, one by one, popping their venomous bodies like fuchsia buds.

Dora tried to say something, but her lips were furred with insects and nothing came out. Time had become demented, as if each second were a furious wasp, darting this way and that way, unconnected with anything else.

Then blue light reared towards them, there were footsteps and voices, and people in neon jackets were gently moving Dora out of the way.

'We've got it, love. Move back, move back.'

'Mo!' Terrence lumbered towards them, his pyjamas creased and flapping. 'I'm her husband! What is happening?'

'She's in good hands, sir, just keep back a second.' The paramedics knelt over Kit and Mo, doing something with sprays and blankets. Terrence craned over them, trying to see his wife. Mo was lifted on to a stretcher. She lolled helplessly, unresponsive to the man leaning in close to her, saying, 'Can you hear me? Mo? Mo?'

Kit appeared beside Dora, wrapped in a blanket. In the pale dawn light, he was almost unrecognisable, his face puffed and covered in weals, as if he'd been whipped. Dora gently pulled him to her and pressed her face against his shoulder.

'Virgil! How did you get out?' Kit bent down to embrace the dog, who leapt and licked at him. 'Bad boy,' he mumbled into the dog's ear.

'He must have jumped on to the door handle; it's not the first time. We're going to have to lock every door now,' Dora said.

'You just can't bear to be apart from us, can you, boy?' The dog panted and sneezed in excitement.

Terrence stumbled up to Kit, in his pyjamas.

'I didn't have my hearing aid in. I didn't hear a thing.' He looked stricken. He reached for Kit's arm. 'Did you save her? I should have heard her!'

Kit flinched as Terrence made contact with his tender skin. 'But what was she doing out here?'

'She wanders sometimes . . . especially lately. She hasn't been able to sleep.'

'But in our garden? In her nightdress?' Dora asked.

Terrence turned on her. 'It's you! She's frightened of you—'

'That's enough, Terrence,' interrupted Kit. 'I know you're upset, but—'

'Damn right I'm upset! She's allergic to wasp stings! Why have you got a wasp nest on your property?' Terrence's fury carried high in the early-morning air.

Kit sighed. 'We didn't have it installed especially, if that's what you're getting at.'

Dora walked away from them both, too close to tears to listen. She noticed Virgil peeing languorously in his favourite spot beside the tool shed, pacing up and down, sniffing.

Suddenly, the dog stopped sniffing and began to gulp at something. He was a born scavenger and Dora or Kit was always hauling him away from dead and rotten scraps out on walks. Instinctively, Dora ran to him, gasping, 'No!' and yanked the thing out of the dog's mouth. She was squeamish about all dead things, and appalled by the rotten dismembered corpses of gulls or fish or hedgehogs that her dog would gulp down with relish. As she lifted her hand to hurl it away, she saw in the poor light that it was a raw steak. A good one – not rotten – still bloody. Dora sniffed it. It smelled like a normal steak. She turned it over, and the other side had a blue-green tinge.

She tossed it into a hydrangea bush in the border and noticed, as she did so, that Terrence was observing her. His eyes followed the steak, then he turned back to his wife, bending over her face with its mask on, her curly hair, usually so neat, matted on the stretcher.

'Come on, Virgil!' Dora said to the dog and nudged him with her feet. He looked at her accusingly and then trotted back to Kit, who was talking to the paramedic.

'Are you all right? I can give you a shot, in case you have an allergic reaction,' the man was saying.

'No, I'm fine,' said Kit. 'I think I just need to rest.'

The paramedic's face was almost entirely made up of smile and glasses. 'Here –' he handed Kit a shiny packet – 'some serious pain relief.' He rested his hand on Kit's shoulder. 'Well done!' he said. 'Times like this, you need your neighbours!'

'What do you think of that, Terrence?' said Kit, looking round for the old man. 'Did you ever think the Fieldings would be saving the day?'

Terrence emerged from the border. He cleared his throat and thrust his hands into the pockets of his pyjamas. Dora was certain she saw him slip something into his right-hand pocket as he did so.

Her neighbour shook his head and climbed into the ambulance beside his wife. The vehicle started up, the blue light circling. For a moment, before the doors were pulled shut, Dora could see Terrence hunched over the stretcher, clutching his wife's hand.

'You're welcome!' cried Dora as the ambulance moved off.

Kit leant heavily on his wife and she led him back into the house. He winced as Virgil leapt and whined. 'Down, boy,' he said feebly.

'We're getting you to bed.' Dora led him to the bedroom and helped him off with his clothes. Wasps dropped from the folds of the dressing gown, some still sizzling with rage. Her husband reeked of insecticide. As he climbed carefully into bed, she went to get soothing cream from the nursery. She paused at the cot and looked down on her sleeping child. It was little short of a miracle that Beatrice would never know anything about this. As she watched her baby's little chest rise and fall in peaceful sleep, she thought about Mo. Terrence had said she was allergic to the stings. Perhaps she had died, right there before their eyes. Dora had never seen anyone die before. It was a horrible, magnetic thought.

She returned to Kit with the cream and, as the painkillers took effect, he began to drift off to sleep. She dabbed cream on to the worst bites. Dora rubbed some cream on her own wounds, but had no hope of sleeping. She made herself a cup of coffee and pulled her dressing gown around her, and slipped back out into the garden, with Virgil padding behind her.

Light was brimming at the horizon and it was, after all the chaos, very quiet. She shivered as she approached the spot beside the tool shed. The dog sniffed about, shying away from the few remaining wasps that were half alive. Dora sank down to the ground, holding Virgil to her.

'I thought . . . I thought it was Beatrice. I thought something had happened to my baby.' Dora began to cry, tears stinging her face. Virgil pressed his warm muzzle to her, briefly, but then pulled away and trotted, sniffing, across to the bush where she had thrown the steak.

Dora followed him. Though the dog could clearly still smell it, it was definitely not there.

So . . . Terrence watching her . . . then hiding the steak in his pocket . . . That was what she had seen!

She remembered the oddness of there being a fresh steak in Virgil's favourite spot. She remembered its strange tinge on one side.

At this, all the peace drained from the garden.

Her instinct was to go straight inside and wake Kit from his slumber. 'This is why Mo was in our garden! She came to lay poisoned bait for the dog. She knows that's his favourite spot. And Terrence knew – *I saw him hide it*.'

But she remained unmoving by the bush as the scene unfolded in her mind.

Kit, always considerate, always reasonable, would drag himself awake, still half delirious from the venom coursing through his veins, and he would try to pay attention as she pressed on him her garbled explanation.

'So . . . there is no steak now?' Kit would murmur.

'No – like I said, Terrence took it.'

'And the dog didn't eat any of it?'

'No! I grabbed it from him! Kit – Mo was trying to poison our dog!'

And he would sigh, turn over, defeated, and collide back into sleep. Or perhaps he would agree that, yes, that sounded really terrible . . . but, in the end, hadn't Mo come off worse? Got her punishment? And if the dog was all right . . . ?

And she would summon up, once more, the energy to protest, but it would do no good at all, because Kit had saved Mo's life and that was all that mattered. Dora had not contributed in any significant way to this heroic act and, therefore, anything she had done, any life she might have saved, any cruelty she now knew to be true, was eclipsed. Dora, now, was nothing and Kit was everything, and any truth that affected that balance no longer belonged here with them.

Dora called the dog and went back in the house and, in the kitchen, she scoured and scrubbed her hands until they were sore and bleeding. When she had finished, they were the roughened hands of a maid below stairs, who observes important events and is unable to change any of them, whose life is invisible to others, no matter how painfully real it may be, and who, above all, has learnt that survival depends on keeping her lips pressed shut.

Part Four

THIRTY-ONE

Wystan

W YSTAN WOKE EARLY THIS morning, intending to work, but, as he stands at his window, lighting a cigarette, he sees Daphne wandering about the misty garden. He blinks and looks again, and there she is, her hair untwisting from its pins and hanging in wet tendrils down her back, her housecoat dragging round her body like a curtain tangled round a pillar. There is something wrong with the scene; clearly, she has been out for some hours. After circling a few times, she starts to climb the massive yew tree in the corner. She vanishes into its knotted arms with just a glimpse of silvery housecoat through the grey of the air.

Perhaps she is undertaking an errand of some sort? He can't imagine what it would be. Daphne has been very listless of late, sitting quietly during their tea sessions, perking up only a little when she takes her inhaler. He has stopped taking this with her, because it moves him too far ahead. Instead, he has a quick breath of it when he is leaving, and then he skips into his room and to his desk.

A few evenings ago, he read her a little section from the long poem he is writing – he shows her a few things, from time to time – and she began to cry.

'What is it, Daphne?' He leant over to her and took her cool hand in his.

'I find it so sad. It's beautiful – brilliant, but so sad . . . I see my own condition in your airman. He will never know love, either, will he? Never have a child . . .'

'Probably not,' Wystan said. 'Although, as I have invented him, anything could happen.'

'But he's you, isn't he, dear? Or part of you, at any rate.'

Wystan blushed. 'I prefer to think of him as my obscure, brilliant invention. Is there nothing you don't see through?'

'I don't want you to have a life like mine, Wystan,' Daphne said. 'I can't tell you how quickly it passes. You look up from your lone-liness and . . . it's like I slept through the play of my life and woke up when the theatre was empty.'

Her eyes were feverishly bright. She leant right into him, close enough for him to notice the bittersweet smell of gin on her breath and the mustiness of her unwashed hair.

'Soon, I won't be myself. You may have to be unkind to me, and I know that is not in your nature.'

He stared at her. 'Daphne—'

'No, dear . . . I want you to know how much . . . how much joy our little chats have brought me. You are such a special young man. And I want to urge you to . . . find your love and hold on to it. Whoever it is. You may, of course, have to leave the country to do it.' She giggles.

'Let's go out. We could walk round the garden.'

'Not this evening, dear. I am a little tired. I am sorry to be so dull.'

Remembering this conversation, he realises he must go to her. He must get her out of that tree before the children see her and her humiliation is complete. Wystan does not bother with shoes or jacket, just shuffles down the stairs in his slippers and follows the trail her footsteps have left in the dewy grass.

'Daphne?' he calls from the bottom of the tree. Her skirts are just visible, and her shoes, with their tidy heel. But there is more up in the branches: planks, blankets, canvas sheeting. Mrs Perkins appears to have made some kind of tree house.

'Daphne? Mrs Perkins?'

She is perhaps fifteen feet above him, and now she is humming. Is it the school song? Or some Scottish ballad he doesn't know? It is quite difficult to tell; after each line, her breath fades and she coughs violently.

'Mrs Perkins, come down, won't you? The boys will be up soon.'

The humming stops and a face appears through the spiny green. It is both Daphne's face and not familiar at all. 'Why, Wystan!' she says delightedly. 'Would you care to join me?'

'I'd love to, of course,' says Wystan. 'But how about a warm cup of tea, first, in the house? We could get proper clothes on.'

'Oh, no, dear. I am really very busy – much too busy, in fact. Well, if you don't want to come up, could you run along?' And the humming begins again.

Jessop is at the rain gauge, taking a reading for his class. He has been there the whole time and has observed this exchange with amusement.

'Jessop, can you help me get Mrs Perkins down?'

His colleague shakes his head, tucking the pad into his waterproof jacket. He is properly dressed for this strange, seeping weather. 'That's where she belongs,' he says, and turns away.

Daphne's face appears out of the branches, suddenly the face he knows, lucid and calm. 'He thinks I am mad. He is a horrible man.'

'I'm going to get your husband—'

'No, don't!' She clambers down to a branch just above him and clutches his hand. 'I need . . . I need to be somewhere safe. High up is safe. Do I look funny? Oh dear. There is no point in getting exercised about it. Jessop is in a very solid position . . . He is marrying Wallace's daughter, Amy, in the summer. He is locked into that family like a jewel in a safe.'

'But—'

'Try to keep one step ahead of him, Wystan. I won't be able to protect you. Mr Perkins and me . . . well, we are on the way out, and Mr Jessop is on the way up.'

'Daphne, you're ill. You really must come inside and get warm.'

Perkins is coming round the side of the building. He has aged, even in the two years Wystan has been at the school. Rain drips from his nose as he shuffles over and peers up into the tree. He and his wife are mirrors, one face above the other, and they have exactly the same expression arranged across their different features.

'Hello, Alby,' she says.

Perkins sighs and plods back to the school building.

'Wait! I'm sure you can persuade her down . . .' Wystan strides to catch up.

Perkins frowns at him. 'It's all gone far beyond anything I can do. We just have to keep the boys out of the garden till she . . . sees sense.' He shakes his head. 'Call no man happy, Auden. Call no man happy.' And he trudges up the steps, leaving Wystan standing uncertainly between the insane humming of his friend and the calls of the school.

He looks back at the tree, whose leaves shake a little as Mrs Perkins adjusts her space. He can still hear her humming and coughing. She is suffering, and making an imaginary world is the antidote to suffering, isn't it?

If he was a true friend, he would join her there, wouldn't he? He would share her little world, even if it is a mad one. Can he not give a little respite to the person who has been kindest to him? He eyes the tree, noting where someone as tall as himself would catch their head, their shoulders. But his feet remain rooted to the spot.

Wystan's kindness is of a different sort. He stares at the shape moving in the tree and imagines a light from Heaven pouring over it, bathing his friend in peace. The thought forces the light into being. He can actually see it, breaking through the clouds and enfolding her as she sings. After a few minutes, he turns and goes in for breakfast.

THIRTY-TWO

Dora

T HE LITTLE BOAT WAS the first thing to make Kit smile in a long time. Someone on the board of La Scala had an old dinghy. Did he want it? It was compact and simple, not unlike the ones he and Dora took out in Oxford when they first met. Kit was determined that they would go out on the water and have some fun as a family. Naturally a sunny person, he knew no other way to go on.

It was a fortnight since Kit had rescued Mo from the wasps. She was still in hospital and Kit had heard from Terrence that she was 'very poorly'. The allergic reaction had been so catastrophic that Mo had developed meningitis. Terrence was away most of the time, only returning late from the hospital, and the house was peaceful. Without the Divines in residence, there were no visitors.

As Dora made a picnic of sandwiches, juice and beer, Beatrice gurgled on a mat at her feet. 'Now *you*,' Dora said to Virgil, who could sense something was going to happen and was sniffing and whining, 'you are staying here.' He was much calmer since the noise upstairs had stopped; nevertheless, if he was left alone for any length of time, he got so stressed he would vomit. Dora made his bed in the kitchen, where it would be easier to clear up the inevitable mess.

It was a spectacular day, perfect to go out in a boat. The sea was a bottomless blue, folded softly like fabric; the surrounding hills were lit up gold by the sun. The sky was cloudless and the shingle dazzled. Beatrice grinned and dribbled as Dora carried her across the road to the steep path that led to the beach. Dora wasn't at all keen on sailing, but her husband was standing, smiling, by the boat, his shirtsleeves rolled up. He looked as Dora remembered him. In marriage, months go by without us looking at our partner, really seeing them. But now she did look at him, with vision unclouded by anxiety or black mood.

Dora slid carefully down the bank, holding her husband's hand, and the baby close.

'You get on first with Bea,' said Kit. Dora cautiously stepped through the shallows to the prow. Once there, she spent the next five minutes attempting to wrestle Bea into a life jacket.

'Na . . . nah . . . yay . . .' said Beatrice.

'Now, no wriggling,' Dora said to her. 'If you fall in, Mummy will have to come in after you.' She sat Beatrice straight on her lap while she tightened the straps around her plump belly. The baby cackled and looked so ridiculous in the orange inflatable that Dora laughed and pressed kisses all over her. Beatrice arched her back and grinned. It was as if her whole body were smiling.

Kit splashed to the boat and started the outboard. In a cloud of blue fumes, they chugged along the estuary, heading up towards Coulport. From the sea, Paradise was even lovelier, standing blue and

279

graceful beneath a sky that seemed to merge with it. Sun caught the windows, and the trees waved their new growth gently in the breeze. Dora felt the return of an old, deep longing. For hadn't she and Kit stood on that lawn together and planned their lives in that house? How they could restore the garden to something like what it once was in its Victorian heyday? It was a house to build a life around.

The surrounding hills grew taller. Blocks of dark green crowned them; almost all this area was maintained either by the Forestry Commission or the MOD. Chunks of forest disappeared overnight when they were felled, leaving a gap-toothed summit.

Kit cut the engine in the loch and took out a beer. They drifted happily, with Bea slurping her juice and gurgling as she pointed at the sea. Kit and Dora exchanged a smile. Today, Beatrice had a mother who was not white-faced and crying, and a father who was fully present. They were, at last, a unit, a family. They were real, they were together, and something in that thought gave her strength. She sipped at her beer and raised her face to the sun. Without Mo, everything was lighter.

Did she see it or hear it first? It was so swift and silent that it was alongside before she had taken in that a boat was approaching. A strange, obsequious smile arranged itself on her face.

It was a navy-police boat, painted black in the truest sense: non-reflective, as if cut out of the sky. On board were three – what were they? Police? Soldiers? – men, anyway, dressed in black flak-jackets, bristling with guns. They stopped parallel with the bobbing dinghy. One removed his shades, stood at the prow of the boat and stared at the family, taking in their appearance fully before speaking.

'Out for a little trip, then?' he asked.

Bea reached towards him, drooling. She was a terrible flirt.

'Good afternoon! Yes, we're just taking our daughter out for a bit of a trip,' said Kit affably. 'We should have rung, shouldn't we?'

'Well, we don't come over and spoil your day, if you do,' said the man, looking with curiosity at the little trio, which Dora had just been loving so much. Older man, pale woman, lone child.

Dora was possessed by an almost unstoppable urge to laugh or to say something inappropriate. The machinery of the state seemed to be following her everywhere, intruding on her most private moments, a hair's-breadth from reading her thoughts. It was so strange that police, soldiers, social workers were everywhere in her life, and nowhere in anyone else's. Dora dug her nails into her palm to distract herself. If she moved her fingers back and forth, they scraped her skin painfully, which slowed down her mind. She wanted to say, out loud, *When will this end?* This resisting of the state, the police of her mind? She seemed to have fought off one incursion: they'd heard nothing from Naomi and Lavender since their visit. Her baby could not be in that much danger if the wheels of bureaucracy could grind so slowly . . . Nevertheless, the need for constant vigilance was exhausting and not a little frightening.

The man said, 'There's a sub coming by shortly, so it would be better if you made your way back.'

'Of course,' said Kit. 'Sorry if we've been a nuisance.'

The man balanced perfectly a few seconds more, then said, 'You have a good day, now,' and sat back down, easing his shades over his eyes.

Dora held Beatrice close as Kit started the engine and they headed home. She wanted to discuss it with Kit, find a way to counter the thoughts in her mind. Her husband was whistling softly to himself as he steered the boat towards the little cove at Paradise. He saw nothing sinister in the police's appearance. It was just an inconvenience, that was all. She could see him forgetting about it – while the fingers of her brain seized on the incident, turned it over and over, trying to understand.

As they pulled into the shallows, Dora knew she didn't want to go home just yet. 'I'll take Bea into town. I need to get a few things, anyway,' she said.

'Of course. Are you all right, though? Did you enjoy that?' said Kit. 'A bit annoying that they came and interrupted us. But it was nice, wasn't it?'

'Yes,' Dora said. She tried, then, to formulate a sentence that would express what she was afraid of, something along the lines of, *I think it means something, means something bad, the way these people appear, and they seem to be malign, all of them.* But she couldn't get the words out – perhaps because she knew what Kit, as the voice of reason in the family, would say.

She gave up trying to articulate her unease and simply squeezed his hand, leaving him standing, a little forlornly, at their front door. She strapped Beatrice into the car seat. 'Let's go to the shops!' she said gaily, turning from the drive on to the road. When she glanced back in the mirror a few moments later, Beatrice had fallen fast asleep.

Dora had no particular plan. She needed some milk and some plasters, so she slowed to pull into the minimart. Beatrice was sleeping so peacefully that it seemed pointless to wake her, so Dora clicked the lock shut and darted through the door of the shop. The line that seemed to crop up in her mind a lot these days started its spin: *That he should seek my hospitality / From out the dark door of the secret earth . . . That he should . . .*

It was momentarily completely dark, as if she had stepped behind a stage curtain. She blinked, trying to get accustomed to the lack of light, and gradually noticed there was a candle flickering in the space. Wystan was at his desk. He smiled up at her as she stepped into his Larchfield bedroom.

Ash spattered all over his front as he stood to greet her. 'I'm so glad you've come. Daphne is so ill. I'm going out of my mind.' He rinsed his tooth-mug out at the basin and pulled a glass from under the bed. 'Stole this from the kitchen. Tired of never having enough crockery.' He splashed whisky into both cups and came up to her, handing her the glass.

'What time is it?' Dora asked. She hesitated, convinced she was late for something.

Wystan glanced at the clock on the mantelpiece. 'Two a.m.' He grinned. 'Usually, I'm just getting going around now, but, for the first time in my life . . . I just can't work. Here . . . sit.' They sat side by side on the narrow bed. 'Let me take your coat.'

The whisky created a trail of warmth, right into her belly, and a sigh escaped her. It was a relief to be home.

'I don't think I can be late for something at two a.m. Or I'm so late that it can't really matter!' A lovely warm dizziness filled her head and they giggled together.

Wystan reached under his pillow and pulled out her notebook, with its pen tied roughly round. 'I think you must have been missing this,' he said.

'Oh!' she cried and grabbed it to her. She leant against him and the tiny crackle of the candle drifted over them.

'Look at this,' he said. 'This is what I've been perfecting, instead of working.' He blew towards the flame. It remained tall and still, and then suddenly, four seconds or so later, bent double and jigged like a Russian dancer.

'But there's more.' Wystan bent a little closer and whistled a tune in the direction of the flame. The flame, after a slight delay, danced sinuously in a rhythmic accompaniment.

'You've been busy, then,' said Dora.

Wystan sat back miserably. 'Daphne's losing her mind. I can't do anything about it . . . can't help.' Dora took his hands and twined her fingers with his. 'And Gregory . . . It'll never be anything. They're after me, Dora.'

'You have to escape yourself. That's it, isn't it?'

Her friend nodded. 'I don't know what to do. Help me, Dora.'

She pressed her lips to him, felt, as he did, the transgression in the kiss. Transgression was what brought one to life. Sometimes, transgression was all there was left.

SOMETHING — A LIGHT, or a blow, or a cry — shook her. Dora opened her eyes and she was standing back outside the minimart, purchases in hand, the door swinging shut behind her. She blinked in the light. Her lips were bruised and sore.

There was a crowd around her car. Gathering herself, she moved towards the angry mob, from which two police officers emerged.

'Are you the owner of the car and the child's mother?' one of them asked.

'Yes?' Dora was completely confused.

'You've left a child unattended in a locked vehicle!'

'I went to buy this! I was gone five minutes. She was asleep.'

'The child is crying. And too tightly strapped in.'

Through the glass, Dora saw her daughter's screwed up, purple face. Dora pressed the remote and the locks popped open. She pushed past the officers, took the baby into her arms and immediately the crying eased. Beatrice began to play with her mother's hair.

'See?' said Dora. 'No harm done!'

One of the spectators, a willowy man in a long black coat, whom Dora remembered as a neighbour from further down the road, said, 'We know all about you and how you treat people!'

'What?'

'You've destroyed the lives of two innocent old people in the house above you – and now you are neglecting your own child. You're evil – that's what you are.'

There was a mumble of uncomfortable assent.

Dora said to the officers, 'Can I take my child home now, please?'

The policemen looked at each other and then at Dora. 'Is there someone at home to look after your daughter?'

'Yes. My husband. He . . . Why?'

'Because we are placing you under arrest for leaving a child alone in a situation likely to cause harm, and you'll need to come along to the station in town after you've dropped her off.'

Dumbly, Dora strapped her daughter back into the car seat. Beatrice had forgotten the incident and was gurgling happily again. Dora kissed her child's soft cheek.

The crowd shifted to let Dora reverse, her hands shaking so much she doubted she could complete the manoeuvre. In the mirror, the police car followed in the languorous way the machinery of the state moves when it has its suspect in its sights.

She was a bad mother. Kit and Beatrice were better off without her.

I get it now, Dora breathed into the car. I'm sorry.

THIRTY-THREE

Wystan

ACCORDING TO HIS FRIEND Christopher, Wystan's sexual appetites are hearty and uncomplicated, like having a good breakfast. This is the reason Wystan returns to Berlin in the summer holidays of 1932. A simple appetite can be indulged instead of repressed, and also, this time, he comes to discuss a new play he and Christopher may work on together.

He wishes he could have brought Gregory with him. Their relationship is so constrained, they have barely been alone. In Berlin, he can have the 'quiet fuck' he wants and return to Gregory with more patience. It is not a matter of faithfulness . . . it is pragmatism.

Four of them are crowded round a table in the Cosy: he and Christopher; Heinz, Christopher's beautiful and rather sullen young lover; and a boy Wystan met on the way in, whose name is Herman. The two boys eye each other in a not-quite-friendly way, trying to assess how serious each is in the life of his lover, while Wystan and Christopher chatter together over the possibilities in their play.

The transient, tempestuous, financially unequal relationships which characterise love in Berlin are easy to present as trivial. Everyone, especially Christopher's mother, is happier with this apparently fluid situation. A fluid situation can change and become normal, after all. But Heinz, despite break-ups, flare-ups and stompings-off, has become a stubborn constant in Christopher's life. Christopher both hates and adores him. The language gap renders them almost unable to talk to each other, although Christopher is paying for Heinz to have English classes and makes a cursory attempt to improve his own German. Heinz is the unemployed son of a labourer and lives in a slum, out towards the east of the city. He has no education to speak of and struggles to pick up even the most elementary English. But these difficulties, combined with Heinz's grumpy beauty, have bound them together. They are inseparable, except when Heinz has slammed out for some reason.

In the overheated conviviality of the Cosy, Wystan has never been happier. His dearest friend is here to talk plays with, and beside Wystan sits a bright and handsome new friend, who is gradually loosening up in the easy atmosphere of the bar. He has removed his jacket and rolled his sleeves up and unbuttoned his shirt, like the other boys. While Wystan talks with Christopher, he keeps his fingers entwined with Herman's. How wonderful it is to show affection. Though the bar is full of boys looking longingly over at them – for they are clearly well-off, clearly foreign – neither Wystan nor Christopher is interested. Every warm feeling surrounds their table: lifelong friendship, lust, romantic love.

It is only a fortnight since Adolf Hitler's Nazi party won enough seats in the elections to make them the largest party, and the holders of the balance of power. In a few months, along with the burning of the Reichstag, this will persuade President Hindenburg to appoint Hitler as Chancellor. Within weeks of that, the first long-planned, systematic attacks on the enemies of the Reich will be underway.

As the four men sit happily in the Cosy, they do not know that what is coming has already begun. Buoyed by their electoral success, and with total victory in sight, the Nazi Brownshirts are raiding clubs like the Cosy, which have, until now, been largely ignored. They are beating Jews in the street and breaking the windows of their businesses with impunity. The storm troopers are the new, albeit unofficial, police force, and the real police force, trapped in the power vacuum that comes with an uncertain leadership, do nothing.

On his way to meet Christopher and Heinz, earlier in the day, Wystan encountered a group of Brownshirts standing outside a Jewish dress shop, letting customers know, pleasantly, that the shop owner was an enemy of the Reich and anyone who went in was, therefore, also an enemy. This was deeply shocking, but somehow so ridiculous that it could not be taken quite seriously. Wystan had pressed on, glancing back only to observe how young the boys were, plastered in their swastikas. How young, how good-looking and how belligerent. It was as if they were away from home for the first time and had gone mad with the freedom to be cruel. It was impossible that it should last. These boys' parents would reel them in. Hitler sounded like a shrieking madwoman on the wireless.

Christopher is more uneasy. Magnus Hirschfeld, the founder of the Sexual Hygiene Museum, where Christopher has his apartment, has gone to Paris and does not dare to return. Soon, the building will be ransacked and destroyed. Brownshirts are often to be seen questioning those who enter the building, as to why they are doing so. Tension crackles in the air, but perhaps because Wystan is used to tension, used to a lifetime of disapproval when it comes to his private life – is used, in short, to being illegal – he does not feel it as strongly as he subsequently believes he should have.

So, when there is hammering on the Cosy's massive front door, neither Wystan nor Christopher immediately pays attention. The play they are planning is very absorbing. It is to be set in a boys' prep school, which Wystan is modelling on a madder version of Larchfield. Heinz nudges Christopher and they all look up as silence falls over the bar and Einrich, the burly doorkeeper, lumbers up the stairs, pulls aside the leather curtain and asks, 'Who's there?'

A explosion of German shouting follows. 'Open up! Open up now!' The door trembles under the kicks and blows. Einrich calls, 'All right! All right!' then quickly turns back to the room to attempt a Nazi salute. This is a warning, not a joke, and his eyes are scared. The boys roll down their sleeves and button up their shirts, and Einrich hurries to the door and slides back the many bolts.

'Don't say anything,' hisses Wystan to Herman. 'Do you have your card?'

The boy doesn't understand, but he has experienced these raids before and, carefully, he slides away from the table and into the shadow of a doorway. The British men clutch their passports. All around them, the Cosy's clientele are separating and rifling in their pockets for their papers, as at least a dozen storm troopers batter down the stairs in their jackboots.

Once there, they stop, blinking, uncertain what to do in this peaceful room full of men not doing anything at all. They are self-conscious in their immaculate uniforms. The brown shirts that form the basis of their uniform are left over from the war, and so are rather rough and uncomfortable, but give these boys a definite military air. In another time, this could be the beginning of a splendid costume party, thinks Wystan.

An older man emerges from the others. Hair immaculately clipped beneath his cap, he radiates cleanliness and anger. These clash visibly with the atmosphere of the room, which is dishevelled and has no anger at all.

The officer scans the room, and his eyes fall on Wystan, who is, as ever, the most unusual-looking person. 'You! Get up! *Hier!*'

Wystan walks carefully to the man. He is about a head taller, but he stoops slightly so as not to emphasise it.

'Name,' the officer says.

'Wystan Auden,' he says.

The officer, hearing the non-German name, scrutinises him. 'Where are you from?'

'England.' Wystan takes the passport from his pocket.

The officer's lips purse crossly. There is nothing he can do with a British national, and, anyway, at the moment, England is an admired friend, as far as Hitler is concerned.

The officer indicates the rest of Wystan's table. 'All English?' he asks.

No one speaks.

The officer's irritation grows. He strides up to the table, puts his face into Christopher's and lets forth a stream of German invective that leaves Christopher doused with spittle and craning back in his chair. He lays out his passport on the table. The officer flicks through it, throws it down and turns to Heinz, who is trying to look invisible, which is impossible due to his six feet of height and his mop of blond hair.

When Heinz brings out his identity card, the officer is relieved to be able to do *something* about *someone* at this table. He calls over a couple of the other men.

'Get up!' he screams. Heinz is pulled to his feet, the chair falling over behind him. Christopher reaches his arms towards the officer. 'No! He's my student!' he cries in his faltering German, but the officer leans in towards him, scowling.

'Get out, you two! Okay, boys, get on with it.'

Heinz is dragged out by the two young Brownshirts, not that he puts up a fight. He gazes back at Christopher with a nervous smile on his lips, because it is so outlandish to be dragged out like a dog. Then the other Brownshirts set to with the batons they carry, smashing the glasses on the bar, raining blows on everyone in it as they try to get past and up the stairs. No blows fall on the British pair as they edge out, Christopher flushed with anguish.

Wystan glances round for Herman, and is relieved that he can't see him. Did he escape through the urinals? This is how they leave the Cosy for the last time. Splintering wood and cries follow them. Wystan puts his hands over his ears and closes his eyes; the dull whacking and the helpless shouts are like a hellish version of public school. He hates himself for walking free while Heinz does not. What will happen to him?

They have their answer at dawn, when Heinz calls up to the apartment window, where Christopher sits, smoking and waiting.

He gallops down to let him in. Heinz's face is bloodied and swollen with two black eyes. He is limping.

'Oh my God!' Christopher embraces him on the step, but Heinz motions stiffly for him not to touch his aching body. Upstairs, in the apartment, Heinz explains to them in his terrible English that they took turns to beat him and that they raped him with a baton – he cries and loses his few words at this. He is so ashamed. His parents will be so angry. He can never tell anyone. But, worse than all this, he is now on a list of sexual deviants, and this list will be passed to the soon-to-be-formed Gestapo, as soon as Hitler comes to power.

THIRTY-FOUR

Dora

DORA GASPED FOR BREATH . . . She was half in and half out of the memory of emerging with Kit from the tall-ceilinged room of Greek statues at the Louvre, headachey and giggling among the marble crowds . . . Unsteadily, they had posed for a photograph at the feet of the giant Athena on her plinth . . .

Lights flashed in her eyes . . . just as they had from the camera of the American in the Panama hat and horn-rimmed glasses. He was the kind of international Everyman that, Dora joked, existed in every sophisticated European city. He preserved forever the image of the two of them pressed beneath the statue, fingers entwined, faces flushed.

Kit had just murmured into Dora's ear, 'Marry me, darling. Please.' The rest of the day unfolded in a private realm that followed them from room to room as they searched for a shadowy place where they could wrap, once more, around each other. There was no such place, not even on one of the back stairways in Egyptian Antiquities. Kissing, halfway down, someone had shouted in French, and they leapt apart and scurried away.

Her eyes were stinging and watering . . . It was just like when they stumbled back into the glass-topped atrium that lay beneath the museum, all that time ago. The pyramid of triangles directed the light fiercely on to the swarms of people. The space was a kind of crucible that compressed the noise and the light together. And now, in the present moment, Dora's senses invaded each other; more, they seemed to be engaged in some kind of struggle . . . Her breaths ran around like stray dogs, howling at her throat, while strip lights passed overhead like a falling ladder.

She was in a room, now, stark as an exhibition room with the statues removed. Its walls, with speckled tiles, were like those she saw at the zoo once – walls that could be hosed down.

She was on a bed, the sheets screwed around her. She looked down at herself and vertigo gripped her. Was she, in fact, made of marble and standing upright? The sheets rippled around her body like a lovely carved robe. Her hand lifted to touch the folds.

There was a sound in the room. Was it the light? Her eyes were hurting. She dragged her head round to look.

It was Kit. He was sitting on the only other furniture in the room, a simple plastic chair, like those exhibition wardens resting in between fielding endless questions asked in bad French . . . Mona Lisa *is Room Six . . . Down to the left . . . No, no, the left . . .*

His head was in his hands and his shoulders were shaking as he sobbed.

'Kit? Kit . . . ?' She extended a plump marble arm out to him. She was as lovely and as permanent as Athena had been that day. She was vast and powerful, and so beautiful that she lit up every room that could accommodate her. Poor Kit. Did he not understand he was safe?

When he looked up, he was not as she remembered him that day in Paris. He was so much older. Wasn't he looking after himself?

'Do you remember?' she asked. 'The Louvre, that time, when we got engaged . . . ?'

'Don't you know what's happened?' he asked.

For her husband, Dora dragged herself into the present moment. The memory of them together that day was so powerful that coming out of it was like throwing herself from air into water. It went against every instinct, for the vision felt more real than this terrible, cramped room and this version of her husband, whose face, now he was near, was furrowed and angry. In that scene, among the Greek statues – which *did happen*, which, in fact, made *everything else* happen – her husband adored her, they had a connection that was so strong it could create life itself. She existed, she was loved, and she had done no wrong.

She took a deep, shaking breath. 'Have they taken my baby?'

'Not yet,' Kit said. He leant over her. 'They didn't take her. But you won't believe what I had to do, to *agree to*, to keep her with me.'

'Where is she now?' Dora began to struggle out of the bed, but her head swam and she sank back.

'She's outside, with a nurse.'

'I want to see her.'

'That's not a good idea. They won't allow it, anyway. Dora, this kind of supervision is what I've had to agree to! You have to stay in here.'

'What do you mean?' It was harder and harder for Dora to breathe.

Kit hissed, 'Why couldn't I just have a normal wife, you know, like all these ones you see around Helensburgh, chatting with their friends in bloody Costa, with their fat, happy babies? Why couldn't I have had that . . . ?' He sank back down on the chair.

'I don't understand. It was Mo—'

'Mo is still in hospital! She's got meningitis! But that's who you are: the sort of person who blames everyone else for their fucking problems.'

'You brought me to that house and left me with a baby all on my own, with no help, no money, no nothing . . . and all the while that . . . woman upstairs . . . It is a miracle I am not mad! I *never* hurt our baby. I never did anything but protect her.'

'The fact is, you locked the baby, alone, in the car—'

'For hardly any time at all!'

'And you were aggressive to the arresting officer. Dora, it is clear to me that you are, and have been for some time, *beyond reason*.'

'You know I'm not mad . . . You know I'm not.'

'You're so distracted I can barely get any sense out of you half the time. I've tried to be understanding, but honestly . . .'

'You don't understand anything! There's only one thing that's kept me going: Auden. *Wystan*. Yes, I'm distracted. He helps me, which is more than you've ever done.'

'What?'

'That's where I've been. That's what has happened. I found a message in a bottle, and I rang the number and it connected! I can travel to Larchfield and be with Auden whenever I want. And he's *kind*. And he *cares* about me. And, there, I am a *writer!*' Dora collapsed into tears.

Kit sighed. 'You need to stay here until the doctors have sorted out whatever is going on in that head of yours. Then we will see where we stand.' He got up to leave.

'Kit, Kit – wait.' She held out her arm to him.

He looked down at her.

'I'm sorry . . . I'll try and bear it. Just don't leave me here . . . please.'

Wearily, he said, 'It's only temporary – till the doctors decide.'

'Till *you* decide!' she cried.

He left the room. The door clicked behind him.

No, no, no . . . Dora turned round and round in the bed, fighting the drugged fog that kept pulling her down. Pain swelled in her belly – an unbearable, anxious pain. She whimpered and began to hit herself on the thighs and stomach as a way to fight it, to stop it engulfing her. No . . . no . . . Kit, please . . . Beatrice . . .

A hand on her arm, stilling her.

She looked up and into the face of Wystan.

'Dora, Dora, dear. Be still . . .' he said.

'But my baby . . . my husband . . . What have I done?'

Wystan sat down on the bed beside her and took her hand.

'You must endure . . . that is all. The time is not right for you.' He pressed her notebook into her arms. 'I brought you this. I think you need it. Everything will be all right. I know you can do it.'

An aching chasm of sadness opened in Dora that she feared would never close or be eased. Wystan gathered her into his arms and held her close to him as she wept.

'I won't leave you, my dear,' he whispered. 'I will never leave you.'

And there they remained, entwined together, until the drugs were brought round and sleep followed.

THIRTY-FIVE

Wystan

WYSTAN'S FATHER HAS ALWAYS said that Auden is an Icelandic name, and Wystan is fascinated by this aspect of his heritage. In a couple of years, he will travel to Iceland with Louis MacNeice and explore the island that seems to have given him not only a name, but a physical inheritance. But, whilst in Helensburgh, it has been playing on his mind that Shetland is within reach – a group of islands with Scandinavian heritage themselves. Why not escape everything: the darkness enveloping his usual playground of Berlin, the claustrophobia of Larchfield? Why not return to roots more ancient, deeper?

And why not take Gregory with him?

They can be alone on these remote islands. No one will know them. No one will be watching. Finally, they can behave like other couples.

Wystan needs a break, also, from his work. *The Orators* is proving hard to finish, partly because of the distractions of starting a new play with Christopher and partly because the paranoia and fear that are part and parcel of Helensburgh life seem to have tipped over from stimulating and into paralysing. Something is stultifying him, making him restless and irritable. Hours spent before a blank page – or, worse, a full page that turns out to be unusable – sap his strength. Daphne's sickness plays on his mind.

Gregory accepted the offer without hesitation. Hesitation followed hard on the heels of the acceptance, however.

'You'll need to ask my ma and pa,' he said.

'But you're eighteen.'

'Aye, but I live at home . . . It will be all right – when they meet you.'

It is true. Generally, people do like Wystan when they meet him. He is charming when he has a mind to be. Although, it has to be said, this observation was more accurate before Helensburgh. In this town, his charm can be hit and miss.

It isn't much to ask of him. It demonstrates, also, that Gregory wants their relationship to be approved of. He is owning it in a way that is sweet.

It doesn't help with first impressions that, when Wystan goes to visit Gregory's parents, he wears his large red sunhat, purchased in Berlin, with not-quite-matching red shorts that stop well above the knee. The outfit is completed with slippers that Wystan insists on wearing because of his corns. With a naïve aplomb that makes everyone stare, he enters the broken-down tenement where Gregory and his parents share two rooms on the second floor.

Mrs Vance's eyes widen as the vision that is Wystan enters the everything room, which she has cleaned as hard as she can. Gregory, mortified by Wystan's costume, which he has never seen before, hangs behind.

'Tea? Lovely!' says Wystan, perched on the sloping couch, in front of which is a deal table on which is laid a single cup with tea in it and some plain cake on a chipped plate. Mrs Vance hogged the communal kitchen all yesterday evening to get this baking done. She stands back, arms crossed, as Wystan gets stuck in.

Wystan says, 'Mmmmm!' and, 'Do you mind . . . ?' as he grabs another slice, crumbs flying from his lips. 'This cake is delicious, Mrs Vance! I've had hardly any cake since I came to Helensburgh; well, nothing like this, anyway.' His vowels bounce around the bare room.

'Mr Auden,' says Mr Vance with a cough. He is a kindling-thin man with a deeply lined face and bruised eyes.

Wystan stops chewing and slurping and, with an unaffected happy grin at Mrs Vance, turns his attention to his friend's father, in the only armchair. The tiny room is stuffed with a number of nice, if decrepit items of furniture. Gregory's father was a foreman at the shipyard, before all this. They have managed to keep the furniture, if not the house. But if the lack of employment continues, the furniture will have to go too. The means test is upon them all.

'What is the purpose of this trip you propose taking Gregory on?'

'Gregory – my friend, Gregory,' Wystan flashes a smile at the boy cowering in the corner, 'is so exceptionally bright, and wants to learn new things. I am in a position to take a guest, and so, obviously, I thought of him.'

Mrs Vance has a mouth whose natural voluptuousness has turned to a fleshy droop. She regards Wystan steadily.

Wystan reaches into his pocket and offers a cigarette to Mr Vance, who takes it reluctantly. He turns it round in his fingers, longing all over his crumpled features. Then he leans forward and accepts a light. There is a silence as Mr Vance sucks on the cigarette. He cannot remember the last decent smoke he had. Usually, he picks up stubs on the street, although there is never anything in them.

'Madam?' Wystan offers the cigarettes to Mrs Vance, but she shakes her head.

'Gregory is our only child,' she says, in a voice that is gravelly and deeper than one might have expected, as if she has long been a smoker. 'How do I know he will be safe?'

Wystan says, 'Mrs Vance, I am a schoolteacher with responsibility for boys every day of the week. I won't let you down. Of course, Gregory is precious cargo. I wouldn't suggest he come, except that I know he would get so much out of a holiday. If we telegraph you from Lerwick, will that be a reassurance?'

'And I will send postcards,' utters Gregory from the shadows.

'We don't want him with a . . . sophisticated crowd,' says Mr Vance.

'Sophisticated? I think it is mainly fishermen and sheep farmers on Shetland, is it not?'

'We don't want him breaking the law,' says Mr Vance, jabbing the air.

'It would be lovely for him to escape everything here for a little while,' says Mrs Vance thoughtfully.

Both parents turn to look at their son, who burns with embarrassment, but also longing.

Mr Vance sighs. The sigh turns into a cough. 'Mr Auden, we are all, of course, very grateful for Gregory's position at the school. To be perfectly frank, Gregory's wage is keeping our heads above water. We are in your debt, of course—'

'Not at all, Mr Vance! Offering Gregory this position was Mrs Perkins' idea. I merely suggested Gregory as the only strong young man I know.'

'This is very difficult for me,' continues Mr Vance, 'because I am sure that, if we say no, you will take Gregory's employment away from him.'

Wystan coughs crumbs all over his front. 'Take his job away? That's not in my power, Mr Vance, even if I would want such a thing, which I don't. Gregory and I are friends.'

'That's what I am worried about,' says Mr Vance. 'I've heard the rumours. I don't want my son to be friends with you.'

Wystan blanches. Silence fills the room.

'Dad!' cries Gregory.

Wystan persists with what he has prepared to say, even while Mr Vance's insult clings to him as if he has been spat on. 'There is, I believe, a good chance of another war, wouldn't you say? Travel may not be possible in a few years – or not the sort of travel you'd like for your son. It will be an education for Gregory and a broadening of his horizons. And some company for me, while I research my book.'

He continues, 'Gregory is a remarkable young man, and this is just a small opportunity that I can offer him to see something of the world.'

The shabby parents stare at this vision before them in the red shorts. They have nothing to give their son. How they wish that someone would offer him something. Why does it have to be a man like this, forcing their hand?

'Mr Auden, why do you not take one of your English friends? I think that would be much better.'

'And why would it be much better, Mr Vance?' Wystan stiffens.

'Because, young man, are you or are you not a damned pervert?' Spittle flies from Mr Vance's lips. 'What do you take me for? Answer me!'

A chilliness comes over Wystan's expression. With uncharacteristic care, he picks the crumbs from his trousers and deposits them on the plate.

'I am very sorry to have troubled you,' he says.

He stands and gives a bow to Mrs Vance, places his hat on his head and shuffles to the door.

'Aye, and I bet you'll be giving our Gregory the sack now, you coward!'

As he passes his friend, Wystan says, 'I made a misjudgement, dear boy. So sorry to have caused this trouble. See you at work tomorrow, I am sure.' And he touches his hat and is gone, trying not to run down the stairs, out of the squalor and sourness.

How has Gregory put up with it? How can he live that way?

He strides out of the dull streets, back up the hill towards Larchfield. Suddenly, he cannot wait to get back. It is a beacon of peace: the trees lining the way, the beautiful frontage, always so easy on the eye. And the people, behind their hedges, in their rooms, keeping their thoughts to themselves.

Underneath it all, of course, burns his hatred of himself: that he could not own his love for Gregory in front of them. And, therefore, that they have over him what they have over him.

THIRTY-SIX

Wystan and Dora

'CAN I STAY HERE?' Dora turned from the window, where she had been looking out on the leaf-strewn lawn. She had come to know the view so well that it was part of her now. It was hers as much as his. Each time she walked through the door of Larchfield, she could remember the last time much more vividly, and the gap in between seemed insignificant.

'Of course you can stay.'

'Forever?'

He smiled at her, but it was a wan sort of smile. 'Well, my plan was to go to Shetland with Gregory at the end of the week, and I think you would be a little extra to requirements then. But, of course – you can be here anytime you want.' He pressed his hands to his eyes in a despairing gesture Dora hadn't seen before. 'But, anyway, I don't think we'll be going now.'

'Why not?'

'His parents loathe the very ground I stand on.'

'What did they say?'

'Doesn't matter, except that they are simple people who don't want their son corrupted.'

'Does Gregory want to go?'

'Very much so. Or, at least, he did before his father called me a pervert.'

'Ah. And do you still want to take him?'

Wystan considered the question carefully. 'Dora, I love the boy. That is my difficulty. Every moment we're apart is a bloody torment.'

'You love him?'

Wystan's eyes filled unexpectedly with tears. He wiped them away. 'I'm being stupid. It's probably just because there's been nothing more than a kiss and it's all I can think about. I don't know what to do. I can't work. I haven't felt like this about anyone.'

The typewriter gleaming on the desk distracted Dora. Sitting before it, she rested her hands on the keys, remembering the wonderful sound they made when Wystan was typing, the great hesitant clump as he whacked them with two fingers. And then the lines emerging, firm versions of his scattered thoughts. Then the sigh and the *rip!* as he snatched the paper from the roller, examined it and threw it on the floor. The rejected sheets were not thrown away, they simply lay on the floor in geographical strata, to resurface later. Wystan would examine them as if seeing them for the first time, and often the sheet would be reinstated on the desk.

'Can I?' Dora rolled a sheet in and began to type some lines from her notebook. She forgot Wystan; she forgot everything except the hammering of the typewriter as it began to construct something coherent from her notes.

'Dora?'

There was no response.

'Dora?' Wystan coughed from the bed and she pulled the sheet from the typewriter and handed it to him.

He read aloud:

'Why were we crucified into sex?
Why were we not left rounded off, and finished in ourselves,
As we began,
As he certainly began, so perfectly alone?'

'Oh, Lawrence, my friend!' he said, smiling.

'"Tortoise Shout",' said Dora. 'I made a note of this, for some reason. This must be the reason.'

Wystan darted to the bookshelf and pulled out his copy of Lawrence poems. He riffled through the pages and declaimed:

'Sex, which breaks us into voice, sets us calling across the
    deeps, calling, calling for the complement,
Singing, and calling, and singing again, being answered,
    having found.

Torn, to become whole again, after long seeking for what is
    lost,
The same cry from the tortoise as from Christ, the Osiris-cry
    of abandonment,
That which is whole, torn asunder,
That which is in part, finding its whole again throughout the
    universe.'

Dora said, 'If you love Gregory and he loves you, then he is your complement. You must take him with you – and face the consequences.'

'I don't think Lawrence meant me to take that from his poem.'

'I think it's pretty clear. We are condemned to long for our complement. To belong.'

'But his parents . . . they'll have me arrested.'

'No, they won't. There will be no proof of anything.'

'It'll be in the bloody *Courier*, at the very least.'

'You'll be hundreds of miles away, on a sparsely populated island. They won't hear about it.'

'The *Courier* is desperate for news. I'm sure they'd go that far.' They laughed at this.

'It's what love is, isn't it, Wystan? Finding your complement and accepting your enslavement. You won't be able to write again until you stop fighting this.'

Wystan lit a cigarette and rubbed his eyes. 'It's true; I can't finish this bloody piece. The aviator. The hero. I can't get him right. My heart's not in it. He loves a man.'

He went to his desk and brought back a newspaper cutting of Amy in the *Jason*. 'I cut it out,' he said. 'I don't know why. Like you, with the poem, I did it for a reason. And this must be the reason.'

Dora held the yellowing photograph in her hand, taking in the bright, pretty face and the small form, seemingly even smaller in the *Jason*'s cockpit. The image was so touching; someone just being themselves, whatever that was. Dora was quiet for a few moments, then said, 'Don't be alone, Wystan. Have courage.'

But Wystan's complement was *illegal*. He had been shamed by his lover's parents and even his bolt-hole in Berlin held no solace anymore.

'Everything's changing, and not for the better,' he said at last. 'I don't want to end up sacrificing Gregory.'

'It won't work out that way; I'm sure of it,' Dora said. 'And, anyway, you'd take the blame if you had to, wouldn't you?'

He sighed. 'Jesus. I'm not bloody Douglas Fairbanks in *Dawn Patrol*.'

'What?'

'Oh, nothing.' He squeezed Dora's hand and picked up her notebook to change the subject. 'Now, back to these line breaks in your own poems – which are *truly* eccentric.'

There was a knock, and Callum Wallace poked his face around the door.

'Dear Lord, it's all happening today.' Wystan seemed lighter. 'Callum, lad, come in! I have some books for you.'

The two young men stood side by side at Wystan's shelf. Dora could see how much Wystan loved to show his books to an interested person. 'How much Lawrence have you read?' he asked the young man.

'Not much. Father says he's a pig.'

Wystan laughed. 'A pig, eh? Well, it might be that your mother is reading *Lady Chatterley's Lover* as we speak!'

Callum decided to let it pass. 'Have you read it?'

'No. I shall catch it on the next round, when all the fuss has died down.'

They talked on and Dora let their excited, youthful voices drift over her. Wystan had cheered up completely.

'I'm going to leave you a key, as usual,' he said to Callum.

'Where are you going?'

'Shetland.' The big face broke into an excited smile. 'A precursor to Iceland. Auden is an Icelandic name. I'm a Scandinavian, you know, in my blood.'

'You're going alone?'

Wystan began to assent, and then he paused, as if considering. Looking round at Dora, he said clearly, 'No, I'm going with my chum.'

'Mr Isherwood?'

'My Helensburgh chum. Gregory.' He looked steadily at Callum. 'You know, the apprentice gardener?'

'The gardener?' Callum was flummoxed.

Dora propped herself up on an elbow to watch. There was a silence in which she could almost hear the cogs whirring in both their brains.

Finally, Wystan spoke again, with a weary edge in his voice. 'Callum,' he said. 'You know that I am a solitary? A homosexual?'

Callum snatched himself back a step. 'No, Mr Auden. I knew no such thing!' His eyes cast about the room for a new space to place himself correctly in response to this news. 'So, you and the gardener . . . are lovers?'

'I hope we will be.'

'And me? All this time spent in your room?'

'Elsewhere in the world, this news is not so shocking as it is in this little corner!' Wystan said impatiently. 'Anyway, Callum, if it's any consolation, you don't have to worry. You're not my type.' He turned, bad-temperedly, away.

'My father . . . if he knew, he would . . . I have to admit it to you . . . it's a shock,' stammered Callum. 'Partly, I feel rather stupid, not to have known. Nothing like that happens here.'

Wystan said, 'Well, that's not true, is it? It *is* happening here. Right now. All happening, right as we stand here.'

'But—'

'If it makes you feel better, who knows, perhaps, when I read *Lady Chatterley's Lover*, I shall be converted! Move seamlessly from perversion to obscenity! But, until then, please, this is the way things are, and I am going to Shetland with Gregory.'

Suddenly quite weary, Wystan sat down on the bed. 'Do you want to go, Callum, dear? I quite understand, if so. It is just so very tiring to carry a secret all the time. I have decided to tell the truth a little more than I have. I realise it may lose me my friends.'

'No, no.' Callum blinked behind his glasses. 'I just need to adjust to the idea, that's all. And thank you. I will come here and read. It is oppressive at home, as you know.'

'I'm glad you'll come. It means a great deal to me.'

Callum looked at his watch. 'I must go, just now. I'm out with a girl tonight!' With some relief, Callum took his leave.

After he had gone, Wystan fell back on the bed and reached for Dora hand. 'Courage, eh? Where does it get one? I mean, really? What good does it do?'

THIRTY-SEVEN

Wystan

G REGORY − SO TALL, so fine-skinned − could be a Scandin-avian too, Wystan muses, as they lean over the rail of the boat to Lerwick. They are wrapped like sausages in coats and scarves and woolly hats. Threads of Gregory's hair poke out from beneath his hat and a tiny reddened patch of his neck is visible. The spray wets and chills the boy's lips, and it is almost unbearable to Wystan that he cannot, right now, reach over and press his mouth to him. The line of properness has reasserted itself between them, stilting their conversation.

Gregory agreed to come, despite his parents being completely against it. Wystan is unsettled by their vehemence, but hopes they won't turn it into a police matter, as that would hurt their son as much as him. Christopher warned Wystan against the trip. *Where will you stay? How will you carry it off in the world of propriety?* Daphne is too ill, really, to understand what he is doing, but it would distress her to know that her plan is causing more problems than it is solving. Wystan has grown more determined. Who are they to tell him who

313

he can go on holiday with? They can all fuck off. For the first time in his life, Wystan feels strong, true, even brave.

The trip hasn't come a moment too soon. Lately, their relationship has consisted of Wystan spying on Gregory from his window, and stilted conversations about plants. Gregory is becoming very knowledgeable about the garden, and, actually, it does seem as though gardening may hold a future for him. He is gentle and good with his hands. He pointed out to Wystan the patches of azaleas he has uncovered, and told him that, in the spring, there will be a carpet of tulips and all sorts of other marvellous bulbs, which he personally intends to plant. 'At least 500,' he said proudly.

The Viking Hotel in Lerwick, a slate-blue edifice looking out over the harbour, does not have two rooms available; surely they should have written in advance? The proprietor has a bush of grey frizzy hair and a beard to match, and the bulk of a bear. 'You will have to share,' he says.

'Oh, how disappointing,' says Wystan. 'But we are really only sleeping here. We have so much to see.'

The proprietor neither believes nor disbelieves, but leads them up a worn staircase, right to the top, and into a large room with two beds in it. 'Bathroom down the corridor,' he says. 'Breakfast at eight sharp.'

And then he is gone and Wystan and Gregory stand and stare at each other. They are alone together. They are *together* with no one watching. He steps towards his friend, who is smiling with the same glee. There is no past or future. There is no this or that. There is only the warm embrace, the chilly sea-lips warming beneath his and the feeling of time itself falling away.

IN THE VERY EARLY morning, he takes his notebook to the window and he writes until Gregory wakes. His focus for work has returned; ideas for *The Orators* are tumbling from him. There is a conclusion to come – that is all. He doesn't know quite what it is. And the best part – there is no hurry to find it. He and Gregory are outside time for three weeks. Three whole weeks. He can hardly believe it.

He lays down his pen and slips back into bed beside his friend. This is how every day will begin for the entirety of their stay. Wystan gently wakes Gregory and asks him to do what Wystan does to the boys in Berlin. There is something sad in the longing being satisfied, because there will be no more boys in Berlin. The world is breaking up, turning dark, and, in the midst of that, this sudden incandescent freedom.

IN THIS GRAZED, RAZED place, Wystan's mind gallops. Poems, or pieces of them, pour from him. They do not cohere, but he is not troubled. He feels he is uncovering the very nature of his long poem: it is a machine whose action concludes but does not end. This machine he's almost made is like an invention to solve a problem no one knew should be solved. His poems seem to him, then, like endless inventions, little machines, running through and over problems, trying to change the outcome.

The sky's endless blue ceiling makes Wystan dizzy. There are no trees. A hawk hangs like a tiny insignia on the air. The wind tears across the – what is it? Tundra? – the land stripped, like a psyche after some catastrophic treatment, leaving space – for what? Thoughts? Yes, thoughts. Instead of flora and fauna, thoughts grow here. It is delicious.

Gregory stops speaking of his wish for a lass of his own. His world has shrunk too, to island-size, to room-size.

There is as much talk as there is sex. There's not much point discussing poetry because Gregory doesn't know much and gets a kind of frozen-rabbit expression when Wystan starts on an exposition. But they can talk about experience, and, at heart, that is what Wystan is interested in. And they can talk about God. Gregory is a Catholic, but lapsed. 'God got the sack when the shipyard closed,' he is fond of saying. Or, 'The means-test man took God away, with Ma's sideboard.' They are simply two young people together in these wandering conversations, trying to understand the world and their place in it, when it appears to be run by some old man or other, either in the sky or in Parliament, who hates the young.

Wystan tries out some of his half-formed communist ideas on Gregory. They gain a certain amount of traction, although, since he has been receiving a regular, if small, wage as Hamish's apprentice, Gregory's manner seems a little harder. Does he see their class difference more clearly? Attempts to talk about that specifically become so stilted that they are dropped. And, anyway, Wystan wants to get away from that. He and Gregory are transcending their class positions. They are in the business, together, of transgression.

A week into the trip, they decide to make the long journey to the northernmost island of Unst. This necessitates a series of carriage, bus and ferry trips, over two days. Not having planned this, they must find their accommodation on the hoof, and there are two nights spent apart, when the boarding houses offer two rooms. Wystan is surprised to find he does not mind. He and the boy stay in the tavern until late, and sit up to watch the day never quite end, and, when he wakes, he slips into the boy's room. Now is the simmer dim, when the sun only touches the horizon before rolling slowly back up in the sky.

'HERE WE ARE – the very top of the island!' Wystan exclaims. 'That's Muckle Flugga – where Robert Louis Stevenson travelled!'

It has been a two-hour trek from Norwick to get here. They lean against one another, pleasantly tired. Wystan feels Gregory's fingers close around his own and stay. There is no need to mention it. It's perfectly natural.

The gulf beneath the cliff top is a vortex of screeching gannets. Their ancient breeding ground is the rough-hewn surface of a vast rock in the sea, whose bulk has been hollowed out over millennia to make a towering arch. The gannets jostle and wail, launching themselves periodically to circle the rock.

Gregory says, 'At school. Long John Silver. I liked that book.'

'Well, it says here –' Wystan pulls out a few bound sheets, purchased in Norwick – 'it says here that he modelled Treasure Island on Unst. The map of Treasure Island is almost exactly the same! Worth the trip, just for that.'

'The rocks, though – look.' Gregory points at the boulders which poke out of the sea. It's as if they have been dropped there from a great height, or there was one enormous one, like an asteroid, which shattered on impact into these jagged lumps. Gregory takes out his own notebook and pencil and starts to scribble. It's a sketch of the sea and the rocks.

'I want to take that home with me,' he says. 'Show Ma.'

A flurry of puffins bobs into the air, their comical toucan-faces turning to stare at the two young men above their nesting sites. They come so close, they can almost be touched, and two land on the grass a few feet from Wystan and Gregory. They look the same . . . Are they a pair? Or two friends, two chums, like Gregory and him?

The men sit side by side, and the puffins sit side by side, and from time to time the puffins and the men turn to look at one another, and the men laugh and the puffins bob and blink.

'What a place,' sighs Wystan, falling back on to the grass. Gregory lights them both a cigarette and they lie, smoking. Wystan considers the feeling, which is not like when he is next to Christopher. When he's beside Christopher, he almost forgets him. They are so in tune with their thoughts that they simply coexist without disturbance. Not even a fuck disturbs the equilibrium. With Christopher, there is no need for *love*. They are such friends that they have passed into deep brotherhood.

There aren't enough words for love. The poet needs to build a machine to make more ways to talk about this.

Beside Gregory, however, every sinew is awake. His touch is electrifying. His roughened beauty jars against the view. The galloping horses of Wystan's thoughts come to a wall, they stop and whinny and jostle – and hang their heads over the gate, because they are horses and they long for touch, for treats, for human warmth.

This is what this kind of love does. It stills the horses.

Gregory gets out the beer and sandwiches they bought in North-wick. They eat the picnic in amazed silence. The sun is warm, but the wind bites and they can't stay much longer.

The land slopes downwards and, as they move further from the headland, there are inlets and tiny coves at the bottom of the cliff. Suddenly, Gregory says, 'What's that?' and points over the edge.

Some sixty feet below, on a patch of sand, lies a whale. It's white and black: an orca.

'Is it beached?' asks Wystan.

From this height, it is hard to tell if it is still alive. Gregory is already scrambling down the rocky face, which is not difficult to descend, with lots of foot- and handholds. Wystan is not so sure and peers from the top. 'Can we definitely get back up?' he asks.

The beast is on its belly, and its blowhole puffs out a feeble spray every minute or two. It has tiny eyes, which are open and weary. The tide is some thirty feet away, and looks to be going out even more.

Gregory shakes his head. 'No way is it going to live until the tide's back in.'

'What do we do?'

Gregory shrugs. 'The sun's up and it's hot. What it needs is water thrown over it, keep it damp – and then, when the tide comes in, we could float it away.'

'How do you know that?'

'Grandpa was a fisherman. Had his own boat, down in Ayr. Always tellin' us stories.'

'So we carry the water in our shoes?' says Wystan doubtfully.

Gregory laughs. 'Could try. Shame to leave it just dying.'

They take off their shoes and socks and run into the waves,

scooping up from the icy surface shoefuls of water and running back. By the time they come back to the whale, most of it has spilled, but they throw it anyway. The whale blinks and groans. Back they go – three, four times; once is aborted because Gregory throws his water at his friend and the rescue mission turns into chasing on the sand and laughter.

After a time, it becomes apparent that this method is going to do little more than soak their shoes. They come to a stop by the whale's head, which has sunk a little further into the sand. Its eyes are closing. Wystan looks desperately around, across the cliff top, in case anyone else is there who can help.

'I think we should find someone,' he says, running back towards the cliff. Reluctantly, Gregory follows, and they scramble to the top and head towards the tiny settlement of Burrafirth. In its harbour, they see a fishing boat and two bent fishermen mending some nets.

After taking in the extraordinary sight of a man in a bow tie in this place, one of them says, in a dialect virtually incomprehensible, that it's an orca – it eats their fish. Why would they rescue it?

'But thanks for the tip. We'll go along and carve it up for eating.'

'Eat it?' Wystan feels terrible that he has secured the whale's demise. How little he knows about the wild places, where real men do unspeakable things with perfect nonchalance. A whale will feed several families for a week or more. It can't be overlooked. The fishermen offer to give some to the young men as a reward, and Wystan is tempted, but meeting the beast and betraying it take the shine off the novelty of eating it.

'No, but thank you,' he says, and turns to go.

Gregory touches his arm. 'Aye, but I'd like some. We could take it back to the hotel. Have them cook it up. It's food, Wystan. You don't pass up food. You never been hungry?'

'Not hungry enough for that,' he says.

'I don't like to turn down food,' Gregory persists. 'It's unlucky. And my grandpa said whale is tasty.'

'It will take ages for them to kill it and carve it up. I don't want to hear it scream.'

'It can't scream.'

'I think that makes it worse. In fact, I am starting to feel nauseated. Come on, Gregory.'

He turns and walks briskly away, giving every impression that he will continue, whether or not Gregory comes with him. After a bad-tempered pause, Gregory follows and they head through the hamlet towards the path that will lead them back up on to the cliffs.

They walk in silence, each alone with his thoughts, a difference between them suddenly revealed. Can love even survive difference, once it's spoken? The question turns in Wystan's mind.

As the poet climbs ahead, he feels a sting on the back of his leg. He wipes it absently away, and then feels another. Gregory is smirking behind him.

'What was that?'

'Nothing.' Gregory drops pebbles from his fingers.

With an exaggerated sigh, Wystan lays down his bag and picks up a few tiny pebbles. He skims one half-heartedly at Gregory's shin and misses.

'Hey, stop throwing stones!' says Gregory, scrabbling around for more pebbles himself. He pings one expertly at Wystan's arm.

'Ow!' Wystan is piqued now. He finds a bigger one, one that will be easier to throw, and hurls it at Gregory's thigh and misses.

'Clumsy!' says Gregory. He is excited now. Chuckling to himself, he picks up another pebble and aims it skilfully at Wystan. It stings his friend in the thigh, ricochets off and disappears into oblivion.

Wystan strains to hear the pebble drop, but it is too small to make an impression. He points to a large boulder, the size of a man, a little way along the path.

'Let's roll that over!' he says, and the two boys run to the rock, apply all their strength and find that it moves, awkwardly, and without life or enthusiasm, but moving nonetheless.

'I bet it smashes,' says Gregory.

'If we get it into the water, it'll make one hell of a splash.'

'Let's get it on the rocks. I want to smash it.'

'What is wrong with you today?' Wystan stops rolling for a moment, reaches out and strokes his friend's hair.

'Nothing! Come on. Push!'

At last, they reach the edge. They each press their fingers under it and, after Gregory's count, they heave at the same time.

The rock rolls over the edge painfully slowly – then plummets. In a flash of black, it hits another rock at the edge of the water and bursts into two pieces, which catapult out into the shallow water of the inlet. A point of each one projects a little way above the surface.

'Look at that!' Gregory grins in satisfaction. 'They'll be there forever. We'll come back and see them in the future.'

Even though the holiday will end soon, Wystan cannot see an end to their story, any more than he can see an end to his poem. He and Gregory are so in tune. They have had such fun. There's a trip by bus to get back to Northwick, and there will be dinner out on the harbour front. They will sit out to watch the day make its dreamy fade, before burnishing itself into a new dawn. It will be magical and unforgettable, as every day has been.

When they leave Northwick the next day, it still feels as if they are heading somewhere. Wystan does not sense that his story is winding to a close. Nor when they leave Lerwick and sail to Aberdeen; nor when the train gasps and belches its way to Helensburgh.

When they arrive at the station, there is a welcome committee of the Vances, Perkins and Jessop, who are standing gravely on the platform. Gregory is whisked away by his parents, without even a proper goodbye, and Wystan escorted into a taxi back to Larchfield and straight into Mr Perkins' study, where he is informed that this is the end of his teaching career at Larchfield and it is time for him to leave. He is not surprised by this, and takes the news very calmly. It does not feel like the end of anything vital.

Perkins ends the interview by standing and walking to the window, which looks out over the garden. He says, 'While you were away, Daphne died.'

'What, sir?' Wystan cannot take in this news. 'You mean . . . When?'

'While you were away! Having your holiday with Gregory Vance. Two weeks ago, now.'

'But . . .' Wystan is sure, then, he is going to embarrass himself with tears. He bites his lip to prevent them, takes his leave of Perkins and retires to his room. The books are disturbed; at least Callum has been here while he's been away.

Even this is not the end.

Alone on his bed, with no job and no Gregory, and Daphne gone, he realises that the end was all those days ago, there, on the cliff top, with Gregory. The final playing out was right there, right then. The two friends admired their handiwork, the impression they'd left on the landscape, and Gregory said, 'We'll come back and see them in the future.'

And how Wystan wishes he had kissed his friend's fingers, held him tight one last time, for he understands it now: they will never go back; they will never see each other again. Wystan's Larchfield story is at an end.

THIRTY-EIGHT

Kit

K IT LEVERED OFF THE lid of the paint with a screwdriver. It was a lovely dusty blue, the colour of the sky reflected in the sea on a late summer morning. Dora had chosen the colour some time ago, but would not be using the paint any time soon. She had bought a trellis too, with the plan that she would paint the trellis and grow honeysuckle on it. Kit was going to do this for her. When she came back to him, she would see it, and it would, perhaps, make her happy. He dipped the brush in the paint and began. Beatrice crawled at his feet, pausing when she found a new branch to pull herself on to, or an interesting leaf. From time to time, she stopped and looked about her, in her baby's face a glimpse of the child to come. From time to time, she cried for no reason in Kit's arms. Of course, there was a reason: she missed her mother.

Kit was going to make it all right. He didn't know quite how yet, but he was going to. He'd wronged his wife. The police, everyone who knew them – all were in agreement that Dora needed to be away, in hospital. But still, as her husband . . . should he have given in so easily? Was there nothing else he could have done?

Dora had created an escape. No one does that unless they are completely desperate. This, Kit understood now. He did not fully understand her desperation, but that did not matter anymore. Surely, what was needed was kindness?

He steered his mind around the edge of this thought. It was too painful to accommodate fully. In part, what was troubling him was that he had made some kind of mistake twice. He didn't think he could live with himself if he failed a second wife, when he did not even have the excuse of youth, as he had with the first.

'Bea, no . . . Be careful!' He crossed the lawn in three strides and scooped his baby daughter up from where she was trying to clamber into the branches of a shrub. She screwed her face into a pout and struggled to be released.

The thing was, the thing that was niggling him, was that if – as he now saw – Dora's life was unbearable – and the evidence for this was right there, in her not being able to bear it – then was it really madness to escape into another world? Didn't it, in fact, show ingenuity and resourcefulness to construct an entire world to give you solace – a world that nevertheless allowed you to care for your child? He wondered, then, if disaster might have been averted if he had tried to understand Dora's private world.

Perhaps she might have invited him to share it.

He'd have liked that. He longed for solace too.

Beatrice cooed at his feet and began to play with his shoelaces. He did not stop her, but watched as she fiddled with great concentration. The realisation slid into his mind: after all, this is what we do with a child, don't we? We enter their reality, and protect them from our own until they're strong enough.

At this, he stopped painting, rubbed his eyes and stared out to sea over the low hedge his wife had created. How he missed her. How he loved that bright, fiery mind. He had married her because of it. It was a mind he could push against, define unclear thoughts by. She had, in truth, scared him a little when they met, and that was a good thing. Without that mind, pushing at the centre of their lives, Kit was adrift. He was standing on the land, but might just as well be lost in that sea.

Beatrice chuckled at his feet. He picked her up, pressed her downy head to his cheek. He had to make this right, for his daughter's sake. Consumed by this thought, he did not hear the footsteps crossing the lawn towards him and, when Terrence spoke, it made him jump.

'Got something to tell you,' said Terrence. He spoke in exactly the same tone he would have used to discuss parking access, or Jesus: even, cool.

'Oh, yes, Terrence?' Kit said, putting his daughter down and picking up his paintbrush again, concentrating the bristles into the corners of the trellis, going over and over the same spot to lift the beads of blue that threatened to turn into dribbles. He expected that Terrence was here to gloat that Dora was no longer here.

'It's Mo . . .'

'Yes . . . How is she doing?' Kit enquired coldly.

Terrence pressed on. 'Very poorly she's been, but there was a complication. She caught an infection . . . made her organs fail . . .'

Kit sought to arrange his face into the correct expression, but found he could not. 'Oh dear,' he managed.

'Anyway, I don't know how to say it, so I'll just say it. She died.

Last night. The strain on her heart, she couldn't survive it. Her . . . heart gave out.' A strange noise, which might have been a sob, remained corralled in his throat. 'I'm letting you know there'll be a lot of folks turning up here. We're having a proper wake, as she'd have wanted. So there'll be . . . cars. Just so you know.'

'I see.' Kit stood with his brush dripping blue on to the grass. Terrence turned to amble back across the lawn. Kit called after him, 'You know what they say, Terrence? Mo was a bitch and now she's dead.'

Terrence stared at him, astounded. He opened his mouth to say something, then thought better of it, turning away with a mutter. Kit continued painting for a decent period, to gather his thoughts, then picked Beatrice up and went inside. He glanced at the upper flat as he did so. Its windows were dark and empty.

IN THE DAYS BEFORE the funeral, Paradise became a place of pilgrimage, with people Kit had never seen before (could there be any left in the whole of Helensburgh?) trailing up and down the drive to commiserate with Terrence. Mostly, they were in tears, and, without exception, they regarded Kit with raw hostility. Beatrice, too, met blank stares when she rolled up to the strangers walking through her garden. Cars crunched up and down at all hours, even more frequently than before, if that were possible.

After their encounter, Kit saw his neighbour alone only once more, when Kit was setting out for a walk. On this occasion, Terrence came striding round the house to accost Kit on the drive.

'You know what happened before in this house? Years and years ago?' he said.

Kit looked questioningly, the dog hovering on the lead and Beatrice bouncing in the backpack.

'There were two families, and the downstairs ones hated the upstairs ones.'

'Ah . . .' said Kit.

'And then, the lady upstairs, she was so frightened of the downstairs ones, she never came out! Died up there, she did.'

'Oh, for God's sake, Terrence. Don't you ever stop?' Kit cried. 'Your wife is dead, my wife is in hospital . . . Can't you . . . ?' And he strode away, too furious to remain in front of his neighbour.

On the day of the funeral itself, Kit piled Beatrice and Virgil into the car and they headed out to one of the far beaches to escape. Beatrice crawled towards the water and Kit scooped her up before she went right in, swinging her high in the air until she laughed with delight. There was a warm, weedy rock pool nearby and he peeled off Beatrice's socks and shoes and let her dangle her toes in the water. She sang with pleasure, but then, again, the serious cloud passed over her face. 'Mama,' she said, clearly, and father and daughter looked into each other's eyes.

'I'm sorry, my darling,' said Kit. 'Daddy needs to work something out, so we can bring Mummy home.' He felt a sudden conviction that it was going to be all right. He knew what to do.

It was a gorgeous, sunny day. The sun was a perfect circle in a blue sky. Kit called the dog and picked up the baby and took them both home. Once there, with them both settled, he pulled the curtains shut and returned, with new clarity and focus, to the notebook with the swirly cover, open on the table.

THIRTY-NINE

Wystan

DAPHNE WAS BURIED FAR away on the east coast, near her hometown of St Andrews. Perkins tells him the location is private, and so there is nowhere for Wystan to go to say goodbye. They say it was a massive stroke, which wiped her out instantly. If one has to die, and reluctantly Wystan accepts this is true, then perhaps this is the best way for the one who dies. She went to bed and did not wake up. It was that simple.

He is leaving soon, having agreed that, to avoid embarrassment, he would start the new term for the boys, to allow time for a replacement to be found. As the holidays dwindle, he has been firing off letters to all his friends to find another position, and yet the place clings to him. So much that is real has happened in what was meant to be a stopgap, an adventure in a foreign land.

On the first day of term, the laughter of the boys settling into their dorms and seeing their friends again after the long holidays claws at him.

He goes to the upper room and sits on the daybed. It is exactly as she left it, but the window has been closed and there is a layer of dust over everything. He goes to the shelf with all the jotters and remembers, with a horrible jolt, that he still has one of her jotters in his room, the one she gave him when he first went to Berlin. She'd asked him to read her poems, and he promised he would, and she asked him to send her a postcard and he promised he would, and, of course, he did neither because he was so caught up with Erich and all his excitements in Berlin. Truth be told, he did not even read the book, though he meant to. He meant to be a friend to her.

It all seems such a long time ago now.

There are at least thirty of the jotters crammed together on the shelf. He takes one down at random and opens it. A dried flower falls out and he picks it up. It's a rhododendron petal, creamy, blousy white. Wystan takes the jotter to the daybed and reads the poems inside.

They are, as he suspected they would be, terrible womanish things, with clunking rhymes and excruciating sentiment. But that doesn't matter; it doesn't matter at all. More petals fall out and some pages have sketches of the garden instead of verses. He comes across a sketch of a figure in the garden, standing alone, and realises it is him. She must have stood quietly at the window observing him. It is quite a good likeness; most of all, it captures his awkwardness. She understood such things.

He rolls the jotter up tightly and tucks it into his jacket.

Perkins has taken to darting around the school like a rat. The rumour is that he is hanging by a thread with the governors. Only Jessop seems to have swelled and grown over the summer. He looks as if he should be commanding a ship. When they encounter each other in the breakfast room or in the corridor, Jessop gives him a huge victorious grin.

One afternoon, in those final days, Perkins scuttles up to him as he emerges from breakfast. The beady face regards him indirectly, fixing on his chin. 'Auden, I should be most grateful if you would write a poem for us, for Mr Jessop's wedding to Amy Wallace.'

'Why ever would I do that?'

Perkins' devastated eyes creep up to meet Wystan's own. 'I know how fond Daphne was of you, Auden. You can't imagine how hard she went in to bat on your behalf.' He draws breath sharply and Wystan realises what an effort he is making to control himself. 'My wife . . . my wife . . . was going to read at the wedding, a poem she had composed specially. I'm afraid I don't know where it is, but, anyway, she can no longer . . . I know she would want you to take her place – for her, if not for Mr Jessop himself.'

Of course, Wallace would not dream of asking himself. He loathes Wystan, but no one can ignore that he has a reputation already as a poet. It would be a coup to have a verse by him at the wedding. Perhaps framed and signed as well . . . ? If Perkins can obtain it, perhaps it will help his case with Wallace, who has influence. Perkins has come up with the only reason that could possibly persuade Wystan to do it.

Wystan sighs and looks down at the little man before him. 'Of course I will, Mr Perkins.'

'And, of course, you know that, if any school should approach us for a character, they will not be disappointed. The wonderful contribution you have made will be described in full.'

'Well . . . thank you,' says Wystan.

'Well, then,' says Perkins. 'I'll leave you to get on.'

Wystan retreats into the garden and finds a bench where he can sit quietly. Out of habit, his eyes drift round the building to catch sight of Gregory, but he knows he will never see the boy again. Hamish told him that the Vances have already left the area. Perhaps to Ayr, wonders Wystan, where Gregory's grandfather lives. Thinking of Gregory is desperately painful, but he surprises himself by his ability to bear it. Deeply engrained is the understanding that he will never have a loving relationship. But his airman in *The Orators* will. Something has unlocked; the chaotic work has come to a close. He expressed what he meant to.

ALL THAT IS LEFT of his happy times is Jamie.

Some boys are good at rugby. Some boys are good at French. Some boys (not many, in Wystan's experience) take a delight in English literature. And some, like Jamie, have only one specialism: to tear at the heart.

For Jamie has not improved. He has not risen from the ashes of his treatment to become a confident little boy. In fact, quite the opposite. Wystan is shocked by the small, pale figure who runs to him on the first day of term. His tin soldier, long stolen, has been replaced with a teddy bear – the one that did not make the initial cut when the major brought the boy to school that first time.

The major does not stay long on that first day. He is of the opinion that this makes settling in harder for the boy. So it is Wystan who carries the case and the box into the dormitory and helps Jamie to unpack. Tied around the teddy bear is a note to Jamie, and the boy asks Wystan to read it. Wystan does so, and swiftly wishes he had not, for the note, written by the boy's father, explains to Jamie that he must harden his heart against losses like that of a tin soldier or a teddy bear. For, in the big world, such things will happen many times, and a replacement will not always be found. Wystan does not agree with the major (harden one's heart against the losses? When one is not yet ten years old?), but does not want to say anything negative to Jamie, so he simply adds, gently, that he will keep a close personal eye on the teddy . . . for as long as he can.

'You're leaving?' the boy asks.

'Yes, I am, I'm afraid. Well, actually, don't tell anyone, but they've given me my marching orders.'

Jamie gives a small sigh and sits quietly on the edge of the bed, with the teddy bear untouched by his side.

In those final days, Jamie goes often to Wystan's room to draw, and, aside from that, keeps himself to the shadows. He has finally learnt the words to the school song and sings them without conviction at morning assembly. Wystan is tormented by his inability to engage the boy, and then irritated by how tormented he feels. If he forbids Jamie to come to his room anymore, will that help him develop a more manly character? What will the boy do when Wystan is gone?

Sometimes, Jamie has bruises, which he explains have come from rugby. As Wystan is often leading the games, he knows this is not true.

And then, that last Sunday, when the boys are getting ready for church, Jamie simply does not get out of bed at all. He is vanishingly slight beneath the sheet and his hair is pasted round his flushed face. Larchfield does not have an infirmary dorm, nor does it have a full-time nurse. Such extravagances were cut long ago. Normally, if a boy is sick, Daphne takes him to the upper room and tends him there, with help from Dr Boyce, who visits. 'After all,' Daphne has always said, 'there's nothing I can catch anymore. And what I have is too busy with me to spread to others.'

But Daphne is gone now, and there is no one to show the boy that kindness. Instinctively, Jamie puts his arms around Wystan's neck and presses his face into his chest as Wystan carries him to Daphne's room and lays him on the daybed. The poet hopes something of her atmosphere will help the boy. Jamie clutches the teddy bear, dampening its fur with his sweat.

Once, when Wystan was a boy, his GP father was called out in the evening when Mrs Auden was at a Women's Institute meeting, and so, reluctantly, Wystan was taken along. He had followed his father discreetly into a tiny Birmingham terrace. There, on a bed of twisted, darkly bloodied sheets, had lain a woman in a fever as wild as Jamie's. His photographic memory for words had imprinted the name on his brain: puerperal fever. His father had spoken softly and gravely to the man of the house, who wept openly into his hands. The woman had moaned and writhed and Wystan had been so relieved when they left that he shook in the car.

'I'm sorry you saw that, son,' his father said. 'Those fevers . . . when they take hold . . .'

Jamie's fever has certainly taken hold. Wystan runs to Perkins' study, stopping on the way to send Olive up with water and cloths. Perkins is staring into space by the window and jumps when Wystan walks in without knocking.

'Jamie Taylor is very ill,' says Wystan. 'We need to get the doctor – and his father must be called too.'

'What? Oh, no, no. It will just worry him.' Perkins looks at his pocket watch. 'You take the boys to church and I will take care of this.'

'Absolutely not. I'm staying with him.'

'Mr Auden, do you really think you have anything to add to the proceedings? I will go and see him straightaway and assess the situation. Where is he?'

'Daphne – Mrs Perkins –' Wystan stumbles for the right phrase – 'the upper room, on the daybed. But I am not leaving him, sir.' He manages a weak smile. 'You can't fire me twice, anyway.'

Perkins regards the young master wearily. 'Very well. I will call the doctor. You wait with him.'

'And the father?'

'That's a different matter, Auden. We need the doctor first.'

To Wystan's relief, Dr Boyce arrives swiftly. Followed by Mr Perkins, he clops into the upper room on raised heels and immediately goes about examining the immobile Jamie.

'Do you know anything about these bruises?' Dr Boyce asks, casually.

'I've not seen anything done to him,' Wystan says, 'but I do think the older boys may be responsible. He's quite sensitive. It's not really a quality boys value.'

'His father is going to ask about those bruises. He's going to be very unhappy about them,' says Perkins.

'Are you telephoning him, then?' Wystan asks.

'We don't want to alarm him unnecessarily,' says Dr Boyce. He has an English accent, with a slight trace of Yorkshire. Wystan's childhood in York is a bright memory and he wonders if this will create a friendly connection between them.

'So it's a matter of balancing little Jamie's need to go home with our need not to alarm the major,' says Mr Perkins. 'You're sure you haven't seen anything when you've been on boarder duty? And you're right above them, of course, in your own room.'

'Mr Jessop also is on duty for the boarders,' says Wystan irritably. He would love to tell them what he caught Jessop doing. But what is the point? These bruises have nothing to do with that, and no one would believe him anyway.

'Oh, yes, we've already asked Mr Jessop and he says he thought you knew something.'

Wystan gives a long sigh. 'Mr Perkins, I have seen nothing. But I know from Jamie that the bigger boys have been beating him. I have tried to catch them at it, but boys are clever, as you know. I suggest you ask Mr Jessop to search his mind a little more thoroughly. He is with the boarders more than I.'

'But you are with Jamie more than anyone else. The drawing in your room and so on.' Mr Perkins' rheumy eyes fix steadily on Wystan.

'And that is how I know what the older boys are doing – from the chats Jamie and I have in my room.'

Dr Boyce shakes his head. 'We're not suggesting anything, Mr Auden. Or, I'm not. I'm just trying to work out the right moment to ring the boy's father, the time to do it when he won't be deflected by something irrelevant.'

'You may know, my father was a GP – in York and then in Birmingham,' says Wystan.

Dr Boyce breaks into what is almost an attractive grin. 'Is that so! Perhaps I went to him when I was a lad! Auden . . . Auden . . .' He is thinking to himself. 'When was that, you say?'

'Around '07, and a few years after . . . But, please, Dr Boyce, I've been out with my father on visits. I've seen these fevers and what they do. And I implore you to call the major and get him here. The failure to do that will be worse than any bruising on his child. You must. In fact, you must or I will!'

'You'll do no such thing, Mr Auden,' says Perkins. 'Now settle down, please. We have to be sensible.'

'Nothing about this school is sensible!'

Dr Boyce is nodding carefully. 'Mr Perkins, I agree with the young man. I've a duty to report this to the father. Let's get on with it.'

Perkins stares at Wystan with ill-disguised hostility. 'I want you to root out and stop whatever is going on. Or, at least –' he adds, half under his breath – 'show them how to do beatings so the bruises don't show! That's how it was in my day.'

Wystan gets to his feet. 'Is that all, Mr Perkins?'

'It is.'

'Goodbye, Dr Boyce.'

'Yes, Mr Auden. Goodbye.'

A few hours later, as dusk is falling, a taxi pulls into the forecourt. Out gets the major. Wystan watches from his window as Jamie's father bolts to the front door and pulls the bell. It clangs through the building. Then he clatters in, calling to Olive, 'I came immediately. Are his things packed?' Up to Daphne's room they go, and Wystan waits as voices blur faintly through the walls, revealing no words, but great consternation.

Wystan considers following, trying to explain to the major, but the man is so distressed it will do no good. Very soon, too soon, there are more voices. Mr Perkins, this time, reassuring, suggesting the major wait and talk with Dr Boyce; they've really acted very swiftly, don't know what it could be. His voice is even more plaintive and infuriating. The major is ignoring him, then he is out of the door, his son in his arms. He's crunching across the gravel, not even looking up. The boy's arms flop by his side.

Wystan turns from the window, unable to watch any longer, and climbs the stairs, once more, to Daphne's room. It is empty. Beyond the window, he hears the car door slam and tyres crunch on the drive. He sinks down on to the daybed and sees, beside him, Jamie's teddy bear, forgotten in the turmoil. Wystan picks it up and holds it to his face. It is still warm.

FORTY

Wystan and Dora

WHILE WYSTAN PACKED, DORA waited for him on the bench in the garden, where a rhododendron had dropped a carpet of white petals. The sun was almost directly overhead and the bush had a crumpled rim of shadow, like the hem of a dress. Dora had packed nothing. She had no need of anything. In her jacket pocket was her notebook and pen. These, and Wystan himself, were all she needed.

And then he was beside her, his shadow hunched like a tiny boy. He was carrying two large cases. Olive scuttled out with a third. 'A cab should arrive in a minute,' Wystan said, consulting his pocket watch.

Dora gazed for the last time on Larchfield. The school had set her free; she was fond of it. She had the bulging notebook to prove it, a mind clear as water. It wasn't easy to leave.

But now that he had decided to go, Wystan wanted it over with. The school was a sullen, empty shell without Daphne or Jamie. No one came to say goodbye. Olive peeped round the pillar as the driver loaded the bags into the boot. And then they were gone, down the hill of Sinclair Street, where they had walked so often, people lifting their heads to see them pass. It seemed as though the world paused for a moment in what it was doing, because it was all over – Helensburgh, Dora and Wystan.

Wystan gazed out of the window. Usually, he shared his thoughts with Dora, but there was no need now. She knew what they were. He flinched as the taxi passed the train station, for that had been where he and Gregory had first glimpsed each other. He said nothing, but his spidery hand reached for hers and she tried to give it warmth.

'Where shall we go?' Dora asked. 'Spain?'

'Perhaps. I should like to *do* something, wouldn't you?'

'I'm sorry about Gregory,' Dora said.

'You know,' Wystan said, thoughtfully. 'It's not him that troubles me the most. It's Jamie.'

'He will be all right. I'm sure he's pulled through.'

Wystan shook his head. 'It's not that,' he said. 'He made me think how it would be to have a child of my own. I could do it, you know. I could love a child, do right by him.'

'Maybe you will.'

He shook his head impatiently. 'You know that's impossible.'

'But, look, your poem.' Dora indicated the sheaf of papers tied with string.

Wystan nodded. 'Yes. It came together. I finished it.'

'And the airman?'

'Well, in my head, he has his boy lover. But I think I may save the details for a later edition.'

They exchanged a glance.

'Dora, I've been as courageous as I can be for now. Like I say, I'm not Douglas Fairbanks. And I've said what I wanted to.'

'Yes.' Dora smiled at her friend.

At the pier, the cab pulled in and the driver got out to unload Wystan's cases. Wystan examined the estuary for the boat; it was a speck in the distance, approaching from Gourock. There were a few minutes spare, so Wystan used them to carry the bags, one by one, to the spot where the gangplank would be put out. The pier master eyed him, his little terrier bouncing at his feet.

Dora was not quite ready to bid a final goodbye. She stared along the front, breathing in the salty air.

There was a future ahead of her – she knew that much. A future where she would be able to be everything she had so longed to be, everything she was capable of being, and where she had done nothing wrong. Dora was excited by what was coming. Wystan was marked by what had happened to him. He was older. He was changed in a way that Dora was not.

'Dora!' She looked up and a man was coming towards her through the crowds. He was waving furiously, trying to run, but impeded by people shoving him back, tutting and grumbling and craning after him. The sun was in Dora's eyes and she shielded them to try to see better . . .

'It's me! Kit!' The man was in front of her now, chest heaving.

'Kit?' The image of the coat as a familiar object solidified in her mind. 'Kit,' she repeated thoughtfully.

'Not easy, I can tell you, to find a way into this world you have in your lovely, strange mind . . .' His hand reached out to her. 'Hang on while I get my breath.' He gazed out to the estuary and observed the ferry drawing near, then held her hand in both of his and smiled.

'Dora . . . I am so sorry.'

'What for?' Dora said this to her shoes. She was suddenly desperately uncomfortable with the swell of feeling in her throat.

Wystan was advancing on them, his expression one of interest in the man talking to Dora.

'I didn't understand, darling. And I let you down.'

'No . . . no,' she mumbled. 'What do you mean?' No one had let Dora down, and she had let no one down. Dora was clean, free, *unhurt*.

The man stared into her face, as if seeing her for the first time. His hands around hers were trembling; for some reason, he was afraid. 'Look, we'll go wherever you want, darling. Us three – you, me and Beatrice – we'll go wherever you need to go and we'll live the life you need to live.'

Dora said nothing, turning over the name he had said. Beatrice. *Beatrice*. The name brought unease, the sense that there was something she did not know.

'Come home,' he said, gently. 'It will all be different. It will all be better. I promise.'

Wystan appeared at her side. 'Hello,' he said amiably to Kit.

Kit stared in amazement at the figure of Wystan, then he said, 'Mr Auden, you have to tell her. You have to convince her to come home, to her family.'

'Don't say that! How can I go back? You're nothing to me—'

'Well, you two have things to talk about, I'm sure,' Wystan interrupted. 'It's just –' he touched Dora's arm and leant in to her – 'the boat is about to dock.'

The late passengers were scuttling past and the seagulls that normally followed the boat in the hope of scraps were wheeling above. Wystan moved discreetly ahead.

'Nothing to you? Darling—'

'Stop it! Stop it! Let me go!' Dora snatched her hand away.

'Dora, please don't say I'm too late.' He ran his hands through his hair in a way she remembered, in a way that hurt to see now.

'*Please*. Dora, *all this* –' he waved his arm at the world of the promenade, and Wystan, and the boat churning against the pier – 'I mean, it's lovely . . . but all this is a fiction. It's your imagination.'

'No, it isn't! How dare you come here and try to take this away from me!'

He buried his face in his hands. 'That's not what I mean to do,' he whispered. 'I've been trying for weeks to reach you . . . to be with you here, where you are . . . but, Dora, if you take the boat, you'll never come back. It won't be possible.'

'What do you mean?' she asked.

'Don't you see what it is? Darling, don't you understand?'

Dora looked once again at the tattered ferry bursting its steam and smoke at the pier's edge, and Wystan, standing carefully by his bags.

'It's the future,' she said.

'No, love.' His warm hands enveloped hers. 'It's the end. It's . . . death.'

Dora pulled away. 'No, it isn't! We're going to Spain.'

'Please, come home, Dora. Beatrice and me . . . we love you so.'

Beatrice? A flash of something. The little girl playing at Larchfield, a baby's face, that smell of milk and sleep. A daughter . . .

The ferry gave an enormous boom and Dora backed away. 'I'm sorry,' she said. The pain on Kit's face was threatening to change her mind. He was going to tempt her from this peace, this *happiness*, back to . . . back to what? A life where she was wrong, a failure as a mother and as a person.

'Dora, listen. It's all different now. Mo has *died*. It's all going to stop.'

Now, that name she recognised. Nausea swept through her, her hand flying to her mouth.

'What do you mean? What are you talking about?' Dora shouted. Passers-by paused in their rush to the ferry to look back at the woman being held to the spot by the man in the strange clothes, who was weeping openly now.

'Sweetie, she had our daughter almost taken away from us. Don't you remember? Now that she's dead, that's all gone.'

'I don't want to remember!'

'Darling Dora, come back with me and you can have a poet's life with the people who love you.'

The image of a little girl with red hair swam up before Dora. She was laughing and running the length of a long lawn. Another, of Dora and this man side by side in bed. It seemed like a future, an alternative future. But the feeling that went with these images was one of overwhelming sadness. Wouldn't you have to be insane to follow sadness?

'I'm sorry,' Dora mumbled and turned to go.

He cried out behind her: 'Dora!' But he was already growing fainter. People swarmed around him.

Dora ran to Wystan at the pier's edge and grasped his arm. 'Please, let's go. Let's go now.'

Wystan held her away from him and looked earnestly into her face. 'Dear friend, are you sure? There are things I can give you and things I can't.'

'*This* is my future,' Dora said firmly, carrying a case towards the gangplank.

Beatrice. Kit. The names were like bruises.

Wystan had never felt more present to her as he walked alongside. The smell of him – of hair grease, youth and cigarettes – was beautiful. Dora reached for his hand and their fingers entwined. When she looked up, a man was getting on just ahead of them. He was wearing a dirty greatcoat and, when he turned and smiled, his teeth were yellow. Wystan froze. But they both said nothing and shuffled on to the narrow gangplank, both knowing it was Florid.

FORTY-ONE

Dora

DORA'S FEW CLOTHES WERE packed in the holdall, her notebook laid on the top. There was no mirror to check how she looked, but she had brushed her hair and cleaned her teeth. The group counsellor, Alice, who now opened the door, had a face that scrunched up like paper when she was pleased. And the sight of Dora made it scrunch.

'Well done,' she said. 'They're here.'

Dora looked around the grim room with its two plain beds and barred window, and took a snapshot of it in her mind. In that bleak space, she had discovered peace. Fragile, but real.

'Ma-ma!' A tiny figure bolted down the long corridor. Beatrice had her arms outstretched for her mother, her red hair flaming around her face. Dora knelt down and opened her arms and the little girl ran unsteadily all the way by herself, falling into her mother's lap with a 'Wheeeeee!' Alice and the various nurses and patients who always turned out to see someone leave clapped and cheered.

Dora lifted her daughter high in the air. She was so happy to see her that she could not stop herself from crying. But she pressed the little girl to her so that she would not see and misunderstand her tears.

Behind Beatrice was Kit. He held back, observing his wife and his child reunited. He'd had his hair cut especially, Dora noticed. And he was wearing a new lambswool jumper, without holes – an exact copy of the original. He picked up Dora's holdall and nodded his thanks to Alice. There had been many long conversations with the staff. He knew them well and there was no need for extravagant goodbyes.

Dora and Beatrice were chattering nonsense to each other. Kit touched his wife gently on the shoulder and she led the way out of the double doors, out to the lift, down to the foyer, and out, out, out into the car park and oxygen.

It was a fresh April day. Kit put the bag in the boot and strapped his daughter into the car seat. Dora hung back, unaccustomed to these chores, unsure of her abilities after all these long months. Kit opened the passenger door for her and she slid into the old Volvo that was so familiar. Of course, it was she who was changed forever.

When Kit had settled beside her, he said, 'We're taking a detour, if that's okay.' Dora nodded. Kit looked extremely nervous as he started the car and they set off.

Behind them, Beatrice demanded music, so Kit put on the Beatles album that had been on a loop in the car since they had got it. It hadn't changed in all the months she'd been away. It made her smile. Kit reached for her hand, but, at his touch, she recoiled.

'I'm sorry,' she said. 'I'm just . . .'

'It's all right. Don't worry about a thing.'

Instead of taking the coastal road, they were entering Helensburgh from the top. Kit drove off to the right, along Montrose Street, and pulled in on the corner with Colquhoun Street.

'Why are we at Larchfield?' Dora asked.

'I've got something to show you.'

Bea was chattering excitedly and desperate to be free of the car seat. Kit popped her out, put her on his shoulders and then took Dora's arm and led her through the gate.

'I don't understand,' Dora said.

She followed him up the steps and into the stone porch. It was so painful for her to step inside the building again, knowing that Wystan was not there and never would be there. The front door was open. Dora followed her husband into the hall and up the staircase. The building was remodelled inside and yet she knew how to navigate it. Up they went, turning on to the landing, and then, there, the door. Kit handed her a key. 'Open it,' he said.

The room was Wystan's room, and yet not. Her boxes were lined against the wall. Her dictionaries were in a low, beautiful case beneath the front window. There was a desk, a bed, armchairs and, in a new addition, a kitchenette and a bathroom through a door.

'If you don't like it, we don't have to do this at all,' Kit said. 'We've had an offer on the house, and we're going to move to the place we talked about in town. But this came up, and I . . . wanted you to have it. As well. Or instead. Whatever you want. Your study. Your bolt-hole. Your place to be yourself.'

Dora stepped further into the room. She felt Wystan there. He was present somehow in the warm, kind walls. She sat at the desk and motioned for them both to come in. Kit tumbled Beatrice, giggling, on to the bed. He perched anxiously on the edge, searching Dora's face.

'How did you afford it?' she asked.

Kit grinned. 'The La Scala project ended up paying well. And . . . I borrowed a load of money.'

Her little girl had found some paper and a pen and went to her father's feet with them. She drew thick, happy lines all over the pages and grinned up at her parents.

Kit said, 'Is he here? In some way? I so want him to be here for you, darling.'

Dora looked out through the tall window on to the beautiful gardens. The immaculately cultivated rhododendrons were in full bloom, their heavy white blossoms bobbing in the sun.

And, this time, it was Dora who reached for her husband's hand. She smiled and held it tightly.

ACKNOWLEDGEMENTS

LARCHFIELD IS SO SOLID and real an object now that it is strange to remember that it was simply an idea for a long time, and quite a mess for a while after that. I owe a great deal to friends and colleagues who guided, encouraged, and, when necessary, scrubbed in and assisted while I sweated with my scalpel. Thank you Jenny Brown, agent and brilliant mind, whose belief went unrewarded for so long but never wavered; Joanne Limburg, my first reader, who has cheerfully endured countless versions of every chapter; and my editors Jon Riley and Rose Tomaszewska who are so very gifted and have taught me so much in a short time.

For vital financial support I am grateful to Creative Scotland and the Society of Authors, and to MsLexia for awarding the novel first prize in their competition, while it was still a manuscript. The prize was a great boost when I really needed it, and bought the whole family a much-needed holiday! Thank you also to my friend Emma MacPherson for reading an early draft and asking all the right questions; Lisa Highton for her insight and kindness; and Margie Orford for her wise advice.

Edward Mendelson responded to early chapters thrust upon him by an unknown poet with transforming grace and enthusiasm. Richard Ford's towering example of how to do the work, as well as his kindness and interest in my writing over many years, have given me everything to aspire to and made me strive to be better. Thank you also to Louis de Bernières for his generosity and gorgeous words. Nearer to home, I am grateful to Lomond School, and its Principal Johanna Urquhart, for their vision and support; Kandy Muggoch, friend and co-creator of the *Lomond Eye*, our historic successor to W. H. Auden's *Larchfieldian*; Professor Malcolm Baird for the Larchfield motto; to my friends in Helensburgh for welcome distraction, and most of all to my husband and muse, Julian Forrester, for our wonderful adventure.

Finally, heartfelt thanks to W. H. Auden himself, a person so complex and fascinating that years spent thinking about him are years very well spent indeed.

POEMS

Daylight, striking at the eye from far-off roofs, why did
you blind us, think: we who on the snow-line were in
love with death . . .

from III of 'Argument', in *The Orators*, by W. H. Auden

*

Will you turn a deaf ear
To what they said on the shore,
Interrogate their poises
In their rich houses;

Of stork-legged heaven reachers
Of the compulsory touchers
The sensitive amusers
And masked amazers?

from 'XXII', in *Poems* by W. H. Auden

It is time for the destruction of error.

The chairs are being brought in from the garden,

the summer talk stopped on that savage coast

before the storms, after the guests and birds:

In sanatoriums they laugh less and less,

Less certain of cure; and the loud madman

Sinks now into a more terrible calm.

from 'XXIV', in *Poems* by W. H. Auden

*

The voice of my education said to me

He must be killed,

For in Sicily the black, black snakes are innocent, the gold

are venomous.

And voices in me said, If you were a man

You would take a stick and break him now, and finish him off.

[. . .]

Was it cowardice, that I dared not kill him?

Was it perversity, that I longed to talk to him?

Was it humility, to feel so honoured?

I felt so honoured.

And yet those voices:

If you were not afraid, you would kill him!

And truly I was afraid, I was most afraid,

But even so, honoured still more,

That he should seek my hospitality
From out the dark door of the secret earth.
[. . .]
And I wished he would come back, my snake.

For he seemed to me again like a king,
Like a king in exile, uncrowned in the underworld,
Now due to be crowned again.

And so, I missed my chance with one of the lords
Of life.
And I have something to expiate:
A pettiness.

from 'Snake', by D. H. Lawrence

*

Some live by *love thy neighbour as thyself,*
others by *first do no harm* or *take no more
than you need.* What if the mightiest word is love?
[. . .]
In today's sharp sparkle, this winter air,
any thing can be made, any sentence begun.
On the brink, on the brim, on the cusp,

praise song for walking forward in that light.

from 'Praise Song for the Day', written for Barack Obama's
presidential inauguration, by Elizabeth Alexander

All the sadness of the hills
was on fire. The swan-galleons
set sail across the grey.
And I ran the length of the loch
to press into your hands this –
for the shining silver of my life.

from 'Thank You', in *Farewell My Lovely*, by Polly Clark

A NOTE ON THE TYPE

In 1924, Monotype based this face on types cut by Pierre Simon Fournier c. 1742. These types were some of the most influential designs of the eighteenth century, being among the earliest of the transitional style of typeface, and were a stepping stone to the more severe modern style made popular by Bodoni later in the century. They had more vertical stress than the old style types, greater contrast between thick and thin strokes and little or no bracketing on the serifs.